ALSO BY PAUL MALMONT

The Chinatown Death Cloud Peril

JACK LONDON IN PARADISE

Paul Malmont

SIMON & SCHUSTER
New York London Toronto Sydney

Simon & Schuster
1230 Avenue of the Americas
New York, NY 10020

First Simon & Schuster hardcover edition January 2009

SIMON & SCHUSTER and colophon are registered trademarks of Simon & Schuster, Inc.

For information about special discounts for bulk purchases, please contact Simon & Schuster Special Sales at 1-800-456-6798 or business@simonandschuster.com.

Designed by Jaime Putorti

Manufactured in the United States of America

10 9 8 7 6 5 4 3 2 1

Library of Congress Cataloging-in-Publication Data
Malmont, Paul.
Jack London in paradise / Paul Malmont.
p. cm.
1. London, Jack, 1876–1916—Fiction. 2. Authors—Fiction.
3. Hawaii—Fiction. I. Title.
PS3613.A457J33 2008
813'.6—dc22   2008009315
ISBN-13: 978-1-4165-4722-8
ISBN-10:   1-4165-4722-3

For Wesley—
My wild child

For Jerry Quartley—
For reintroducing me to Jack

And for
Andrew Marshall and Homer Bass—
Two men who answered the call of the wild. One survived, one did not.
Both lived.

But above all the voices there rose one sweetest and clearest of all, and going up into heaven, as it seemed, as a lark's does on a summer morning. He was only a little fellow that sang—a little boy of the Lastra a Signa, poorer than all the rest; with his white frock clean, but very coarse, and a wreath of scarlet poppies on his auburn curls; a very little fellow, ten years old at most, with thin brown limbs and a lean wistful face, and the straight brows of his country, with dark eyes full of dreams beneath them, and naked feet that could be fleet as a hare's over the dry yellow grass or the crooked sharp stones.

He was always hungry, and never very strong, and certainly simple and poor as a creature could be, and he knew what a beating meant as well as any dog about the farm. He lived with people who thrashed him oftener than they fed him. He was almost always scolded, and bore the burden of others' faults. He had never had a whole shirt or a pair of shoes in all his life. He kept goats on one of the dusky sweet-scented hillsides above Signa, and bore, like them, the wind and the weather, the scorch and the storm. And yet, by God's grace and the glory of childhood, he was happy enough as he went over the bridge and through the white dust, chanting his psalm in the rear of the priests, in the ceremonies of the Corpus Domini.

For the music was in his head and in his heart; and the millions of leaves and the glancing water seemed to be singing with him, and he did not feel the flints under his feet, or the heat of them, as he went singing out all his little soul to the river and the sky and the glad June sunshine, and he was quite happy, though he was of no more moment in the great human world than any one of the brown grilli in the wheat, or tufts of rosemary in the quarry-side; and he did not feel the sharpness of the stones underneath his feet or the scorch of them as he went barefoot along the streets, because he was always looking up at the brightness of the sky, and expecting to see it open and to see the faces of the curly-headed winged children peep out from behind the sun-rays as they did in the old pictures in the villa chapels.

The priests told him he would see them for a certainty if he were good; and he had been good, or at least had tried to be, but the heavens never had opened yet.

It is hard work to be good when you are very little and very hungry, and have many sticks to beat you, and no mother's lips to kiss you.
—OUIDA, *SIGNA*

Because he was alone
He became the world we see,
At the root of the earth, there is Kanaloa
In the earth rocks, there is he,
Kanaloa, great voice of the ocean
—FRAGMENT FROM A HAWAIIAN MYTH

Part 1

THE FOREST PALACE

—A VALLEY OF THE MOON EXPRESSION

CHAPTER ONE

L OS ANGELES WAS FREEZING but Hobart Bosworth was drenched in
his own sweat. His undershirt was plastered to his body and droplets
ran like spring-fed creeks down his back. He had run down Spring to
catch the little Central trolley, which was already trundling away from
its most recent stop, nearly certain that Rhea Haines, one of the Famous
Player starlets, but more importantly one of Rudisill's girlfriends, had
seen him outside the Alexandria Hotel. As she was across the street and
not on guard, as he was, he had spotted her first. The cab he had been
hailing was more than a block away, and her motion indicated she was
turning and would have seen him before he could escape in it. So he ran.
He hadn't heard his name called out, which made him think that perhaps there was a slim chance he had slipped out of her sight. It was hard
to tell. He was one of the tallest men in Hollywood, and he was certainly dressed like the movie star he was, in a tan wool suit. Normally a
slender part of his vanity would have been pleased to have been noticed by
someone he knew. But these times were extreme and he was desperate.

Gossip. That's what he was worried about. The path of gossip was
like a lit fuse heading toward a keg of TNT. Or a snowball rolling down-
hill, gathering more snow. Or maybe a snowball made of TNT, he wasn't
sure. Whichever it was, if she had seen him she would certainly gossip
about it to Rudisill. Rudisill would tell Garbutt. Garbutt would tell
Zukor. And his proverbial dynamite snowball would explode. Garbutt

and Zukor, and probably Rudisill, all thought that he was in Arizona. Because that's what he had told them. When they found out he was still in Los Angeles they might find out where he was really going. Which could destroy everything he had worked to build.

As he reached for the brass rail of the trolley the thought crossed his mind that he should have given Rhea that part in *Pretty Mrs. Smith* that she wanted. Instead he had cast Fritzi Scheff as the eponymous heroine, after all, she was prettier. Maybe if Rhea had been cast she would have been so grateful that Hobart would fear no malice in her heart that would cause her to gossip about him. His actresses trusted him and he could trust them. There was a bond that formed. He knew how to make them look good and draw great performances from them, make them shine.

Rudisill, Garbutt, Zukor; these were powerful, rich men. More powerful than he even though he was a studio company owner and picture star. They were certainly wealthier. Wealth and power was what mattered to Rhea and other girls like her—the ones who weren't going to get the big roles and become famous. The girls who were flooding into Los Angeles as if the dam holding back beautiful girls had burst somewhere just outside the town limits. She was looking out for herself the way a pretty girl with not much acting talent had to. That's how it worked out here in Hollywoodland and he couldn't blame her. He didn't have to like it or her. But he couldn't blame her. And she just hadn't been right for the part, after all.

His tortured lungs raged against the abuse. He had fought back against the years of tuberculosis with vigorous exercise, and the warm, dry California climate had helped immensely. But for some reason, running turned breathing into an agony akin to inhaling fire. He slid onto an empty bench and sat up against the window, closing his eyes. He focused on slowing his breathing down, the way he had been taught in the sanatorium back in Arizona, by inhaling through his nose and out through his mouth. With any luck the ache would soon recede. His eyes closed, he listened to the sounds of the city: the beeping of the automobiles, the grinding of the streetcar wheels on metal, the clip-clop of a horse-drawn delivery wagon, the murmurs of the other passengers near him. He could smell the city, too—a familiar blend of dust and ocean, laced with a hint of orange. He never grew tired of the smell of Los Angeles. It seemed as if it was the fragrance of promise, and as he considered himself an optimist, whenever he caught a whiff of that particular blend, he always felt a little inward surge of forward momentum, a burst of hope. Even now, with threats of disaster hanging over him, he couldn't help but feel a little bit better. After all, he had a plan.

When he was finally able to inhale deeply and exhale through his mouth, he opened his eyes. The tall buildings of downtown, the Security Savings Bank, the Grosse Building, the Lankershim Hotel receded as the streetcar came up on the new auto-dealership district. After this, he rode past large tracts of undeveloped land interrupted by periodic eruptions of new small neighborhoods. If it weren't for the quality of the light, which was much brighter, this terrain could be Ohio, his boyhood home. It was at once attractive and repugnant.

He breathed a healthy-sounding sigh of relief as the streetcar bounced roughly onto the Electric Avenue line. The winter of 1915 had rolled in early and hard, and the orange trees had quickly been stripped of life and reduced to their twisted, gnarled bones. Hobart loosened his necktie and settled back against the rattan seat, letting the cool breeze blowing in from the Pacific dry his damp clothes. The more he pieced together the moments of the encounter—separating it from his emotions—the more confident he became that Rhea had not seen him. But that didn't change the fact that he still had to hightail it out of Los Angeles.

The trolley crested a hill, and from this vantage point he could see the sharp ribbons of glittering cobalt blue cut into the landscape just above the shoreline. It was a fascinating sight to Hobart. Only in Los Angeles, he thought. Only in a town in which the stock in trade was dreams could a man like Abbot Kinney have realized his vision of recreating the canals of Venice. And only in Los Angeles would anybody have ever thought it was a good idea. On close examination the genuine city of Venice, rising from its azure lagoon, was in and of itself a horrendous idea but at least its inspiration had been grounded in something resembling sense—to provide a natural defense against marauders and easy access to the commerce that traveled by sea. But this California Venice had been built ten years ago as an adventure in speculative real estate development—acres and acres plowed under and dug up, millions of dollars spent, all to create an interesting destination for the trolley. The imaginary made inevitable.

By the time he disembarked at the small station in front of the Lagoon Amphitheater opposite the amusement pier, only his damp collar remained as a reminder of his earlier mad dash. The thrill rides were shuttered for the season, the massive Ferris wheel, the twisting Automobile Races, the Mill Ride, and the Journey through Hades. A few old men dangled fishing lines from the pier into the calm waters beyond the surf. Hobart had never seen one fish caught from a pier in all the time he had spent on waterfronts in his life. But he always admired the optimism of the fisherman.

He turned his collar up and pulled his hat down against the chill wind that was blowing in off the ocean. Overhead a biplane bounced through the bright atmosphere, heading toward or coming from Ince Aviation Field in the distance. Behind him the imported Venetian gondolas tied to posts at the boathouse and grouped together like a log jam on the river thumped hollowly against one another. There were no lovers to ride today, nor gondoliers to serenade them.

Hobart walked east along what the residents referred to as the Grim Canal. The sea pumps that kept the lattice of carved waterways filled appeared to be under repair—their natural state it seemed—and the water was turning brackish with the waste from the settlement. It was one true thing, he noted, that Venice had in common with its namesake. He was grateful for the cool air. When the temperatures rose, so did the open sewer smell. Already there were community voices calling for filling in the canals and paving them under. He passed a flier drifting just below the surface of the water—a call to rally against the Kaiser in the great war raging in Europe. There were always people calling for change of some kind or another—pave Venice under or save Mother Russia—all the same.

He made a left and took the bridge that crossed the canal past the shuttered summer cottages, over another bridge across the Altair Canal, until he reached the small cluster of bungalows on U.S. Island. At the door of one, nearly hidden behind the great ferns in the small front yard, he gave the knocker a few loud taps, then waited for the footsteps. Soon enough the door swung open. Willoughby Hollis blinked and squinted into the sudden sunlight, trying to focus his bloodshot eyes on the figure on his doorstep.

After a long look he nodded, smiled slightly, and said, "Hullo Bosworth." He took a step back and let Hobart enter. The stuntman smelled of juniper berries and strong pipe tobacco, and so did his small house.

"How have you been, Champ?" The lights were off and the curtains were drawn. Hollis shut the door with his left hand, keeping his right arm tucked tightly against his body.

"Better than ever," he replied, seemingly unaware of the spastic twitch his head gave as punctuation to his sentence.

"I was just over at the Alexandria looking for you. Allan Dwan's there rounding up every cowboy he can find for his new Fairbanks picture. *The Good Bad Man.*"

Hollis shrugged with disinterest.

"Working much?"

"Keepin' my head up," he replied, shuffling toward the kitchen. "Want some java? I got some on."

"Sure." He sat down in a club chair, recognizing it as one of the pieces he had used a few years ago when he had first started Hobart Bosworth Productions with the film *The Sea Wolf*. Willoughby had taken them away when the wear and tear began to show on film. Now the leather cover was cracked and the cotton stuffing was leaking out in tufts. Willoughby came back carrying two large clay mugs, more props that Hobart recognized—these from his Canadian stories. Again, Willoughby kept his right arm close, even though it made holding the mug awkward. He handed Bosworth the other mug from his left hand.

"Busted rib?" Hobart gave a slight indication to Willoughby's right side.

"Ribs," he said with a groan as he lowered himself into the club chair's twin on the other side of the small coffee table. "Three of 'em." His head snapped spastically again and he grinned, revealing the bloody gap between his incisors. "A rough shoot."

He was lying. Hobart knew that if Willoughby had been injured in a fight scene that he would have heard about it on the grapevine. His old friend's injuries were not the result of a staged bar fight gone out of control and they weren't from a fall off a horse. Willoughby had been picking up money at the Friday night fights.

Hobart had met Willoughby in a match in Chicago years earlier when they were both in their early twenties—before Hobart had heard the call of the stage lights. Willoughby was the more experienced of the two, and slightly bigger. But the difference then, as it was now, was that Willoughby seemed to like the punishment of the ring and used it to fuel his combat, whereas Hobart avoided pain at all costs by striking earlier and faster. It was one of the reasons why Hobart's nose remained straight, and long, and handsome, while Willoughby's was spread across his face like the flattened mesas in Monument Valley. It was also one of the reasons why he had been, at least at one time, one of the most in-demand stuntmen in town.

In their first meeting, as in their second and third, Hobart had left the bigger man drooling on the canvas and fumbling for his mouth-piece. To Willoughby, the only man he could respect was one who had whupped him, which meant that he respected very few men. To those he did, his loyalty was deep and faithful and always earnestly surprising. When Hobart had succumbed to the lure of the movies, his friend left the fight and rodeo circuits behind to join him. As Bosworth's star had ascended, so did his need for a stunt double. Willoughby's physique was enough like his that he could pass on film. Hobart's hope was that there was still enough of that resemblance now for him to fool another more perceptive and less forgiving audience.

"I'm hoping what brought you out here was some of that money you owed me," Willoughby said, the missing teeth turning his "s" sounds into sputtering lisps.

"To my recollection we're all square. The lawyer that kept you from going to jail on a drunk and disorderly didn't come cheap."

"I'd have taken my pinch. At least I'd a had some of my life savin's waitin' for me when I came out."

"You made an investment in my company, same as others have."

"And when's that gonna start payin' off for me again exactly?"

"You know, it's not a sure thing, show business. We're doing about as well as anybody else. But the houses take their share, and the distribu-tors, and then there's equipment and the Teamsters."

"And you haven't had a hit since *Sea Wolf*."

"My pictures do well."

"But you haven't had a hit in two years. And hits pay the bills. And pay back investors. So I haven't got my money back." He rubbed his left hand over his right side.

"There's a gig," Hobart said. "A good one."

"So. So what's the gig? I don't know if you could tell by lookin' at me, but I ain't in shape for fallin' down right now. Or much of anything else."

"It's a part," he replied. "A real part."

Willoughby laughed. "Acting? I'd rather fall off a roof. You can't put this mug on film. You'd scare away the audience. We're trying to make money, remember?"

"It's a part you can play. I know you'll be good at it."

"What is it? The part?"

"Me."

"Come again?"

"I need you to play me."

"That's gonna be some kind of picture."

"It's not a picture. I need you to move into my house and pretend you're me."

"Over in Westlake? And give up all this? Okay."

"Listen to me. There's more to it than that."

"I said okay."

"Hang on, Champ. I've been putting it out that my tuberculosis is back. I've been out to Arizona for some treatment and now I'm shutting myself in to recuperate."

"You ain't sick?" Willoughby drew back slightly.

Hobart shook his head. "No. But you were right about needing a hit. In fact, we need a hit real bad. *Birth of a Nation* big. But without the troubles. One hit will put us in great shape. Hobart Bosworth Productions will be the going concern in town. Bigger than Biograph. Bigger than Famous Players. There are people who know that. People who want a piece."

"Other investors?"

"Something like that."

"Jesus, Bosworth. When are you going to realize that you're just an actor, not a businessman?"

"I have a plan and I need your help. I need for people to think that I'm still in town."

"Where are you going to be?"

"North."

"Where?"

"Will you do it or won't you?"

"Well, hell, brother! I already said I'd do it."

"So you'll lay low and let people think it's me holed up in my home?"

"With this face the way it is right now it's just as well I stay indoors."

Hobart stood up and fished for his keys. "You're the only one who knows. I've had to let the servant staff go." Willoughby, taking the keys, shook his head at the word "servant." "The larder and bar are fully stocked. There's everything you need plus five hundred dollars in cash in an envelope in the desk in my study." He didn't want to mention that the sum amounted to a little more than half of his overall current worth; the rest he carried on him. If his plan worked as he hoped then the money would be flowing again soon. "If anyone calls you just answer the phone, sound like me sick, and tell them to go away. Don't let anyone in at the gate. But let yourself be seen by passersby and delivery boys at the head of the path."

"How long will you be away to the north?"

"Only a week or so, I hope." He heard the distant buzzing of the bi-plane again. He hoped his gear had arrived at the airfield safely. He'd had to use a courier service that wouldn't recognize his name instead of the regular studio messenger. He would know soon enough; a quick glance at his pocket watch showed that he was due to meet his charter in half an hour. "You'll do it?"

"How many times do I have to say I'll do it? I'll do it."

"Okay. You'll go today?"

"As soon as I wrap up my affairs."

"I'm serious."

"Relax, chum," Willoughby said with a horrifying grin. "I'm on my way already."

Hobart opened the door and the brightness startled him. He had grown accustomed to the darkness of Willoughby's home. He felt Willoughby moving up behind him.

"What's your big plan for getting a hit? What are you going to do?"

Hobart Bosworth watched the small red plane on the horizon head in for a landing. "I'm going to catch a wolf."

CHAPTER TWO

THE STOMACH CRAMPS SEIZED Hobart three hours later about a thousand feet above the California coastline. Nerves. He had always had a vaguely nervous stomach and had to be very careful about what he ate, and for breakfast he had taken his usual fresh fruit and farina. But here he was flying through the clouds, squeezing his buttocks together as tightly as he could as the sweat streamed around his leather goggles and the lenses fogged up. He held himself rigidly, breathing in through his nose and out through his clenched teeth. He twisted in his seat, looking back.

"How much longer?" He pointed down toward the ground for added emphasis.

"What?" The Jenny rocked a little as the pilot looked up from his dead-reckoning chart. His own eyes looked like pupils inside the larger lenses of his goggles, making him resemble a strange owl that Hobart would have found hilarious under other circumstances.

"How long?"

"Soon!" Gerald Ruby cried over the wind and the roar of the biplane's engine. Ruby was not a particularly well educated man, nor would he ever be called clever. Nevertheless he was one of those lucky native-born Californians who became rich selling their parents' vast and once worthless ranchland to Los Angeles developers and now had the money, time, and passion for expensive hobbies. In this case the three converged around flying. Ruby had purchased one of the first JN-3s off the assembly line, and his offer to take any member of the Los Angeles Golf Club for a flight was a standing one. When he'd heard about Hobart's destination, he'd leaped at the chance to put his prize to such a test. He'd even refused Hobart's weak offer to pay for fuel and lodging on the way, and gone so far as to pack a lunch for them both.

Money. That was the cause of Hobart's nervous stomach today, he thought as he closed his eyes, waiting for the spasm to pass. He was worrying about money all the time now. How much did he have left? How much had he spent on this film or that contract? How long could he go? How much could he borrow? How much could he owe? How much could he lose? How much did he spend yesterday? That much? How? Had dinner cost that much? Why did he have to have that suit? That membership? How deep in shit was he?

A lot, according to his gut.

The money would come, he told himself. It always seemed to. He wouldn't have made it this far if he hadn't managed to squeeze blood from a stone. He knew how to be poor if he had to be. There was always a way to rustle up some cash—a poker game, someone interested in investing in motion pictures, a soft touch. He looked back again at Ruby. The man was younger than Hobart's forty-eight years, in his midthirties Hobart guessed. Hobart also knew that he didn't look much older than Ruby ("boyishly handsome" had been a recent *Variety* assessment) though he had started recently feeling his age on cold mornings and once in a while in bed with one starlet or another, he found he'd rather sleep than screw.

"If the wind and fuel hold," Ruby told him in a loud voice, "we should raise San Francisco by nightfall."

Hobart nodded.

"Hey," called the stout man. "I saw *The Sea Wolf* a couple of months ago at the Egyptian and you weren't in it. I thought you were Wolf Larsen."

Hobart sighed. "Yes," he called back, "I am Wolf Larsen. In the *authorized* version, which I produced and directed as well," he added for emphasis. He watched their shadow zooming over the ground below. The airplane ride was as thrilling as he had hoped. "That's an illegal production made by swindlers who did not have the rights from Jack London, as I did, to make that picture. We fought the Balboa Amusement Company in court over their version and we've just been recently vindicated completely. Those pictures are to be confiscated and burned. Thanks to us, you'll have to own the rights to a book, Jack London's or any others, to make a picture of it."

"Well, I thought it was pretty good anyway," the man said, somewhat defensively. "It's just a great story."

"My version was better," Hobart muttered, loud enough to be heard. "Definitive."

"Well, I liked your *Martin Eden* picture," Ruby shouted. "But I thought the fella that played him, Peyton, seemed a little stiff."

"I wanted to play the part myself but I just didn't have time," Hobart acknowledged.

"You're a little old for Martin Eden, ain't you? I mean he's a young fella."

"I'm an actor," he said, feeling a little hurt. "I could have played Martin Eden had I so chosen. Of course, anytime you want to come into the picture business with me, I'd be happy to let you consult on casting decisions like that as soon as your check clears. In fact, we've got an interesting project in development."

"Oh no, no, no." Ruby waved off that suggestion. "If I've told you once I've told you a thousand times, pictures are too risky for my blood."

"Safer than airplanes, though."

"At least my Jenny only has one pilot."

The perspective on clouds was like nothing Hobart had ever experienced before. They were mountains of gray spun glass, distant islands to remain ever unexplored, continents of dissipation. In his early twenties, before the boxing, before the vaudeville and the acting, he had gone to sea, working on cargo ships in an effort to put as many miles as possible between him and his father's horrible little farm in Ohio. The vista now reminded him of those days when his only burden was an uncertain future, as opposed to now when his certain burden was his mishandled past.

"Those fellas with the other *Sea Wolf*," Ruby hollered, "they really burned your ass, didn't they."

"Not that you'd notice," Hobart lied loudly and cheerfully. Hobart's first rule of the picture business was that you never told anyone the truth about the bottom line.

But the losses had been staggering. Although it appeared that his *Sea Wolf* had been a blockbuster, the money he had spent to defend his ownership of the rights to make the film from the popular book had wiped out any profits that had made their way to him. In fact, the battle to be proven right had driven his entire studio to the brink of failure, and he'd had to mortgage it to the hilt—to Rudisill, Garbutt, and Zukor.

"I bet old Jack London is sure gonna be happy to see you when we get there."

Hobart watched a single massive thunderhead form far to the east of the Jenny. Its dark edges were trimmed with the slightest highlights of pink. The whole colossal shape appeared to be painted on a backdrop of unimaginable scale.

"Sure."

"I can't wait to meet him. He's my favorite writer."

"Mine too." Hobart grinned to himself. It wasn't just because an airplane would provide the swiftest transport to San Francisco that he had called upon Gerald Ruby. As he'd learned from many years as an actor and director and finally producer, he had a canny, or uncanny, ability to find out what truly motivated people. Gerald Ruby always called the office of Hobart Bosworth Productions for passes to the premiere of a Jack London picture.

"I've read all his novels. *White Fang. Call of the Wild. Martin Eden.* All of them."

"Really? I lost count after his first dozen."

"Well, I've read a bunch of them, anyway. The story collection, too. You're positive he won't mind if I stay at his ranch with you all?" He sounded like a little boy asking his father for permission to get an autograph from a famous ballplayer.

"Are you kidding? Jack and Charmian love company. There are always people from out of town visiting at the ranch. Charmian calls their new mansion the Jack London Traveling Road Show Wolf House; it has over a dozen rooms just for guests. It's absolutely magnificent. Built of massive native redwoods and stones carved from local quarries. He's designed it himself. Last time I saw him he showed me the plans and we walked the foundations. It looks as if it has been there for a thousand years. As if Vikings had landed in California ages ago and built a great lodge in Glen Ellen before sailing into history leaving it for Jack London to discover on his Beauty Ranch."

"How much land does he own now?"

"Well, he's bought a number of farms and a vineyard over the past decade. I'd guess around two thousand acres."

"How long have you known him?"

"We went into business about five years ago. I licensed the film rights to some of his books. I've made *The Sea Wolf, Burning Daylight* parts one and two, *The Valley of the Moon, Martin Eden, An Odyssey of the North*, and *John Barleycorn*."

"Sounds like it's working out well for both of you."

"Absolutely." The thundercloud loomed larger. "It's been great."

Except for the swindlers.

And Garbutt and Rudisill.

And Adolph Zukor.

And Jack.

"My favorite hotel in the world," Hobart said, jumping from their hired car to the curb in front of the Palace. "As a young sailor on shore leave I used to stand on this spot and dream about staying here. I wanted to slide my hands over the brightwork and polished redwood, to shuffle my feet across the carpet. To rub elbows with the swells." The remembrance of those days—nearly thirty years past—filled him with a happy sense of warmth. The camaraderie of his waterfront friends, the companionship of the prostitutes, the songs, the liquor, the freedom of being young, that was what San Francisco used to mean to him. "Four years ago when I first came up to meet Jack London I finally got to stay here. It hasn't changed a bit from my younger days."

"Oh, yes it has," Ruby said, struggling with a heavy case bound with leather straps. He refused the driver's help with a curt, "Get the other things." He lowered the heavy case to the sidewalk with a grunt. "It was burned to the ground in the fire after the quake. It was rebuilt completely from the ground up. Then there was another fire on the inside in 1909 so they had to rebuild again."

"I hadn't heard."

"Really?"

"I don't follow the news much. Too busy working."

"So, this is not the Palace of your youth. Well, one thing they always did right was steak. Let's go check in and see if they still do."

"Do you need some help with that?"

"I got it," he said, hoisting it up to his chest and refusing the bell-man.

"What's inside?"

"Nothing really." He hoisted the box up on his shoulder and Hobart followed him and his mysterious cargo into the rich, glowing amber warmth of the hotel. The lobby was civilized—the original builder had feverishly pursued the European ideals of taste and service and the management had maintained or even exceeded the original vision. Hobart gestured for the bellman, the same one Ruby had brusquely dismissed moments before, and gave him command over his trunk and bag. He may not have known about airplanes and Ruby may have known more about the city than he did, but he had spent years touring from one theater to another and he knew how to get the best from the best hotels. Like many rich people who had grown up with service, Ruby merely expected it, unlike Hobart, who had learned how to demand it. He guided them both quickly through the process of checking into their separate rooms even though they had no reservations. Then he sent a cable to London at the Beauty Ranch, notifying him of their arrival in San Francisco and letting him know what time they would be arriving at Glen Ellen. The two men then adjourned to their rooms.

From his window, he could see the incredible rebirth of San Francisco. The city skyline was a skeleton of construction and scaffolding. Any building that didn't look as if it was being built looked new and clean and modern. As darkness settled across the city, Hobart could see strings of Christmas lights coming on, wrapped around numerous houses. It made the city seem alive and glittering in a way that Los Angeles never did.

Before long he had washed and changed into suitable dining clothes. For Hobart this meant a gray worsted suit, the wool from a small ranch nestled deep in the Scottish Highlands, crafted for him by his own studio tailor—the crisp, razor-sharp English style perfectly draping his tall, fit frame. They met under the Maxfield Parrish mural of the Pied Piper leading helpless village children to an uncertain fate, then were shown to their table under the curved arcs of cut glass that swept up to a ceiling that dripped heavy chandeliers in the crystal pavilion of the main dining room.

"I want to hear more about London," Ruby asked as they were seated. "Is he as strong as they say? I've heard he only eats raw beef that he raises himself on his ranch. Does he talk much about his hobo days? Did you ever ask him about the Gold Rush?"

Instead of answering Hobart politely turned his attention to the hovering waiter and began ordering the meal for both of them in a polite and knowing way. Ruby, a man who loved his food as much as the next gourmand, looked stricken at not being consulted. "But I was going to have a steak," he interrupted as Hobart began to order their third course.

"Trust me about the chateaubriand," Hobart responded. "The way they make it here, you'll never suffer a plain steak again." He turned to the waiter. "Ask the chef to be judicious with the béarnaise sauce, please."

"Of course," the waiter replied.

Ruby might have mastered the buying and selling of the earth and the art of flying over it, but when it came to fine living few had made such a study of it as Hobart Bosworth.

It was well known among show folk that Hobart Bosworth was exquisitely enlightened when it came to knowledge about wines. He had realized early on that educating himself about certain aspects of culture would make his ascent up society's ladder easier. He had quickly learned that wine was one of those areas, like opera, where people acted as if they knew a great deal, when in fact, they did not. So he had applied himself to studying wines with the same vigor with which he had later studied fashion, food, literature, and, ultimately, picture making.

If, in the course of his self-education, Hobart had learned one thing about the rich and the powerful it was that they loved to be told what to do on occasion. It was as if they spent so much time ordering others around, that when the tables were turned and someone took control in a surprising way, they were almost relieved not to have to make another decision. Ruby appeared to be no different—his proud shoulders sagged somewhat at his having ceded control of his food. But it only took a sip of the '03 Heidsieck Brut before he regained his focus and began asking about London again. Was he really six foot five and had he really celebrated his eighteenth birthday in the Yukon by wrestling a grizzly bear? Did he really have twenty unpublished novels in a vault? Was it true that President Roosevelt had placed a call to the Japanese to have him released from prison? How had Hobart Bosworth come to know him?

Finally a question Hobart could answer. He thoughtfully chewed on a slippery Olympia oyster, swallowed it, cleared his throat, and paused for a long moment. "I wrote him a letter." He signaled for the maître d' and then continued as the man headed across the large room. "I had fallen in love with his books—I explained how I shared his love for the greatness of nature and his loathing of the worst aspects of civilization. I, like him, had spent years of my youth on the seas or on the road. I had turned to art, first acting the classics and then directing moving pictures, as he had turned to writing to tell the truth. And I was successful, though by no means as successful as he."

"Sir?" The maître d' had arrived in answer to his gesture.

"There should be a message addressed to me. By wire or phone. Would you ask after it at the desk?"

"Absolutely, Mr. Bosworth. I'll take care of it. How is everything?"

Hobart immediately identified the gentleman's accent as Romanian. "Everything's fine, thank you. Oh! Please tell the steward we're ready for the Château Montrose."

"Immediately, sir." The man melted away.

Hobart focused for a moment on the music drifting through the room—a soul-touching melody drawn from a harp, flute, and viola. He loved bringing musicians on set to help set the mood and edited his scenes to music as well. He wished he could attach music to his pictures. It would add so much. Often he would choose an accompaniment for his pictures with cues for the musicians. The results were less than satisfactory. No two theaters ever played it the same way.

"I wanted *The Sea-Wolf.* Griffith had made a one-reeler of *The Call of the Wild* and had done so fairly well. But I knew *The Sea-Wolf* for what it was, London's masterpiece. I told him how the conflict between the mighty Wolf Larsen and the intellectual Van Weyden was the most perfect illumination of the struggles within human nature itself ever written in America. I knew not even Griffith had the ability to tell such a story on film. I begged him for permission to tell the tale. He wrote me back promptly."

Ruby looked up from his chateaubriand, which he had attacked with delight. His face had taken on the color of the wine. Hobart's meal remained mostly untouched; he had ordered it mostly for show. He hated to see it sitting there untouched—it had cost so much—but his stomach was in no condition to accept it. He deducted the cost of the meal from his overall capital and forced himself to take a few bites.

With only a few hundred bucks left, food like this would be scarce from now on.

"You know that Jack London receives a tremendous amount of mail from all corners of the world because his works are published everywhere, and he is famous everywhere. He writes his new works in the morning. One thousand words a day, every day. If he misses his target, then he makes up the difference the next day in addition to his daily one thousand. In the afternoon he attends to his correspondence, answering all his letters personally. Whether you're a comrade socialist seeking encouragement or a young writer seeking advice, if you have written to Mr. Jack London, you will receive a letter in return. And so he wrote me back as well. He knew of my pictures and recognized in my love for nature and beauty that I was a kindred soul. He extended an immediate invitation to visit him and Charmian at the Beauty Ranch. And I caught the Pacific Coast Express up here.

"Beauty Ranch in the Valley of the Moon, well, you'll see it for yourself tomorrow. It is an astounding experiment in utopian vision. A convict on parole from San Quentin can find a job there, as can any Joe down on his luck. He is pioneering farm sciences from around the world; terracing from the Orient, plowing under crops and letting the fields sit fallow for years as they do in France. He has dammed up a creek to create a lake that provides irrigation for his crops. The design he has created for a hog sty is a model for cleanliness that Sinclair Lewis would admire. He is breeding beef cattle from the finest California stock. He is even attempting to revive the dormant local industry of wine making with his acres of grape vines. All this while still setting the pace for American writers."

The maître d' appeared as smoothly as he had recently vanished. "I'm sorry, Mr. Bosworth, but there is no message of any sort for you at this time. However as soon as it comes in I have asked them to let me know."

A small icicle of anxiety pierced Hobart's nearly empty stomach. "All right," he said, dismissing the messenger.

"No word from London?" Ruby asked.

Hobart shook his head. "But I did send the message late. He may not have received it yet, or Nakata, his manservant, may be waiting until the morning to give it to him." That was the best situation he could hope for, the icicle reminded him. The apple dumpling dessert was draped in a warm brandy hard sauce. He poked the pastry around on the dish and sipped his port.

"Jack London greeted me as a brother. I spent a week on his land, riding horses with him, watching the progress of Wolf House, listening to him read from his latest works at night before he disappeared to research the classics or read the latest from the fields of science or literature or philosophy. By the end of a week in his presence I had decided to form Hobart Bosworth Productions, Inc., in order to go into partnership with him to create a series of pictures based on his works. And over the past three years that's exactly what I've done."

"So what explains the urgency of our trip today? Why not take the train again?"

"I thought you wanted to meet him."

"Of course I do!" Ruby was slurring his words. His being seemed to have settled in a place of contentment.

"Well, I'll tell you what I'm after. I want a Jack London story that's exclusive to me. I don't want to be chiseled by the phonies again. Now that we've won our copyright battles, it'll be even harder for them. And they can't shoot a competing version if I have the original screenplay. An original Jack London story written expressly for the pictures is bound to be as close to a sure-fire hit as one can have in this crazy business. No one can walk into a bookstore and buy a copy of it—they'll have to see it in the theater. I'm in a hurry because life is short and I want to get Jack excited about this as quickly as possible."

Ruby's eyes were bright with enthusiasm. "Jack London writing original moving picture stories," he whispered.

"Stimulating, isn't it?" Hobart sat back and watched his companion closely.

"Incredibly."

"Just think. In a few short hours you're going to be party to the birth of a new Jack London work—a new chapter in his amazing career. You and I are going to turn Jack London into a picture writer."

"I can't believe it."

"Believe it. It'll be better and bigger than *Birth of a Nation.* I guarantee it."

"What's the story?"

"I'll leave that to Jack. He'll do what he does best, and then I'll do what I do best."

Ruby nodded eagerly, and Hobart knew that the hook he had been trying to set all day was in. It was only later, when he was alone in his room, with the chill wind blowing wisps of fog through the open floor-to-ceiling windows that looked out over the bay, as he held the receipt for the massive dinner he had just paid for, that he vomited up the little food he had eaten. But even that hadn't purged his gut of the growing, digging, twisting icicle.

CHAPTER THREE

Hobart awoke just after dawn still perturbed by the fact that, too old or not, he should have played Martin Eden, the fictional hero of the story of London's own rise from poverty to fame. He'd wanted to, but the pressures of adapting the book for the screen, as well as producing and directing, had seemed too much of a burden at the time. He could see himself in the part; worn shoes, holes in every pocket, cigarette burns on the sleeves, a notebook full of story ideas, a handful of rejection letters from publishers in his fist, the writer on the eve of the success that would transform his life. Hobart knew he could transform from that Eden to the one full of weariness, the one who carried the disillusioning sickness with the world and from the world that gnawed at his coiled innards, the dying of his soul preceding the dying of the flesh. Martin Eden became a young man without hope. He was a character for whom suicide was the preferable choice to life and suffering. At least in the final plummet from a ship's stern, all would be still and dark and bliss.

He sat up and poured a glass of water. Were things so desperate that some part of him was contemplating suicide? He thought not. He had hope. He was an actor at heart, after all. And what was an actor, if not ever hopeful—that there would be another play, another part, another audience? He lived on hope.

He knew how to create characters beyond what was written on the page. During the rehearsals of *Hedda Gabler* in New York he had had the critical insight that Lövborg, the drunkard intellectual, must stand ramrod straight at all costs and at all times in order to preserve his dignity. It was understood in the theater that drunks must always be played as swaying, loose-limbed wastrels, and the arguments with his director had been epic. But he was so sure he was right and the audiences and critics bore him out. No one had seen the pride of a man crippled by alcoholism so realistically portrayed before. He often found himself praised in the reviews before and above the grand Mrs. Minnie Fiske herself. It was the role that had made him a star.

He set down the empty glass and muttered to himself what he had divined to be the proper interpretation of the dream; *I should have played Martin Eden*. He swung himself out of bed. *Then it would have been a hit*.

He bathed while waiting for his breakfast cart to arrive, letting the warm water wash away his stress and the remaining wisps of the dream that still clung to him. He then ate in his robe, sitting on the edge of his bed, watering down his coffee to a weak brew, and dipping the edges of his sourdough toast in the running yolks of the poached eggs. Years of traveling and touring had taught him that you couldn't poach a rotten egg, and they had the further virtue of being well tolerated by his stomach. Then he dressed, today in a soft brown wool suit, appropriate for both the season and the occasion. He packed up his case, rang the desk for the bellhop. Upon exiting the room he found the copy of *Variety* he had requested folded neatly by the door. He scanned the headlines, then tucked it under his arm and descended to the lobby to wait for Ruby and his mysterious case to make their way down. When he finally arrived he was cheerful but bleary eyed, indicating the anathema of the idle rich to the early morning hours.

Together they rode in a taxi to the busy waterfront and caught the ferry to Sausalito, then another north to Petaluma at Sonoma Landing. The bay traffic was a riot of massive steamships, the ocean liners and freighters, marching relentlessly out to sea, and the smaller local craft, fishing vessels and merchant craft of that sort, that shot about the larger boats' shadowy wakes and played before their looming prows like speedy, insolent waterbugs. Upon reaching the small ferry outpost at the point where city began to give way to country, they headed to the station servicing the Southern Pacific Line. Before long the small train left the station and they headed into the low rolling hills of the Sonoma Valley. A light rain began to fall over the farmland.

Hobart opened his *Variety*. It was the only paper, other than *Film Daily,* that he read on a regular basis, even though he was far removed from the theater scene of the East Coast and the vaudeville circuit in general. Here was news of his old friend, Lowden Adams, opening to-night in *Our American Cousin* at the Booth while Grace George's presence had contributed to the extension of the run of *Major Barbara.* He had worked with her before and would love to see her in the pictures. But film acting was beneath top stage actresses such as herself in spite of all he had done to prove its worth. Tucked here and there throughout the paper were ads for pictures in circulation, including the ones from Para-mount, which distributed the pictures of Hobart Bosworth Productions, Inc. The biggest of these by far was the ad placed by Fox Films for *De-struction*, starring Theda Bara. Hobart made a mental note to send her a bouquet when he had the chance, and to make sure Paramount bought a bigger ad for his next picture. When. And if.

Ruby sat for a little while with his hands in his lap. He seemed slightly anxious, as if debating whether to ask a question or take an action in the brief times when Hobart stopped reading and began flip-ping pages. Finally, he stood and opened his case, which he had placed on the rack above the seats. Hobart feigned a lack of interest. Ruby pulled an object out, closed the case, and sat down. Hobart could see that it was a book.

"What are you reading?" he asked innocently, putting down the paper.

"*Valley of the Moon,*" Ruby replied, holding up the copy for Hobart to examine. "First edition. I, uh, thought this would be a good time to reread it."

"How many of his books are you carrying?"

Ruby cleared his throat and made a hand gesture of surrender. "All of them," he said at last.

"All first editions?"

Ruby nodded. "I told you I had all his books."

"I didn't know you meant with you."

Ruby sat down, clutching the book. "I was hoping I could find an opportune moment to have him sign it. Or a few. I went a little over-board probably, didn't I."

"I wouldn't worry about it. I'm sure he'll be flattered. If I know Jack, he'll happily sign them all and throw in a few copies of his latest to boot."

His traveling companion's face lit up like a child who had been given a full sack of Christensen glass marbles.

"When we arrive," Hobart told Ruby, "Jack should be waiting for us either on his trap or in one of the Glen Ellen taverns. If he is late then we will hear him coming because of all the bells he's fixed to his wagon. Then we'll see something wonderful as the townsfolk turn out to wave as the emperor of Glen Ellen drives his team through town. It's a sight to behold. I almost hope he's late so we get to see it. We'll have several drinks in his favorite tavern, so I hope you're thirsty. Jack will have his own bottle of whiskey, but he'll buy for anyone in the saloon. Since the people of Glen Ellen know this they will crowd the bar. Fortunately for Jack, it's a small town. After much singing and storytelling, hopefully more of the latter and less of the former, we'll race up the mountain as fast as two horses can and there we'll be, guests of the Beauty Ranch in the Valley of the Moon." He took the book from Ruby's hands. "Shall I read to you some of my favorite passages?"

"Yes, please." Ruby settled back. And as they rolled toward the knobby hills covered in spruce and oak, Hobart read the romance of Billy and Saxon as they left the hardships of city life behind them for a new life of freedom and love in this very land.

The rain was falling steadily as the train arrived in Glen Ellen just past two o'clock, as scheduled. The deluge had swept the streets clean. There was no one to be seen, and no horse-drawn carriage waiting any-where along the street as Hobart had expected. Across from the train station were several low-storied buildings, including the post office, a hotel, and the general store. The rest of the buildings, from where the road turned into town to where it turned left and away toward the Valley of the Moon, seemed to be the other outlets of support for the local economy.

"Sure is a drinking town," Ruby said, stating the obvious. Hobart peered to the end of the road. London had preferred the tavern just at the end of the street on the curve, the Overton, on his last visit. But again, there was no sign of his customary vehicle in front.

Ruby looked at him with raised eyebrows. "Should we wait?"

"I want to check out a few of the bars first. He might be having a drink."

Ruby took off his coat and wrapped it around his case. "Let's go!" he cried cheerfully. Hobart grinned. He had chosen his traveling companion well. Off they sped into the downpour, dashing into one saloon and then the next, each time to be greeted only by a dour bartender who had only the shake of a head for them at the mention of London's name. Finally, breathless and wet, they stood on the porch of the yellow brick hotel.

"Let's see if they have a phone we can use," he told Ruby, sweeping the water from his face. Ruby nodded. As they entered the lobby Hobart paused for a moment at the familiar sign that hung over the doors: No Dogs—No Actors. He sighed inwardly. If only John Wilkes Booth had been a lawyer.

He let his eyes adjust to the gloom of the lobby. Old gas lamps and a dying fire in the fireplace provided illumination that barely cut through the murk of deep red rugs and old dark wood. The front desk was empty and there were no other souls in the room. The faint scent of roasting fish hung in the air. Ruby went to the fireplace and stamped his feet, rubbing his hands near the flames to dry and warm them, casting his eyes over the photos framed and placed on the mantle. Hobart approached the front desk and rang the bell. The pathetic chime echoed once and then died a lonely death, unable to rouse anyone. He rang again and the sound followed its predecessor into the darkness.

"Maybe we should just head back over to the Overton," he said, walking across the lobby to Ruby. He had to appreciate the decor; the furniture was rustic yet expensive, and well chosen. Glen Ellen had the reputation for being a country retreat for the wealthy of San Francisco and Oakland, and the hotel lived up to it.

"Right now? It's pouring out." Ruby was right, the downpour had turned torrential, biblical. "I'd just as soon wait here until the rain lets up a little."

The warmth of the fire was attractive. It pulled the cold dampness from Hobart's bones.

"I wonder what happened to the third floor?" Ruby was pointing at one of the photos of the hotel. "There's a third story here, but this building only has two stories now. Wonder what happened?"

"Quake happened."

The two men spun around from the light of the fire and peered into the dark room. The creaky, laconic voice that had answered Ruby came from somewhere just beyond their vision.

"The 1906 quake flattened out the top floor like a flapjack."

Now Hobart could see a figure moving toward them. The man was short but still lost in the shadows.

"Lucky any of it stood at all."

Hobart cleared his throat. "Jack?"

"Excuse me?" The man who stepped into the light of a gas lamp was wizened and brown like one of the countryside's many Joshua trees.

"I'm sorry," Hobart said. "I thought you were . . . I was expecting someone to meet us."

"Ain't no one come in here today but us," the man replied, stepping into enough light that Hobart could see his crooked smile. "You two lookin' for rooms? Plannin' on stayin' with us?" He walked back to the front desk.

"Actually, we just came in to get out of the rain and to use your telephone."

"Phone's out," the innkeeper said, taking up his post behind the desk. "Electricity too. Happens every time it rains. Weather never seems to affect the whale oil, though." He nodded at the lamp on the desk.

Hobart looked out the window at the street. The train had departed and the small station was deserted. There was no sign of London's trap anywhere up or down the street, that much he could see at least through the sheets of rain.

"Maybe we should wait down at the tavern?" Ruby suggested, interrupting Hobart's train of thought.

Hobart held up a finger to him, then turned back to the innkeeper. "My friend and I are on an errand of some urgency," he said. "Maybe you can help us. Is there anywhere in town I can hire a pair of horses? We can return them tomorrow without a doubt." A burst of lightning followed by a crash of thunder startled the old man. Hobart could tell because the man blinked, twice. This was a man who liked to believe he had seen it all. "Or an automobile."

"I can do for you both or one or t'other," was the drawled reply. "Which one d'ya want?"

"The auto," Ruby quickly spoke up, as the thunder rumbled again. "Definitely the auto."

The truck was a Ford Roadster, which was, for all intents and purposes, Mr. Ford's basic Model T with the back shorn off for light cargo hauling. Even though the innkeeper, Mr. Chauvet, had affixed a tarp to cover the back, Ruby insisted on keeping his heavy case of precious books on his lap as they bounced their way out of the village. Their luggage, on the other hand, he had no problem stowing behind them. Hobart found himself doubting that all of those books, signed by the author and God himself, would be worth as much as the hand-tailored clothes he had packed in his trunk. Because the back of the car was so light, the rear wheels bounced and skittered through the muddy furrows worn deep in the dirt that the road transformed into beyond the limits of the village. Hobart struggled to keep the vehicle from fishtailing out of control as they climbed up the mountain. Low branches hung heavily, drenched with rain, sweeping across the roof with a whispery caress, leaving behind the thick, heady scent of eucalyptus.

"It'd be a real hoot if we ended up having to hike back into town," Ruby chuckled as Hobart pulled them out of a skid. A short while later he said, "I know we're moving forward but it seems like we're moving back. I can't tell how you can see anything," he added.

Hobart felt his hands tighten on the wheel and he clamped his jaw shut. Nothing looked familiar. He had been up here on bright summer days. Now the dark gray of the storm was giving way to the darker gray of impending night.

"I wonder how far down it is?" Ruby wondered aloud, looking over the edge just beyond the road.

Hobart was opening his mouth to invite Ruby to find out for himself when he saw something he recognized. The ranch arch, made of redwood, standing over an inviting path, the letters twisted from wood into the single word "Beauty." He hit the brakes.

"We're here," he said. "We're here."

He turned the wheel and pointed the flivver up the path. The redwoods lining the road formed a strange gauntlet of silent guardians, stoically holding a verdant roof above the road. Hobart quickly drove to a fork in the road. "The old cottage is up that way, by the lake," he said, pointing to the right. "But Wolf House is down this way." He turned the car to the right and headed up another small hill. "It's set back by the edge of a ridge." The going was even rougher than it had been on the worst of the road out of town and several times he had to wrestle with the truck's tendency to wallow helplessly in the mud. Now Ruby braced himself, wild eyed, against the dashboard. At least he was quiet. "Just ahead," Hobart grunted as they topped the hill and a clearing opened up before them.

The truck skidded to a stop, cutting the engine off, its roar replaced by the low steady drumming of the rain on the roof, the hood, and the tarp behind.

"Jesus Christ!" Ruby said. "What the hell?"

Hobart fumbled for the door latch and it flew open, banging against the front of the truck. He stumbled out, stepping into the mud and the rain. He hadn't even put on his hat, and the rain spattered down on his bare head, plastering his hair to his skull.

What lay before him was no tribute to man's desire to live a modern life in concert with nature, no story of London's writ large across the land, no fruit of any imagination save the damned. Wolf House, the glorious expression of triumph, the cathedral to writing that was to stand a thousand years, was a ruin.

The gorgeous, hand-hewn redwood walls that Hobart had seen being erected with his own eyes were gone, leaving behind a haunted shell. Only the great stones, carved from nearby quarries, were left standing upon one another as they had first been set by the hand of man. Stone fingers, the shattered remainders of supports, reached skyward, straining in agony toward the heavens. Even in its gloom, its silence and form told a story of intent, of rooms laid out, of floors once lofted, of massive chimneys rising to the level of the great trees surrounding it. The corpse of the great house still spoke of dreams of home and happiness gone as dark and hollow as the vacant, black fireplaces, as empty as the deep meditation pool that was the centerpiece and the soul of the design.

A sensation gripped Hobart, as if the land he was standing on and surrounded by were swirling around him with the pivot point buried deep in his gut. A low, deep hum, a vibration that rose and fell, tickled at his ears.

"What happened here?" Ruby shouted at him.

A dank air of despair hung in the air over the ruin, dripping from the branches of the eucalyptus trees even as the rain did. Hobart was filled with dismay that something that had promised such beauty had been reduced to such devastation. He could barely hear Ruby over the rushing noise that filled his head.

"I . . . I don't know." He gestured futilely. "I just don't know."

"I thought you and Jack were friends! How could you not know about something like"—Ruby threw a wave toward the ruin—"like this?"

Hobart's world suddenly stopped spinning and he felt very small in it. "Because," he said, "Jack London stopped speaking to me last year."

"What?"

He took a few steps toward what was left of Wolf House, stopping when he slid on loose shards of slate roofing tile. "Zukor put it around that I was holding back money owed to him. I wasn't. But he thought I was chiseling him. I just found out about it a few weeks ago and I was coming up here to clear things up because he wasn't responding to my letters and cables."

"Well, obviously, because he's got other things on his mind! And what the hell is that racket?"

Hobart hadn't realized that Ruby could hear the strange noise as well. Up until that moment he had thought that only he could hear the sound of his life falling apart. They both turned to look back up the road behind them. Over the hill came a coughing and sputtering truck, older and in much worse shape than theirs. Its engine was creating the sound they heard. It drew to a stop and the air around them grew still; even the rain seemed to fall more quietly. A woman stepped out of the cab. The woman's simple ranch garments, a faded canvas skirt and vest, cotton blouse, round field hat, hung over her squat form. Her eyes were set in a face so hard that it looked as if it had been molded from cast iron.

"Mr. Bosworth," the old woman called to him in a voice that sounded like cracking wood, "you'd better come along on back to the house."

CHAPTER FOUR

WITHOUT SPEAKING A WORD, and with Ruby sitting quietly seething beside him in the passenger seat, Hobart followed the truck back up the road. Eliza Shepard was not a woman to be crossed. Hobart knew her to be stern, hard in the way of a woman who had spent her life in hard, resentful servitude to the classes above her. He also knew she could hold a grudge and was protective of Jack. As the ranch overseer she only had his best interests at heart. As his step-sister, older by more than ten years, she also had his ear. Hobart knew better than to get on her bad side. Only problem was, he couldn't tell if he was already there. Her sour expression never changed, and the funereal air that surrounded her never seemed to dissipate.

After traveling some way he could see two stone cylinders rising over the trees like defensive towers guarding a medieval fortress. But when the car turned the bend there was no fortress, only a large, modestly styled white ranch house. Hobart parked in the gloomy shadow of the pair of silos—the largest in California, or so Jack had told him when they had been in the planning stages. Hobart noted the other ranch vehicles, a tractor, several wood wagons, and the rig in which he had expected to see Wild Jack make his town appearance. Once handsome with trim, the wood of the wagon's railings was split in places and the harnesses of silvery bells, which deserved better reward for providing their simple pleasures, had been slung over the bench to rust.

The rain had stopped falling in torrents and become a more reasonable shower. Hobart and Ruby got out of the car and headed across the mud-filled flat toward what was affectionately known as "the cottage." To the left was Jack's state-of-the-art concrete pigpen known as the Pig Palace in local parlance, which featured individual rooms and play areas for each sow and her litter. A creature sat on its haunches in one of the pens, swaying gently and making no effort to get out of the rain. At first Hobart thought it was a large pale dog, but as he drew closer he could see that it was an emaciated pig—something he hadn't even known was possible. Her pink skin pooled in folds around her haunches and her nipples drooped like tired fingers. The pig looked at him through bleary red eyes, sneezed, then turned and wobbled on loose limbs back toward the center building and out of view.

He heard the sound of coarse laughter coming from the stable to the right of Jack's Pig Palace. The stable, and older buildings behind it, were all that remained of the ranch's previous incarnation as a failed winery. Several ranch hands were standing under the eaves, smoking cigarettes and telling one another crude jokes in an indolent, ill-mannered way. They grew silent as Eliza mounted the steps to the cottage, glaring at her with heavy-lidded, stubborn expressions. She met their gaze with as much scorn. One of the men spat, and then they turned back and disappeared into the darkness of the barn.

"Jack's gone, isn't he?" Hobart said, standing below Eliza on a stone set before the steps up to the porch. For a short woman she towered over him, droplets falling from her prairie hat, brown eyes focused darkly upon him. "He's not here."

"That's right," she said. "He's gone away and God himself only knows if he's coming back. Now why don't you and your friend come inside before you catch pneumonia like those damn pigs."

They followed her inside. Hobart's eyes adjusted to the warm but dim interior.

"Electricity's out," she said. "Hang up your wet things and take your shoes off, please."

As they slipped out of their jackets and hung them on pegs, Hobart introduced Ruby. He set his case of books down on the floor and shook her hand, apologizing for their intrusion. She brushed it away with a flick of her hand.

"Did you get my cable?" Hobart asked.

She shook her head. "One of the hands saw a truck head down over to Wolf House. I thought you might be one of Jack's readers come to bother him so I went down to fetch you," she said.

"Eliza," Hobart said, "what happened to Wolf House?"

"Ain't it obvious?" She shrugged and shook her head. "Fire. 'Twas in the papers." She turned and beckoned them to follow. "I've got some coffee made and there's some stew so have a seat." She swept aside a heavy ornate drape to reveal the dining room. A chandelier made from a ship's wheel hung from the ceiling over a large square table covered in some kind of tropical cloth or tarp. Lining the opposite wall were dark cabinets full of china, silverware, and enough service settings to entertain a small division of hungry visitors. Several large rocking chairs, composed of wide pieces of a soft light wood, were comfortably placed around the room. A door to the right led to the kitchen, while on their left was a large window that looked out upon the small, algae-covered pond.

"Make yourselves comfortable," she said. "I'll be back in a few."

"May I smoke?" Ruby asked.

"If that's what it takes to make you comfortable," she replied, then swept from the room. Ruby lit a cigarette and then strolled to the cabinets, examining the collections. Hobart sat in one of the rockers, which accepted him with a welcoming squeak. He watched the rain make dimples in the pond. A family of ducks searched its surface for food, oblivious to the heavy weather.

"How could you not know that his dream house had burned to the ground?" Ruby asked, without looking at him.

"I don't follow the news much," he replied, exasperated at having to repeat something he had already told the man. "I determined a long time ago that most news didn't have much impact on me, and I didn't have much on it. So I gave up reading about it."

"So there's a war on the horizon and yet you choose not to know about it?"

"Oh, I know about it. I have conversations with people. I hear the latest at parties and on my sets and such. It's like a book that I choose not to read though many others have."

"But the war will affect you. Don't you want to know about that?"

"It hasn't affected me so far. I'm too old to fight. I have no children to go off and fight. War. People will still need to be entertained, I've found—in wartime and in peacetime, in good times and bad. That's what I do. I provide them with entertainment so they can forget about those things in the news.

"On the other hand," he continued, "you're a loyal reader of Jack's and you follow the news. Had you come across this incident in your papers?"

Ruby finally met his eyes. "No."

"Well, then," Hobart said and left it at that.

Eliza entered with a tray holding a carafe of coffee, mugs, cream, and sugar, and set it on the table. The two men took seats and let her pour the dark brew into their cups. "This is Jack's favorite Kona coffee. He has it sent to us from Hawaii." The aroma, carried up on wisps of steam, was rich and soothing. "The cream is from our own cows, who only eat the grass we grow here following Jack's natural techniques and philosophy." Hobart added some cream and sugar and had a sip. Maybe it was because he was chilled, or perhaps because the flavor was strong enough to draw away his attention from his concerns, but it seemed as if he had never had coffee so good before in all his life. It was, quite simply, the best he had ever tasted.

"Though there's only three cows left in the herd. All the rest died during the summer." Eliza stopped speaking and was staring at a spot on the carpet. Hobart followed the path of her eyes but saw nothing other than the pattern on the floor.

"What is it?"

"I was just recalling that on the night that Jack completed *White Fang* he called us all down, everyone who was on the land. The property was much smaller then, only two hundred acres or so. There might have been fifteen or so guests in all and Charmian and myself. And Jack sat on the floor right there. And everyone sat around him. And he read that story. He read it all night long and no one moved, it was that good. I was just remembering that night. Ten years ago. Only ten years. So much has gone right and so much has gone wrong."

"Eliza, what happened to Wolf House?"

"Somebody set fire to it. Ain't it obvious? Took more than two years to build and more money than I ever earned in my entire life. Then, one August night, the night before we were all to move from this house down to there, I heard voices shouting and saw people running and saw the flames rising over the trees and the clouds above turning orange and

I ran. I ran over the path in the dark night with men ringing bells and hollering and I ran through the darkness and I got there and Jack was standing silently with tears streaming down his face. Then Charmian turned up and she had to show how it affected her most deeply of all of us. Oh, the weepin' and carryin' on.

"Someone had gone through Wolf House with a torch in the middle of the night spreading fire from room to room."

"Who?"

"Ask *her*," she spat.

"Charmian? You're not saying his own wife burned it down? I don't believe it."

She clenched her jaw, the skin like worn, oiled leather drawn taut over wood, and whatever emotion might have been welling up in her was swallowed back. "Sometime you ask her what happened."

"Poor Jack," Hobart said, trying to imagine the man's disappointment.

"Why not rebuild it," Ruby stated more than asked. "The insurance companies must have paid off royally. Why not rebuild?"

She turned to look at him. "We hadn't yet insured Wolf House. So much money was going to the house and to the ranch. For all the money Jack earns, we live in debt and on credit, most of the real money spent before the check ever arrives. In the months leading up to the completion of the house there wasn't a cent to spare for insurance what with all the extra hands, and Jack's not been selling books as well as he used to, though he can still sell a story to a magazine just by holding it up in the air when he's done. But we didn't have a thin dime to spend on insurance, and Jack told me, 'Eliza, don't you worry about it now. I've designed Wolf House to last for a thousand years. She'll certainly last a few months until we're on firmer ground and then we'll insure every brick, stone, and tile.'" She had a sip of her coffee. "He talks about rebuilding, says it's not about the money, but his heart's not in it. His heart's broken. It was his curse again, and this time, for the last time, he couldn't overcome it."

"What curse?" Hobart asked.

She waved her hand as if brushing away a fly. "Plume's curse," she said with a bitter chuckle. "Plume. You know, mother was a spiritualist? She was very popular for her séances. People would come all the way across the bay to receive answers from beyond the grave from their loved ones, hear their knockings, feel their cool breath, watch their ectoplasm flowing from mother's mouth. What they didn't know was that the knockings were Jack under the table, the whispering breath on their necks was me, and the ectoplasm? Silks soaked in olive oil that mother regurgitated to their horror. I always felt for poor Jack, just a boy, hiding in the darkness listening to mother fill her mouth with the dead. I know he tried hard not to believe, but mother was very good.

"Plume, she told her guests, was the spirit guide who led their loved ones from the lands beyond the grave to our parlor. She claimed he was an old Indian from before the white settlers came to California. I never knew how real mother considered Plume, but I know that when she took his voice, it filled me with dread.

"One time she wouldn't let Jack buy a book he wanted. He must have been about seven. He chose to sulk under the table during one of her sessions instead of responding to her and the customer left without paying. I knew she was furious. And when she started using Plume's voice, so did Jack. I never heard her as mad; we needed the money that had just walked out the door. I hid in the pantry, afraid to attract her attention, but that voice followed me. It was the most fearsome thing I've ever heard. I can't imagine how it must have seemed to my brother. She began speaking in tongues like a revival preacher. I almost believed the spirit of an Indian chief had entered our house. No mother could say the things she said to him.

"Plume laid a curse on Jack. A curse of failure. Mother claimed not to remember the curse and it's a hard thing to believe in. But I know Jack never forgot. He could never forget. I know the curse, whether Plume's or his own mother's, still rings in his ears. Somewhere in the back of his mind I believe he blames it for how it ended his first marriage to Bessie and drove his two daughters away from him. It was the curse that nearly ruined his dream boat before she launched on a seven-year voyage that lasted barely a year. It struck him with an illness that laid him out in an Australian hospital for five months. It cheated him of the son he always wanted, killed his third daughter after only three days of life, the only fruit of his second marriage.

"The curse ensured that the market for the first cash crop he would plant here, the twenty thousand eucalyptus trees, would fall out, that the herd of prize cattle would die on the terraced fields, that the pigs would catch pneumonia and die in his scientific piggery, that the peaceful socialistic community he hoped to found on the Beauty Ranch would devolve into brutality and anarchy. And Wolf House would burn. If he were to build it again, it would burn again. And again and again and again."

"That's some curse to turn him into the most famous and successful writer in America, if not the world," Ruby said.

"You mean to say that the fame and the money aren't part of the curse?" Hobart answered, holding Eliza's eyes with his own sympathetic ones. He could tell that she knew he understood what she was talking about in a way that Ruby never could. "He has to write now to support this life. He's like Karen in the fairy tale about the red shoes, the vain girl who couldn't stop dancing—he couldn't quit writing now if he wanted to. Isn't that right? Isn't that the worst part of the curse?"

She nodded.

He stood up. "And what has the fame brought him but that the eyes of the world are upon him in all matters at all times. Allowing lesser minds to mock him and taunt him about the failures that this curse, Plume's curse, has laid upon his doorstep. Inviting every Tom, Dick, and Harry with a pencil, paper, and a stamp to write to him asking for advice, a hand, a dollar, an endorsement. No. Fame and fortune can be their own curse. Though I'm sure that Jack would embrace that curse all over again if it meant that otherwise he would never have escaped the poverty and crushing work of his early life."

She broke her eyes away from his and bowed her head.

He looked out the window again. The heavy clouds had made the dark of night fall quickly over the ranch. "Where has he gone, Eliza?"

"Paradise," she said with an envious tone.

There was a rustle across the room and they all turned to look as a young Oriental man entered carrying a tray that held an ornamented tureen—Hobart could see mermaids holding the bowl aloft from the base—and a large round loaf of fresh brown bread. Hobart recalled that Jack had had a Japanese manservant, Nakata, but this fellow was younger than that other Asian. He set the tray on the table and went to the cabinets for some china and silverware.

"Thank you, Sekine," she said to the young man as he went about his tasks. She turned her attention back to her guests. "We have some wonderful beef and pork stew if you're hungry."

The smell of the bread in particular made Hobart's stomach gurgle, and he could see Ruby lick his lips in anticipation. But as he looked at the chunks of roasted meat floating in the rich brown sauce and thought of the dying herd and the sneezing pig, his appetite died away. He tried to caution Ruby away with a subtle gesture, but he only received a quizzical look in reply as his companion allowed himself to be served by Sekine.

"Eliza," he said, leaving Ruby to his fate, "I've written Jack a number of letters over the year and sent him some packages but he hasn't responded. Do you know if he's ever received them?"

She rose to her feet and picked up one of the lamps. "Follow me."

She crossed the room and for the first time, as the light from the lamp fell onto that corner, Hobart noticed a door set between the cabinets on the far wall. He walked after her as she opened it and left the dining room. Behind him, Ruby stood and followed them, bringing his bowl of stew along.

They entered a drafty hallway that led to a heavy wooden door set in a stone wall. "This is the old stone winery," she told them. "Jack uses it for storage." She felt inside the door and clicked a switch, but nothing happened. She beckoned them into the darkness and they watched as she drifted into the emptiness. After some fumbling, several lamps were lit and a glow filled the room.

The room was unadorned and had no furniture of any kind. Instead it was filled with crates and boxes.

"This is where we keep the mail and gifts Jack receives after he's written back or sent a note of thanks." She went to a wooden case and Hobart recognized it instantly. It was emblazoned with the logo of his own studio. She lifted the lid, but he already knew what was in it.

"Keep that lamp away," he cautioned. In its illumination he could see two expressions turn identically quizzical. "Silver nitrate film is extremely flammable. Burns up like that!" He snapped his fingers causing both expressions to blink simultaneously.

Inside the crate were the familiar (to him at least) round and flat aluminum tins, about the size of a dinner plate and the thickness of a steak, that contained reels of film. He picked up the top one from the two dozen or so inside. It was marked with his label and identified as *Burning Daylight* Reel 1." The seal on the side of the can was unbroken.

"He never even opened it." Hobart tossed the can back into the box. "None of them?"

She shook her head.

"I sent another box, too. Is there another . . . ? Ah! Here it is." He had found another large crate. Its lid had been loosened and he opened it. "I thought for sure he'd love this with the way he feels about progress and technology. This is a feat of engineering."

Ruby looked into the box with great interest. "What is it?"

"This is the latest invention from Mr. Edison's magical factory. It's a transportable motion picture projector." Inside the crate were several large cases and empty take-up reels.

"It's transportable if you have a staff, I suppose," Ruby sniffed.

"Are you kidding me?" Hobart cried. "This contraption weighs only eighty pounds, yet it's as steady as ones weighing hundreds more." He felt genuinely sad. "I really had hoped Jack would love it."

"He's never recovered from the burning of Wolf House," Eliza said. "I won't go so far as to say that it's broken his spirit because the spirit of Jack London could never be broken. But that someone would burn down Wolf House . . ." She drew the lid over the crate of film cans. "All of these boxes hold souvenirs of his travels, rewards of his career, which were to be displayed in the rooms of Wolf House. Now he can't bear to know of them, so they sit here until I decide what to do with them."

Hobart gazed around the room wondering what treasures could be found in the boxes. He could see crates indicating that they had been shipped from Fiji, Tahiti, Hawaii, Australia, Korea, Japan, London, New York, and Africa. "If only he had written to me. Sent me a letter or a cable. Instead of this passive, white silence."

She drew herself up imperiously, glaring at him and letting loose the words she seemed to have been holding back all evening. "Your partner indicated that you were chiseling Jack out of money and that was another betrayal he couldn't face. He trusted you, Mr. Bosworth. Of all the many people he has known he thought of you most of all as a kindred soul. How you could cheat him?"

"Your partner?" Ruby asked.

"Rudisill." Hobart sat on the edge of the film crate. He was feeling very tired.

"You're in business with Rudisill?" Ruby exclaimed. "But he's Frank Garbutt's man."

"That's right. He is. And Garbutt is Zukor's man. I borrowed some money from Garbutt—in exchange I had to put Rudisill in as my business manager. I didn't know that behind it all Zukor was brokering the deal."

"I never knew that Zukor was involved with Hobart Bosworth Productions."

"That's why they're called silent partners."

"Well," said Eliza, "I've never met a Mr. Rudisill nor Mr. Zukor, but Mr. Garbutt was the one you introduced us to at the *Sea Wolf* premiere over in San Francisco. And he's the one who came up here to see Jack just this past fall."

"He did?" Hobart was surprised.

"Yes. At first he said he came by to talk about the lawsuit against Balboa. But then he told Jack that you were defaulting on your agreement with him, that you were withholding his fifty percent of the profits for yourself. Then he asked Jack's blessing to try to remove you from the company so that he could clear the way for a new deal."

Hobart rubbed his hands over his face. "When I first wanted to make Jack's stories into pictures, I needed money. And Garbutt's the wealthiest man in Los Angeles." Ruby acknowledged the truth of this statement with a little bob of his head. "I mortgaged all of the property Adele, my ex-wife, left me, and my studio to Garbutt, through Rudisill, for twenty thousand dollars."

"Typical of Garbutt to keep his hands clean of a deal."

"So I received forty-nine shares of my own company. Rudisill acquired another forty-nine, with Garbutt and Zukor each receiving one, thought I didn't know about Zukor at the time. Once Rudisill had access to my books he was able to say that my movies, and I, have been nothing but failures and that the only way to get Garbutt's money back is to sell my studio. And Zukor is the buyer waiting in the wings."

"Those two know how to play both sides against the middle," muttered Ruby.

"That's it exactly. Garbutt has a lot of money invested in Zukor and he wants to help Zukor expand his business. He's already made Rudisill force me to distribute through Pallas and now Paramount. But my pictures have to get in line behind Zukor's own Famous Players and Jesse Lasky's Feature Play Company so there's not many theaters left so my pictures don't make money. What Rudisill says Garbutt and Zukor will distribute is more Jack London pictures—that's what the public wants and they'll clear out the theaters for a new one. But I don't have the rights to any more London stories. My only hope in coming here was to convince Jack to stand with me—two great artists against the capitalists—the Oligarchs, as Jack would call them. I had a feeling that Garbutt or Rudisill, or even Zukor, had reached out to Jack. But I never expected him to listen to them."

"It's hard not to listen when the words are about money," Eliza said.

"Adolph wants to rule Hollywood. Frank's tougher than Zukor but not as ambitious," Ruby said. "I've heard a story that at his first studio he wanted to fire an expensive film developer but couldn't because the man held the secret formula. So Garbutt had his kids sneak into the lab and weigh all the chemicals one night. The next morning he told the man to make him ten pounds of his solution that Garbutt was selling to another studio. Then, while the man was delivering it, Garbutt's children reweighed all the chemicals, which gave them the exact amounts that the man had used. Garbutt was so quick to fire the developer that the poor man couldn't even get back into the building when he came back that afternoon."

Hobart nodded. He'd heard the story, too. From Garbutt. It hadn't stopped him from getting involved. "So," he asked Eliza, "what did Garbutt ask from him in the end?"

"He wanted Jack to know that if he ever wanted to make more pictures that he would be better off selling his rights to Famous Players than to you. He wanted Jack to know that he would never see a dime as long as he continued his association with you—that you were a poor businessman and your company would soon go under."

"And what did Jack say?"

"He said he was disappointed to find that you, of all people, who was most like him of all men, was a plain thief and liar."

CHAPTER FIVE

HOBART AWOKE LATE IN the morning after a night of dreams that he couldn't remember. His head was clear and he felt remarkably unburdened for the first time in months, even years. His body was free from the usual aches and pains that plagued it early in the day. And he was suddenly aware of a stabbing hunger in his belly, as if he hadn't eaten in days.

He became aware, as he got out of the old bed in one of the London guest rooms, of the sound of young girls laughing. It was the sound of pure happiness and it made him smile. He went to the window and gazed out upon the low mountains. The day was bright and the sun was warm, filling the valley with the light mist of yesterday's rain evaporating. At the end of the distant meadow he could see the origin of the laughter, two young girls, holding baskets and seeking late grapes on the bushes separating the meadow from the forest beyond it. He made a mental note to re-create the imagery in a scene sometime; perhaps a tale of two woodland sprites celebrating spring; a scene from *Midsummer's* perhaps. Filming Shakespeare would be a provocative challenge. Could the tales have meaning without the words?

He followed the smell of bacon down to the dining room again. Ruby was there, filling his plate from the platters of scrambled eggs, biscuits, bacon and sausage, porridge, and fresh oranges set in the center of the table. On the sideboard was a carafe of coffee and hot water for tea. Ruby's general good nature seemed to have asserted itself and he greeted Bosworth through a mouthful of food.

"The Turks are really giving the Brits what for in Kut," he said, indicating his newspaper.

Hobart poured some hot water into a cup and filled the tea strainer with some dried brown leaves. Dunking it into the water he turned to the table. "There's always some war somewhere."

Ruby sighed, shook his head, and turned back to the paper.

Hobart shrugged and sat down. "A lot of food," he said, sampling a biscuit.

"Leftovers from the field hands' breakfast."

Hobart nodded and popped the rest of his biscuit into his mouth. He was still very hungry and cast his eyes over the things he wouldn't usually eat but was looking forward to today. They both heard a clatter down the hall as the front door was thrown open, then the pounding of feet and the two young girls Hobart had seen from his bedroom window burst into the dining room, out of breath and flush with the fervor of the morning's explorations. Both girls were pretty and slight and appeared to be in their early teens. Obviously sisters, they shared long, brown curly locks of hair and deep, hazel eyes. The hems of their white dresses were wet from the damp grass of the field, and their feet were bare; part of the clamor of their entrance had involved the kicking off of muddy shoes.

"Good morning," Hobart said.

"Hullo," the one whom, through her stature and demeanor, Hobart judged to be the eldest, said boldly to them. She set a pail upon the table while her sister ran around to the sideboard to fetch a bowl. "We've brought grapes from the field." She poured the purple fruit into the bowl, still glistening with drops of rain.

"My name's Hobart," he said, "and this is Mr. Ruby."

Together both girls curtsied in a well-mannered fashion. "I'm Joan," the one who had spoken said.

"And my name is Bess," said the second one.

Hobart scooped up several small globes and popped them into his mouth. They were woody and bitter, the last survivors of the late season. "Delicious," he told them.

"Girls?" Eliza entered the dining room through the doorway that led to the storage hall. "Let your father's guests eat in peace."

"May we take the boat out on the lake?"

"Change into dry clothes first."

The girls squealed with glee and set off for unknown parts of the house. Their footsteps could be heard throughout the rest of the meal until the girls finally burst free from the house.

"Jack's daughters," Eliza said, pouring herself some coffee. She was dressed again for field work and appeared to have been up for hours. "Their mother, the first Mrs. London, lets them come up from Oakland and spend time here when *she* isn't on the ranch." The emphasis on "she" was accompanied by a look of distaste.

"She?" Ruby asked.

"The second Mrs. London."

"Well, they're lovely young ladies," Ruby said.

"Bessie comes from a good family and has raised them in the traditional ways." Eliza sighed. "If only Bessie had given Jack a son, chances are *she* never would have stolen him away. Jack never would have divorced Bessie if there had been a son." Again, the bitter emphasis on "she."

"For that matter," Ruby said, turning to Hobart, "why didn't you tell me you and Adele had divorced?"

"We had a much better love affair than a marriage," Hobart said with a shrug. "It's difficult for an actor and actress to marry because for both it's a performance for which there's no script, rehearsal, or intermission, and the curtain never falls." He chewed on a thick piece of bacon. It was splendid, salty and crisp with a hint of the smokehouse intertwined with maple. He found himself eyeing the biscuits now. Where had this tremendous appetite sprung from? "My wife"—he swallowed and corrected himself—"my former wife finds picture acting somehow less than authentic. She feels that for a performance to be truly remarkable it must happen live on a stage, and in front of people. That the audience itself provides such a critical element that the actor responds to it in all sorts of little ways; timing and emphasis and the like that shape the role in ways an actor never expects and that the pictures cannot provide for.

"I set out to challenge her on each and every point. To prove that picture acting was as truly creative and enveloping for an actor as the stage. Not only to prove that, but to show that it was even better and more fulfilling for an actor's talents. And I never failed to show to her when and how I thought I had proved another point. I wanted to bring to the pictures what Jack brought to literature, natural truth.

"I don't know why I nicked and nicked and nicked away at her. Have you ever spent time around one of those marriages where one partner makes little jokes at the other's expense? I'm not talking about bickering or sniping. Just little jokes that indicate superiority, told maybe just a little too often. Nothing too hurtful. In fact, they're almost funny. Almost. It turns out I did a lot of that," he said, reaching for a biscuit. As he pulled at it, it came apart in fluffy, dry crumbles, which he easily popped into his mouth. "Things like, 'You'd never get a second chance to get that expression right in a Broadway show' and 'Broadway audiences would never be able to see that bit of business.'"

"What'd the poor woman do?" Eliza asked.

"She went back to Broadway." Hobart popped the rest of the biscuit into his mouth. Too bad the eggs were hardening; they looked quite tasty. He speared another piece of bacon with his fork as Sekine came into the room and began to clear the table. "I expect we'll be leaving after breakfast."

"I expect so," she replied.

"If Jack ever returns from Paradise, I hope you'll spend some time convincing him that I never intended our business dealings to be thwarted the way they have been. It'll take more than a letter on my part."

"I will."

"Paradise," Ruby said. "That came up yesterday as well. What do you mean?" He dropped his voice conspiratorially. "He's not . . . dead, is he?"

"Hell no," Hobart said. "Paradise is Hawaii. He calls Hawaii Paradise, or Aloha-land, quite often."

"Must be in the magazine essays," Ruby said. "I didn't count those."

"Well, the Hawaiian Islands are where you'll find him."

After breakfast, Eliza showed them Jack's library. The electricity had been restored early in the morning and the lightbulbs were blazing away as they entered. She shut off the electricity and let the natural light, diffused through the curtains, fill the room with a pale, golden haze.

"Seventeen thousand books," she said in response to Ruby's open astonishment. "He's been collecting them all his life. Even when we were stone poor he'd find a way to get his hands on a book to read. And it didn't matter if he was pressing laundry or canning salmon to support mother, there was always the books. He always says that the reason he only spent a year at Berkeley was because he realized he'd already read everything they wanted him to read. I thought it was such a shame at the time 'cause he worked so hard to get in. He'd had to finish all his high school work he missed when he dropped out to go adventurin' and take care of the family and that took almost two years. And then one year at Berkeley. When he made the decision to quit I thought his heart was broke." She excused herself, citing urgent ranch business, and left them to explore.

"Look." Ruby held up a worn cloth-backed volume from the small writing desk. *First Principles.* A note of awe crept into his voice. "His very own copy of Herbert Spencer. And it's full of Jack's notes in the margins."

Hobart was handling a model of a small oyster boat. It was a replica of London's first skiff, the *Razzle Dazzle,* a vessel he had set out in upon the bay to become the prince of the oyster pirates—raiding the oyster beds and selling the spoils along the docks of Oakland and San Francisco. "Who's Spencer?" he asked. The model recreated a sleek little boat with curvy lines, painted white with red trim. It was the same that the boy would use a year later when he switched to the side of the law and joined the Oyster Patrol, rounding up the same poachers, the Russians, Chinamen, and assorted ruffians he had learned the devious trade from to begin with. He had been sixteen the first time a man took a shot at him. Hobart realized there had been no answer to his query and he looked up to find Ruby staring at him.

"How could you adapt *Martin Eden* to the screen and not know who Spencer was to London? There are entire chapters devoted to how Eden adopts Spencer's philosophy as his own, idolizes him, discovers the evolution of his life, the connections of all things, the survival of the fittest. Without Spencer there's no Martin Eden. Or Jack London."

"I cut all that bunk out. It wasn't dramatic," Hobart said, putting down the model, "and it made my eyes glaze over. Like the newspapers."

Ruby shook his head. He let his fingers linger on the cover, as his eyes roamed eagerly around the room, memorizing everything as if discovering more gems like the Spencer book that would enhance his future readings of London's works, providing deeper understanding, a more personal and direct connection. He paused before one solid cabinet filled with the hundreds of magazines in which Jack had been published. Jack had mastered the art of selling both to the many magazine publishers that had sprung up as publishing and circulation costs had dropped at the turn of the century and then to the book publishers. This skill, in addition to his prolific output, accounted for his tremendous income.

"Jack London took adventure from the dime novel to the library. He's been famous for half of his life," Ruby said. "It all happened so fast, once he cracked it. Within a year he had gone from nothing to everything."

Hobart picked up the first edition of *People of the Abyss* and paged through it as Ruby prowled through the library. Bosworth had heard that this book, Jack's investigation of the London slums, was one of his very best and most passionate works. Jack had lived in disguise in the streets and slums with the wretched poor and reported back to the world with outrage. Or so Bosworth had been told; he very infrequently read anything that wasn't fiction. His training in the theater had taught him always to look for the grand themes in story, in characters; to draw them forth and illuminate them. His chosen art had been to reveal the Lessons of Hubris, the Fall from Grace, the Death of Innocence, the Comedy of Sex, the Immutability of Destiny, and the Tragedy of Love. He had a hard time applying those fundamental lessons to books that were factual in nature because facts often did not lend themselves to the grand themes. Oh, it was always possible to find aspects of the grand themes in biographies, and Hobart occasionally read those. He had even gone so far as to adapt, direct, and star in London's drinking memoir, *John Barleycorn.* After all that was a series of small morality tales, easy to dramatize. In the long run, however, he much preferred a tale in which the author had control of every aspect of the story and the grand themes were writ large.

Since Ruby seemed to be interested in examining every last corner of London's library, Hobart had a seat in a comfortable leather club chair and began reading a chapter in earnest. After reading several pages, his first thought was how expensive it would be to shoot.

"I didn't realize he was such a short man," Ruby said as he examined London's wall-mounted photos alongside the posters printed for his two campaigns for mayor of Oakland. Hobart knew the photos. There would be teenage Jack, eyes glittering and full of eagerness at the base of the dreaded thirty-five-hundred-foot Chilkoot Pass, over which a man had to carry a ton of supplies as his ticket, his grubstake into the Yukon and the golden treasures that surely awaited on the other side of its wintry ridge. It had taken the young man more than sixty trips up, over, and back again to move the grubstakes of him and his three companions. Another photo would show Jack, again under the age of twenty, in the midst of a bloody seal hunt on rocky Japanese shores. Then there were his famous photos of San Francisco after the quake, and still others documenting his tour of the Russo-Japanese war. Each of these photos, and the others beside, contained the elements of the stories London told, of men alone in the wilderness, of the cruelty of one man to another, of the struggle and joy of survival.

"My father always said, 'Beware the short man,'" Ruby said as he came to the photos of London and the wife he called Mate-Woman. Arm in arm together, her broad life-loving smile and his dark eyes leaping from the deck of a yacht, or the shore of a tropical isle, from astride horses upon the land of the Beauty Ranch. "Is this Charmian?"

Hobart looked up from his book and nodded. As he watched Ruby prowl through the library he felt some stirring in his heart and mind of his original plan, the one that had required Ruby's presence here but that he had felt dashed last night upon Jack's absence. The plan, the idea, begged to be heard out, to be given one chance after having been carried for such a great distance and for such a while.

"You know," he said in a calm, confident voice, as if the thought had just come to him, "if you were to buy out Garbutt's shares then we could settle any misunderstanding with Jack himself, and continue to bring his stories to the screen."

"I've tangled with Garbutt before and lost a bundle," Ruby said, not looking away from the framed fliers announcing Jack's various speaking engagements on behalf of the Socialists. "I won't do it again."

"If Jack stood with us . . ."

"The pictures ain't for me, Bos." Hobart could tell it was his final word on the matter.

He let the idea die and stared out the window. If only Jack had been here. He heard the roar of a car engine and moments later saw a ranch hand driving their hired car up the lane. "Guess it's time to go," he said.

"Right."

Hobart replaced the book where he had found it, cast a quick eye around the room, and then walked into the hall and toward the front of the house, where he found their bags packed and waiting on the front porch. Two hands were loading the crates of film into the truck beside the projector, which they had already placed there. Eliza turned to him. "You may as well take it back because if he ain't opened it yet, he ain't never gonna and it's just taking up space here."

"Sure," he shrugged. "Don't know how we're going to get it on the airplane but we'll figure something out."

"Actually, I'm going to stay around for a week or so and visit some family in Frisco." Ruby stepped out of the dark foyer onto the porch. He carried his case of books with him, setting it down only to shut the clasp, which had sprung open. "So you'll have to take the train back." The clasp clicked sharply as it fell into place, punctuating his direction. His eyes were set and cold.

Hobart shrugged. "I'm in no hurry to get back."

The hands finished settling the luggage and Eliza bade them farewell. Hobart tried to take in as much of the Beauty Ranch as he could before they made the turn and headed back down toward Glen Ellen. Part of him felt that the worst injustice of the past twenty-four hours was that he would never see the completed Wolf House. Then he remembered that that was the least of his problems.

Ruby remained mostly silent throughout the trip back to town and the subsequent train and ferry trips. He didn't even pull a book from his case, preferring to hold it tightly on his lap and stare out the window at the countryside and bay views. Hobart tried to engage him several times but it was evident that the man's feelings had been hurt as he had figured out what he assumed was his only value to Bosworth. In the end Hobart settled back with a newspaper he had purchased at the train station. This time he read it from first page to last. Just as he feared, the war news depressed him even further. It was only upon reaching Oakland, while waiting for the ferry back to San Francisco, that Hobart shook the webs of despair. Even before they had landed he had spotted Heinold's First and Last Chance Bar, actually built into the wood of the pier, perched mere feet away from the water's edge in the shadow of the mighty ships. At first Ruby declined the invitation to a drink but Hobart insisted.

"It's known in town as Jack's Rendezvous," he explained. "It's been his favorite watering hole since he discovered booze."

"The bar of *John Barleycorn*."

"The very same and no other."

Leaving their luggage in the care of a porter, except for Ruby's case of books, the two men headed toward the low building. Before the door stood a lonely Anti-Saloon League soldier wearing a sandwich board reading JOHN BARLEYCORN MUST DIE. The evangelist stepped up to confront them but Hobart slipped to the right, Ruby to the left, confounding him and leaving him unsure of his target. Hobart's mind was racing as they entered the small, one-room tavern—a bold new plan was taking shape. Johnny Heinold's bar had been built from the planks and beams of whalers that had sailed their last and the ache and slaughter of those voyages still moaned in their grain and fiber. The noxious tar from years of whale oil lamps, cigarette and pipe tobacco, and stove coal had coated the walls and ceiling with a foul, thick, yellow-tinged black. Ruby skidded as they entered, as unprepared for the gloom as he was for the downward slope of the floor; the building had settled at an odd angle when the earthquake struck and ever since then guests had to be wary of releasing their drinks only to find them sliding away down the bar or table and crashing to the floor. The bar was closer to empty than it was to full, the lunchtime drinkers having returned to their posts and the early afternoon drinkers yet to leave them. As Ruby set his case upon the bar, Hobart ordered a couple of noxious, bitter pints of warm steam beer.

"Excuse me," Ruby asked the bartender, "but where does Jack London set when he come in?"

"He don't come in no more," was the growled response. The bartender's face grew dark. "He ain't allowed."

"Really? Why not?"

"See that fella outside?" The man from the Anti-Saloon League was warbling "Onward, Christian Soldiers" at the top of his self-righteous lungs. "That book London wrote about his drinking here was like lighting a candle to a moth. From the moment I open now until the moment I close there's somebody out there tryin' to scare away my sons of bitches who want to drink. Now Jack'll tell you he only wrote that book as a cautionary tale about hisself, but I hear it's bein' used to rile up the faithful at Women's Christian Temperance Union meetings from here to there. Jack's gonna put us all outta business."

"I don't know about that," Ruby said. "It made me want to have a drink, not give up drinking."

"Well, since he wrote that book, whenever he shows up here, that fella out there goes out and gets all his brethren to come a-runnin' and pretty soon I got a whole congregation out front raisin' holy hell. So Jack can't come in no more."

"Well, here's to Jack anyway," said Hobart, encouraging Ruby to drink up as the bartender wandered away to help another customer. He had to get a little alcohol into Ruby and there wasn't much time. He looked at the clock on the wall; through the grime he could see that it was 3:15. There wasn't much time at all.

"The thing about my deal with Rudisill, Garbutt, and Zukor is that I can make one picture a year outside of that deal if I can raise the money on my own. If the only pictures of mine they'll release are Jack London ones then that's what I'll give 'em to release."

"Too bad about you and him, then," Ruby said, ordering a second round with a wave of his fingers. "Too bad."

"If he's as sore at me as Eliza says, it's gonna take a real man-to-man palaver to straighten things out."

"So hop a ship to Hawaii."

"That's exactly what I was thinking."

Ruby finally turned to look at him. "Seriously? You're out of money, Hobart, you told me so yourself. I don't even know if you can get yourself back to Los Angeles, let alone Hawaii."

"True enough. That's where I was hoping you could spot me a little capital."

Ruby sputtered and slammed down the second glass of beer on the bar. "Goddamn you, Hobart!" he coughed. "You really must think I'm stupid, don't ya?" He rose but Hobart put a hand on his forearm, stopping him.

"If you would be good enough to loan me some money for this venture, I promise you I will never tell Jack that you lifted his copy of Spender." He nodded his head toward the case.

Ruby sat down heavily on the wooden bar stool. "Spencer," he grunted.

"Spender. Spencer. I don't really care," said Hobart. He released Ruby's wrist and pointed to an ad in his paper. "All I care about is that the *Falls of Clyde* is sailing for Hawaii on the evening tide and that's enough time for you to cash a check so I can be on it. Oh, and I'll make sure Jack signs all of those books for you. So what do you say, Gerald? Are we in business?"

CHAPTER SIX

HE WOULD HAVE ENJOYED nothing more than inhaling the fresh ocean air early in the evening, if it weren't for the stench of the oil that came with each breath.

Oil. Oil was the cargo the *Falls of Clyde* hauled over the Pacific. The reek of it permeated everything from his cabin to the galley to the deck. No matter how hard the crew worked to keep the ship scrubbed fresh, there was no avoiding its metallic tang.

Hobart watched the sun setting into the western edge of the sea from the foredeck while the Dutch crew busily worked on trimming sails for the night wind. Twenty-four hours had passed since he had bid his farewell to Ruby on the docks and set sail with two thousand borrowed dollars in his pocket. He would have to make sure that Ruby was added to the books for payback. He didn't feel too bad about putting the squeeze on the man; Ruby never should have lifted something that belonged to Jack in the first place. After all, had that been appropriate behavior for a guest? Hobart considered the loan absolution.

He'd had time before the ship sailed to put in a call to Willoughby. It had been eerie to hear a reasonable facsimile of his voice answering the phone, complete with pained wheezing and coughs. He'd explained the situation, that he'd be gone at least three more weeks (figuring on one week out and one week back, with a week to take care of business) and was pleased that Willoughby hadn't broken character once, even to say how much he'd been enjoying himself and that Hobart should take as much time as needed and that no, no one from Garbutt's or Zukor's offices had called.

The *Falls of Clyde* was an old ship; he would have much preferred to be sailing on one of the beautiful ocean liners like those glorious floating palaces of the Matson Line. But she had been the only vessel sailing for Hawaii at the moment when he needed one and the round-trip fare had only cost one hundred and fifty dollars. She had long beautiful lines in the old schooner fashion, which reminded him of his early days on the whalers—he had always envied the crews of those graceful clippers from his vantage point on the stumpy, yet hardy, tubs. The sails spread across the four masts were supplemented by a temperamental engine. Even now he could feel its irregular thumping beat vibrating through the wood under his feet.

He wasn't the only passenger aboard; there were a dozen or so paying customers, and all were fascinated to have a genuine star of the pictures sailing with them. For example he was aware that Mrs. Holdings, the wife of another fellow traveler to Hawaii who himself was set to work for Benjamin Dillingham's railroad and sugar concerns as an assistant manager, was even now considering whether or not to approach him. He had been introduced to her at the captain's table during dinner the night before. She was long limbed, fair skinned, and quite lovely; Hobart instantly wanted to film her. Very badly. Her newlywed husband had turned green at the sight of the food set before him and today she was on deck alone. She held a parasol against the sun's strength but as he had seen earlier, her skin was already reddening. He had caught her sneaking little glimpses at him from across the table, and all this day he had felt like a Ziegfeld beauty haunted by a stage-door Johnny. And she hadn't been his only silent suitor; he had noticed a young fella, a cabin boy, who hid behind any object he could find whenever Hobart passed, yet had taken an undeniable interest in spying on him. Of the two, the boy was a mere irritant; the Mrs., on the other hand, could turn a restful voyage into a most entertaining one, if she finally got around to finding her courage.

He found himself contemplating the rigging. He dearly desired the captain's permission to ascend to the top spar but the old man had yet to be assured of his nautical skills. Up there, high above the creaking of the wood and the smell of the oil, he knew he would find a sense of his younger self, which he had been craving more and more since his return to San Francisco.

"It seems strange that we should be celebrating Christmas at sea." He tried to suppress his smile of certainty. While his mind had been aloft, she had crossed the deck.

"When is it exactly?" He turned to look at her. She was freckling and it was hard to tell whether the blush on her cheeks was from the sun or from her boldness.

"This Saturday," she said as if he should know. Her hair was straight and blond, and every now and then the wind would catch a lock and toss it across her face, where she would retrieve it with slender fingers. He couldn't imagine that she was more than twenty-two years old.

"I'm a poor excuse for a Christian, I suppose. I've lost track of the days, it seems, with all the rushing here and there."

"Yes, we've traveled a lot as well. All the way to San Francisco by train from Wisconsin. We had a sleeper car. It was small and hot so we had to open the window, then smoke and ash blew in every time we passed through a tunnel."

"And how are your accommodations aboard *Clyde*?"

"Small, as well. I thought we were supposed to be on the upper deck, but the captain explained we had to move just before we set sail. We're one floor below in the front and there are some officer's quarters on the same floor as us. They stay up late drinking and they're rude men."

"Sailors usually are. It's the lack of civilizing influences and what becomes of men when they're left to their own devices."

"My husband, Wayne, he's down there now. At least the engine smoke doesn't blow into the porthole. He's become quite seasick, you know."

"I thought I saw that coming on last night at dinner."

"And where are you staying? I haven't seen you below."

"They've found a place for me." He didn't have the heart to tell her that he was the cause of her displacement. "Up there. I think the first mate had to give up his quarters."

"It looks like it has a fair number of windows, and some space."

"You know what's funny, Mrs. Holdings?"

"Alice, please."

"Good. What's funny is that as a star of the stage I've bunked in louse-ridden boarding rooms sharing beds with other men. I've slept on park benches and in dressing rooms. I've huddled over furnace vents in the cold weather waiting for the important hours when I could bring the words of Shakespeare or Marlowe or Ibsen to life. As a star of the pictures, Captain ten Broeke insisted that I do his ship the honor of taking the first mate's quarters, which were comparable in size to a suite I recently rented at the Palace, and the first mate be damned."

She laughed.

From the cut of her fine clothes and the styling of her white buttoned shoes he knew she was of her community's moneyed tribe. "Walk with me," he ordered, pleased to see her blink twice before falling into step at his side as they toured the deck. He continued talking, as the sound of her skirt rustled quietly next to him. "Now I've always failed to see the difference between my acting for the stage and my acting for the silver screen. Honestly, picture acting is so much easier. But others seem to and I've slept on more than enough benches to know better than to turn down fine accommodations just on principle."

"I've done a little acting," she said, and then seemed embarrassed to have mentioned it. "Oh, really, it was nothing at all like what you do, Mr. Bosworth."

"You can call me Hob, if you'd like. Tell me about your performances."

She smiled. "Well, they were more like pageants, if you will, in which we enacted, or brought to life, great works of art by the masters such as Vermeer or Rubens. For example, one season we presented *Bacchus and Ariadne* and *The Feast of the Gods* and *The Worship of Venus* by Titian accompanied by a dramatic reading of Catullus."

"You were Venus."

"And Ariadne."

"Seems like some of those masterworks are a little racy for Wisconsin sensibilities. I recall being closed in Milwaukee for the lewdness of a controversial production of *Midsummer*. I played Bottom."

"Oh, these were very discreet, but thoroughly accurate," she said with an uptilt of her chin. "And the audiences were more enlightened and sophisticated than what one may have found usually in Milwaukee."

"It sounds very entertaining."

"I suppose." She looked out over the ocean. "You can feel it growing warmer already."

"The weather changes fast at sea. We're in the trade winds now and making good time. Once we cross the thirtieth parallel we'll have warm weather. Then soon after we'll cross the line and see the tropics."

"The line?"

"The Tropic of Cancer."

"How will we know when we cross it?"

"There'll be a little ceremony to mark it. Mostly for any new sailors who haven't crossed it before. With this crew I can't imagine there'll be any. See that dark line on the horizon?"

"Yes?"

"That's a storm front. Unless I'm mistaken, the captain will shortly give the order to take in some of those sails and we'll be in for a blow."

"Will it be bad?"

"No storm at sea is ever good. Keep your eyes on the whitecaps and color of the water. When it turns from blue to black and the whitecaps blow off the top of the waves like blowing foam off the head of a beer, we'll be in for it."

"That should be hard on Wayne," she said with a sigh.

"Not the maiden voyage you've been expecting."

She shook her head. "Quite the disappointment, all in all. Wayne's very sensitive. His family's very worried about how he'll handle the jungles of Hawaii and frankly, so am I at this point."

Hobart laughed. "Well, Hawaii's hardly the heart of darkness that you may have imagined. It's actually downright civilized since the Americans annexed it—shame though that all was."

"You've been there?"

"Twenty years ago. Before the annexation. But Paramount distributes my pictures there. And in my younger days I sailed the South Pacific and we made port several times in Honolulu. At the time, while Hawaii was still for the Hawaiians, they were the warmest yet most fierce of all the Pacific savages. But that was nearly thirty years ago, before a group of American businessmen toppled the monarchy, brought in the marines, and forced the annexation of Hawaii."

"Before I was born."

He looked at her, trying to discern what she had meant by that. "And yet the world has changed so little in that time but for your presence." He thought he detected the pursing lips of a challenge accepted. "Incidentally, your husband's employer, Dillingham, wasn't one of those Americans who participated in the shameful act of toppling the Hawaiian Queen in the name of better business. A very sad affair for the Hawaiians who had wanted her to fight back against the whites."

"Why didn't she?"

"Imagine the bloodshed. A few thousand Hawaiian warriors against the entire American nation. When last I was there she had been made a prisoner in her own rooms within her palace."

"I'm sure the Hawaiians are better off with the United States looking out for their best interests."

"Have you ever been to one of the Indian reservations near you in Milwaukee?"

She shook her head, an innocent expression upon her face.

"Then I'm certain you'll find a comfortable place in the new Hawaiian society," he said.

"I should hope so. We're giving up so much comfort back home."

They watched the approaching dark wall. Indeed, as Hobart had predicted, there were already calls back and forth in Dutch and men climbing the rigging. "I feel like that storm's been chasing me for days," he said. "I think it's going to be a hell of a night."

"I should see to Wayne," she said after a long moment.

"You know the thing about seasickness is that it can turn a man into a dog. He'll lose all sense of himself. Before that happens try and coach him to breathe in through his nose and out through his mouth. After a while that'll be all he'll concern himself with. He'll talk of wanting to die before he loses the ability to communicate, but once you get him breathing properly, he'll do that for hours and hours. And he won't die. No one's ever died from seasickness. And for yourself, if you feel the desire to move about the ship, be sure to keep one hand for the boat and one hand for yourself. There is no proper sense or rhythm to a ship in a storm and you can never predict which way she'll pitch next."

"Wonderful," Alice groaned. "What a honeymoon."

"Didn't anyone tell you that marriage was an adventure?"

She smiled. "I didn't know they meant literally."

"What other way is there? Here, put your arm in mine."

The sensation as she followed his direction was quite enjoyable. The tips of her fingers fluttered against his for a moment. "Shall I take you back to your cabin? There are many sailors between here and there and they would respect an escort."

"Thank you," she said as he began to guide her toward the stairs.

"Still," she said, sighing a little as she gazed at the sea, "it will seem strange to have Christmas without snow."

"I live in Los Angeles. Not only do we celebrate Christmas without snow, we manage to celebrate it without Christ."

He led her down the flight of steep metal stairs, moving aside to allow a pair of sailors to rush up past in a blur of blue uniforms. At one point the ship took a steep pitch forward and her body fell against his for support and his arm went around her waist. He could feel the heaviness of one of her breasts against his arm and he slid his hand slowly away before drawing her down the final few steps. "The sea's already getting rough," he said. "We're going to be in for it for at least a full day. Maybe two."

Electric lights led the way through the wide corridor toward the forward cabin. At night there would be men sleeping in the bunk compartments along the sides. Right now there were great coils of rope and other materials essential to the smooth running of the ship. The roof above their heads was curved to support the deck.

"Tell me, Hobie," she said, "why are you going to Hawaii? Are you going to be performing there, something I could see you in, perhaps? Or are you going there to make a picture?"

"Well, I'm going to see a man about a picture," he replied as they reached her cabin door. "Jack London."

"The dog writer?" She placed her hand on the knob.

"Wolves, actually. And he's written about much more."

Alice made a slight face of distaste. "I heard he married his second wife on the day he divorced his first. Scandalous."

"Which? The divorce or the marriage? Now then, let's see how your husband's doing."

She swung open the door and they both recoiled.

"Finally," he said, placing his hand over his mouth, "a smell to take my mind off the oil."

"Wayne?" she called.

From the dark room came a weak, petulant voice that failed to add emphasis to the string of curse words hurled at them.

"Let me apologize for my husband's temper," she said, embarrassed.

"I'm dying," the voice moaned.

She grimaced and hesitated. "For better or for worse, right?"

"That's what they say."

She raised her eyebrows in a look of resigned acceptance. "Let's get some of the worst out of the way, then." She took a deep breath and stepped over the rim of the doorway and pulled the door shut behind her. He listened for a moment but beyond the pained tones of invective in the man's voice, he could make out no details. With a shrug he turned back toward the stairs.

The ship lurched again, heavily to starboard. As he steadied himself against one of the support columns he heard voices shouting on deck; men suddenly under stress calling directions to one another. The oncoming storm was of greater concern than they had first thought.

Hobart heard another sound, a crack as of a piece of wood breaking, and a sharp, high-pitched cry of pain accompanied by cruel laughter. These sounds came from below, not above. He paused at the staircase that led to the bowels of the ship. He heard a repeat of the sounds of violence. It sounded all too familiar; he had taken enough beatings at the hands of his father to know by sound when one was being delivered. He was halfway down the steps and heading into the darkness before he even realized it.

There were fewer electric lights down here, and his eyes adjusted as his feet hit the floor. The lower floor was a cargo hold; underneath its boards were the tanks holding the thousands of gallons of oil. There were crates stacked upon crates down here full of supplies and more bound for the islands. Also down here were the chicken coops that provided fresh eggs and meat for the crew and passengers, and the unpleasant smell of caged chickens fused with the oil reek to become a stink that made his sinuses ache. He heard the whistling crack again and another squeal coming from the far side of the near set of crates. Quietly he removed his jacket and tie and laid them on top of one of the boxes. Then he stole forward until he could clearly see the two figures caught in the glow of a lightbulb that weakly illuminated a large space clear of boxes.

The galley cook was a thin, hard man with a gray, bristling mustache, like those found on walrus. A cigar was clenched between his teeth. His forearms, wrists, and hands were enormously out of proportion to the rest of his body, corded with veins, layered over muscle with leathery, tattooed skin covered by thick hair. In one of his fists he had clenched the bitter end of a heavy cord of rope that fell coiled by his feet and ended in an ugly and heavy knot.

The victim of his wrath was the halfwit boy Hobart had noticed skulking around in his wake. He stood on the far side of the open space, his back against the crates. Hobart put his age around ten or eleven. His pants were off, his shirttails covered his groin. His skinny legs were picket-fence white crisscrossed with lattices of old bruises and rising welts. While tears streamed down his face he jumped from one foot to the other as if he wanted to run but knew he could not. This was not his first lashing.

The cook lifted his arm and began to swing the rope so swiftly that it became a blur. The boy held his hands to his face but made no attempt otherwise to protect his body. He began to moan. Hobart noted that the dance his feet were making was leaving bloody footprints on the floor, a gruesome tarantella. The cook took a step forward in preparation for his next launch.

"Hold on there, God damn you!" Hobart's voice, stage trained to reach the far seats with rousing speeches to troops on St. Crispin's Day, cracked across the man as sharply as his whip had struck the boy. The cook staggered sideways in shock and surprise, and the cable fell from his hand. "What the hell are you doing?" Hobart advanced on the man.

"He busted the damn eggs!" came the reply. "The eggs, he fell and busted 'em up. I'm teachin' 'im to stay on his feet no matter what."

Hobart knew that passions about the larder rode high on a ship; the sailors' work was hard and relentless and solace could be found at the mess table. The loss of provisions through destruction or theft was a chief concern. But he also knew that this example of corporal punishment was cruel and out of proportion to the loss of however many few eggs. And there were the other marks, penalties for other crimes long since forgotten.

"Hey, you shouldn't be down here," the cook now shouted, regaining some of his bravado.

"Make me leave."

The cook evaluated the situation. Hobart could see the wheels turning slowly behind his dark, menacing eyes. He was evaluating the risks of tangling with this new man. Obviously he felt that he could beat him in a fight; the question he was pondering was what would be the repercussions of a paying guest of the ship turning up bloody at the captain's table. The ship lurched again, struck by a wave. Now Hobart could see the man formulating a solution in which he could be made to disappear during the storm. The cook sneered at him and slowly bent down for his rope. Hobart stepped forward, putting his fists up.

"You want to fight, eh?" The cook straightened up and took a swing with his right fist that Hobart backed easily away from. The change of expression on the cook's face was dramatic; in one instant he had gone from formulating murder to realizing he was in a fight for his own life. He took another swing, again with his right, and Hobart stepped to his left, avoiding it. He could tell that the cook had been in fights before, but sailor brawls were different than standing toe to toe with a former professional boxer and someone trained in stage combat. The right-hand strike had left the man's entire right side unprotected and as Hobart centered his feet under him he launched a punch to the man's spleen. The grunt of pain was satisfying. He followed that up with a right to the diaphragm, just below the sternum. The blow knocked the wind out of the cook and he stumbled forward against Hobart, clutching at him for support. He could feel the cook's fingers grasping at his shirt and he pushed the man away before he could rip it—this was one of his favorites: creamy yellow heavy cotton with a monogrammed pocket. The clawing fingers reminded him that brawls of this sort often ended in grappling and wrestling when the combatants grew weary and forgot their skills, and that's when things got dangerous and knives came out. As much as he was enjoying torturing the abuser, he knew he had to draw the fight to an end with haste. He quickly judged the man's weakest point and planted a fist heavily into his nose, feeling it mash like a boiled potato. The brute dropped to his knees, blood and snot oozing through the fingers of the hands he had brought to his face quicker than his punches had flown. If a person had never been hit in the nose before, the pain would be surprisingly unbelievable. Tears leaked from the sides of his eyes.

Hobart leaned down and grabbed a thick tuft of mustache between his thumb and forefinger, yanking it so hard the man nearly toppled over. He now had his weight supported by only the hairs on his face. "Leave the boy be," Hobart spoke, and as the cook nodded his acquiescence, the boy, too fearful to move until now, snatched up his pants and disappeared into the darkness of the cargo hold as quickly as a cat disappearing over an alley fence. "And I'll tend to my own meals from now on." Hobart tossed the mustache loose with a snap that rocked the cook's head. Then, removing his handkerchief from his back pocket and wiping the sweat from his brow and the blood from his knuckles, he made his way back to where he had left his articles of clothing and climbed heavily up the stairs. The energy of the fight was quickly leaving his body and he was feeling drained. He wanted to get some fresh air and clear the clouds of anger from his brain.

The sight of the sea he discovered upon reaching topside took his breath away. There was not a straight line to be seen anywhere beyond the borders of the ship. The waters rose and fell in great heaving erratic breaths, deepening into yawning valleys one moment then rising to snow-capped mountains the next. Somewhere far away the end of the ocean had merged with the curtain hem of the sky to become a solid wall of murky black ink. The wind was blowing so hard that it had begun to make the rigging sing, an unpleasant high-pitched whine.

He had to see more.

He made his way to the forward upper deck, a small slightly rounded roof over the forecastle. Although the ship could typically fly four sails from the bowsprit to the fore topmast, currently there was only the storm jib raised and reefed. He struggled up the small stairs to his left; directly above the small compartment below this deck was a brass bell supported by two copper fish, green with age. Weirdly it made no sound, tied down unless needed to sound an emergency. His feet under him on the upper deck, he wound his forearm through a sheet and held fast to the line with another. Huge droplets of rain fell on him now, bearing the warmth of the tropics from whence they blew. He kept his face pointed, like the ship, directly into the wind and closed his eyes. He could feel the pull of gravity as the vessel slid down the slope of a wave, slippery as an icy road. Then he felt the racing momentum grind to a rocky stillness as they plunged headfirst into the rising surge of another great wave and the pilot fought to keep them pointed into it. Cold spray and foam broke over the deck and moments later he could hear men's voices. He turned and realized the merchant sailors were waving a lantern, beckoning and calling for him to return to safety. He turned away from them and faced another drop and rise and another. It was his storm, he was its creator and master. Its power rose and fell with the howling of his voice, which it stole from his throat. He felt the maelstrom enter his chest, his breath becoming the gale. They would not founder or sink, the storm was delivering him. Finally, he turned and made his way back, past the astonished faces of the sailors who had no choice but to be on deck, to the comfort and warmth of his stateroom.

Here he unpacked a bottle of scotch he had borrowed from Jack's liquor cabinet and had a quick snort, shaking the fire from his throat and the water from his hair in a single motion. Stripping from his wet clothes, hanging them carefully to dry, he then slipped on his warm Egyptian cotton robe, toweled his hair, and sat on the edge of his bed. From beneath the bunk he pulled out Ruby's case of books, undid the straps, and flipped it open. He looked through the collection he had agreed to have London sign, wondering what he should read. At first he was most eager to pick up *The Son of the Wolf,* a collection of Jack's earliest published stories that also contained the short novel *An Odyssey of the North,* one of Hobart's favorite tales, not least of all because of the fond memories he had of directing and starring in the filmed version of it. It was a damn good story of adventure in the Klondike that had the accuracy of Jack's own adventures there. But authenticity based on experience was Jack's stock in trade, after all. In the end he opted to read one of London's newest novels, *The Star Rover,* published earlier this year. Of the book he knew very little, other than that it was twice as big as *The Son of the Wolf;* he chose it in the hopes it might help him divine some insight into where Jack's passions might currently lie.

As the *Falls of Clyde* rocked and skittered its way across the hellish seas he lay upon his bunk hours into the night reading the book, which unsettled him more and more with each turn of the page. It wasn't that Jack wasn't as compelling a writer as ever; his mastery over his language was nearly complete, and his ability to spin a yarn was still powerful. The book could even be considered adventurous, if somewhat outside the normal physical boundaries that defined adventure. It was just— Hobart thought long and hard before he could define it appropriately— oddly spiritual. Through intense meditation forced upon him by a torturous prison situation, Jack's latest hero had learned how to launch himself out of the confines of his body and to travel through lives lived in the past and experience planes of existence that exposed the wonders of the universe. His hero even claimed to be a Roman soldier present at the Crucifixion in one lifetime while claiming to be a childhood victim of the Mormon Mountain Meadows Massacre during another. It was deeply puzzling, yet cast such a heavy spell over him that he was easily startled by the soft knock at the door.

He rose, expecting either to be confronted by the cook, the cook's friends, or emissaries of the captain set to clap him in irons for the remainder of the voyage. He drew himself up to a regal height as if he were playing an unwritten Lear in his prime and opened the door.

She was wet from head to toe, her hair hung in her face, her soaked clothes plastered to her body. Her face was flushed and her eyes bright and hungry. She was shivering.

"Wayne's asleep," she whispered. "The captain gave him laudanum."

"That'll be good for him," he started to say when she slipped into the room, pushing him back and closing the door, "and good for us as well." She pressed herself tightly against him, opening her lips to meet his, devouring his, drawing them together. Her breathing was hard, deep, and fierce. He was pulling her into the warm embrace of his open robe. He turned away from her to place a bookmark at his page. Then, after closing the book and putting it in a safe place on his dresser, he looked at her as she stood swaying near the door, noting that her blue eyes though filled with desire were now also showing a hint of what he had been waiting for, confusion. "Alice," he told her, "take off your clothes."

CHAPTER SEVEN

HAD THERE BEEN ANOTHER ship on the ocean that Christmas Eve, one driven by steam power, as there was no wind at all, her crew would have beheld the strangest sight. The *Falls of Clyde,* her engines swamped and quieted by the storm, still in the water. One mast extended over the water with one sail hung taut over it filled not with air but with light. They would have seen words magically appear on the improvised screen, painted by a spectral cone of light emerging from a magical device newly bolted to the ship's pilot house.

A Hobart Bosworth Productions Inc.
Filmed Presentation

Another ship would have heard the distant sound of applause and cheers rolling across the still waters.

Hobart Bosworth
as
Jack London
in Jack
London's
John Barleycorn

And then, as that ship would have passed over the horizon, just at that point where the stars in the clear sky met their own reflection in the black sea to create a seamless wall of brilliant diamonds, they would have seen the sail filling with the moving image of a man, handsome and vital, smiling in slight embarrassment.

Hobart had trained the camera on Jack London when the author and Charmian had visited the set of *The Sea Wolf.* The image had been a signature touch to the opening of all of Hobart's London pictures. While the on-screen Jack laughed at some off-camera joke, Hobart now checked to be sure that the feet of the Edison projector were securely fastened to the blocks the ship's carpenter had fashioned to his specifications.

"You love the pictures, don't you?" Alice said from her seated position on the rug the officer had laid for Hobart's comfort on the roof of the pilot house. Her husband remained belowdecks, his condition of seasickness only made more severe by the storm, which they had only passed out of just this morning. The passengers and the available crew, those who weren't toiling to repair the engines, had settled comfortably on the deck for the show, which had been Hobart's suggestion.

"There's nothing better," he replied, finally satisfied enough with the crispness of the image to stop fiddling with the focus ring and have a seat beside her. "Nothing." There was nothing to be done about the occasional ripple in the sail caused by the occasional breath of wind. "Nothing compares to making a picture. It's sculpting in time and light."

As the story began to play he made sure they were out of view of spying eyes, pulled her close, and kissed her. Then he gently turned her face toward a slight breeze. "Smell that?" he asked.

"What is it?"

"Paradise," he answered.

"I think this is Paradise."

"That's Hawaii out there, ahead, in the dark. The perfume on the wind."

"I wish we'd never get there. That this ship would just sail on forever like the *Flying Dutchman* and never reach shore." She shivered and pressed closer against him. He kissed her again. "Don't you want to watch?" she whispered, as he studied her face.

"I've seen it all before."

"And you know how it always ends."

"Yes."

The ship swayed every so slightly on the calm seas, each gentle rise and fall bringing them closer to the Hawaiian Islands. And as they kissed again he kept one eye on the improvised screen as the next title card appeared:

Jack London—The Birth of a Legend

The Sonoma hills are bathed in a warm silver glow of happiness and nostalgia. A young boy, about seven, rides his bicycle down a country lane until he spies a festive gathering at the side of the road. The trees are strung with banners. He dismounts and watches for a moment. The people are free and dancing and wild. The boy has a seat by the road flowers. The men all wear mustaches and their hair is slicked, black and glistening. The women are full and sensual, loose haired and barefoot. As the boy spies, two large men slam their bottles, from which they've been taking drink, and rise angrily exchanging words. They grapple and brawl while the men cheer and the women wail in horror. Then, abruptly, both men are embracing and tears are pouring down their faces and all resume their celebrations.

An Italian Wedding

A girl about Jack's age finds him in the flowers and invites him forth. She wears a frilly white dress and has a flower in her black hair. At first he resists, but her fair charms prevail. Holding hands, they trip down the hill together and are welcomed to the party. Jack is swept up into the dance. First the delighted dancers clear a space for him to dance with the young girl, then the bride snatches him up and spins him around, and when he's almost exhausted, he is clapped upon by a grandmama of great age and bosom.

Jack's First Drink

He is rescued by the gleeful menfolk and seated at one of the benches. An astounding platter of spaghetti is set before him. As he is about to eat, a bushy-browed, glittering-eyed representative of the race sits down across from him. His mustache is bristling. He pours a glass of

*wine and sets it before the boy, urging him to drink it. Young Jack
shakes his head. The man leans forward, insistent.*

His Mother's Warning:
Beware Crossing the Italian for Fear of the Evil Eye

*The lad is obviously terrified of the fierce Sicilian, not comprehending
his good-natured intent. The man's eyes under his heavy brows certainly seem full of evil. The glass is thrust upon him and he takes it.
Trembling he raises it to his lips. Then, in one smooth motion he
pours the liquid down his throat as quickly as possible and brings
the glass down on the table.*

*The Italian is stunned. Amazed. His jaw drops. He calls for his
paisanos, who gather round. The Italian pours another glass for
Jack and gestures again that he drink it up. Again Jack is fearful of
the Evil Eye and swallows the draught in one gulp. The Italian men
find this hysterical and heroic. They clap Jack on the back. Another
drink is poured and set before the boy. This one he raises, more em-
boldened than before by spirits or bonhomie none shall ever know, and
again downs the wine. Again the men laugh uproariously and now
drinks are poured all around. Jack grins, growing heavy lidded and
stupid. Now he tries to snatch the bottle away from his new friend,
who teases him before giving it up.*

Jack Meets the White Light

*The lad staggers through the party drinking and singing like a
sailor. His little girlfriend tries to take the bottle from him but he
pushes her away, hugging the bottle to himself. She watches him
make his way down the country lane alone, weaving as if storm
tossed.*

An Illness That Rages for Days

*Jack's mother tries to restrain the raving, fevered boy while the doctor
tends to him. Finally the boy passes into a slumber that seems relaxed. His eyes open and he sees his mother. He throws himself into
her embrace and tries to tell her about the Evil Eye. She leaves the
room to find him some food. He stands and weakly moves across the
room until he finds what he's searching for: a jug of hooch marked
with three X's, which he hugs to his body.*

In one magical instant, the boy Jack is transformed into a handsome young man surrounded by genial friends in a warm tavern and is pouring drinks for all from the jug into awaiting glasses and then his own mouth.

John Barleycorn—a New Lifelong Friend.

"Why is there a bowl of eggs outside your door?" she asked.

"I think it's my Christmas gift."

He told her about the boy and the galley cook. He had asked the captain about the lad and he had responded by saying that the boy, who had no name other than Kid, had been found stowed away a few voyages back and as no one at any port knew of him or stepped forward to claim him, he had simply been added to the crew roster and set to work. Since he was obviously a feeb, the logical place for him to apprentice was with the cook. "It's a story that happens all too often," he told her in conclusion.

It was soon after he had cooked the eggs on the cabin's small stove that the cry of land sighted was raised. They joined the small crew assembling in the ship's prow.

Smoke seemed to rise like a chimney from the dark shape on the horizon. "Big Island," an old sailor croaked. "Hawaii."

A light flurry of fine white flakes swirled around them, making Alice laugh delightedly. "Snow!" she cried. "Snow for Christmas after all."

"No," Hobart corrected her, catching a flake in his hand. "Ash."

The storm had blown them a few minutes of latitude south and the crew spent the day working north to raise the windward side on their way to the port at Hilo, and now, long after the sun had set, the crew and passengers again lined the rails to watch a light show even more spectacular than the one Hobart had conjured up. A scarlet glow seemingly from the center of the landmass still miles distant illuminated the low clouds. Thin red tendrils of light bled down the black cliffs, which soared straight up from the ocean with no trace of beach at all, consecrating their union with the water in plumes of steam.

"The Goddess is angry," the old sailor muttered. "Figures. My last voyage an' the old volcano bitch, Pele, is tight an' steamin'." Hobart had known a sailor like this one on every ship he had ever crewed upon. Hell, for all he knew it was the exact same man. The white beard was always thick and stained yellow around the mouth with tobacco juice from his pipe. The squint was perpetual from having stared into the sun rising ten thousand days over the ocean. An old sailor like this knew all the lore of the sea and dispensed it without provocation. If one wanted to know all the traditions of the ceremony for crossing the equator line, this would be the one to go to. Likewise if one needed a few words in the tongue of a local dialect, he would tell the proper way to locate the local tavern and negotiate with its whores.

"Maybe it's not you she's tight at," Alice muttered in a tone that roiled Hobart's stomach.

"It's me all right. She's been waitin' for me for all these years. Knowin' I'd come back sooner or later. 'Cause I stole from 'er. Let me tell you about my lady, Pele," the old salt began. Hobart had always admired his type. Illiterate and uneducated, somehow they always were the ones who knew the laws of each port, the customs of its taverns, the negotiatings of its ladies, and the legends of the lands. It didn't matter if they were right or not, what mattered was that they knew and their shipmates believed them. "She was a wanderin' beaut, the daughter of the god who created the heavens and the earth. But she fought with her brothers and sisters and one day her father, he threw her out to sea in a canoe. An' she came to Hawaii an' she brought fire to the savages livin' here. But her sister, Namakaokahai, who ruled the oceans, was in a twist because of the stolen fire and chased her from island to island. Ever' time Pele found a place to hide she turned it into a volcano. You see, your Diamond Head and Punchbowl craters are just some of her old homes. Finally, her sister caught up to her and rent her limb from limb an' her bones became Maui. But since she was the daughter of a god she became a goddess herself and made her home in a lake of fire on Kilauea. An' that's where she lives to this very day. An' when I was a young pollywog I wen' to visitin' her and that's when I stole from her and that's why she knows I come back. 'Cause it's a curse, y'see, to steal so much as a grain of her black, black sand from 'er."

"Come on there, Old Skuse," one of the other sailors scolded, "what'd you ever steal from the Goddess?"

The old sailor reached up and withdrew from around his neck a thin strand of leather from which dangled a black pendant, glossy as if it had been dipped in oil, then frozen. "One of her tears," he replied. "One of her tears."

"Aw, you ain't got no curse on you, you old coot," the sailor snapped at him.

"An' what you call a life spent on the sea with no home nowhere to ever go to? No wife nor no little ones? My own ship sunk out from under me? Not a captain no more, an' no teeth left in my head what's mine, just another man that gone bust on the ocean an' if that ain't cursed I don't know what is."

"Why ain't you brought the rock back before now?" the sailor asked.

"I been tryin', damn it! I can't tell you how many years I thought it was just the worse luck I was havin'. It weren't until I met an' old Hawaiian woman in New York City, an' she recognized this tear for what it was, that I heard about the curse. So I made my way aroun' the Horn, an' as fast as I could it took me three years of voyagin' to do it, for one thin' or another. A hurricane in the Gulf of Mexico. War in South America. Fever in San Diego and Teamster strikes in San Francisco. A couple of times I set off on ships bound for Hawaii and I thought, Well, old-timer, this is it. But one ship had to turn back when the boiler blew, and another had to outrun a typhoon clear across to Japan. Then it was all hell to get down to Tasmania and we put in at Tahiti instead of Hawaii an' there I was back in Oakland. Almos' as if old Namakaokahai wanted to keep me from completin' my task. So I made a deal with Pele then and there by the dock and said if I brought her tear back that I would leave the ocean to her sister and never leave Hawaii. Then I caught wind of this run and signed on. Old Namakaokahai tried one more time and there were moments during that blow that I thought she had me. But Pele kept our fire hot and we saw to the end of that storm. But here I am an' my sailorin' days are at an end."

"Well, if the problem's a curse, let me get rid of it for ya. I'll throw 'er overboard right now!" The sailor snatched for the pendant but the old man swatted his hand away with a deft smack.

"This old tear's gonna be returned proper," he muttered, securing the stone beneath his shirt again. He squared his hat upon his head and muscled through the small crowd until he reached the stairs and disappeared belowdecks.

As he turned from the old man to Alice, Hobart was hoping that the seafarer's tale had taken her mind off her emotions, but her thin-lipped expression and stony gaze was enough to dissipate that hope.

"You're mad at me," he said, feeling as if a statement of the obvious was what was required of him. She had been peevish toward him ever since he had come on deck this evening. This following an earlier incident in the morning when he had suggested she leave his bed to tend to her husband, so that he could get some sleep at last.

"Well, why shouldn't I be?" she shot back. Her anger seemed well seasoned.

"Think of yourself, Alice, for a moment." He took her arm and walked her out of earshot of any sailor, up to the forward deck. "You're young and newly married. There's still time to make something of that. I'm just an old actor. I can't offer you any of the comforts your husband is offering—respectability, family, status. You're setting off together on an adventure in a whole new world."

She leaned in against him, put her cheek against his, her jaw clenched, her lips breathing warmly near his ear, stirring the small hairs there. "But I want you."

"Alice. Sweet delicious Alice. I want you, too. But you deserve better. You're generous and warm and witty and you'll make Wayne a fine wife. And you have some new pleasures to show him once he finally rouses himself." He cupped her cheek in his hand, drawing the thumb across her lips, which parted slightly, releasing a sigh. He let his hand drift down her body, rising over the soft curve at her breast, then sliding down her slim waist and over her hips and around to rest on her bottom. "And what of me? Imagine my reputation back on the mainland if I were seen in the press as some kind of homewrecker and adulterer. That kind of scandal can ruin someone in pictures. They'd run me out of Los Angeles."

She placed a hand over his heart. "I feel as if the whole rest of my life is now going to be different than I ever imagined it to be."

"Would you say it was a mistake?"

"No."

He wanted her now. He wanted to take her roughly and drag her down to his stateroom one last time, to feel her nipples between his lips, to run his hand down her belly one last time. Instead, as she leaned in for a kiss, eyes closed, he let his hand drop from her backside and pulled away. Her eyelids fluttered open, her eyes full of cold and distant starlight.

"Good night, Mrs. Holdings," he said.

She bit her lower lip and she turned from him, putting both hands on the rail. The shore wind tossed her hair; otherwise she stood as still as a statue. Without looking back he returned to his cabin.

The *Falls of Clyde* dropped her anchor into the waters of Hilo Bay at the Big Island of Hawaii on Sunday morning, the twenty-sixth of December, just past dawn. Hobart was already awake and dressed. Although he had seen no sign of the galley boy he had found another bowl of fresh eggs outside his door. It then took several hours for the ship to negotiate customs, but eventually the gangplank was lowered and he disembarked. The day was bright, the sunlight diffuse through the low layer of silvery clouds; one hand shaded his eyes as he tottered his way down the dock, his body still under the influence of the sea. He quickly found the office of the Inter-Island Steam Navigation Company, where he was momentarily discouraged to discover that he had to wait until Wednesday for a trip on the steamship *Mauna Kea* to Honolulu, on the island of Oahu.

It was only upon his return walk to the ship that the reality of his new environment struck him. The tangy smell of sawgrass in the air reached him and he stopped where he was and looked around. He had only ever made landfall in Honolulu before, never Hilo, and though the towns were very different there was no mistaking the thrilling fact that he was in Hawaii again. In many ways Hilo appeared like the very model of Western frontier towns such as Reno or Fresno he remembered from his traveling days. Low and wide buildings with ornate brick or wood fronts with colorful trim shaded by palm and monkeypod trees. As if to emphasize the extremes found in the Hawaiian lands, the tropical forest at the edge of the town rose swiftly toward a distant snow-capped mountain range. An air of industry hung over Hilo as motorcars and horse-drawn wagons raced busily along wide paved avenues leading away from the waterfront. "God damn!" he cried with a laugh. "I'm in goddamned Hawaii!"

He set off at a trot toward the ship's anchorage to collect his belongings. The damp warmth and the tropical fragrances brought him closer to feeling young again than his return to San Francisco or even lying between Mrs. Holdings's soft thighs had made him feel. He felt his age dissolving from joints newly lubricated with strength and vigor. A small group of passengers was clustered at the foot of the gangplank and he drew up short as he saw Alice among them, the man who must evidently be her husband by her side. He was ghastly pale but in many other ways he and his wife seemed very much a match. They were exactly the same height though his similar blond hair was slicked and styled with pomade. He wore a stiff brown suit. She was wearing a light white blouse and long white skirt. Her hair was up and under a Western-style hat. Her eyes met Hobart's and narrowed just as her husband's face turned toward his and registered an expression of surprise.

"Mr. Bosworth!" her husband cried and Hobart drew to a halt. Alice remained motionless; he could tell nothing from her eyes. Hobart felt his right hand curl into a fist, just in case. The man reached a hand out, an open hand. "Wayne Holdings," he said, breaking into a grin. Hobart was immediately reminded of a weasel, for the man's face was long and pointed. He relaxed his fist cautiously, took the man's hand and shook it. "I believe you know my wife."

"She's a charming woman," he replied with a nod to her.

"Thank you, Mr. Bosworth," she replied stiffly.

"Please, call me Hob," he answered, causing her to purse her lips in an attempt to hold back a frown. "It's good to see you've regained your vigor."

"I am a man reborn," Holdings replied. "I spent plenty of time on the water at Princeton crewing but I suppose it was no preparation at all."

"It happens to all men at one time or another."

"I swear I kissed the ground just now. Didn't I?"

"He fell to his knees," she affirmed.

"Right here on the dock," he laughed. "You know, I loved that picture you made of *The Sea-Wolf*. I saw it three times. I'm sorry I felt so ill; I would have loved to talk to you about that. At least you were able to keep my wife company."

"No trouble at all."

"I hear you'll be traveling on with us to Oahu?"

"In fact, I've just come from the Inter-Island office. I'm afraid we won't be able to leave until Wednesday."

Holdings turned to his wife with an eager, surprised expression. "Why that's a break, isn't it?" He held up his left hand in which he had several envelopes. "The office here has just sent my mail over and there are arrangements by my employer, Mr. Dillingham, for us to see the volcano should we have the time. And now it appears that we do. You should join our expedition."

"Oh no," Alice said with a nervous laugh. "I'm sure Hob has been to Kilauea on one of his other Hawaiian voyages."

"Actually I've never been to the Big Island before. Or the volcano." He returned Alice's steely gaze with bemusement. "I hear it's something to see. And I have absolutely nothing else to do while I'm here."

"Delightful." Holdings clapped him on the shoulder. "Let me just send word back to the man at the Olaa Sugar Company. Shall we rendez-vous again here in an hour for the car?"

"It'll be a pleasure," he said, breaking into a big grin.

"Do you have to come?" she asked.

"I want to see the volcano," he answered honestly.

He opened his cabin door for the last time, softly singing the same verse of Billy Murray's "Hello, Hawaii, How Are You?" that had gotten stuck in his head, over and over again:

> *Hello, Hawaii, how are you?*
> *Let me talk to Honolulu Lou*
> *To ask her this*
> *Give me a kiss*
> *Give me a kiss*
> *By wireless*

He froze. Someone had been in his room. His bags sat on the bed; the drawers were open and empty. His bags appeared to have been packed for him. He threw open the wardrobe door and Kid stumbled out, blinking rapidly as his eyes adjusted to the light. His expression was fearful and he stood softly rocking from one foot to the other.

"Did you do this?" Hobart asked. The boy didn't respond. "Have you taken anything?" Again there was no answer and Hobart began to wonder if Kid understood him at all. "Well, then. If you're here to help then help. Take these up onto the dock and wait with them. Don't muck it up and I'll give you two bits."

The kid sprang into action, a smile flitting across his face. He scooped up the cases—everything, including the one containing the books—and tottering under their weight clumped out of the room.

Hobart took a final cup of tea with the captain and exchanged some words of thanks with the crew and then checked his watch and headed down the steps from the pilot house to the deck. It was there that someone reached out and grabbed his forearm. Instantly he clapped his other hand over the one that had stopped him and, closing a fist over the thumb, twisted.

The old sailor shrieked, "Jesus God!" and stumbled out of the hatch from which he had reached out to Hobart. Seeing that the threat was no threat at all, Hobart released the man's hand.

"Hey there, sorry, old-timer." He patted the old man's shoulder. "I thought you were someone else entirely come to see me off in style."

The old man massaged his thumb with his other hand. Hobart could see that it was bandaged. "I guess you thought I was Cookie," he muttered and cut Hobart's protestations short. "It's hard to keep a secret on a ship, son. F'r instance I hear you're making a trip to the volcano with the married woman and her husband."

"So?"

"So I'm wonderin' if you'd do an old man a favor and throw this back to the bitch." He lifted the necklace over his head and held it out toward Hobart. The black stone caught the sunlight and seemed to absorb more than it reflected.

"After your tale last night I would have thought you would want to do it yourself. Bringing it so far and all the hardships."

"I come far enough," the old man said, his shoulders sagging as he stared south, down-island. "I can't go no farther. I don' want to look on her ever again. She'll understan'. Just so long as she gets back what's hers in the end. What needs to be done needs to be done. I'd hate to meet that woman and her husband at the volcano and have your name come up. The old Hawaiian woman told me I should wrap it in leaves and just heave it in. Can you do that?"

"Why not?" Hobart said, appreciating the touch of blackmail, and the old sailor dropped it into the palm of his hand.

"Who's this?" Wayne asked him as the driver from the sugar company turned the Pierce-Arrow seven-seater into the traffic stream.

"This is Kid," Hobart replied about the boy sitting in the far back with the smaller of his bags. The rest the sugar company had entrusted to the City Transfer Company, which would deliver them to the steamship on Wednesday.

"What's he doing with us?" Alice asked coolly.

"He wants to see the volcano, too," Hobart replied. Nothing was going to be able to dampen his mood today. He was back in Hawaii.

They ran south and were soon beyond even the outskirts of the large town. They were surrounded by a marvelous forest of giant fern trees, which bathed the world and everything in it a green aura. Through the trees they constantly glimpsed the great blue expanse of ocean, somehow even more entrancing and promising from the land than it had seemed aboard the ship. And all the while they were climbing the low slope of Mauna Loa. Then, as quickly as they had left Hilo behind and entered the forest, the forest disappeared from around them and they found themselves in lands covered by thick, fleshy-leaved agave growth, scrub, and anemic trees. The air began to reek of a new smell. Sulfur.

Along the way, listening to Holdings's relentless chatter, Hobart had learned the following things about the man: He was a lawyer. He came from a long line of lawyers. Alice was lucky to have married him. He played rugby and crewed in college (but he had already mentioned that) and boxed as well. Wayne was a Republican and was looking forward to getting involved in the party here. A backwater like Hawaii was in desperate need of his abilities. If he were driving he would have had them there by now. He admired the cut of Hobart's suit. He was hungry for lunch. He thought Hawaii would be more of a jungle. He was a Republican (had he already mentioned that?) and had a great interest in national politics, where he thought his views had value. He thought the volcano would be more of a classically pointed mountain with its top chopped off instead of this great bump.

Hobart found it only took a little of his mind to keep the man engaged in conversation; the rest he could focus on the countryside as well as the slender enjoyment of Alice's quiet discomfort and disdain, which her own husband seemed oblivious to. Perhaps that's only how Wayne knew her to be. Hobart knew his presence had unsettled her and he had no real answer as to why he had decided to come (although he really did want to see the volcano) other than this: he felt challenged by her husband. He was tempted to invite him to a bout of sparring to teach the Ivy League man some lessons about the sweet science. The first being that no good boxer ever went to college, let alone Princeton.

In less than two hours they crested a ridge and arrived at the Volcano House, the small wooden hotel that sat on the rim of the caldera. Kid immediately headed into the underbrush along the path toward the volcano. In the parlor the proprietor, a middle-aged Greek who insisted on being called Uncle George, informed them that, among other things, the fire in the great stone fireplace had never been extinguished since the hotel first opened in 1866 and that Mark Twain had once warmed his heels before it.

Next they lunched in the cozy dining room, Wayne scarfing down fire-roasted pig and fresh fruit like a man who hadn't eaten in a week, which was in fact the case. As they drank some ouzo punch, the young lawyer finished going through the pouch of mail that had greeted him at dockside. "Look, darling," he exclaimed excitedly, pulling a thick, cream-colored square of embossed parchment from an envelope. "Mr. Dillingham has arranged for us to attend the governor's New Year ball on Friday night. I'm sure this will be the perfect way to introduce ourselves to Honolulu society. Not even here one day and we're starting at the top. Didn't I tell you that's how it would go? Didn't I?"

"You're halfway to the presidency already," Hobart said, relishing the punch, which had been strongly flavored with fresh pineapple and something Uncle George had called dragon fruit.

"Well, I'm sorry you're not invited, Hob," Alice said, sliding her hand into Wayne's. "It promises to be quite the exclusive event."

"I'm sure I'll find some way to interest myself," he replied.

Alice had completely stopped communicating with him as they trudged over the barren land in the heat of the afternoon, following their guide from the hotel, and he'd laughed to himself as he overheard Wayne chastising her impolite behavior. The ground had turned gray, spotted with thin patches of high grass, and though the air at the elevation was chilled, he could feel heat rising below his feet.

"We are entering Kilauea Crater," the guide announced shortly, his voice sounding flat and small in the great rocky space. Soon they were on the plain of a vast desert from which sprouted mountainous tumbles that piped forth dense steam that filled the valley. The pungent odor of brimstone surrounded them. Before them he heard a low roar that reminded him of the approach of a storm. They crept over great twisted ropes of smooth black rock. With one step Hobart would find himself feeling as if he were treading upon the new earth of creation, and with the next he could imagine himself marching through Hell itself. The land seemed to drop away ahead of them, a great rift in the surface of the earth from which steam and smoke poured forth, and yet the guide drew them onward toward it, though instinct said to flee.

"Behold," the guide said at last, with a flourish of his arm, "Hale-maumau Crater. Home of the goddess Pele."

It was long moments before anyone could speak, and even longer moments before any chose to. It was a greater sight, by far, than any Hobart had ever seen before.

They stood on the brink of a lake of fire. Great swelling domes of red filled and then burst, scattering dense bloody droplets, releasing an ink-green gas. Rock melted and churned like boiling iron in a vast steel mill. The heat billowing up seemed impossible and he saw Alice turn her face away. White veins of superheated ore coursed through the red and the black of the lava. The far side of the cauldron was too distant to see.

There was nothing to say. In time and in silence they made their way back. Later he couldn't recall just how long they had remained there, nor how long it took to return. But he had found Kid sitting by the automobile, dirty faced and sullen with that same gaze he had seen in his companions' faces. Farewells were bid, though he wasn't sure if he had spoken or if they had been heard. And it wasn't until later that night, as he stumbled from the auto to the door of the Hilo Hotel, that he had thrust his hand deep in his pocket and realized that he had forgotten to return the tear to Pele.

CHAPTER EIGHT

J ACK WAS CLOSE NOW and Hobart knew it.

The S.S. *Mauna Kea* steamed northward out of Hilo Bay into the bright blue waters of the Hawaiian Pacific on Wednesday morning, steam pouring from her single chimney in the center of the ship, her two small sails fore and aft filling with steady wind. Hobart stood at the rail on the top deck watching the passengers mill about on the two decks below him. Even though he had been at sea mere days ago, he was still excited. Each launch was altogether different and each voyage promised new adventures. He loved being on a ship almost as much as he loved being on a stage.

Below him on the main deck he caught sight of the Holdings, arms around each other watching the crescent of Hilo fall away. They whispered conspiratorially to each other and acted in every way as if their marriage had at last been consummated. Hobart felt satisfied with that. Of course, Alice would not have tossed her marriage aside for him and he knew for certain now that she would never betray her misadventure to her husband. Still, he would miss her lovely companionship, especially because his new sidekick was silent and otherwise altogether incompatible.

"Major," Hobart sighed, using the name he had chosen for him. The boy materialized as if by magic at his side as he had done countless times the day before. Hobart would exit a door and moments later discover he had a second shadow. The only time he hadn't been followed was when he'd boarded the *Falls of Clyde* to return the volcano stone to the old sailor, but the rightful owner had apparently disappeared into the saloons of the waterfront to celebrate his emancipation and was nowhere to be found. This morning on his way from the hotel and as he boarded the steamship, he thought he had finally left the boy behind. Surely he would be drawn back to the *Falls of Clyde* in the end. Instead, here he was again, as silent, persistent, and annoying as gout. "If I wanted a manservant I'd hire a Chinaman."

Major stared out at the dolphins racing the waves created by the ship's progress.

"Isn't there anybody on this earth looking for you?"

Major remained mute.

"Because I've got people looking for me." He sighed. "Okay. If you're going to travel with me I want my shoes shined every night. You take care of dirty laundry. You don't hang about when I'm speaking with anybody else. You don't curse, spit, or break wind around me. I take my meals alone, though I'll pay you a dollar a week so you can find your own food. You sleep on the floor and you run any errands I may need. And the first thing we have to do is get you some new clothes. Can't have an employee of Hobart Bosworth Productions dressed like a sea urchin. Now go get lost until we reach Oahu. I want to be alone. And don't spy on me either!" he called as the boy dashed away. He wasn't sure how much the boy had understood; his eyes had remained dull throughout, but he was certain the boy would be waiting for him soon after they reached Pearl Harbor.

As the day passed, the island of Maui slipped by, impossibly green with mountains that clawed at the sky, followed soon by the rocky coast of the island of Molokai, which reminded him of the Seaton Cliffs where Scotland meets the North Sea. All along the way the ocean was dotted with small islands, like rocks strewn about a puddle. Then in midafternoon the great wall of the Koolau mountain range rose up before his eyes, a sight he hadn't seen in ages and had neither forgotten nor ever thought he'd see again. Clouds swarmed against the range, which seemed to stretch from the foot of the shore and then disappeared into the distance like some great backbone fin of a beast from antiquity.

The *Mauna Kea* drew in closer to the shore and the passengers rushed to the starboard side to gasp as Diamond Head came into view, a great brown sawed-off cone that rose up from the body of the main island. After rounding that all could see the soft warm sands of Waikiki Beach and the tiny forms of distant people walking upon it. There were buildings to be seen as well, buildings made of stone and designed by architects as opposed to Hilo's wooden frontier construction. This was Honolulu. Hobart felt the shock of surprise; the city had grown so much since his last visit. There were even lanes cut into the rising mountains that backed the city and houses set along those very same lanes. Soon the steamship turned east and made its way into Pearl Harbor, a sheltered ocean port on the leeward side of the island protected by gently sloping green shores.

The OR&L train station was conveniently close to the docks and Hobart headed there, while the kid followed behind struggling only a little with the luggage. He heard his name called and turned to find Wayne Holdings pulling his bride toward him through the small throng gathering under the green awning, many of them young American Navy sailors disembarking from the nearby cruisers.

"We wanted to say good-bye," the young man said, and his wife looked as if she couldn't agree more. "We're off to Ewa," he said, pronouncing it with a "v" in place of the "w" in the Hawaiian fashion while indicating the northbound train.

"My journey is almost done. I'm off to find Jack London," he replied.

"You're taking that kid with you?" Alice sniffed.

"This is Major Domo. He's my *chargé d'affaires,*" Hobart said drily. He held out his hand and Wayne shook it, then he extended it toward Alice. After a moment in which she stared at it, she gave her hand to him and he placed a gentle kiss on it. "It has been my pleasure," he told her.

The little train pulled out from the Pearl Harbor depot, first rising up over several small hills and then turning to the south, keeping the ocean to the right. The sunset was an astounding mixed palate of scarlets and vermillions but Hobart was too distracted by the changes to the land that drew his attention. Automobiles had invaded the island like a swarm of hornets that had moved into an old barn. They roared along every road Hobart saw, coughing up clouds of smoke and dust, and those roads, most paved and some lined with strings of electric lights, were new to him as well. American flags seemingly hung from every building.

When the train reached the end of its rails with a whistle and blast of exhausted steam, they transferred to a nearby streetcar bound for the downtown area, the boy's head swiveling back and forth as he took in the sights. At Queen Street they hopped off and walked several blocks on narrow, clean-swept sidewalks until they reached Hobart's destination on Beretania Street—a granite office building. He looked up and saw the light on behind the second floor window, illuminating the golden words:

Paramount Pictures, Distributor

"Keep an eye on my bags," he told Major Domo and entered the building.

The effect his entrance through the office door had on Ben Morosco was worthy of being captured on film. The man spilled a good portion of the bottle of rye he was holding onto a pile of receipts and ad clippings. Then his jaw dropped open in outright amazement and his eyes filled with tears. On his rush to embrace his old friend, he stumbled on a pile of round metal film canisters, sending them skittering across the wooden floor as he fell like an ingenue into Hobart's arms. Hobart waited until the last canister stopped spinning in place, a surprisingly long moment, before looking down, smiling, and saying, "Good to see you too, Ben."

He helped the heavy man right himself. In fact, Morosco was not much older than Hobart, but since his thirties he had carried himself with an air of gravitas that overcame his stout, ill-kempt appearance. Theater owners treated him with more respect if they thought he had twenty more years' experience under his belt than he actually had, and in his way of acting like an old man he was able to drive harder bargains for bookings and was able to be less patient about payments as he gave the various owners of the vaudeville and Broadway stages the impression that he might expire right there in their lobby while the evening's take was counted. It didn't hurt to be the cousin of the most feared showman on the circuit, Oliver Morosco. Hobart had known Ben as one of the best bookers in the business for many years and when he had moved his talents to Los Angeles he had called upon the man to get his pictures into the palaces being built at a rapid pace around the country. He had done this job so well that when Hobart had been forced into his alliance with Zukor, Morosco had been promoted to the Paramount distribution team. Poached, both Hobart and Morosco had agreed. Morosco, unhappy at the turn of events, had bucked for the position in the Pacific territories and Zukor had agreed, consigning him there and evidently forgetting about him.

"My God, Ben," Hobart said as he took a seat in one of the upholstered chairs, which seemed to sigh happily under his weight. He took quick note of the melted candles frozen in the menorah on the windowsill. "How can a man live in the tropics for two years and still be as white as a sheet of paper?"

"It's true, Hob," replied the man, finishing pouring his rye into a cut-crystal glass and pouring another for Hobart. "Hard to believe." He carefully removed some papers from the other chair, setting them on the small table between the two chairs, and had a seat. "Had I known you were coming, the reception I could have arranged for you. No matter, tomorrow I'll talk to my people at the *Pacific Commercial Advertiser* and before you know it you'll have this town at your feet."

"No press, I'm afraid." Hobart held up a hand to stop his friend's planning. "This is a personal visit. The less Zukor and Garbutt, or anyone else back there, knows about it, the better. If you can do that for me, I'd appreciate it."

Morosco's eyes grew steely at the mention of the names and he nodded in agreement. There was no love lost there.

"How are you doing here, Ben?" he asked.

"The islands have gone crazy for the pictures," the man replied. "If I had five more movie theaters I could keep them filled. I just finally got the Popular to move *Birth of a Nation* out—that played for months."

"The Popular—is that a good house?"

"Very good. Owned by two wealthy widows. It used to be a real theater but they converted it. Give the people what they want, I suppose."

"Hmm." Hobart was beginning to formulate a plan. "I might like to meet the widows."

"That can be arranged."

"What are you showing now?"

"Now? *Kilmeny*."

"Ugh. Lenore Ulric as the lost gypsy child. Bathetic."

"Yeah. The locals eat it up, though. Plus I'm showing the travel pictures of South America and the latest chapter of *Diamond from the Sky*."

"You should have *Seven Sisters* soon."

"Marguerite Clark, right? I can't wait. It'll do great after the holidays."

"I'm not sure how long I'm going to be here, but I need a few things to help me while I'm here and you're the one to help me out."

"Anything. Name it."

"I need the name of a good hotel."

"Hau Tree Hotel," he replied without dropping a beat. "The finest hotel in Waikiki. I know the manager, he owes me some favors for the business I throw him. I'll have him set you up with a great deal on the best suite straightaway. Now what else can I do for you?"

Hobart plucked up the familiar cream envelope he had spied among the papers Morosco had toppled over. "I'd like one of these," he said, reaching for it. "I don't yet have plans for New Year's."

Morosco screwed his face up in a caricature of concerned thought. "That's a little more difficult," he said. "Those invitations are hard to come by. Really, it's just another boring old party."

"I hear it's the social event of the season. Do me a favor and see what you can do."

"What I can do," the man echoed. He picked up the telephone. "Let's see about your hotel first, right?" He hesitated, studying Hobart's face. "There's something more you want?"

Hobart nodded. "I want to know where I can find Jack London."

The small brown cottage with the white trim stood by itself at the end of Beach Road not far from the hotel. Surrounded by palm trees it faced the long white beach where great waves, which started rising far out in the harbor, driven by the strong winter winds, finally broke and crashed away to nothingness. The woman sat on the bamboo recliner, positioned on the open lanai to catch the breeze. She wore a simple, tasteful dress, gray with brown trim, and a blanket was thrown over her curled legs. She wore sunglasses, her eyes hidden behind their green lenses as she read a book. Her brown hair was worn tied back to keep it from being tossed about.

Her face was tanned and smooth, with only a few smile lines around her broad mouth betraying any sign of age. She hadn't sensed his approach and was startled when he had quietly said, "Hello, Charmian."

She set her book down and looked up at him, studying him. He would never describe her as pretty in such a way where he would want to put her in front of a motion picture camera and capture her beauty. Her features were, in fact, rather plain. But when she spoke, her voice was deep and enticing and conveyed a sense of her fierce vivacity. "Hobart Bosworth," she said simply, adding no meaning, positive or negative, to the name. "You're a long way from home."

"I brought some books for Jack to sign," he said at last.

"He's not here," she said, again displaying no emotion, only conveying information.

"Where can I find him?" he asked.

"Oh, you know Jack," she said, closing her book at last. She unfurled her legs slowly from under the blanket, like an awakening cat, and stood. Her feet were bare. She was fairly short but that was only apparent up close. She waved toward the ocean. "He's out there walking on water."

Shading his eyes he looked out in the general direction she had indicated. Far out on the ocean, where the waves began to rise in great blue lines crested with white, he could see a scattered group of men bobbing up and down as they sat on long wooden boards. As a wave rolled in and grew in size, one of the men swung into a prone position on his board and began to paddle with his arms as the other men moved out of his way. The wave lifted the man's board up and over their heads and in an instant the rider had fluidly leaped to a standing position and was rocketing down its face.

"Wave sliding?"

She nodded.

"I've read his articles about it but it's amazing to see it for myself. Is Jack out there?"

"He is."

She handed him a worn pair of field glasses. The lenses brought the wave riders into sharp focus. They were all dark-skinned young Hawaiian men, fit as if sculpted by a Renaissance artist. The one white among

them was easily apparent; his skin was the color of fine leather but nowhere close to the dark nut brown of his companions.

"That's him, right? The one smoking the cigarette."

"He's surfing with Duke and his beach boys right now. Won't be in
for hours."

He lowered the glasses as he heard the screen door from the house
behind him squeak open. A young but stern-looking Japanese man
stood in the doorway.

"All right, Mrs. London?"

"Fine, Nakata. You remember Mr. Hobart Bosworth? The man
from Hollywood?" Hobart was about to greet Jack's manservant but
she continued, a new sharper tone to her voice. "How could you possibly ever forget the man who robbed Jack of fifteen thousand dollars."

"That's one of the situations I've come to talk to Jack about."

"Do you have fifteen thousand dollars on you?"

"Of course not."

"Then there isn't much to talk to Jack about after all, is there." She
removed her glasses and her eyes were blazing with anger and hurt. "He
considered you his friend, Hobart, and when Mr. Zukor and Mr. Garbutt explained how you had stolen from him he was too broken up even
to consider suing you even though that's what I wanted him to do and
would do in a heartbeat." She advanced on him.

"Your shenanigans and those of others have just played hell on
poor Jack's health, and I won't have you ruining all that we have
done to put him on the road to recovery. Am I clear about that? Now
you stay away from my husband or there will be even more hell to
pay."

Hobart backed off the porch onto the lane. "I just want to explain
myself to Jack."

"Stay away from him and stay away from us," she snapped, standing
above him on the lanai. Her hair had come loose and the wind was tossing it around wildly. He had forgotten what a striking woman Charmian London was.

"There's one more thing," he said before turning away. "The Popular is going to screen all of my Jack London pictures. I hope you can
both come." He smiled to himself as he walked away. Not even in

Oahu twenty-four hours and he'd already figured out a way to make some money, though the actual details of the Jack London screenings and the associated benefit party had been left to Morosco. If convincing Jack London meant convincing Charmian, then he might be here for a while. At least he'd be able to afford it. The money would come.

Part 2

WESTWARD
THE COURSE OF EMPIRE

—PAINTED ON A WOODEN SIGN AT THE OPENING OF PEARL HARBOR

CHAPTER NINE

CHARMIAN LONDON'S HANDS SHOOK as she prepared Jack's medicines.

Hobart Bosworth was in Hawaii.

To begin with there was Algospasmin for his stomach pains. Next she steadied her nerves and carefully tapped out a few milligrams of Salvarsan prescribed for the pellagra into the silver measuring spoon she had kept with her since Sydney. She sprinkled the white powder into his tart fresh-squeezed noni juice and used the spoon to dissolve it. He had already taken his Benzedrine with the first strong cup of Kona coffee Nakata had prepared for him when he had arisen, as always, before dawn. He called those his "energy pills." The Veranol he would use later that night to fall asleep. There were other bottles, filled with various pills, powders, and liquids to be administered for a variety of his illnesses as needed. But not today. His days had been very good since they had arrived in early November, and the majority of the medicines remained untouched. Still, it was reassuring to see those little bottles every day because when his days were bad, they were bad indeed. Then she checked his vials of morphine sulphate and atropine sulphate as she did every day. Untapped, they had rested in his case for a long time in case of a dire emergency during one of his adventures when a doctor would be out of reach. She closed the lid of the wooden case and noticed that her hands had stopped trembling. It was amazing how soothing a little bit of routine could be.

Charmian wondered if she should tell Jack about Hobart and then realized that she would have to. He hadn't come all this way to Hawaii to be turned away at Jack's door. He would be back. Forewarned is forearmed she decided. She was still filled with disbelief at the actor's sudden appearance. She tried to not get involved too much in Jack's business dealings; one of the benefits of marrying a rich man was not having to worry about money anymore. Eliza capably handled all of their financial affairs, and though Jack often complained of having money troubles due to the ranch or his adventurous whims, Charmian felt certain that his sister always had the situation well in hand. If Jack wanted Charmian to be more watchful with their money, she certainly would be—all he had to do was mention it. As little as she cared to know about Jack's various business ventures, though, she fully shared with him his sense of betrayal by Hobart. It wasn't about the money. He had charmed them both. Jack had often said to her how he felt Hobart was a kindred spirit in so many ways, from their similar youthful adventures to their achievements in their art forms. He and Hobart were equals, he had told her, in a world where he had few equals. She saw it, too, the electric light in his eyes that spoke of daring and adventure.

Charmian took her cup of coffee and walked over to the sleeping porch that Jack had claimed as his writing space. He had set up a small desk at which he wrote and another desk to hold his research books and his correspondence. She had set herself up with a desk in a room down the hall where she sometimes wrote herself, but more often typed, his scrawled words into manuscripts to deliver to his publisher or the many magazine editors who awaited his dispatches. Though they were not so numerous as in years before. She sighed as she looked about the room. Poor Jack. He had taken lately to describing his writing room, whether this lovely lanai or the one at the Beauty Ranch, as a prison cell. He said he felt as if he were only writing to keep ahead of the banks. And yet he could still afford to winter in Hawaii so she assumed that there was a measure of joking to his complaining.

The ashtray at the small desk was full of the stubs of his little hand-rolled cigarettes, evidence that he had sat there this morning. His special pen, connected by a tube to the inkwell so it never needed dipping and never ran dry, lay undisturbed in the same position it had rested in yesterday. She looked over the books he had set aside for special research; on top of the thick stack of books on Norse mythology was his much-read copy of Freud's *Interpretation of Dreams* and his latest obsession, Jung's *Psychology of the Unconscious*. A quick scan showed her that he had been underlining passages again last night.

She checked his papers to see if the day's output included anything for her to transcribe. She expected to find a few pages for his new novel, *Cherry,* but there were no new additions to the small stack of pages full of what felt to her to be half-hearted effort. He was trying to create yet another woman hero. It was as if he was flying directly into the face of his critics, who hailed his books about men but derided his attempts to characterize the fairer sex. There was no solid progress to speak of. Instead there was simply a list of seemingly random words that were scrawled in his cramped, angular cursive.

moon

sun

fenrisulfr

wolf

They had no meaning for her. But there was no reason why they should. He had told her that his thoughts were concerned with enjoying Hawaii and the holidays and that he would resume his customary thousand words a day in the new year. But she had never known him to go this long without writing in the ten years that they had been together. He had even written during that horrible voyage on the *Snark* when he had first been stricken with the tropical disease that still plagued him. He had even written in the aftermath of the Wolf House fire. The only time she had known him to take this long a break from his schedule was after Joy's birth, and days later, her death. She ran a hand over her flat, empty belly. He hadn't written for a month then.

She thought about updating her Hawaiian journal, or sending some letters. If Jack wasn't going to write, at least she could put some words on paper for the sake of family honor. But with the sun streaming through the windows and the warm breeze coming in from the ocean and a beautiful day stretching out before her, it seemed as if there was too much else to do. She heard the distant roar of the voices of men in high spirits and she knew that Jack and his clan were coming in from the surf. She could hear them as they congratulated themselves on successful rides and taunted one other about the waves that had crushed them, Jack's booming voice and boisterous laugh rising confidently above them all. That made her smile. It meant he was having a good day.

Through the window she could see them as they approached the cottage. The Hawaiians were not tall men, which meant that Jack, who was short among the Caucasians, could see eye to eye with them. To a casual observer, only the lighter coloring of the skin, a fair teak when compared to their mahogany richness, differentiated her husband from the natives. She let the lace curtain fall back and went to get the mixture of aloe and kukui-nut oil that soothed his skin after being out in the sun. They had been introduced to this island mixture a decade before during their first visit when Jack's eagerness to learn surfing had caused him to be stricken with a sunburn so bad that the skin of his back and shoulders had split open. Yet another one of the misadventures the *Snark*, had brought them to.

Nakata had heard the approach of the men as well and he entered the room with coffee and cakes for all. She smiled at him and the handsome Asian gave her a smile back. How many years had he been with them now? Nearly ten. He had been their cabin boy on the *Snark*, since signing on during their first trip to Hawaii, and he had stayed by Jack's side ever since—unafraid of any adventure Jack could conceive of. After surviving the *Snark*, how could he? While Jack had been laid up in the Australian hospital for month after month, struggling with the sunsickness that tore at his tissues and the malaria that racked him with chills, both she and Nakata had been stricken with neurasthenia and they had supported each other through the aches and the weaknesses and the spells that accompanied it. After her, Yoshimatsu Nakata was Jack's most trusted. He had grown into a handsome man who must be nearly thirty by now. Hard to believe Nakata was now the age Jack was when she had married him. That reminded her that Jack's fortieth birthday was only two weeks away.

"Nakata," she said, "what do you think London-san would like for his birthday? I'm a little stumped."

The man thought for a minute and then replied in his soft, slightly accented voice. "Perhaps a new fishing pole? He wants to fish from the jetty." He indicated the narrow wall of boulders that jutted out into the harbor.

She heard a thunder on the front porch as the surfers laid up their heavy wooden boards, each about fifteen feet long and crafted from holy koa wood, once grown exclusively for the Hawaiian monarchy. Then again, Duke Kahanamoku, the leader of the pack of the beach boys who were following Jack to the cottage, was considered royalty even by what was left of the real Hawaiian aristocracy. Not only was he the best wave slider on Waikiki Beach, but he had won gold and silver swimming medals at the 1912 Olympics, forever endearing him to the islanders. Jack had only burnished his luster by writing tales of Duke's surfing prowess. The two had been friends since the *Snark* visit when Duke had taught Jack the art of riding the waves.

Now Jack was describing in vivid terms his last wild ride down the face of a wave, how he had skimmed along for what seemed like forever. She smiled to herself. Although he was aging and his belly was growing, and he fought a variety of plagues that sapped him of energy, there was still in the sound of his voice and bearing the fire and crack of Nietzsche's *Übermensch* he had once held as his ideal.

There was a pause in his story-telling interrupted by a great trumpeting blast. This was followed by gales of hysterical laughter from all on the front porch. Some jokes needed no translation. Yes, she thought to herself, Nietzsche's *Übermensch* suffered from occasional gastric distress. Still laughing, the men tumbled through the door into the house like a pack of overgrown boys. Jack led the way, tears spilling from his eyes. Then Duke, the Olympian, and his brother Samuel followed. Behind them were four of the ever-revolving group of young Hawaiian men who followed Duke everywhere and made pocket cash teaching the *haole*—the white visitors—how to ride waves. She recognized only a few of them today, including the heavily tattooed Mano, one of Duke's more constant companions and the tallest of the group. On her travels through the South Pacific she had decided that the Polynesians were a most perfect race, and as if to prove that point these Hawaiians of that line were spectacularly beautiful men, with physiques seemingly carved by the hands of an artist out of the same sacred wood as their boards. Even the one who was fat, the one they called Johnny the Samoan, when compared to the others was still a strong specimen of man. Water drops beaded on their smooth, dark skin, and their straight white teeth gleamed from their dark faces. Jack had met Duke on the first visit, years before he had won the gold and silver swimming medals. Funny how even though there were so few men in the world that Jack considered his equal, there were now two on this tiny Pacific island.

"Charmian," Jack cried, still boisterous from the attack of laughter and coming toward her quickly. "Did you see us out there? I had the most intense ride of my life today. It must have been something to see."

"I'm afraid I missed it," she said, letting herself be swept up in his arms. She could feel his ocean-dampness seeping into her clothes, but she succumbed, as she almost always did, to the force of his strong body against hers. She would have to change soon anyway. She brushed the thick locks of his dark wet hair from his prominent forehead so she could see his wild eyes, which were brimming with the Irish in him today. She tilted her face ever so slightly for a kiss, but he turned instead to play host, while keeping one arm around her waist. She should have known better. Although he would stay in almost continuous physical contact with her, Jack hardly ever kissed her in front of anyone else and certainly not in front of his Hawaiian friends. It had just felt at that moment as if he might have.

"Take your medicine, Jack." She indicated the pills and potions she had so carefully laid out for him, while Nakata went about serving up the coffee to the surfers.

"You know, Mate-Woman, I'm feeling as if I don't need them today." She felt his chest puff and his shoulders rise. "I swear I feel as if I could have surfed all the way to Tahiti."

"That's how you know they're working, Mate-Man," she replied. "Now come. You know I'm right."

His shoulders fell. "Of course you are," he said. As his friends laughed and joked in their native tongue, which sounded more like singing than any language she had ever heard, he eyed his medications but didn't move to take them.

"The incredible thing I find about surfing is that the minute I catch a wave I lose the ability to form words. I mean, I can still think. I'm aware of the thought process of my brain. But I'm more aware of feeling. It brings me a feeling of fear and of power and beauty. And finally it brings me a feeling of accomplishment. I see the reef sliding beneath and I can talk about it now, but I can't recall being able to speak about it while the board is in motion. It's like I have become a part of the wave. Part of the ocean. An insignificant droplet cascading down the face of the wave. What say you, Duke?"

"You celebrate the wave, brudda Jack," Duke said in his low, smooth voice, "and the wave celebrates you."

"That's it exactly," Jack said. "That is it. It's the wave. We're celebrating the wave and the ocean from which we rose. We're celebrating us. The all of us. And risking our lives to do it."

"It's just fun to me," Mano said, with such earnest seriousness in his deep low voice that it stirred the other men to laughter.

"No writing today?" Charmian quietly asked Jack as he wiped the tears of laughter away.

He shook his head. "It's New Year's Eve. I decided to take the day off and enjoy myself. To free myself from the shackles that keep me chained to my writing desk all day every day. To hell with writing. Today," he announced to his friends as much as her, "I am celebrating myself! After all, what's the point of being a celebrated writer if I don't celebrate once in a while?"

"Now does that sound like something Mark Twain would say?" she joked.

"Mark Twain didn't surf!" he said with a grin. "I've written fifty books in twenty years. I think I've earned a vacation."

"You have some gift for the words, brudda Jack," Duke said, shaking his head in admiration.

"Ah, a gift you say? I say that gift comes with a curse as well. You know the gift, too, Duke. The fire that needs constant tending. Look! The fire grows low, you have to put more wood on and more and more. And where does that wood come from? From your own life."

"I just do what comes naturally," said the surfer, his dark eyes twinkling.

Jack sat down on the couch and propped his feet up on the coffee table. She could see that his ankles were swollen.

"How big would you say that wave was? I say twelve feet easy," Jack said.

Mano burst into a laugh, which he choked back. Duke slapped Jack playfully on the leg. "Four feet. Maybe three."

Jack was aghast. "What?" He looked at the others for support but saw only that they were in agreement with Duke. He settled back into a slightly sullen pose. "It always seems bigger when you're on it."

"And bigger still when it's on you," Duke pointed out.

After lunch and more surfing tales, the Hawaiians departed. Nakata had left earlier on some errands and they had the cottage to themselves, which seemed a rarity these days. Jack stretched out on the couch with a groan while she rubbed the scented oils into his skin. His shoulders were still firm and muscular and the cords of his neck were thick and heavy like oak. He was still a fine man in spite of his illnesses. She found herself embracing him suddenly, her cheek against his neck. The warmth of the sun radiated from his skin. She felt his hand on her arm.

"How did you sleep?" she murmured.

"The worms were at my brain again," he sighed.

"That's what your medicine is for."

"I know." He twisted around so they were nearly nose to nose. It seemed like it had been a long while since she had captured his eyes and attention so completely. "But sometimes, here in Paradise, I feel so like my old self that to admit that I have to take medications is admitting that I'm not that old self at all and that I'm just old."

"You're not even forty."

"Well, I'm feeling my age. You've been caring for me in one way or another since I broke both my arms. And that was a dozen years ago. I must seem like such an invalid to you. Aren't you sick of it?"

She gave him a small kiss on the lips. "No. You're still my wolf."

"Did a Dr. Homer send word this morning?"

"Who?"

"Never mind."

"Why are you seeing a doctor? Is there something wrong?"

"He's not a doctor really. Nothing to worry about. I'm just doing some research for a book and need some expert advice."

"About what?"

"Nothing. Never mind about it." He nuzzled against her, his head against her breast, while she stroked his hair. She put a little pressure against his head, hoping to coax his lips up to hers, but he resisted. Instead he inhaled deeply; she could feel the press of his nose against her blouse. He whispered something, his hot breath seeping through the fabric, warming her nipple. A rush of involuntary, urgent excitement flooded through her core.

"What?" she murmured back. Her voice suddenly sounded thick and husky to her own ears.

He tilted his head back a little. His eyes were dark, the pupil and iris nearly the same deep shade. "I can still smell *him* on you."

"No, you can't." She shook her head, suddenly feeling small, the tingling inside her suddenly ebbing. She placed a hand on either side of his face. "That was an ocean away and a lifetime ago," she said. "I am yours. There is nothing of that man, nor any other man on me. My old skin is burned away by this tropical sun. This is new skin and it belongs to you."

She felt his hand suddenly upon her breast and his mouth was crushed against hers. She rose to her knees to meet him. In a moment he had her swept up in his arms as he carried her toward the bedroom. The outfit she intended to wear this evening was laid out across the bed so she could examine it later and be sure it suited her mood.

"Be careful," she laughed as he made ready to toss her down. "My dress!"

"To hell with it," he growled, sweeping it to the floor as he threw her to the mattress.

"But it's for the ball tonight! Don't you want me to look pretty?"

"I can't wait," he said, ripping her blouse open from her neck to her navel. She sighed, releasing months of pent-up frustration as he rolled her over so her face was against the soft coolness of the sun-dried linen. It smelled faintly of lavender. His hands were on her back, around her waist, his lips on the nape of her neck now and she sighed again and for the moment she felt forgiven. She heard him grunt, then whimper, felt his hands leave her body. Her ache for him remained unsoothed: she knew how to push it all away.

With a mournful groan, he slid onto the bed next to her. Without looking at him she placed her hand tenderly on his belly then slowly slid it down to where everything remained soft.

"Will you still love me if I can't love you?" he said, moving his arms to cover the frustration on his face.

"I love you," she said, turning to kiss those very hands. "You're growing healthier by the day. I can see it. Here in Aloha-land you'll grow as strong again as you ever were and more. My Mate-Man. My Jack London. My wolf."

CHAPTER TEN

"MOTHER SPENT THE DAY helping the Queen prepare," Harry Strange said. "Mother said the Queen is quite upset with you."

"With me?" Jack said. "What have I done?"

"It's what you haven't done," their friend replied, the starch of his British accent not the least softened by his years in Hawaii. "You haven't called upon her."

"Oh dear," Jack replied. Charmian felt him squeeze her hand a little more tightly as they moved through the New Year's carnival crowd gathering on Hotel Street. "I didn't think she'd care about me."

"Liliuokalani is very fond of you, it turns out." They stopped before the great iron fence that separated Washington Place, the Queen's home, from Iolani Palace, now the headquarters of the territorial government, across the street. They stood watching the nenes and moorhens scratching around the roots of the canopy-like monkeypod trees and the great stalks of wild ginger topped with flaming red spear tips that grew in front of the golden statue of Queen Liliuokalani's ancient predecessor, the great King Kamehameha, the man who had united the Hawaiian Islands. Charmian wondered if the Queen, in her exile, took some strength from the idol, now glowing in the light of the setting sun. Living in the shadow of her former home had to be difficult. Knowing she was the last queen of the islands, with no children to succeed her, to carry on her struggle for justice, to care for her, had to be nearly unbearable. At the thought of the old woman living alone, surrounded only by the remains of her court, Charmian felt the hollow ache of her missing womb. Now it was she who squeezed Jack's hand.

Jack, always one to get swept up in the jolly spirit of camaraderie, found himself unable to refuse any stranger's hail-fellow-well-met, and so Charmian and Strange waited patiently for the frequent interruptions to pass, as Jack drank from proffered hip flasks and open bottles, danced to fiddlers and ukuleles, and laughed at jokes too numerous to recall.

"It's almost seven," Harry said finally as the last group of well-wishers, American sailors who had recognized Jack, staggered off to join the swirling throng. He tucked his pocketwatch back into his vest pocket. "I'd plug your ears." This friend of theirs had been an administrator for the Honolulu Gas Company when they had met him, and his mother, years before. Now he ran the company. As a British citizen he had a unique perspective on the territorial annexation of Hawaii by the Americans: he could condemn their actions at the same time he could profit from them. Of course as a son of the great empire, he fully understood the American position as necessary for the best interests of the nation and for the native Hawaiians. Trim figured and debonair, he was quite popular among the females of Hawaiian *haole* society. The silver that now wove through his sandy brown hair only seemed to increase his desirability. Though he had been engaged several times, he was currently unattached to any one woman. Therefore he was free this evening and had taken it upon himself to bring the Londons to the New Year's Eve ball to witness the return of the seventy-seven-year-old Queen to the palace for the first time since she had been banished by the island's new masters. Since Harry knew everything about, and everyone in, Honolulu, he was the perfect choice to guide them through the crowded streets—jam-packed with sailors and soldiers, Asians of every creed but especially Japanese, European businessmen, vacationing Americans, and hundreds of others dressed for various masquerade balls. Indeed there seemed to be so many *haole* that Jack had commented he was hard-pressed to find any *kamaaina,* or native Hawaiians. Another reminder, Charmian thought, of just how much Oahu, the "Gathering Place," had changed since their first visit.

On their way to the ball Strange had pointed out the 20,400-ton Delaware-class Dreadnought USS *North Dakota,* anchored in one of the

deep-channel piers at Fort Armstrong and told them of the noisy part
the vessel was to play in the evening's festivities. She took his warning
seriously, releasing Jack's hands to place her fingertips in her ears just as
the great ship fired her ten twelve-inch guns and fourteen five-inch guns
one after another. The explosive outburst caromed from the lowlands of
Pauoa Valley at one end of Honolulu to the hills of Palolo Heights at the
other end and everyone who heard it knew that the evening's celebration
had begun. Even as the booming echo faded away, and she and Jack lowered their hands, the gates to Washington Place opened to allow the exit
of an ornate carriage drawn by four horses, the red, white, and blue flags
of the Territory of Hawaii that adorned its roof fluttering merrily in the
evening breeze.

"Come on," Jack said, his dark eyes glittering. She wasn't certain but
the energy in his gaze made her think that perhaps he had helped himself to an extra dose of medicine, perhaps the Benzedrine. A small pro-
cessional had followed the carriage as it exited the grounds of the
Queen's home and Jack led them into the street to join it. They walked
in the street as the parade passed the new library under construction.
The assembly then turned right onto Punchbowl Street, in sight of
Kawaiahao Church, built from coral rocks that Hawaiian divers had ex-
cavated from the harbor.

"Listen," Jack said, as ever the first to notice something of interest.
Now, as each person on the street and sidewalk heard the footfalls of
the horses' hooves, they were falling silent, standing somberly, until
the whole of the route had grown as still as the stalks of sugarcane
standing in the plantations on the other side of the mountains. In silence the procession turned right again on South King Street and, as if
following the outstretched arm of the golden statue of the king
Charmian had seen earlier, the carriage passed through another set of
gates and up the lane toward the palace. As the gates closed the crowd
began to cheer for Her Majesty one last time. It was a roar that rose
with such lusty, vibrant power that, Charmian heard later, the men of
the USS *North Dakota* thought it a long-delayed echo response to their
salute.

Having followed the carriage in and presented their invitation,
Charmian watched as the Queen and her entourage, including Harry's
mother, a woman nearly as old as the Queen who threw her son a
happy wave, disembarked from the carriage. One of the other women

in the Queen's company, a lovely young Hawaiian, looked familiar to Charmian but her memory would not serve. The Queen and company were greeted at the great palace door by the governor and his wife and the sugar baron Benjamin Dillingham with his wife, Emma Louise, by his side. The Queen, weary in step but proud in bearing, took the arm the governor offered and allowed herself to be escorted into the house along a paved path lit by hundreds of colorfully glowing Japanese lanterns.

As they smoked cigarettes under the coronation pavilion on the northwest corner of the palace grounds Charmian studied Jack, whose own attention was focused on his conversation with Harry about the current rash of reports coming from soldiers on the European front of great visions of the dead appearing over the battlefields. Jack held his cigarette tightly between his forefinger and middle finger, his arm locked somewhere between raised and lowered as if his body had forgotten about it. His other arm was wrapped tightly around his body, which leaned against one of the columns of the gazebo. He wore a navy blue smoking jacket with matching trousers he'd had made for himself several years before on a trip to New York to speak at Columbia. He hadn't been able to button it across his protruding stomach tonight so it hung open casually. His eyes were glassy yet the pupils were dark centers of studious concentration as he took the antisupernatural side of the discussion. Charmian was about to offer her opinion when the conversation was interrupted by the appearance of another friend of theirs from years before, Judge Wilder, whose sad demeanor and hollow eyes showed that the death of his wife still weighed heavily upon his heart. The price of his admission to the conversation was to compliment Charmian on her dress and ask her if she had found it in Hawaii.

"God no," Charmian replied quickly. The dress, chartreuse satin with sleeves of silver lace, which she accented with a twisted braid of pearls that had belonged to her mother and a matching silver headband, had cost a fortune back in San Francisco. "It's just something I had a friend make for me back home. I saw a picture of it in a magazine and had to have it." What she spared the men, and Jack, was that while that much was true, she had had the fabrics shipped to her from Paris. She knew at the time she had the dress made that Jack would have disapproved and she would have fessed up to it had he confronted her but he had never asked. She could only assume that Eliza had paid the balance due and buried the receipt so as not to disappoint her step-brother. Besides, Jack had complimented her on how beautiful she looked this evening, so he had noticed. She always wanted to look her best for him when they went out in public.

She had heard him muttering something as he eyed a group of carousing soldiers in the street beyond the palace gate. They were trying to climb the statue and hang Old Glory from the king's arm.

He shook his head. "All those boys, they're just spoilin' to get into the war. They don't know. They think it's all a glorious adventure. They don't know what they're in for at all."

"Well, no one is saying for sure that America is going to war," Harry said. "Though with England in, can America be far behind?"

"Right," Jack said, dropping his cigarette into the grass. "When the time comes to go no one will have to say anything because they'll be singing it from the rooftops. One great voice raised against the Kaiser— the Beast of Europe."

"I think they look very dashing." Charmian took his hand and gave it a tight squeeze. "And tonight I'm sure the last thing they're thinking about is going off to war, so why should you be?"

He shrugged.

"Come along," she said. "It looks as if the governor is about to open the armory for the ball and we haven't even formally entered the party yet." She invited the judge to join them but he insisted on waiting until the crowd had cleared somewhat before venturing forth so they bid farewell to him and headed inside. A steady stream of costumed guests, some wearing simple feathered masks while others dressed in the elaborate costumes of French clowns in whiteface, or cowboys, minstrels, and harlequins, were flowing down the stone staircase at the rear of the palace, following Honolulu's mayor. On the lawn the Hawaiian band played a waltz as they made their way under a white canvas arch that was illuminated by even more lanterns and toward the guest entrance to the palace. From inside she could hear the sound of another band: the guests would be surrounded by music all night long. Jack seemed to fixate for short spells on the decorative palm fronds draped with golden leis that rose like great blooms from the lawn and were lit from below with hidden lights that cast mysterious shafts of shadow and light.

With most of the guests now on their way to the armory for the ball, the receiving line had grown short. They took their place behind a dozen others, mainly American naval officers, in the entrance to what had once been the throne room to the right of the great hall.

"The first time I ever came here was for the coronation of her brother, King Kalakaua," Harry said to them as they waited. "In the old days when Hawaii was a kingdom. They're not descendants," he added in a conspiratorial whisper.

"Descendants?" Charmian asked.

"Of the true line. Kamehameha's. After the death of his last descendant the Hawaiians held an election to choose their next king. Isn't that so wonderfully egalitarian?"

"An elected monarch," Jack murmured, staring at the gaudy banners of red, white, and blue, a sad attempt to decorate a once-regal hall that had been worn down from its former elegance by years of civil service audiences. "What an oxymoron."

"The first king they elected, King Lunalilo, he was such a handsome and fine man. He ran against David Kalakaua. Both of them were *ali'i*, chiefs of ancient lines. But not royalty. And he was a cousin of Kamehameha the fifth, so the Hawaiians loved him for that. But he died after only a year and then the legislature appointed David the king and he named Liliuokalani to be his successor. And she lost the whole kingdom. Poor dear. Look at her now. She seems so tired."

The Queen sat on a padded chair on the opposite side of the large room from the raised dais upon which the thrones of the kingdom had once rested. She was dressed in an evening gown of rose satin with a bodice of black and white brocade. This she had adorned with a colorful sash indicating her royal status. Although they had had audiences with her several times over the years, Charmian was always flustered by the power and sadness surrounding her like a darkly glowing aura. She found herself unbalanced in the presence of living history, a woman who had been vested by her people with the responsibility of representing them all, who had suffered for them and still embodied their hopes. The Queen's skin was the color of caramel and her face was carved with deep lines of age and care. The eyes were dark, full of empathy and still touched with a glint of fire. Charmian tried to imagine her as a young woman, then as a woman the same age as she was now, and quickly came to the opinion that the old woman had never been a beauty. In fact, she looked no different than the wealthy widows who used to spend afternoons in the parlor of the aunt who raised her, gossiping about nothing and doing less.

"Do you think," she whispered to Harry, "that if she had been of the Kamehameha lineage that she would have been made of stronger stuff? That she never would have allowed the lands that her very own ancestor had united to be handed over to the *haole* without so much as a drop of blood?"

"Oh Charmian," Harry whispered back, as they were very near the spot where the first member of the Queen's retinue stood behind her. "Don't you think she did what was right and necessary at the time?"

"I don't think a true queen would ever choose surrender no matter what the odds." She said this meaning simply to be cavalier, but her voice carried a little too far. The green eyes of the young woman at the end of the receiving line flitted from inattention to latch on to hers.

"I'll be damned!" Jack had just noticed the young island beauty. "Leialoha Kaai! Good God, girl! You're all grown up." He extended his hand past Charmian, who could only stand before the girl as if her feet had taken root.

Now Charmian knew her, the Queen's most favorite, though distant, niece. Her presence startled Charmian a little. When last she had seen Leialoha, she was merely a little girl who sang traditional island songs for the pleasure of the Queen's guests. There was no denying now that the girl had grown into a strong and poised island beauty. Nineteen years or maybe twenty. Her black hair, thick and glossy, fell in loose curls around her long neck and over her collarbones, and an orchid was tucked behind her ear as a graceful accent. She was dressed in a white beaded gown, with long gloves up past her elbows that glowed against her tanned skin. Leialoha's cheekbones were prominent, giving her lush features a slightly feline grace.

"Mr. London," the woman said, in a civilized tone tinged with only a lilting hint of the islands. She ignored Charmian completely. "Aloha."

"Aloha, indeed," he said, giving her hand a proper and gentle shake. "I am so delighted to see you. I said to Charmian during our voyage here on the *Mariposa* that I had hoped to see the progress of such a promising young lady, and here you are. Quite progressed."

"Here I am," she nodded. "And, of course, here is Mrs. London, too. I should invite you and the Queen to discuss *aloha 'aina* some afternoon over tea." The girl's eyes (for that's what she was, after all, just a girl) sparkled at her.

Charmian matched her gaze; she was holding up the line, Jack and Harry had already moved on to the Queen herself. She smiled as broadly as she could. "My days here are open and I look forward to your invitation."

At that moment several gasps from the attendees still in the great hall interrupted them. Charmian saw the girl's mouth slacken, the confidence vanish from her eyes, and she turned her head to see that the Queen had risen from her seat and was clutching Jack in a quiet embrace. Finally, she released him, whispered several words to him, then sat again, nonplussed, as if she had warmly hugged each and every visitor. Charmian took her offered hand and received a pleasant nod and slight smile in return.

"What on earth did you say to her?" she asked Jack as he led her away from the receiving line moments later, after they had spoken briefly with the governor and his dignitaries. Of course they all knew Jack. Everyone knew Jack, or knew of him. At the line they had parted with Harry, who had joined his mother in a conversation with the Dillinghams. "That was remarkable."

"I told her her dress was more beautiful than a Waikiki sunset. What?" he said, as she gave him an elbow nudge and a grin.

"You're an old dog, you know that? You're such a flirt."

"It's not what I said. She's just happy to see an old friend—a friend to her Hawaiians, after all."

"I say you were flirting with her."

"Of all the hundreds of hands she had to shake tonight, I bet not one of the people those hands were attached to took the time to tell her that she looked nice. I thought she did so I told her. Sometimes a woman likes to hear that. Even a queen. Especially my queen. You look absolutely splendid tonight."

"Aha! You are a shaggy old dog after all. I'm shocked, Mr. London. Making love to me out in the open like this."

"That dress is spectacular and more so for your wearing it."

"Too little too late." Arm in arm they walked toward the rear door.

"Your jewelry is only superseded by your eyes."

"Superseded! My, my, my. Such a fine word for love. Superseded. Somehow I expect better from America's foremost man of letters. Shall I compare thee to a summer's day? Thou supersedes it. What a ring that has to it, Jack! Bravo."

He was grinning sheepishly. "Well, not every note Mozart struck rang true either," he said and then shook his head. "That's not the case at all. Of course, he always rang true, that's why people worship him. Ah, well. I never meant to say that I was a Mozart. And I certainly could never supersede him. Particularly because I can't play the piano at all."

They stood on the open patio listening to the music. "Shall we dance?" he asked her.

"I would love to." As they walked down the steps to the lantern-lit walkway she remembered Leialoha's phrase. "Jack, what does *'aloha 'aina'* mean?"

"It has a couple of meanings. First, it means a passion for this land." He used his open hands, palms down, to indicate the earth around them. "It's how the Hawaiians keep Hawaii in their hearts. It describes their spiritual feelings about their place alongside the wind and the sky and ocean and the trees. It's such an important concept for them that the movement to return Hawaii to the Hawaiians has taken it as their name and their rallying cry. But I think the window of opportunity for that has closed. The old chiefs, the *ali'i*, have sold their properties to the *haole* and so have the *kamaaina,* and now the businessmen own more Hawaiian land than the Hawaiians themselves do. *Aloha 'aina* may mean love for the land to the Hawaiian, but the businessman might say *mana 'aina,* which is to say that the land is the power. And that power is political. No one knew that better than great Kamehameha himself."

She nodded thoughtfully. "I didn't like Leialoha's dress at all. It was too old-fashioned. She needs something more modern and fashionable." They started down the steps. "What did you think of it?

Jack shrugged. "I didn't really notice."

"What did she say to you?"

"Leialoha?"

"The Queen, silly. I saw her whisper to you. What did she say?"

"Ah, she said, 'Thank you.'"

"Well, you've been a good friend to the Hawaiians. You've certainly written enough about them."

"I think she just meant to thank me for the compliment about her dress." He let his hand slide down to take hers as they entered the armory. He whistled. "Say, this is something."

The mass of dancers swirled like colorful leaves swept before the wind in great spirals around the tremendous hall. From the center of the floor rose an enormous replica of a Moorish pavilion; four great ornate columns supporting a platform surrounded by wrought iron and topped by a cupola under which sat the Twenty-fifth Infantry regimental band, which provided the music for the dancers below. Great ribbons of streamers had been stretched across the hall, all coming together and bound at the spire of the cupola. Hundreds, thousands of colorful balloons bounced among the streamers like bubbles on the head of champagne. Occasionally one would bounce against one of the scores of Japanese lanterns where it would burst from the heat, and the audience would cheer. The walls all around were covered in muslin upon which was painted a seamless mural representing a secluded Hawaiian grove, and the scene was dressed with strategically placed potted plants and fronds of palms to create the effect and depth of a diorama.

"What time is it?" she asked.

He checked his wristwatch. "Nearly eleven. Time enough for a dance or two."

"I'd love to."

She let herself be swept away into the dizzying mass of dancers. Jack had always been a terrific dancer, something he had taken the time to learn to do well in the saloons of Oakland and the Yukon, as well as the salons of the San Francisco intellectual society that had adopted him as its own and inspired him to better himself and lose his rough edges. Something caught her eye and she planted her feet, stopping suddenly, causing Jack to stumble.

"What's wrong?" He followed her gaze.

Across the yard, illuminated by torchlight as if he were caught in the glare of a spotlight, stood Hobart Bosworth. He was caressing the hand of a lovely blonde, her feathered mask pushed up on her forehead. They watched as the woman yanked her hand back and, turning from the actor, pushed her way into the crowd. Charmian felt Jack's hands dig sharply into her sides and she heard him snarl through gritted teeth.

"Son of a bitch!"

CHAPTER ELEVEN

WITHOUT ANY WARNING CRESCENDO, the band ended its song abruptly, only a few brass instruments allowing some lonely, fading notes to escape and die above the heads of the dancers. The dancers ground to a stop like the wheels of heavy factory machinery turned off at the end of a day. Charmian lost sight of Hobart and the woman who had just deserted him, though Jack was craning his neck, searching the crowd as well.

"Was that really Bosworth?" he asked her.

"It was," she began. "He—"

A primal howl rose over the great lawn, startling her. For the longest, strangest moment, she thought Jack had made the sound. The gathered crowd grew quiet. The cry rose and fell with a control that indicated that its origins were human in nature. It ended with the sound made by the tongue vibrating against the roof of the mouth; other voices, making a similar sound, joining in to create a chorus. Cheering wildly, the assembly surged as one toward the door. She and Jack found themselves helpless against the tidal force and joined the movement. All the while the harrowing squall of voices filled the air, now suddenly joined by the relentless pounding of wooden drums. It drew them on into the night, where they found that the canvas walls of the covered promenade from the palace to the armory had been removed.

A volcano erupted through the earth of the great lawn. Great flames leaped toward the sky. Then she realized that the flaming mound was, in fact, a tremendous bonfire. Charmian could feel the heat of it even at a distance of fifty yards. And still the crowd moved toward it. Now she could make out shadows dancing in the glare of the blaze, men naked but for loincloths, whirling long poles, the ends of which had been used to snatch flames from the bonfire. Faster and faster the men spun their fiery torches until each one of them appeared to be surrounded by a continuous swirling loop of dazzling orange.

Jack pulled her roughly through the crowd, barely taking the time to apologize to those he was colliding with. His clenched hold on her hand was a reminder of the great strength he still possessed in spite of his recent ailments; she wondered if she were to be suddenly trapped between two people whether his forward momentum would pull her arm out of its socket. "Jack!" she called to him, dragging back against his pull. "Jack!"

He stopped suddenly, catching her deftly as she stumbled into him. "Where is he? Did you see him? It was him, right?"

"It was," she said. "He came to the cottage today."

"Why didn't you tell me!?" His eyes were wild, catching the reflection of the blazing whorls created by the spinning torches, turning his pupils into flame-tinged coals.

"Jack. Honestly, I forgot all about it. He was only there for a moment. There was a lot to think about and do today." She placed the palms of her hands on his cheek to help him focus on her. His skin was cool, yet slightly damp, and she could feel the pulse of his heartbeat. It startled her. "Jack," she said, trying to approximate a soothing tone. She couldn't seem to get him to look at her for more than an instant before his eyes went roving again. "Jack, darling, which medicines did you take tonight?"

He took her wrists, gently fortunately. "I took the ones that make me feel good. I'm all right." He kissed her fingertips. "I'm damn all right."

"Excuse me, Mr. London," a man said directly behind Jack, so she couldn't see who it was. Jack dropped her hands and she caught a glimpse of ferocity crossing his face as he turned away from her. She reached for his shoulder, felt the muscles coiled. Then he lunged for the man who had spoken his name.

She laughed with relief as he caught the little man up in a great handshake that separated him from his wife, a woman of the exact same stature and middle age. The woman's close-set eyes were mirth-less, and Charmian had the impression that she was being scrutinized. Was it because her laugh just now had been too loud or too long? Jack's behavior had created anxiety within her, and his sudden turn to cheerfulness had released it. Why couldn't she predict which way Jack's moods were moving? It concerned her. For the first time in years she felt as if, since their arrival on Oahu, she had lost something of her sense of him.

"Mate-Woman," Jack cried, releasing the man's hand at last. "This is Dr. Homer."

"Professor is fine, please, Mr. London." The professor was smaller than Jack, trim and healthy looking. What was left of his hair was lac-quered down with a silver sheen, and the flames from the bonfire filled his glasses with a reflection that made it hard to see his eyes. He straightened his jacket with an attention to the detail of every proper fold and crease. It was apparent that this was a man not accustomed to Jack's brand of manly gregariousness. Or possibly anyone else's for that matter. He seemed to be all tension and formality. "Mrs. London, a plea-sure to meet you," he said, and there was such a slight tone of wry affa-bility that Charmian instantly abandoned her suspicions about him. "And this is my wife, Martha."

"How do you do?" She greeted both of them with firm handshakes. "And you must call us Jack and Charmian."

Jack, impatient for the formalities to be done with, changed the sub-ject instantly. "Have you read the books I've sent you?"

"I have. I must admit they're very intriguing."

"The professor teaches mythology at the University of Hawaii. Ha-waiian mythology. He's made the most extensive and fascinating study of it, in fact."

"That's quite an accomplishment."

"Well," Professor Homer said, clearing his throat with some embar-rassment. "Somebody has to capture the mythologies and oral traditions for future generations. Since no one else cares to write them down, I do it."

"Are you a born islander?" Charmian asked.

"No. Actually I'm from Ohio. Martha is, though. The daughter of missionaries. I came here about eighteen years ago to be a minister to their church. As it just so happened I had studied various mythologies at Oberlin, which developed into a passion here. And since I appeared to be the *only* white studying in all the islands, I somehow became the de facto expert."

"He's being modest," Jack said. "He's on his fourth volume of the most wonderful collections of island stories. And I'm hoping he's going to agree to help me out with a new endeavor."

"Oh?" she asked. "What's that?" Again she felt that growing sense of unease. Jack had conceived of a plan and begun to put it into action without telling her about it. It wasn't like him to be so discreet; he usually couldn't wait to share every fleeting thought or passing fancy with her.

"Mr. London's proposal is largely outside of my purview," Professor Homer protested.

"I thought you might need a little of the old arm twist," Jack said. "What if we published our work together? Your side of it and my side, together. Like I did with Anna Strunsky and *The Kempton-Wace Letters* with our discussions of the reality of love."

"That book brought you nothing but grief," Charmian said, bristling. She hadn't known Jack when he had written that book with his platonic lover. But in the outrage over his divorce from Bess, the young society intellectual had been named as the "other woman" and, to defend her honor, Jack had been forced to drag his and Charmian's relationship into the glare of the spotlight, where Charmian had endured the wrath of so many people merely because she loved Jack. It was a painful introduction to Jack's stratospheric level of fame; it was hard to ignore the vilification, being hated. Jack had been so disappointed that the world hadn't loved her as he had, and he never acknowledged the pain it caused her. But he obviously still thought about it. Maybe he still thought about Anna, as well. "Will you please shed some light on this project for me? It all sounds so mysterious."

"Well, you know of Freud's work in curing neurotic complexes, right?"

"You read me passages from one of his books a few years ago."

"One of his students has recently published his own theories on the nature of the mind, in particular expanding greatly, and deviating from, Freud's concept of the unconscious, the things we've forgotten or hidden away that persist nonetheless. We," he indicated the professor and himself, "have been reading the book by this student, Carl Jung, and I have been trying to coax the professor into applying those analytic precepts to an exploration of my own mind."

"Are you serious?"

"Absolutely. I could probably do it myself. In fact," he turned again to the professor and spoke to him as a conspirator, "I have already begun exploring some free association. We should talk about that."

"But why, Jack?" She hadn't seen him so excited in quite a while.

"Individuation," he replied. "Look here, Charmian. If a man gave you a map to buried treasure, you'd go dig for it, right? Even if you didn't know what was in the chest exactly. Well, that's what Jung's theories offer—a map to find that inside myself."

"Still," said the little man, "from what I know the process itself is difficult and even potentially dangerous. It appears to be a medical treatment to be used in cases of deep neurotic crises that cannot be treated with conventional medication. It's not a quest for treasures, Mr. London, but a confrontation of one's secrets."

"Aw," said Jack with a snort. "My life's an open book already. I don't hide anything from my readers or my mate or myself. I need your help to translate my symbols. I think I know what they mean, but I want to bounce them off someone else."

"What symbols?" Charmian asked. "And why do you think a mythology professor can help you. No offense, Professor."

"None taken," he said with a gentle nod.

"Because mythologies are metaphors for the human experience. And as a mythologist, he knows that, and I think that in telling my own life I am creating my own mythologies. He can help me understand my own metaphors. He's captured the mythology of an entire race. Can you help me capture the mythology of one man? Really, I don't see much difference and, practically, it should be somewhat easier, right? I'll just talk and you help me separate fact from metaphor." He grew quiet and looked from face to face. "Oh dear," he said. "I've been on a rant and I'm afraid I'm ruining your evening."

"Not at all," the Professor demurred, though his wife's pursed lips told a slightly different tale. The professor thought for a moment and then asked, "Jack, what do you expect this exploration to lead to?"

"More stories to tell," Jack said with a shrug, as if the answer were obvious.

The professor nodded, almost more to himself than to Jack.

"Would it be all right if I came by your office next week and at least talked to you about my plan? I've really put a lot of thought into this—how to proceed and all."

"I really don't know what I have to offer. Perhaps there's someone with psychological training in this on the island?"

"There isn't," Jack said, with a sigh. "You're the closest thing to an alienist in Hawaii."

"Why don't you wait until we return home?" Charmian suggested.

Jack clenched his jaw, unable or unwilling to answer.

A chorus of warlike shrieks rent the air and they all turned to watch as the fire dancers finished their performance by throwing their blazing torches into the air and catching them repeatedly.

"Is that Mano?" she asked, pointing to one of the men.

"Indeed it is," he said after a moment. "That big fella there is a friend of ours. I surf with him."

"He's very impressive," Mrs. Homer noted. "Fewer and fewer real Hawaiians know the old arts," she sighed. "Not to mention their own language. It's kind of a shame that when we brought the Word of God, the price was so high."

"Well, the Word did come with smallpox and measles," her husband said. "It's one of the reasons I feel compelled to record as much of their culture as I can."

"Guilt?" Jack asked.

"A kind of complicity, I suppose," he replied.

The fire dancers, carrying their torches, ran with light-footed speed to the palace staircase. There they formed a parallel line with members of the U.S. Army. The Queen appeared at the top of the stairs on the arm of the governor. Slowly, he helped her down the stairs to the patio while their combined entourages followed. The crowd assembled on the lawn cleared the way, and together the Hawaiians and the soldiers led the procession slowly across the lawn, the Queen setting the pace, and into the armory. All the while the band played an incongruously spirited march. "It just seems so sad to drag her about in front of everyone like this," Charmian said to Jack. "She's just an old woman now."

He nodded and took her hand, then tenderly rubbed his other hand over hers. "Compared to some of the other cultures we Americans took over, the Hawaiians got off lucky. Can't tell you how many Indians I knew in Dawson City who had no home nor people to go to. Couldn't speak their own tongue any more and could barely speak—" He paused. Something had caught his attention.

She saw Hobart Bosworth near the bonfire, a stout man by his side. There was no sign of his earlier, more lovely companion. They were speaking with two elderly women. Hobart's head turned and she watched as his eyes made contact with Jack's. He gave Jack a slight nod. At that moment Jack dropped her hand and she watched as his lips curled back over his teeth and a growl rose in his throat.

"Jack," she called, but he was off and pushing his way through the crowd again. She turned to the Homers. "Excuse us," she said with her most disarming smile. "An old friend." She left them quickly before they could say anything and set off after her husband, raising the front of her dress so as not to stumble over its hem.

"Say, Jack!" She heard Hobart say, and then Jack was upon him. Jack gave him a shove squarely in the chest that sent Hobart stumbling back. One or both of the women shrieked but as the night was full of similar noises, no one paid particular attention. Hobart pushed back, causing an object to fly out of Jack's mouth. The projectile dropped to the ground in her path and she stooped to pick it up.

Hobart held his hands up and out at shoulder's height. "I'm here to palaver, Jack." Charmian stepped to Jack's side and tried to put a calming hand on his upper arm but he shrugged it off. His eyes were filled with a wild fury. She caught a glimpse of Hobart's short companion and the two old ladies looking on in astonishment. A small crowd, realizing a fight might break out in their midst at any moment, began to gravitate into a circle. Because of the glare of the bonfire, she did not see the figure come up from out of the crowd behind Jack. Mano, still dressed in ceremonial garb, had thrown a convivial arm around Jack's shoulders, and only the observant would notice that the muscles were rigid and corded, the fingers digging deep into the joint, holding Jack back. To anyone else it appeared that a friendly native was supporting his little drunk white friend. Jack seemed to accept his fate.

"Not tonight, brudda Jack." Mano's tone was agreeable, cheerful, and firm. "Tonight's for the luau and the Queen is here. You fight some udda time, right? There's plenty of time for fightin'."

Jack made no response, but his expression never softened. Hobart lowered his fists. "I came all this way to mend fences, Jack."

Finally Jack spoke, his voice deep and fierce, but at the same time slightly comical because of the slight lisp created by the large gap in his teeth.

"You've got nothing I want to hear and I've got nothing to say to you."

"Hobart, will you please just leave us alone," Charmian pleaded, quietly. At least the small crowd was already drifting away.

"I have business with your husband," he said. "Jack, you've been sold a bill of goods all right, and I've made mistakes, too. But I'm just as much an injured party here as you and I believe we can make things right."

Jack twisted free suddenly and dashed forward as Mano clutched at the empty space just at his back. Another figure threw itself between the two men, smaller than both. Jack drew up short and stared in surprise at the young boy who had appeared out of the night. The boy bared his teeth at Jack. After a moment of shock, Jack burst into a sharp laugh.

"Ain't this some picture?" he cried to all of them. Then he turned to Hobart and the lad put up his fists in a fair representation of the action Bosworth had taken moments ago. "In the spirit of *auld lang syne* or what have you I'll palaver like you want."

"Thank you," the actor said.

"But not here and not tonight. You want to talk to me, meet me Monday morning, eight on the button, at the Outrigger Canoe Club on the beach at Waikiki."

"I'll be there."

"It's no loss to me if you're not."

"I said, I'll be there." He straightened his jacket. "Major, come on, let's go and find a good spot for the fireworks."

The youth dropped his guard and instantly darted to Hobart's side. "I think this is the second time today I've wished you a Happy New Year," Hobart said to Charmian with a nod. Then he turned and walked off into the night, the boy at his heels like an obedient dog.

Jack shook off his anger with a whoop that mingled with similar cries as the minutes wound down to midnight. He turned and found that Hobart's stout friend and the two old women were still rooted to their spots, eyes and mouths still wide.

The man sprang to life as if his key had just been wound tight enough. "Mr. London," he said, extending his hand, "I'm Ben Morosco with Paramount Distribution. And this is Mrs. Mae Blaisedell and Mrs.

Anita Wildemann. Owners of the Popular—Honolulu's finest picture house—and hosts of the first ever retrospective of the Hobart Bosworth Jack London pictures."

"We're big fans," one of them said. Charmian wasn't sure which was which. Whichever it was, the other one was the one who said, "We just love *The Sea Wolf*," while the first added, "And I adore your dog stories."

"We can't wait to screen them all together. We're thinking of calling the event 'Jack London's Days.' We are over the moon to have both you and Mr. Bosworth attending. It's incredible that the stars have aligned so."

Jack rubbed a hand over his face and collected himself. He seemed to realize at that moment he had lost his teeth. He kept his hand to his lips as if he were being thoughtful and muttered how-do-you-dos as he shook their hands with his other. He walked from them toward Charmian and Mano, his bashful smile faltering momentarily as his eyes locked onto something just behind them.

She turned to see the young woman, Leialoha, appear at Mano's side. She must have heard the slight disturbance and left the Queen's entourage. She touched Mano's arm and he looked at her and smiled. In those two small moments Charmian saw that Leialoha was fond of Mano and that Mano was in love with her. The young lady spoke to Mano in Hawaiian and he nodded with assurance. "No worry," he said in English, "Brudda Jack just run into his old friend. Run into him hard."

Charmian turned to Jack, who had completely regained his composure. He leaned forward and whispered into her ear, "I loshed my feef."

"What?" she said, all innocence.

"I lost my teeth," he struggled to say.

"You know, I should throw these on the bonfire," she said, displaying the spring-loaded wooden dentures that had flown from his mouth. "What were you thinking, fighting here at this wonderful occasion? Honestly, Jack. What will they say? You're just lucky there were no reporters around."

"There hasn't been a reporter interested in me in years," he muttered, plucking his teeth from her fingers. "Haven't you heard? I'm just Jack London, dog writer."

"Well, if it weren't for those dog stories we wouldn't be here in Hawaii," she said.

He shrugged, adjusted his teeth with his tongue and finger and then said, "Cloudesley Johns always told me I could find someone I knew at the Great Wall of China," he said with a shrug as he came up to Charmian. Then turned to Mano and Leialoha. In the glow of the bonfire their skin took on the luster of the prototype of all Hawaiians, she thought, strong and fine. As if carved from wood, they could be the parents of all their race. Somewhere the countdown had begun, all up and down the lawn, and in the street beyond the fence, she could hear voices calling out the seconds.

"Thanks Mano," Jack shouted over the chanting. "Thanks for keeping me out of trouble tonight."

"No worry, Jack. We bruddas. Happy New Year!"

"Happy New Year to both of you," he answered. He turned Charmian around in the direction of the armory but stopped short. Professor Homer was standing nearly behind him. How long he had been there, how much he had seen of the confrontation, she had no idea. But he was studying them, of that she was sure now. He looked up at Jack. Fireworks exploded in the sky above them, reflected in his spectacles, filling the glass with green and gold. Then with a thoughtful nod, he withdrew into the crowd.

CHAPTER TWELVE

A T FIRST SHE WASN'T going to come. But Charmian London had always liked a good fight.

Now, as she stood outside the boxing ring in the gymnasium of the Outrigger Canoe Club watching Nakata lace up Jack's leather gloves, part of her wished she had heeded her first instinct, while another part wanted to see what was going to happen. And that was the part that always seemed to win out—especially when it came to her husband. She tried to recall when she had ever been so angry at him as she had been on New Year's. Perhaps never. She had been disappointed by him before, and even hurt, especially by the rumors of his infidelity. But that was just the work of people trying to come between them for their own sport and she had learned to ignore their hubbub. She and Jack knew what they had between them and that was all that mattered. Had any of his actions left her as angry as his provoking a fight on the palace grounds, even if his own wrath was partially justified by the presence of Hobart Bosworth? She had been angry at his stubborn refusal to abandon his quest for global circumnavigation aboard the *Snark* when his health had demanded it. But he had invested so much of himself in the vessel and the voyage and they had traveled so far—from Oakland to Hawaii to Fiji to Tahiti and on to Australia—on his wits alone she could understand how he hated to quit when they had finally figured out what they were doing. Ah, but then there was the time he had rushed off for three months without consulting her to cover the Mexican Revolution and contracted dysentery in Veracruz. She had been quite stirred up by that, not that she was afraid that he might die in some godforsaken field hospital but that he would consider the whole experience such a damned amusing inspiration for a story while he did so.

Hobart sat on a stool in the far corner of the ring. When he had arrived this morning he had been surprised to find out that a boxing bout was Jack's solution to their situation. He had protested, claiming a stomach ailment. But Jack had threatened to end any discussion then and there and so he had accepted the challenge and withdrawn to the locker room. Like Jack, he now wore light cotton trunks to his knees. Neither wore an undershirt and both wore Canoe Club robes loosely over their shoulders. Hobart's companion from the ball, the stout and swarthy man named Mr. Morosco, stood by him but was leaving the binding of the gloves to one of the club regulars who had happily interrupted his morning exercises in favor of the surprise match. In fact, almost every member there that morning was slowly drifting his way over to the ring as word spread that the world-famous author Jack London was about to box the world-famous actor Hobart Bosworth.

The actor kept himself fit, she had to admire that in spite of her bitter feelings toward him. His stomach was as flat as a surfboard and his legs were long, carved like a runner's. His chest was covered with a sprinkling of salt-and-peppery hair now dewy with perspiration. Jack's torso had always been hairless and smooth, a legacy from the Irish father he had never met.

The building that housed the club lay behind a long, high row of immaculately trimmed hedges. It was nearly brand new, having only just been finished the previous year, and was situated enviably at the edge of Waikiki Beach. It was no small tribute to Jack that it had been deemed necessary by Americans who had fallen in love with surfing due in great part to his wildly popular musings on the sport in *The Cruise of the Snark* and elsewhere. Alexander Ford, a local, and Jack had founded the club together in 1906. Ford had once told Jack that every time he published an article in a magazine, membership surged. As at most athletic clubs, women, and in particular wives, were not welcome as a rule. However, an exception had been made in Charmian's case because, well, because Jack was who he was. Children were also generally not welcome, but a youth had entered with Hobart and Mr. Morosco and waited in a corner by the lockers, silently guarding Hobart's garments.

Jack held on to the ropes and did some deep squats. She could hear the joints in his hips and knees crackle like a piece of steak in a hot frying pan.

"How're you feeling, Jack?" she asked.

"Fit as a fiddle," he replied, with believable nonchalance. He looked rested and strong today. His eyes were clear and focused. "I'm going to take our fifteen grand out of his hide."

She didn't beg him to stop. There was no way to stop Jack from doing what he wanted to. That was one of the qualities that was so attractive about him; he did what other men couldn't or wouldn't. All the same she didn't want him to box Hobart. He hadn't boxed in a while and she was worried for him. "Watch your kidneys and protect your chin," she said. Hobart was watching her, an eyebrow arched. She realized why the actor was a star of the stage and screen; he was truly a handsome man. As Jack crouched down, his face between the lower two of the three ropes, she reached through, took his face, and kissed him. He smelled of bay rum and sweat and she loved it. Catcalls rose from the swelling gallery; word seemed to be spreading rapidly through the ranks of the members, and she slowly pulled away. "You do him."

"I'll do him all right," he said with a nod and his cocky grin.

Scattered applause broke out as the attending club officer, Taylor Boone, stepped through the ropes and into the ring. He was one of those Yankees who had lived in Hawaii for years but still looked as if a blizzard was imminent, while his skin never tanned but turned from pink to grape purple. He was a popular man and waved to the group as if he were the reason for the assembly. "No wagering," he called, to rousing laughter. Bets were being placed all around Charmian. Hobart appeared to be an odds-on favorite. "And don't forget the vig."

He drew the two fighters to the center of the canvas and the crowd grew relatively still. "What we're here for this morning is a gentleman's match between Surfin' Jack"—roars of approval from the crowd as Jack raised an arm—"and Hollywood Hobart!" An ovation nearly as loud. "The match is to last until one of these men is down or is done. Is that clear?"

They both nodded.

"Each round is to last three minutes with a one-minute break in between. Is that clear?"

Again, nods of agreement. She hadn't realized how much shorter Jack was than Hobart.

"No seconds will be allowed in the ring."

"That's clear," shouted Mr. Morosco to general amusement.

"You know, Jack," Hobart said in a low voice, "we could just as easily hash this all out over a hot breakfast."

"There's plenty of time to eat, Hob. I want to know what happened to my money."

Boone interrupted by placing a hand on a shoulder of each man. "Gentlemen, to your corners, please." Hobart retreated first and she was sure it was due to Jack's righteously withering gaze. A moment later Jack turned to his corner and let Nakata remove his robe. Twisted scars—from his appendectomy and the surgeries on the intestinal fistula he had developed in Sydney—crisscrossed his belly like the map of a train route. Nakata whispered a few words in his ear, something along the lines of hit him hard and fast then get out of there, she hoped. Boone gave the signal and one of the club men brought the hammer down on the bell.

The two fighters sidestepped out of their corners. Their techniques were nearly identical: each led with his right shoulder, right fist held palm up and slightly extended while the left was positioned in front of the chest. They circled round each other once, then twice, and the third time, Jack reached out with several right-hand taps against Hobart's glove. Hobart jabbed back with a left. "I didn't steal money from you, Jack," he said.

"Frank Garbutt says otherwise." Jack blocked the exploratory blow. Neither man had the grace of the real fighters Jack had taken her to see, like Tommy Burns or Marvin Hart, or the Negro champion Jack Johnson. Though both had skills and training, their footfalls were heavy and each constantly had to use a forearm to wipe the sweat from his eyes. It did not seem to matter to the crowd, however. They cheered each blow and feint with the delight of a heavyweight title bout audience. Even though she was in the front row she could barely hear the men's conversation above the calls.

"Garbutt!?" Hobart said. "Garbutt is the one who holds the purse strings." He kept his left arm in, elbow down, covering his belly.

"Garbutt's not the one I have a contract with. You are." He landed a thumping blow to the side of Hobart's head, staggering him. The bell rang as Hobart regained his feet, before Jack could follow up with another punch. The two men retreated to their corners. Jack, sauntering, threw her a wink. Hobart rubbed the side of his head where the punch had connected. Nakata spoke a few words to Jack and he nodded in agreement.

The bell rang and they both bounded back into the center of the ring. Hobart wasted no time in placing a few punches to Jack's torso. He stepped back out of Jack's immediate range.

"I read *The Star Rover* on my way here," he said. "I didn't get it." He sidestepped a swipe. "The prison scenes were vivid and cruel and some of your best writing." He planted a left and a right on Jack's rib cage. "But astral projection? That just seems so *au courant*. Are you courting the café society?"

"I wouldn't expect you to understand," Jack grunted, lunging and missing.

"Having your character revisit the Mountain Meadows Massacre, now that was intriguing." The hits took on a flatter, more painful tone. The padding wrapped around Hobart's fists was getting wet, making the gloves themselves heavier and denser. Hits that had sounded like taps now sounded like dull thuds. "But sending him back to the Crucifixion? As if you all of a sudden believe in Jesus Christ? It smacked of pandering."

"It'd make a helluva picture, wouldn't it?" Jack threw a punch that connected neatly with Hobart's stomach. Hobart gasped and clutched his gut with both arms. Jack had tagged something sensitive; the flush of color left Hobart's cheeks and he turned away from Jack. "Maybe I'll let Griffith do it," Jack growled, curling his upper lip.

Hobart's left came at him so fast that Jack never saw it before it knocked into the side of his head. He dropped to his knees. The crowd roared. The referee stepped in and began to count. Hobart's left hand stayed against his stomach. She saw the rage leave his face as Jack hit the canvas, showing her a glimpse of another emotion. She couldn't tell for sure what it was before his expression turned to one of exhaustion. What had she seen? Compassion? Resignation? Hobart shook his head and as the bell rang, he parted the ropes and climbed out of the ring.

Seeing this, reason returned to Jack's eyes and he struggled to his feet. "Hey!" he called. "It ain't over yet."

Hobart waved him off. The crowd began to boo and call fraud.

"I don't gain anything by hurting you, Jack. I just want to talk with you."

Jack slipped between the ropes and landed in front of the actor. The spectators roared their approval. Boone tried to call for order. Jack gave Hobart a shove in the chest. "This is your opportunity. This is your chance to come clean. Just be straight with me."

"I have been, Jack. You're the one who favored Frank Garbutt before me. Took his word over mine. He and Zukor have made fools of us both. At least I know I've been made a fool of."

"Don't pity yourself, Bosworth. Even you're not such a good actor that you can play the injured party. Why don't you hit me? Some touch of morality?"

"I don't want to fight."

"And because of that you don't think I'll hit you."

"No, Jack. I don't."

Jack drew back his fist and punched Hobart in the face. The actor staggered back, scattering club members. Boone shouted at them to stop. Jack advanced on his opponent. Hobart drew himself up.

"I'll hit you again," Jack said, and then did. Hobart stumbled against the door that led to the beach. He used the handle to pull himself up.

Charmian, followed closely by Nakata, fell upon Jack. "Jack, darling," she cried, "please stop!" Without taking his eyes off Hobart, he gently removed her restraining arm from his chest.

"I've had enough of bum luck and people exploiting my name," he said. "Come on, Bosworth. Let's take your measure. See if you've got any true stuff left in you. That's what I want to find out."

Hobart turned and glared at Jack. The bemused and charming gleam in his eyes was gone, replaced by a dull anger. He swung and Jack leaped in to catch him in an embrace. Their momentum carried them against the door. It swung open and the two fighters staggered out into the brilliance of daylight.

She grabbed Nakata's arm. "I've never seen him like this, have you?"

Nakata shook his head. "No. The anger of betrayal burns hottest of all."

The throng had grown to more than fifty and as a mass they surged onto Waikiki Beach, sweeping Charmian and Nakata along. The two men grappled and swung at each other while white sand flew from under their feet. Men quickly surrounded them in a tight circle, while other early morning beach visitors ran up the shore to witness the commotion for themselves. Punch after punch was thrown by both, each receiving as well as giving. Blood spurted from a gash above Jack's right eyebrow, the skin torn from the skull by Hobart's sand-covered leather mitt. Any pretense of boxing was lost, its learned formality replaced by each man's formative memories of street brawling. The tone of the spectators had changed as well, from that of amused gentlemen to the harder edge taken by those men she had known who worked the ranch or the ports. Theirs was an uglier sound, one that called for domination and pain rather than for points won or scores settled. She tried to get through it to get to Jack, but the men had formed a hard knot she couldn't push through. She saw Nakata trying to pass as well and meet the same resistance.

With a roar, Jack caught Hobart around his waist and heaved him up into the air. The two men crashed heavily into the surf of an oncoming wave, emerging from its foam coughing and sputtering, yet still floundering to engage. Both men had reached the limits of their endurance, both breathing in great ragged gasps of air. Jack's punches were little more than feeble roundhouse slaps and even these Hobart was hard pressed to bat away with any vigor. Each struggled against the rolling surf; first Jack fell then rose, then Hobart did as well. Suddenly Jack threw his right around Hobart's neck and pulled their heads together. "You ready to give?" Jack wheezed.

Hobart placed his fists against Jack's chest, weakly trying to push away. "I'm just getting my second wind," he gasped. His knees buckled and he fell to a sitting position in the surf.

"You gonna whup my knees from there?" Jack asked. Before Hobart could reply, a wave had knocked him off his feet as well. Hobart helped him rise from the surf. Jack was laughing. Hobart began to laugh as well and within moments both men were racked with great gales of humor, as much as they could muster in their weakened states.

She ran onto the wet sand, her feet sinking and losing traction. Jack looked up at her, helpless in his mirth, his face glistening with tears, sweat, seawater, and blood. Behind her, the crowd suddenly seemed to regain its sense of civilization, and though there were some sour grapes

about the absence of a winner or loser, a general round of approving applause broke out for the two fighters, and almost all seemed in agreement that it had been a damned fine match. Jack was gesturing toward
Hobart as the spectators began to disperse, but not before Hobart's
second implored them all to come to see "Jack London's Days" at the
Popular.

"What?" she demanded. "What's so funny."

"Sweetheart," Jack said, trying to catch his breath, "we're having a
guest for dinner."

"I'll have to cancel my plans," Hobart snorted, doubled over.

Jack eased himself out of the water and lay on his back in the sand,
looking up at the clouds. "Welcome to Hawaii," he said at last.

CHAPTER THIRTEEN

"WE'RE GOING NORTH TO Haleiwa for my birthday—my fortieth—next week. Have you ever been there? You should come with us."

"I've never been," Hobart said.

"We're going to see the waves," Jack continued. "At this time of year they're the biggest, most spectacular things in all of Hawaii save for the volcano, I hear. Everyone says it's a sight to behold, especially the beach boys. Even Duke stands in awe of them and dreams of a day when he could ride them. You'll have to give wave sliding a try."

"I'd like to."

Night was falling over the island and the sky looked as if a jeweler was scattering his diamonds across a piece of navy blue velvet for inspection. The moon was full as it rose above its brilliant twin in the dark ocean below. From several directions at once came the mournful note of conch shells being blown and they could see in the distance, from where they sat on the lanai, brown-skinned men clad only in loincloths racing along the beach bearing flaming lances, which they used to light the torches along Beach Walk for the amusement of the guests of the hotels and restaurants of Waikiki.

"It is Paradise."

"That it is. The Hawaiians considered Waikiki a sacred place, a healing place. This beach used to be strictly the preserve of the royals." Jack was dressed in his familiar blue silk kimono, now fraying at the sleeves. Somewhere inland, behind the cottage, wild chickens squabbled. Hobart slapped at a mosquito. "What you need to keep those skeeters away is one of these cigars." Jack motioned toward the open cigar box.

"Can't smoke 'em," Hobart replied. "Bad for my lungs. But I love the smell." He took one from the box and sniffed its length. Jack watched him eagerly. Suddenly Hobart laughed and Jack broke into a grin. "I'll be damned! Is that a Jack London brand cigar?"

"Can you believe it?" he said. "And a fifty-cent one to boot. I make a dime every time a fella lights one up."

"Or a lady," Charmian added. She was sitting on the railing that bordered the porch, catching the breeze and puffing on her own cigar. She hadn't felt like being part of the conversation until now, preferring instead to watch Hobart's young friend play fetch on the beach with the stray dog Jack had christened Jerry. She found herself irritated at the two men on their wicker plantation recliners. They had spent most of the day recapping the details of their bout until it had reached the proportions of a Wagnerian epic. The recalling had lasted longer, by far, than the fight had. They had both nursed their wounds and bruises, Jack with a cold piece of steak against his head, Hobart occasionally staunching the blood flow from his nose, drinking bottle after bottle of cold beer. How could they have been ready to murder each other only hours before but now relaxed together like brothers? Well, she was not going to forgive Hobart so easily.

"How are you finding the hotel?"

"It's very nice. Though having seen the Moana Hotel, I'm thinking of switching."

"Don't bother," Jack dismissed the thought with a wave of his arm. "Past its prime. And the Hau Tree is so close."

"Must be costing a pretty penny," Charmian said.

"Fifteen bucks a night," he replied. "Not too steep. Ben has me speaking at a number of ladies' garden parties. The fees are quite generous."

Nakata stepped onto the lanai with a platter of the sliced raw fish he had first introduced to them aboard the *Snark* and of which they had become so fond. "Ah," said Jack, clapping his hands, "this you must try. This is the true taste of the ocean."

"I've heard this is how the Japanese eat it all the time."

"True," said Nakata in his soft gentle voice. "Fresh from the ocean and caught this morning. This is wahoo, this is mahimahi, and this is moi, my favorite."

"*Mahalo,* Nakata."

"Yes, London-san."

"You make sure you take the day off Wednesday, son. Right?"

"Yes. I will spend the day with my uncle and his family in Ewa."

"Take those bolts of fabric we bought to your niece."

"I won't forget."

Nakata withdrew. "He's happy to see his family here," Jack remarked to her.

She nodded. "It's nice, isn't it. Though they're putting quite a bit of pressure on him to find a wife."

"Lord, I hope not." Jack popped a piece of fish into his mouth. "All I need is yet another mouth to feed."

"Hobart," she said after a moment. "Who is your young friend?" He was following the dog as it snapped after the night crabs streaming from their sandy burrows toward the safety of the water.

"I don't know his name but I call him Major," he said. "He's a fellow traveler who's fallen in with me for a while. He doesn't have much to say. At least to me. But he has his uses, and quite frankly, I can't get rid of him. He's taken quite a shine to me, I'm afraid."

"What about his mother?" she murmured. "Something dreadful must have happened for her to let this happen to him."

"He appears to be one of those driven by life's circumstances to seek his way in the world earlier than others his age."

Jack, too, studied the boy. "He's about the same age I was when I had to leave school and start work in the canneries."

"It wasn't right when you did it either," she said.

"He gets to make his own way in the world."

Hobart gave a whistle and both the dog and the boy ran up the beach to their cottage. "Say Major," he said. "Fancy some Japanese fish?"

The boy grimaced at the flesh on the platter and his expression made her laugh.

"Okay then. We'll shove off soon and fetch you something more suitable on the way to the hotel." The boy nodded and then dashed off again with the dog.

Jack rose, groaning with exaggerated exertion, and shuffled inside, to the bathroom Charmian guessed. She puffed on her cigar and wondered about Major's life. She had thought children going off to work as something from history, that social conditions had changed since Jack's youth. But sadly, this appeared not to be so. The dog, a large black and tan Airedale, leaped up, placing his paws on Major's shoulders and licking his face, making the boy laugh and fall over.

"You know, Charmian, I can see your smile even in the dark."

Even though she had known he was there on the other side of the porch, she had hoped he would have read her mood and left her alone with her thoughts. The sound of his voice was as startling as it was invading. And yet it was a harmless compliment, wasn't it? She found herself blushing and pulling a lock of hair down as if to cover her cheek so he couldn't see, though it was dark after all. "Nice of you to say so."

"I didn't mean to make you uncomfortable."

"You didn't."

"I did. I'm sorry. Since I started making pictures I think of everything in terms of how it would look projected and that image of your smile against the darkness struck me as one I would like to see on screen."

"It's no big deal, Hobart," she said, though the tone was sharper than she'd intended.

"Good."

"But *mahalo* all the same."

"What does that mean?"

"It's Hawaiian for 'thank you.'"

"*Mahalo,*" she heard him repeat to himself. He sniffed a piece of fish and nibbled on it; appearing surprised at the taste he tucked the rest into his mouth.

Inside the house, Jack turned the gramophone on and the sounds of Irving Berlin's "When I Leave the World Behind" drifted out into the night. Jack, who had left them creaking and bent with aches, now waltzed onto the porch, his kimono swirling comically, almost girlishly around him. His face was filled with the romance of the music and she let herself be swept up to sway gently to the melody. She would present nothing less than a united front to their guest.

"Don't try to charm me," she whispered. "I'm mad at you."

He twirled her around. "Still?"

"Yes." She could feel Hobart's eyes on them.

Hobart leaned forward. "I want a Jack London original. A new story, written exclusively for the screen by you. That'll create the kind of event that my publicists will love to get behind and the public will flock to see. It'll make news from coast to coast. Hell, around the world!"

"But why not just adapt one of Jack's books? Isn't the audience already there for those?" Charmian asked.

"Well, there's a case to be made for that and I've given that a lot of thought. It just seems to me that the effort that goes into adapting one of Jack's books, stripping out all of the musings on philosophy, nature, civilization, and all those literary stylings to get down to filmable action, is almost more trouble than it's worth." To Jack directly he said, "Remember how much of *Martin Eden* we had to leave behind because we couldn't figure out a way to film it? We wouldn't have that problem this time."

"Jack," Charmian said, "please tell me you're not considering working with Hobart again? After all the heartache he caused us."

"I do apologize about that," Hobart said again.

"So," said Jack, sitting down at last and rubbing his thigh in a gesture she knew meant he felt uncomfortable. "What was your idea for this cinematic epic of ours? What story would I even tell?"

A look of worry furrowed Hobart's brow. "Don't you have any?"

She awoke late that night to find Jack's side of the bed empty, but damp from sweat. "Jack," she called and there was no answer. The bones of the house creaked in the ocean breeze. She rose, put her slippers on and moved through the house, following the fragrance of cigarette smoke and the scritch-scratching of pen tip on paper. He was scribbling at his table, using the light of several small candles, which he preferred at night to the harshness of electric lightbulbs, hand cramped around the pen. At her approach he discreetly drew a guarding arm over the paper, something he very rarely did; she almost didn't notice the motion. He looked up at her and his eyes were sunk in the dark sockets in an otherwise bruised and swollen face. But still handsome. So handsome.

"Are you in pain?" she asked. She ran her fingers through his thick brown hair, admiring its coarseness. If she was ever envious of Jack for anything, it would have to be his hair.

"Not so bad."

"Your fighting days are over, Mate." She plucked one of his rolled cigarettes from the desk and lit it.

He sighed and ran the fingers of both hands through his hair, smoothing where she had ruffled it, then held out his left hand and tried to bend his thumb for her. "Look at this, will you?" The joint refused him, though the tip trembled mightily. He grinned at her. "It went during one of the punches."

"You want sympathy?"

"My thumb doesn't work. So, sure, maybe a little."

Now it was her turn to sigh. She slid herself onto his lap and caressed his cheek.

"I keep thinking I'm going to feel better. I feel like I've been sick for such a long time. And instead new things keep breaking." He wiggled what he could of his thumb. "You know I keep taking my medicines and they keep adding new drugs, stronger stuff all the time, but it's been ten years of misery. Am I wrong to hope for a cure? 'Oh, Jack, the trouble is in your kidneys so don't drink and you'll get better.' So don't drink is what I do and I don't get any better. 'Don't eat this food, don't eat that food. Stay out of the sunlight.' What kind of life is that for me to live and write about? I'll be turning out drawing room comedies."

"But you took a little something extra tonight. I could tell."

"I had to get a little aggressive about the pain tonight. It was a rough day. I took some codeine pills."

"Did it help?"

"It did. But now I'm up in the middle of the night and I'm full of energy but I can't really write and the White Logic is filling my mind and it's telling me to take more. That I am a slave to pain and life but I don't have to be. That I can clear my head and free my mind from the concerns of my flesh and bones. I'm only thirty-nine and I know I've lived a hectic life but I should be doing better and I keep thinking that maybe it's something serious."

"The things you did when you were twenty, most men could never do at any age. Maybe your body is just settling into being an ordinary forty-year-old instead of a remarkable one."

"Is that it, you think?"

"I don't know. But we'll keep looking for a cure, okay? I won't give up on that. And you shouldn't either. Though I know it's easy for me to say you should since I'm not the one in pain."

"Ah, but you've been with me every step of the way. I know it's been hard for you, too."

"Only hard to see you suffer and not be able to help more."

"Duke says there's a holy man Mano knows, or maybe he's related to, who lives up in the mountains, one of the last true *kahuna la'au lapa'au*, the old medicine priests. Duke says he has knowledge of the ways before the missionaries came. Do you think it would be worth trying to wrangle an invitation?"

"Of course," she said. "We should try everything, right? As long as you continue to take your medicines. Even the painkillers if they help."

"I will."

They nuzzled for a few moments and she began to touch him, tenderly. Intimately. Caressing him. Letting her warm breath tease his ear, but after a shiver he gave her a rueful shake of the head. "Wishful thinking tonight, Mate-Woman. I'm banged up."

"Are you sure? Do you want to come back to bed? I could make you forget about writing for a while."

He shook his head and his eyes fell away from her. "I think I'm going to get a little more work done."

She let her hands drift away from his body, crossing her arms over her breasts. "What is it? Your secret memoir?" She hated the tone of her voice.

He shrugged. "Thinking if I have anything for Bosworth, actually."

"So you're seriously considering his offer?"

"He has made some magnificent pictures out of my books. And, after all is said and done, I do like the man. I think you do, too."

"Whether or not I like him has little to do with how I feel about you working with him. But you do what you want, give him a second chance if you feel you must, just as long as you don't expect to see any money out of him." She slid out of his lap. A gecko ran across his desk. As she stood she caught a glimpse of the page he had slid over his night's work. It was the sheet she had seen several mornings before, only more words had been added to the column:

grapes
bacchus
zeus
lightning

hammer
thor
odin
wotan
joy
bess
joan
john
all-father
chaney
gjöll

"What is that word?" she asked, pointing at the last one.

He looked at the paper with what seemed to her feigned indifference. "It's a word from Norse mythology," he said after studying it for a moment. "It's the great rock that tethers the great wolf, Fenrir, until Ragnarök—the Twilight of the Gods. At which time he will slip free and devour first Odin the all-father, and then the world."

"Are you going to be writing about that?"

"It's just some notes," he replied with a dismissive shrug.

After a moment she kissed him on his head, then left him at his desk, as she so often did, staring at an empty piece of paper and waiting for more words to come. She closed the door to the bedroom so he wouldn't hear the tears she knew were about to come.

CHAPTER FOURTEEN

THE BUICK HOPPED AND skittered like a shiny green beetle in and out of the deep ruts cut by the sugar trucks that ran endlessly day and night along the road to the plantation. The taut leather canopy shielded Charmian, the driver; Jack, her navigator; and Hobart and Major, her backseat passengers, from the otherwise numbing intensity of the sun. Ewa, on the arid leeward side of Oahu, was flat, dry, and brown, much like the landscape of her beloved California during the summer and fall months. And winter, for that matter.

Between Hobart and Major rested several large bolts of cotton fabric she and Jack had brought with them from Glen Ellen for the purpose of having Nakata's relatives tailor them new clothes. In his haste that morning, Nakata had left them behind, so Jack had volunteered them as a delivery service. Since Jack had already planned to spend the day with Hobart discussing picture ideas, it was not hard to convince him to spend the time on a car trip. And, of course, Major Domo had flung himself into the car even before Hobart had entered. It was two days after the fight and both men's bruises had spread like spilled ink into ugly purple stains that would last for weeks. Secretly she had to admit to herself that watching their discomfort, the slowness of rising or sitting, the wincing of turning heads, gave her a sense of quiet satisfaction. She had found herself growing less angry about the fight but more annoyed at Jack's letting bygones be bygones.

Jack's mood, which had improved steadily since the morning, had taken a turn for the worse again as they had passed a morning drill of a squadron of sailors and marines at Pearl Harbor, hundreds of identical, eager-faced young men moving in lockstep.

"Look at them," he had muttered. "Ready to fight for the Oligarchs. The very muscle and sinew that could ensure that no Americans fight in Europe, the labor that could end this war in a month, through a general strike, is the one that most wants to die. I'll never understand."

She was driving faster than she should. Jack had disappeared yesterday after his morning work, which he had hidden away in the locked drawer of his writing desk. She hadn't seen him on the waters with the beach boys and even Nakata had no idea of his whereabouts. He had returned late in the afternoon, appearing just as the black storm clouds opened up over Waikiki, his mood unsettled, his attitude irritated. She had found him at his desk in much the same state this morning and he had been so distracted that she'd insisted, gently so as not to provoke a scene, that she drive. Now the almost reckless speed released the tension in her chest that had been building over the secrets that Jack seemed to be keeping.

"You know, Jack," Hobart leaned forward and shouted over the roar of the engine, "Oahu seems so settled now. What happened to the wild jungle lands of my youth?"

"On the other side of the mountains, my friend. There you'll find your pockets of uncivilization, small though they may be."

"How long are you thinking of staying?" she asked.

Hobart looked discomfited for a moment; she saw it in the rearview mirror. It was nice to see a look on his face that didn't look rehearsed. "I'm not sure yet."

The only cloud in the sky today was the low black one that hung heavy and low directly ahead of them, immobile, nearly blocking their view of the Waipahu Hills. As they drove toward it they found themselves brushing away strange, warm snowflakes that appeared in a flurry and surrounded the car. An aroma of cotton candy which she had first experienced at the Pan-Pacific Exposition only last year, filled the air. The fragrance reminded her of San Francisco, and she felt a pang of homesickness. Major plucked a soft flake from his nose and rubbed it between his fingers for a moment, watching it disappear. He held up his blackened fingers.

"Ash?" Hobart asked, brushing the flakes from his linen suit.

"They're harvesting one of the sugar fields," Jack replied. "You have to burn down the heavy plants to get to the sweet cane."

They rumbled through the gate for Ewa Plantation and the sky grew considerably darker as they began to drive down into a small valley. At the top of the hill they passed the administrative offices, then the mansions of the owners and the smaller but comfortable manors of the managers and overseers. As they reached the valley floor the residences became a series of identical wooden frame homes on one side of the road housing workers and their families and military-style barracks on the other side for the single men who worked the fields. Everywhere she looked she saw the inscrutable, yet somehow accusatory, faces of the folk who lived and worked there. An overwhelming majority of the workers on the plantation were transplanted Japanese. Nearly fifty thousand in all, Nakata once told her, had traveled over the seas to take up the work from the Chinese, whose second generation had migrated on to Honolulu to create a middle-class merchant community of their own.

Past the cluster of housing was a small main street bordered by a barber shop, a social hall, the camp office, the Latter Day Saints church, a schoolhouse, a garage, and the infirmary, which was their destination. She turned the headlamps on against the unique blizzard, not that it would help her see but to enhance the visibility of the car— the sidewalks were filled with mothers and children. Looming over all the buildings and set solidly at the end of the road was the sugar refining plant where the stalks would be brought in from the fields by the small train engines, sent up, and boiled down, the bagasse devoured in furnaces.

"Plenty of Mormons, huh?" Hobart said, noting the small, clean church.

"More than Hawaiians now, I think," Jack said. "They're building an immense temple on the other side of the island at Laie. Old Joe Smith was here himself last summer to break ground. Seems like religion is the only thing that man spreads to man faster than germs. You know they've converted the Queen?" This he directed to Charmian.

"I didn't know that."

"Yep. It's true."

There was a clearing behind the post office, which she pulled into.

They got out of the car and stood at the edge of a vast field of black and red land—black from the ash and charred remains of the thick-leaved sugar plants, and red from the rich Hawaiian land shot through the scorched earth like scarlet veins. In the distance they could see the line of firemen moving behind a low wall of fire, driving it before them as cowboys back home herded steer to the stockyards. After them followed a steady line of harvesters, cutting down the smoldering stalks and hauling them in an endless line to the refinery.

"Welcome to the edge of the Pit," Jack said, staring at the black-streaked faces, downcast under the heat and their burdens. "They pray that each day they work brings them escape, when actually it brings them only closer to the shambles of the bottom. Slowly their strong bodies will twist and wrench and distort, by accident. By hardship. And when that happens they will be cast aside like an old shoe. I've done their work, in far-off fields, and I've swapped stories with those that have been broken by that work. I learned that the only way out of the fields for an individual like myself was to use my mind and never do another day of hard labor. Of course, only lately have I discovered that the labors of the brain are even more taxing in some ways than the labors of the muscle. But my decision was still sound as I don't think I shall ever find myself sliding down the side of the Pit to its bottom."

"Is there a way out for these men?" Hobart asked him.

"Brotherhood," he replied, as she knew he would.

"Forever the Boy Socialist," Hobart smirked.

She smiled a little, for that had been Jack's nickname in San Francisco long before she had first met him, when she had only heard from her friends of the handsome, magnetic youth with the powerful point of view and words to match who spoke in the park and caused such a scene and set girlish hearts aflutter.

"That Revolution's lost its power as well as its morality," Jack replied.

Each of them stepped over a dog dozing in the building's shade and headed toward the infirmary. Inside, as Charmian's eyes adjusted, she quickly recognized the long, narrow hall filled on both sides with beds for the ailing, separated from each other by a curtain. There was a single occupant today, an elderly Japanese man, skin browned into leather by the sun. He was sitting up and speaking with an elderly woman who bounced a toddler on her lap. Toward the back of the hall she saw several other figures huddled around a ladder, watching and lending moral support, if not actual help, to another man at the top of the ladder attempting to hang a new set of venetian blinds. As they came closer they could see that the man wrestling with the wooden slats was Nakata's uncle, the small hospital's caretaker, and the group of three younger men at the foot of the ladder included Nakata himself. Nakata was suitably embarrassed to realize he had forgotten the fabric, and Jack had to reassure him multiple times that it was fine, that they were out for a drive anyway.

"Is that Jack London?" a voice roared. Charmian turned, as did they all, to see the familiar rolling gait of their immense friend. His stride was as confident as his face was red. His lab coat, never clean, was a mottled mosaic of queasy colors.

"Dr. Belko!" Jack hollered back, and the two men embraced each other. The effect was almost comical as Dr. Belko, the infirmary's physician, was nearly twice as big, in every direction, as Jack.

"Good Christ," the doctor said, looking from Jack to Hobart. "I heard I missed a hell of a fight, but I had no idea. Hello, Mrs. London, my tropical beauty."

"Hello Ken," she said, hugging him warmly. The man was so good-natured that just being in his presence could make one feel better. She introduced Hobart and Major.

"I hope you didn't come too close to this fella." The doctor indicated the old man a few beds away. "I'm suspecting dengue fever." He laughed as they took a few reflexive steps back. "I'm just kidding. He's got an impacted tooth. What I wouldn't do to have a dentist here. And what kind of scratch a dentist could make here, you wouldn't believe. How have you been feeling, Jack?"

Jack shrugged. "Fine."

"Any chance of taking the *Will-o'-the-Wisp* to Molokai sometime soon? I've got a delivery you could help me make."

"If you want to go, we'll take the old girl out. Just let me know when."

"Okay, as long as you promise to keep your hands covered. How are they, anyway? Any swelling lately?"

"They're pretty good." Jack showed his hands, which had once painfully swollen to twice their size due to exposure to the tropical sunlight.

Since then he had always taken care to protect them during extended outdoor sessions. He clenched his fists a couple of times. "They can still throw a roundhouse."

"How's everything else?"

"Like I said, pretty fine."

"He has his up days and down," Charmian said, shooting Jack a pointed glance.

"You want I should give you a quick look-see?" the doctor asked.

"No."

"Great," he said, ignoring what Jack said and throwing his arm around Jack's shoulders. "Why don't you come up the street with me to my office. It's a far more appropriate setting to examine a world-famous author than what we have here." Then he said in a low-voiced whisper that was only meant for Jack but carried to the four corners of the infirmary, "We can discuss your urine in private."

He led Jack out much the way a father leads a young boy into church on Sunday. Nakata left right behind them to retrieve the fabrics from the car, and his uncle and his companions sat on a bed in a corner, lit their cigarettes, and drank tea from a china pot and small chipped cups they had brought with them.

"Now they'll come back and be lit," she sighed. "Everyone wants a drink with Jack. It's like the tales of the Old West where everyone wants to test themselves against the best gunslinger in town. Jack's legend precedes him."

"Well, he is good at it. I've seen him drink a full bottle of whiskey in one sitting and leave all other men lying on the floor and him as steady as a rock," Hobart replied.

"Thankfully, those days are over."

"Something to do with his urine, I gather."

A moment after she shrugged, unwilling to discuss Jack with Hobart anymore, the door to the infirmary burst open and three field hands staggered in under the weight of the fourth who was shrieking in hellish agony. Wisps of smoke trailed his entrance and the skin of his face and hands was as black as the charred field clothes clinging to his body. It was immediately apparent what had happened; the men had lost control of the fire and it had turned on them like a cornered beast and caught one in its jaws. She felt her hand go to her mouth, but otherwise she found herself frozen, physically and mentally. It was as if she was aware of her mind receiving sensory input but was incapable of acting on the information in any way.

There was movement. Hobart had left her side. Hobart was easing the man onto a bed. Hobart was looking at her. Yelling.

At her.

Why?

Her sense of self snapped back in a sudden rush, forcing the horror to recede somewhat. He needed her help.

"Scissors, Charmian! Scissors!"

"Scissors," she repeated as if she had just learned the word. Scissors. He wanted scissors? Feeling herself slipping away again, she forced herself to focus on looking for the common tool. A scissor was something she could comprehend. She heard Hobart call again, this time for Major, to run and find the doctor and Jack. She heard the crash of the door, saw the brief flash of daylight. Why wouldn't the man stop screaming? Couldn't they do something about that first? Instead of spending time looking for . . . ? Scissors! But there they were lying on a silver tray alongside other instruments. Might he need all these? She grabbed the tray and rushed it across the hall.

Hobart was using his hands to rip the tatters of smoldering cloth from the man's body. As she set the tray down on the side table with a "Here you go," she became aware that Nakata's friends and relatives had quickly come up behind her. Hobart plucked up the scissors with a grunt and used them to cut through the heavier parts of the fabric. She began to pant through her mouth—the smell rising from the man, vaguely reminiscent of roasting pork, was nauseating. His white eyes stood out in stark relief, rolling wildly with pain and panic. His hair, eyebrows, even his eyelashes, were gone. As the fabric fell away under Hobart's hands, she was relieved to see that some flesh had emerged unscathed.

Hobart turned to her. "I need buckets of cold water. Take these men, get buckets of cold water and as many clean sheets as you can find. Bring them back here."

Nakata's uncle understood and spoke in Japanese to the other men, including the three who had brought in the poor unfortunate. They scampered out of her sight. She recognized a white cabinet. She had seen nurses stocking it with linens on other visits. Opening it, she was relieved to discover that at least her memory was intact. She arrived back at Hobart's side with a stack of white sheets that smelled of Mrs. Stewart's bluing and sunshine. She inhaled as deeply as she could, trying to replace the other odor, which seemed to have settled into every crevice of her sinuses. Hobart had the man's clothes off now and she was relieved for the man to see that his penis and testicles were untouched. If he lived he would be glad of that, at least.

She heard the door slam and looked up, hoping to see Dr. Belko and Jack. Instead Nakata stood silhouetted in the light, his burden slipping from his arms in his astonishment. His uncle arrived with a dishpan full of water, the first of the men returning.

"Nakata," Hobart said in a loud, stern voice that demanded attention. "Find some whiskey." Nakata instantly began inspecting cabinets. "Soak the sheets." Hobart was using the same tone to her. It helped keep her mind from wandering again.

She plunged a sheet into the water, which was cool, not cold. Nakata's uncle grabbed the next sheet and plunged it into the dishpan currently being delivered by the next man.

"Now what?" She looked up at Hobart.

"Is it good and wet?"

"Yes."

"Unfold it and give it to me. We're going to spread it over this man."

She handed him an end and rose, unfolding it rapidly, the water sluicing out.

"Gently now," he said. He nodded at her and they let it come to rest on the man's body. He screamed again at the contact. She helped Hobart unfurl the next sheet and spread it over the man's legs.

"Nakata," Hobart called. "Find any whiskey?"

"No," was the response.

"To hell with the whiskey," she heard a familiar roar, and her eyes were blinded by the sudden light flooding in through the open door. "Morphine's what's needed."

Dr. Belko, who had arrived with Jack, hastened to another cabinet, withdrew a key from his coat pocket, opened it, and pulled down several bottles and needles. Then he was at the injured man's side with a speed that was impressive in such a big man. Moments after he jabbed the needle into the man's arm, the screams and wails began to subside and the man's cracked eyelids began to close with relief.

"Did you do anything else?" Dr. Belko asked, busily setting about examining the man by strategically lifting off pieces of linen. She was appalled to see hunks of flesh being stripped off, more married now to the wet sheets than to the form that was shedding them.

"Got the clothes off. Started with cold wraps."

"Good. Can you stay and help? I can use the extra hands."

"I'm not a doctor."

"Of course you're not. Otherwise you would have soaked these cloths with picric acid. But you did the best you could and I'm a little short-handed today. And obviously you're not put off by the sight of blood."

"Fine."

"Where'd you learn about the wet sheets?"

"I'd read about it in a book about coal mining I was thinking of adapting. There was an explosion in the book."

"Well, it's nice to see a little veracity in literature, eh, Jack? Another debt we owe to you."

"If you say so," Jack replied, his face grim.

Charmian could smell whiskey or spiced rum on his breath, even over the smell of the burned man.

The door swung open and shut again. A handsome man in a dark suit that was well made but inappropriate for the climate had joined them in the infirmary. "Dr. Belko?" the man spoke. "I've heard there was an accident?"

"This is going to be a long afternoon but we may save this man to harvest more sugar for Dillingham yet, Mr. Holdings." Belko kept his back to the man, rolling his eyes. "I'm glad you're here to help—I'm sorry, investigate—but we'll have to save that for later, shall we? For the time being everyone has to leave except my assistant." He looked to Hobart, who nodded back.

"Is that . . . ? Hobart Bosworth?" The sugar plantation executive appeared confused.

"Hello, Wayne," Hobart said through gritted teeth, struggling to subdue the man's suddenly thrashing leg. "Not the best time for introductions all around, I'm afraid."

"Out!" Belko roared. "Out you damned sons of bitches. Each of you is crawling with germs and disease and that's what we're fighting now more than the burns."

"Can you stay?" Hobart turned to Charmian. "You've got your head about you."

"Really?" She couldn't believe he actually thought her competent, as up until now she had only felt useless. His blue eyes were filled with concern.

"A woman's hands would be useful and welcome," Dr. Belko added.

There was something else in Hobart's expression. Something that asked her to join him in sharing the man's fate. As if by acting in concert, with no one to guide them, they had created an ownership over it. It was in their hands.

She turned to Jack. "I want to help."

CHAPTER FIFTEEN

"THE OTHERS, HIS COMPANIONS, his brothers, had left his bedside. After all, at dawn they would have to be in the sugar fields again. And there would be a new man in his place already, tending the elemental fire, earning his daily seventy-seven cents.

"He raised his hands and wondered at the thick bandages already soaked through with his life's blood. There was no pain in his extremities; the nerves had been burned away. He called out but he was alone in the hospital and it was the middle of the night. His hands fell back to the bed; he was unable to support their weight any longer. The hands with which he had torn a living from the earth. His eyes strove to shed a tear but, of course, his body was dry. He felt the world swirl around him, slipping away. It was time to surrender to a greater knowledge. He stared up at the ceiling, at a spider slowly spinning a web between the rafters.

"His last thought as he fell away from himself into a black whirling void was that the boss-san would only count his day as half worked. His last day of life had only yielded a worth of thirty-eight cents with a half cent credited to his next day's pay of which there were to be no more. At last, he shed a single tear. He had died for a half cent that would never be paid."

Jack put the pages he had written during the last two mornings in order. It had been a long time since he had read a story out loud to a group that included herself, Mano, and Hobart. There had been no room in the Buick for Major today.

Charmian caught Hobart's eye. He shrugged. If it hadn't exactly happened the way Jack had described it, and he hadn't been there so he wouldn't have known, then the telling of it was truthful enough. The field hand had died in the middle of the night. But he hadn't been alone. Not exactly.

They sat as a group, protected from the wind on the shelf cut into the side of the mountain, known as the Pali Lookout. They were on their way to see Mano's *kahuna* relative on the windward side. In typical Jack fashion he had invited everyone along on another one of his private missions. After the morning climb up rough roads through the jungle that Hobart had asked for, they had stopped at the lookout for a picnic and Jack had introduced the story, which he had begun the afternoon of the incident, now three days past. It was the first time Charmian had seen Hobart since a plantation driver had dropped him off at the hotel at dawn at the direction of the manager whom Hobart knew, Mr. Holdings.

"Crackerjack story, Jack. Really tops," Hobart said and Jack looked pleased. The only thing he loved more than reading his stories to an audience was to have them favorably received.

"It reminds me of 'Koolau the Leper,'" she added, one of Jack's favorites among his stories. She was looking forward to reading it again when she typed it up.

"It's a little like that, isn't it?" Jack nodded. The wind tousled his thick dark curls. He had worked with a blazing passion on the story for the past few days, and except for another somewhat upsetting unexplained absence, had spent far more time on it than he usually allowed himself. Instead of just trying to reach his daily average, he had plowed through it until he had finished. He next turned to Mano. "And now to put you on the spot, comrade, what did you think?"

The big man shifted awkwardly. "It was sad," he said.

"It's supposed to be."

"But why did he let the *haole* cheat him again and again?"

"Because he felt that earning money was the same as earning a livelihood. You see, Yamada was a wage slave, like so many in the world today. One payday away from ruin. And before he is paid, the sugar company deducts his room and board and expenses him for everything he purchases at the company store so he is left with little to call his own. Here he is surrounded with nature's bounty and he has forgotten all his forefathers ever knew about the land and foraging for fresh fruit and sleeping under the stars and all those skills that could have provided him with a means of survival should he have slipped the bonds of servitude."

"My bruddas and I would have gone fishing and let the *haole* pick his own sugar."

"Yes, well you and your brothers share a tribal, familial loyalty that places one another ahead of lesser needs. Your wage slave, even your union man, no longer shares that instinctual sense of brotherhood. The only interest served anymore is that of the self." He looked sadly at Hobart. "It is why, in fact, I am no longer 'the Boy Socialist' as you reminded me of my old moniker. I no longer believe that Socialism will inspire the worldwide Revolution of labor."

"I find it hard to believe you're giving up the dream of Revolution." Hobart raised an eyebrow, in that way he had when he sounded quite serious but was having a little fun.

"I still believe that labor will one day find a way to force capital to share equally in the rewards of the system. But instead of open revolution, I think that men should turn their backs on the system entirely and force capital to acquiesce. Every man and every woman should seek their Valley of the Moon and let capital come begging for their services. Just as Mate-Woman and I have done."

From the overlook, which was on the side of the first mountain in the Koolau Range, the land seemed to her to be miles below, though it was only because of the sheer drop down. The landscape leading to the ocean was a green and blue patchwork quilt of rice paddies and fish ponds crisscrossed by sandy roads that led to pockets of small villages on the shore of the great ocean.

"And now," Jack said, putting on a comically exalted air, "having stood on the very spot of Kamehameha's great triumph, I shall go commune with nature." He strode off into the thick grove behind the dirt turn-off.

"What was Kamehameha's triumph?" Hobart asked.

Mano swept his arm around the panorama. "This is where King Kamehameha defeated Kalanikupule in spite of the betrayal of Kaiana, to become *ali'i nui,* which is the king of all Hawaii."

"Try runnin' that past me again?"

Mano sighed and nodded. "Kamehameha had fought many wars to become king." Pride filled the Hawaiian's voice as he spoke, his accent turning his "th" sounds into soft "d" s. "Kaiana was always by his side, his trusted *ali'i*. After conquering Big Island, Kamehameha built a great navy, twelve hundred canoes, which he filled with ten thousand brave warriors. They quickly captured Molokai and Maui. Then they set their sights on Oahu, where Kalanikupule ruled. But Kaiana wanted Kamehameha's power and wife for himself. So he took his boat, and the soldiers loyal to him, and came to Kalanikupule with all of Kamehameha's plans. So Kamehameha knew he had been betrayed, and he came up with a new plan and his invasion set Kalanikupule's army running for the hills. They retreated up this mountain, with Kamehameha in hot pursuit, until they came to this spot, where there was nothing for them to do but turn and fight. So then they fought. But in the end, Kamehameha forced hundreds upon hundreds of his enemies over this cliff here, the Nuuanu Pali. And not just soldiers, but women and children, too."

She tried to imagine the terror of falling from such a great height. It was a drop of more than a thousand feet.

"Sometimes, down there, your *haole* scientists will find the bones of those who opposed Kamehameha. But it was here, on that day, that the wars ended and Kamehameha became king of all the islands. Now sometimes lovers come up here and jump when their hearts get broken or when they can't be together. Sometimes they fall all the way to the bottom, but if they were really in love then the spirits of all the dead carry them away across the sea so they can be together. They say the same thing happens when people have a hex on them from a witch lady."

"Whatever happened to the fella that betrayed him? I'm not even going to attempt to say the name," Hobart asked.

Mano walked along until he found two indentations in the earth in which he planted his feet. "These are the footprints of Kaiana the traitor. This is where he stood when the king cut him down. Nothing ever grows here."

Charmian could do without the violent imagery. The thought of all those people tumbling to their deaths had deeply unsettled her. She wanted to get off this cliff as quickly as possible. "Jack's been gone awhile. I'm going to make sure he's not lost." She left Mano and Hobart at the edge of the lookout discussing Hawaiian military tactics and followed the trail into the jungle. It was moist and dense among the thick, magnificent fern trees, dripping with lianas. "Jack?" she called, her voice falling flat. She walked farther down the trail. The Nuuanu battlefield had disappeared from sight. "Jack? Mate?"

She heard a groan from off the trail and stepped off to see Jack, his back to her, leaning against a tree.

"Jack?"

"Mate-Woman?"

She rushed to his side, slipping a little on the moist leaves covering the jungle floor. He gave her a wan smile as she reached him. His face was pale and drenched with sweat that had soaked through his collar and into his necktie. She noticed scraps of paper around his feet. In his clenched fist was the remains of his story. It had been rolled into a tube, ripped apart, and what was left of it was riddled through with tooth-tears. She put her hand on him. He was shivering, though not fevered.

"What happened?" she whispered.

"I'm having a devil of a time taking a piss," he said. His fierce grin faded as he stuck the pages between his jaws again and clamped down against the spasm that shook his body. As it passed, he spat out another part of his story upon the jungle floor.

He hadn't wanted to let the other two men know there was a problem. "After all," he had told her as they limped back along the trail after he had finally finished what he had come out to do, "we're on our way to see a healer, aren't we?"

"You brought all your medicines, right?"

"The whole case."

"Is there something in there you can take?"

"Well, it's going to have to be something strong. The codeine's not going to be enough. I think the time has come. I'm going to have to ask you to inject me with some of that morphine sulfate once we get back to the car. I can't stomach doing it myself."

"Oh, Jack, please," she blurted out. "Don't make me. You know how I feel about needles."

"Yep," he said. "Same way I do. Can't stand 'em. But it's either that or I'm taking Kalanikupule's way off this mountain."

"You know that story?"

"Sure," he said. "I was there."

"What do you mean?"

He shook his head and he pulled away from her, standing upright and planting his feet more firmly, as if nothing were wrong. They had arrived at the clearing. Close to the edge of the cliff, by the low stone wall, Mano and Hobart were engaged in a heated discussion. It appeared that Hobart was trying to restage the battle. Jack tossed off a casual wave, then cupped a hand around his mouth.

"If it's all right with you fellas I'm gonna take a few moments and dictate some notes. I'm feelin' inspired."

They waved back and went back to their talk. Jack squeezed Charmian's hand, making her bones ache. "You can do this," he said, his voice full of confidence. "I've made a study of it. It's no harder than threading a needle."

He had a seat in the back of the car while she opened up the trunk. Next to the picnic basket was a small leather case about the length of her forearm. She picked it up and set it on the front seat beneath the steering wheel. Opening it she was surprised to see just how much medicine he had brought along. She began to cry; she couldn't help herself. The tears just welled up and rolled out.

"All right. Take out the needle and the morphine," he said. "And help me take my leather belt off."

She couldn't see through the tears. Her fingers fumbled with the glass vials. "Maybe I should—maybe I should call Hobart?"

"Charmian." He placed his hand gently on the side of her face. She leaned against the palm; it was cool and warm at the same time. His thumb gently brushed away the tears from her cheek. "You won't hurt me any more than I already hurt. Understand?"

She nodded. He explained to her how he would bind up his arm with the leather strap, making his veins bulge, and then how he would point out the vein and she would gently slide the needle on a nearly parallel angle. He filled the injector with a little of the morphine, his hands remarkably steady, but then he always had had strong nerves. He handed her the needle and pointed out the vein. Then he rubbed a cotton ball that he had daubed with alcohol on his arm. She heard the sharp intake of air through his teeth as she slid the slim tube into the spot he had indicated.

"Did I get it?" Her voice was high and distant in her own ears. "Should I push it in?"

Gently he probed at it with the forefinger of his free hand. "Pull it out and let's try again," he said after a moment.

She pulled it out. A small, perfectly circular bubble of dark, rich red appeared instantly.

"Close," he said. "Let's try a little deeper this time."

"Did it hurt?"

"Not even a little. And you see how easily it went in? You can do it again, right?"

She nodded. She could. "I love you," she said.

"Then here we go."

She punctured his arm again. There was more resistance than she expected. He nodded after a moment. "I think you've got it."

"Are you sure?"

"I think so."

"Jack! Please tell me if it's for sure."

"Yes. Go ahead and press the plunger. Quickly."

She exerted pressure with her thumb—less than she had thought—and watched the clear liquid vanish.

"Pull it out!"

Alarmed, she jerked her arm back. Jack threw off the leather band and curled his arm up, flexing his fist.

"What happened?" she asked. "Are you okay?"

He closed his eyes for a moment and she watched as color flooded back into his cheeks, which had been pale and gray only moments before.

"Jack?"

His eyes remained shut for a long moment and then he inhaled deeply and opened them. He blew the air out of his lungs in an immensely long sigh. "That's better," he said at last, relief welling up in his eyes. "That feels great. I hope I didn't have you overfill it by accident."

She slapped his thigh.

He grinned. "You did all right. I knew you could. I love you, too."

"Well, don't make me do it again."

He lit a cigarette and puffed on it as she packed up the medicine kit. His eyelids were heavy.

"You've been doing too much," she chastised him. "Boxing and surfing and going off God knows where on your secret missions and doing what, exactly?"

He shrugged. "I can't sit around like a veal."

She took the cigarette from his loose fingers and took several deep puffs of the rich, peppery smoke. "I think we should go home."

"What's the point now? We're more than halfway there."

"The point is I want to know what's wrong with you."

"Pfft. Dr. Belko's already told me what's wrong. He knew as soon as he saw me. That's why he took me away—to make sure."

"What is it then?"

"Kidney stones."

She stood up and placed the medicine kit in the back again. "Why didn't you tell me?"

He gave a sharp laugh. "I didn't want to worry you."

"Well, what does he think you should do?"

"He wants to wait and see if it passes in a few days. Otherwise if I start to pass blood or get a fever, or if I can't piss or get too many more attacks, he'll have to operate."

"Jesus, Jack."

"It'll be okay. Why do you think I'm pushing to go see Mano's *kahuna*? We're supposed to go to Haleiwa in a few days and I don't want to spend my fortieth birthday having surgery. And if this works the way Mano thinks it will then I don't think I'll need another surgery."

"Drunk physicians and now a witch doctor?"

"*Lomilomi* was practiced here long before white medicine showed up, and it managed to keep the Hawaiians alive." He winced. "Just because it was outlawed doesn't mean it doesn't work."

"Promise me you'll tell me if it gets worse."

"I don't think I'll be able to hide it from you."

"And I don't want to have to give you another injection."

The trip across the other side of the Pali was no less strenuous than the ascent had been. Especially now that Hobart had taken the wheel. They found themselves on a concrete ribbon carved into the side of the mountain, hundreds of feet in the air. She had always liked heights, and speed, loved pitching down a steep hill in a wooden carriage behind two horses running for all they were worth. But as a hairpin turn again brought them near the edge, she found herself eager for a hint of the descent to come. To pass the time she had told Jack of the legend of the Pali and how the lovers and the hexed came there to cast themselves upon the winds of the spirit ancestors.

"You know, Jack," Hobart said breezily from the front. "The battle of Kamehameha—that would make one helluva picture now, wouldn't it?"

Jack, who had been resting his head on Charmian's shoulder, grunted, as he did when she disturbed him from a dream.

"You could turn that into a great script. I can see it now. A cast of thousands."

"I'm still on the fence about writing you a picture, Hob." He sounded churlish and tired. Jack's eyelids were low and his eyes were hard to see, but when their glances connected, he winked at her. She could sense that he was still feeling the effects of the morphine, perhaps even more so now than immediately after the injection. "Maybe I should just let you try and make *The Iron Heel.* No one could make a picture of that."

"I could make a picture of that," Hobart said with confidence.

"Seriously?" countered Charmian. What was it about his arrogance that seemed so challenging. "The story of a three-hundred-year global war against the Oligarchs culminating in the ultimate triumph of the Socialist Revolution told as a world history? Even Griffith couldn't do it."

"I could."

"How?"

"By focusing entirely on the love story of Ernest and his wife, Avis. The brilliant revolutionary and his romantic convert at the heart of the action. Folks love a good love story. That's what *The Iron Heel* is at heart. But I warn you, Jack, if you let me have the rights to it, the first thing I'd do is lose all the speeches."

"But that's where the message lies," Jack insisted.

"Then there's plenty of message in your book 'cause there're a whole lot of speeches. Too damn many for a picture, though. In a picture or on the stage the message lies in what the characters do. Yes, a play. I could even tell your sprawling epic as a play."

"How?" Charmian asked, now growing rather interested in his explanation.

"The only part that really made an impression on me is the part I remember the best—the Battle of Chicago."

"That's all anyone ever talks about," Jack said, distressed.

"Because it's an amazing piece of writing. The police and the military against the people. Brilliant. Imagine a room that overlooks State Street, where the battle rages. Periodically a newspaper boy shouts out the headlines, which tell of the progress of the battle across the whole of the city. Avis, the young and beautiful wife, waits in the room for word of her husband, leader of the Revolution. Friends and enemies find their way to her, telling her why the battle is fought, how it began, who is winning, what's at stake. She waits for Ernest to fight his way to rescue her. Of course, he reaches her as Chicago burns and the revolutionaries are routed. At the moment of their reunion, they are betrayed and taken away to die together. But wait! One of their compatriots, perhaps a character who was unsure of his place in the Revolution, has escaped with a manuscript Ernest has written, his detailed plan to guide the Revolution over the long years triumph will take. Hope lives.

"Then again, audiences may want a happier ending, so perhaps Ernest and Avis shall escape at the last moment to live and fight another day. I'm not sure what would play better. I'd have to think about it. Anyway, Charmian, there's nothing that can't be staged."

"You made it sound very exciting," she admitted.

"*Mahalo,*" he said with a sly smile and a tilt of his head.

Jack's face had brightened as it did whenever anybody spoke well of his writing. "I'm sold. Go make that."

Hobart shook his head. "Oh no. I just meant to show you how I could make it. I could never actually get it made."

"Why not? You said you could. And what you described would make a great picture."

"Wouldn't it? But tell me, who is going to give me the money to tell the tale of the violent overthrow of the capitalists and the U.S. government? I may as well be asking my Zukor and Garbutt to clean and load the guns that they will be executed with. Artistically I could make it. Realistically is another story altogether."

Jack settled back against Charmian, his head resting comfortably on her breast, as they rode on in silence for a little while. She stroked his hair. As they rounded a switchback the whole of the Pali came into view.

Hobart slowed the car down to a crawl as Mano pointed out the lookout to them. "What a terrible sight that must have been. Hundreds of warriors sweeping up through the jungle while their foes struggle to make their final stand with that fall at their backs. And at stake, nothing more than a kingdom. It must have been something to see."

"It was a horror," Jack murmured.

"What?" Hobart said. "I didn't quite catch that."

"I was there!" Jack snapped. "It was a bloodbath." His eyes were glazed and unfocused. Charmian made a mental note that some of the effects of the drug were delayed. Nobody spoke for several long moments and the valley floor finally began rushing up to meet them. Jack began drifting away again, as if to doze.

"I'm Kamehameha, you see," he said. "I was there and I was the king. I am the king."

"Of course you are," she said, adding, "You've had a bit too much sun and beer today," and hoping that they would overhear and accept her explanation.

"I am the king," he said to himself. He muttered something else in the self-important yet nonsensical tone that a child has as it falls asleep.

"What?" she whispered quietly and leaned in to listen.

"I miss my daughters. I wish they were here."

"I know."

Then he murmured something else. For the next part of the drive, as they slid off the mountain into the green of the windward side she tried to convince herself she hadn't heard properly. But her brain clarified his words, eliminating the dreamy chaff, until she had to admit to herself that he had said what she had hoped to God she hadn't heard him say. The empty pit behind her navel ached as it hadn't since her womb had been removed, and no matter how hard she pressed against the spot, she couldn't make the pain go away, nor remove his words from her mind.

"I want a son."

CHAPTER SIXTEEN

TWO DAYS WITH JOY. That was all she'd had.

The baby had seemed all right at first but had quickly turned listless. Her little girl's tiny mouth was unable to latch onto Charmian's nipple and her breathing was quick and shallow. She was already in the hospital because her water had broken weeks before the baby was due and the midwife had been unavailable. The doctors and nurses had swooped in and plucked the gasping infant from her breast—she could still feel Joy's lips sliding away. She watched helplessly as her baby's warm pink skin turned shockingly gray while the doctors administered medications and the nurses provided massage. She burst into tears when Joy finally began to cry—the sound was such a life-affirming sound, a wail of protest and defiance. In time, her color restored, they had returned Joy to her arms. Nurses hovered constantly nearby and doctors whispered urgently in Jack's ears. She ignored them all, focusing all the energy of her soul and heart upon the tiny babe with the thin wisps of black curls like her father's. Each time Joy faded she would be plucked away. Each time she was returned the light in her eyes had faded more.

All the while Charmian had bled. Not much, but steadily. It wouldn't stop. Two days after the birth the doctors told her there was nothing left to do but a hysterectomy. She had refused. Joy needed her. For another long night and day she held her baby until the nurses and doctors left them alone. She was dimly aware that even Jack had slipped away. She hadn't cared. Joy had become her entire reality and anyone else was an intrusion—even Jack. This one thing, this precious little life, was all she wanted in the world. Joy would be hers and Jack's, their love made real, their future personified. This little girl would be the most perfect thing ever made, the best thing Charmian had ever done. She hadn't know it was possible to fall so deeply in love with something that hadn't even existed days before.

Charmian had felt the baby's last breath leave her little body as the sun had set on the third day. When the night nurse had asked how they were doing Charmian had told her that she thought Joy was doing better. She wanted to hold the tiny hand forever. It was only at the next dawn when she had finally passed out from the loss of blood that the doctors and nurses discovered the cold form at her bosom.

Charmian had awakened to find that her daughter was gone and so was her womb. Jack was gone, too. He hadn't shown up for days and when he finally did he looked as if he had been in an accident, covered in bruises. He never spoke of where he had been nor what had happened to him. She didn't care to know. She hadn't wanted to share Joy with him. She still didn't.

A strange tree-covered cone rose above the shallow, startling blue waters past Kualoa Point. To Charmian it resembled the fin of an immense dolphin slicing through the ocean. The *haole* called it Chinaman's Hat because it resembled the traditional straw headgear of the field workers. Some people told their children that the rock sat on the head of a Chinese giant who used palm trees as chopsticks to feed the wintering whales rice from his great bowl. That, as Mano pointed out as they caught sight of it flashing in and out of view beyond the coconut trees, was a typical white man's tall tale. The little island, which he called Mokolii, was sacred, a place where, long ago, a condemned man could seek asylum even from the greatest of the *ali'i* and *kahunas*.

She was tickled at how the immense Hawaiian, usually so reserved, even shy, had grown comfortable with them and opened up. She knew how it was to stand in the shadows of living legends, even ones with generous personalities like Jack and Duke. And if one already had a tendency toward introversion (as she most certainly did not), that kind of presence could be completely overwhelming. Sometimes people interested in Jack would have entire conversations with him without even acknowledging her presence.

Mano described the Hawaiian legend about the island, that it was formed from the hump of a dragon slain by Pele. At the mention of the goddess, Hobart's double take caught her attention. She watched him as he reached into his pocket and pulled out a smooth black stone, rubbing his thumb over it in the manner that Nakata worked his jade worry stone.

"This man we're going to see?" Charmian asked Mano. "Is he a relative?"

"No. He was a friend of my *makua kane's,* my father's."

"Was? Mano, is your father dead?"

"Yes. He was shot in the rebellion of 1895 when I was less than a year old."

"I'm sorry."

"He died trying to restore the Queen to her throne. He's a hero."

"How about that, Hob?" Jack said. "Can either of us say we had heroes for fathers?"

"Not my father," Hobart agreed. "But I am a descendant of Miles Standish."

She caught Jack pursing his lips. She knew how much he hated his own illegitimacy, that his origins provided no clues to his destiny. That he had no ancestry of note or renown rankled him so much that upon occasion she had known him to take the achievements of his adopted father, who at least had been a soldier of the Union Army, as part of his heritage. That he claimed John London's lineage as his birthright gave him legitimacy as a man, and an American.

The village had no real name and had been built for and by the Hawaiians who fished the coast and worked the ranch. Some of the well-kept little houses, built along the road, were constructed of brightly painted wood planks, while others were built of thick thatches of dried palm, which hung over the windows the way Jack's unkempt bangs sometimes fell over his eyes. Black roosters sporting high and proud purple tail feathers strutted arrogantly across the road while their hens could be heard clucking judgmentally from the bushes.

The Polynesians roaming the village displayed none of the cowed and sullen attitude of despair of the Japanese workers at the Ewa Plantation. Perhaps because, as Hawaiians, they could come and go as they pleased without the burden of indenture, but she was also quite certain that the native disposition of the peoples was, in general, lighter than that of their far-Pacific cousins. Small children ran alongside the car, laughing, while the adults met her eyes with boldness and bemusement.

Jack, rousing from his doze, must have noticed something similar because he sat up and after a moment said, "What a beautiful people. In form and attitude they are so splendid you have to consider whether Adam and Eve were white after all. Maybe this is the image of God. Look at them. They live in a state of grace with nature, wanting for nothing and owing no man a tithe."

Mano laughed. "That's not true, brudda. All these men, they rather be rich like you and live in a big house than live here."

"Shall we put that to a test?" Jack responded. She knew by his tone that, coming off his nap, he was a little irritable. "Perhaps I should trade places with that big fella over there?"

"Absolutely not," she insisted.

"Then I could write the opposite of *The People of the Abyss.* Explore the reverse side of the horror of the slums by living among the natural people."

"And would you have that man and his family come live with me at the cottage while you displaced them? Or should I sleep on his mat alongside you? And besides, it was easy for you to pass as a stranded sailor in the West End; after all, you were a white among whites. How you would disguise yourself among the Hawaiians, I have no idea."

"Perhaps Bosworth could teach me some theatrical makeup secrets."

"But then they wouldn't be secret anymore, would they?" Hobart said.

"Brudda Jack, you the only rich man I ever meet who want to be poor again." The thought of Jack living in the village seemed absurd to Mano and caused him to laugh.

"I'm not rich, my friend. I make a good living. And I still say I'm not as rich as those fine folks."

Now it was Hobart's turn to laugh. "You own thousands of acres of land and employ dozens of men. I don't know any poor men who could do that."

"Well, you're looking at one," Jack said. "For I am the kind of man who shares his wealth with others. Those workers you say I employ, they will share in the profits of my ranch—if I ever see a profit. Until then they make more in wages than any other rancher pays his hands. I'm not keeping my money in some bank so the capitalists can use it to exploit others. I'm spending it on projects I deem worthy and I'll spend as much as I can make and I'll die penniless but satisfied. Isn't that right, Mate-Woman? Haven't I always said that?"

"That's the plan," she said.

As they talked they had passed the village and left the children behind. Now there were only a few houses, of the palm thatch model, along the road and Mano interrupted to point out that they should stop in front of one. He had them wait in the car while he went inside. Jack sighed and rubbed his palms into his eyes.

"How are you feeling?" she asked. She wondered how many times she had asked him that question and realized more and more how she braced herself for the answer.

"I have a headache," he said. "It'll pass."

"Okay," she said.

After a short while Mano came out of the house onto the lanai and was followed several moments later by a hale but wrinkled old man. His face was creased like the wrinkles of the side of the very mountain he lived upon. He gave them an impatient wave and Jack leaped out of the car, always eager to make a new, interesting acquaintance. "This is Mr. Pehu," Mano announced, with more than a hint of importance. "He is the *kahuna la'au lapa'au.* A healer." The little man resembled nothing so much to her as an image of the *menehune*—the magical elves of old Hawaii—she had seen at Honolulu's Bishop Museum. His upper body and arms were free of tattoos, unlike Mano, but his legs were so densely encircled with tight lines of tribal calligraphy that they appeared to be nearly solid blue.

"I'm Jack London." Jack extended his hand.

"I know," the wizened man said in an accent heavy with the islands. "I've read your books." He shook the hand in welcome. "I like *Burning Daylight.*"

"Ah!" Jack exclaimed. "One of my favorites."

"Sometimes I try to imagine snow from here to here the way you saw it in the Yukon." He swept his hands dramatically to indicate all that they could see. "But I can't. Too much green."

"Well, you're still a young fellow yet, and there's still time to get you up to the northlands for some prospecting."

The ancient Hawaiian chuckled and spoke his native tongue briefly to Mano in a good-natured tone. Then he turned to Jack again. "Mano, he is a big man. Like Burning Daylight."

"The very model," Jack affirmed. "Like a tree."

"Come in. Come in," the man beckoned to Jack, who then turned to Charmian and gave her a little nod of invitation. "No, no. Only you," he said, smiling, though he held up a wavering hand at both her and Hobart. "I'm sorry. It's *kapu*."

"*Kapu,*" she said, even as the three men were disappearing through the doorway. "Taboo."

"Damn!" said Hobart. "I really was looking forward to seeing the shrunken heads."

"Why don't you grow some kidney stones so you can have your chance?" She swung around and had a seat back in the car.

"Is that what's wrong with Jack?"

"Today it is."

Hobart explored the edge of the jungle, which began right at the road's edge. It was apparent that someone occasionally tried to clear some growth to create a shoulder, but the thick trees and vines would not be beaten back. "I shouldn't have boxed him."

"No kidding." She rifled through the pocket of Jack's coat until she found his tobacco pouch. She rolled herself a cigarette, moistened the paper, pulled out the loose tobacco, then lit it. Throughout the process Hobart continued to examine their surroundings, sometimes touching the flowers shaped like red lobster claws, sometimes peering through his thumb and forefinger at some visual detail of interest. Every now and then though, she noticed, he would cast a glance at her. After she had blown out several puffs, he wandered back toward the vehicle. She noticed for the first time that Hobart had the same arrogant self-assured swagger that Jack had when he was healthy. The resemblance in attitude between the two men was unnerving.

"How long has he been ill?" he asked, his voice conspiratorially low so as not to carry into the small house.

"You know, I really don't feel like discussing Jack's health with you, Hobart." She flicked some ash away. The old man stepped out onto the porch and she stood up, awaiting Jack, awaiting anything actually. He smiled warmly but waved her off just the same. Stepping off the lanai he took up a machete and began carving thick serrated leaves from plants growing in the garden beside his house. The harvested shoots left behind hollow wounds that oozed a clear gel. The man kept the leaves inverted so as not to let their precious contents dribble out. All the while he sang a tuneful Hawaiian song and the happiness that the song filled her with reminded her of the church hymns of her childhood when her aunt (her parents had died when she was very young) had taken up with the Universalists of Oakland. There was no sound from the house the whole while the *kahuna* went about his task and soon he reentered his abode with his harvest in his hands.

She watched Hobart for several moments. "How much longer are you planning on staying?"

"I can't go back without a Jack London picture to make," he said. "I'm afraid I'm not leaving without one."

"You know he's going to do it, right?"

"He hasn't said as much."

"But he will."

"I hope."

"He will."

"Good."

"What if I ask Jack not to do it? What if I say, 'Jack, if you don't write this picture, Hobart Bosworth will go away and leave us alone'? What if I say that?"

"Then I'll be ruined. Is that what you're intending to tell him?"

"I don't know," she shrugged, feeling weary. "I need to think about what's best for Jack."

"And isn't that his work?"

She shrugged again. "Maybe we'll see what the witch doctor says."

Hobart smiled at that. It was damp and hot where they were, and condensed droplets fell from the thick leaves all around them. Hobart took his jacket and tie off, then loosened the top button of his linen shirt.

"You're tanning already," she said. "I'm envious. Jack and I always have to burn terribly first."

They listened as off in the brush a hen scolded a rooster for some offense or other. When the hubbub settled down Hobart turned to her. "There's something I've been meaning to ask," he said. "What happened at Wolf House?"

"I wish we knew."

"It's just that Eliza said I should ask you as though you knew."

"Oh, she did, did she?" She stood up and stepped out of the car. "She hates me. She really hates me." She walked up the road, away from the car and Hobart and the little house. She ground the palm of her right hand into her mouth as if to press back a scream. As if deprived of an outlet, the suppressed emotions turned to tears that brimmed over her eyelids. She heard the crunch of his feet on the dirt behind her.

"Charmian," he said softly, "I'm sorry. I wasn't trying to goad you. She just led me to believe there was more to know." He gave her his handkerchief, which smelled faintly of bay rum.

"Oh," she said, wiping her tears away. "She has her reasons for hating me, I suppose."

There was a sudden switch in the quality of the air surrounding them and then it began to rain heavily, as if a squall had just blown in from the ocean and crashed into the side of the mountain. It had been so humid up until that point that there didn't seem to be any reason to escape the little additional moisture.

"I'll always be 'that woman' who stole Jack from the mother of his girls, I suppose. That's how the whole world sees me and I don't see why she's any different. But I'm not, y'know. Jack was ready to leave Bess. He was just looking for me and he didn't know it. He wasn't happy with her. I made him happy and he made me happy and that's not something that someone can be at fault for. And that was eleven years ago anyway—you'd think she'd forgive me for that, at least.

"I love Jack, you know? I love him. But there are things that can happen in a marriage. Hard things. You asked how long he's been ill. Hobart, it's been nine years. Nine years of one travail after another since he was first brought down aboard the *Snark*. You know, every morning for nine years I've awakened and asked him how he was, hoping for just a simple 'fine' or 'good.' If I hear that, I'm so happy. I'm almost afraid even to ask anymore because I can't stand to hear about this ache or that hurt, any of which could be the signal that today might be the day that I lose him. You can't imagine how frightening it is, and how I hate myself for losing sympathy sometimes. But you know what?"

"What?"

"I do ask him. I ask him every morning. And I make him take his damned medicines and I drag him to his damned doctors."

"It must be very hard for you."

"Harder for him. He's the one suffering."

"You've suffered along with him."

"In some ways, it's been hard. It's not as if there's anything wrong with me and yet I'm deprived of certain qualities of life along with him."

The rain began to pass away as quickly as it had come upon them.

"At least Hawaii's better for him. In particular, it's less stressful than Glen Ellen. He can write and not worry about the ranch or projects like Pig Heaven or Wolf House. It's very hard to be married to a famous man, you know? The world opens itself up to Jack and he accepts the invitations, sometimes to distraction. Sometimes . . . It's a matter of attention really. He has more attention for me here, too. At the Beauty Ranch—" She stopped.

"You don't have to tell me about the Beauty Ranch."

"I know what Jack's sister thinks happened."

"What?"

"She thinks that a ranch hand burned it down in revenge."

"For what?"

She stared at him coolly. "Do I have to spell out all the sordid details for you, Hobart? Because I'd had an affair with him and Jack found out and had the man driven off."

"Oh. Does Jack suspect the man?"

"Does he share his sister's suspicions? You'll have to read his latest novel, *The Little Lady of the Big House,* to find out. It's going to be published any day now. It's about a wife who takes a lover. Her penance, by the way, is suicide. I think it was an accident. It would break my spirit if

I found that my actions had led to this disaster. I hope you won't admit
to Jack that I've told you all this."

"Now we have another secret between us."

"The infirmary," she nodded. "I didn't tell Jack about that."

"I gathered from his story that he didn't know what had happened."

"The man was going to die anyway, right?" She searched Hobart's
face for an acknowledgment that he felt the same. "Dr. Belko did all he
could do."

"I'm not saying there's more he could have done. The man's suffering
was enormous. I think Belko did what he had to do. It wasn't murder,
you know. It was a merciful act."

She nodded. "Then why does it still feel like I've witnessed a sin?"

He put his hands on her shoulders as if to reassure her, she thought.
She stood eye to eye with Jack but she had to look up into Hobart's. She
took a step back, away from him. "I know Jack invited you but I don't
want you to come to Haleiwa."

He was about to ask her why.

"I want Jack to rest. And you're just another distraction."

"You're still considering telling him not to write for me?"

"Even if it means your ruin. I'm going to wait until after his birthday
to make my decision. You'll know when we get back."

Hobart nodded, then snapped his head in the direction of the new
sound, a bestial roar, ripping and flowing through the jungle toward
them. It echoed up the mountainside and down the valley. They started
and stepped away from each other. Another bellow ripped up the mountainside.

"Jack!"

She was aware of Hobart following her down the muddied slope back
to the house of the *kahuna*. But she was swift and light on her feet. Always
had been. At the side of the porch she nearly lost her footing in a decep-
tively deep puddle, but a wild leap cleared it and her momentum brought
her into the house a moment later, *kapu* be damned.

It was much brighter inside than she had expected and there were no
shrunken heads in the neat, open room. Sure enough, her husband was
the source of the cries. Jack lay face down on the floor atop a straw mat.
He was stripped down to his undershorts. The two Hawaiians crouched
on either side of him, both of them driving their elbows deep into the unprotected flesh of the small of his back. All three looked up in surprise.

"What's wrong, Mate-Woman?" Jack said with a guileless smile, grunting even as the other men continued to press into his spine.

"I thought you were in pain."

"Pleasure, Char. Pure bliss." He let out another rafter-rattling howl as the old *kahuna* ground into a sensitive nerve. Then his head settled, cheek first, against the floor, an expression of empty ecstasy written across his face. "I do love me some *lomilomi,*" he sighed.

CHAPTER SEVENTEEN

"I'VE NEVER SEEN A green lemon before," she said to Jack. "What's next? Yellow limes?"

He squeezed the juice from the two halves he had just separated from each other into the tumbler, which was partially filled with the fluid milked from the aloe leaves the *kahuna* had been harvesting. Into this he added several drops from a vial of tonic. Mano had later told them that it was called *maluhia,* and according to him it contained extracts of olena plant, bitter melon, and awa root (which, they had discovered in Fiji, was also known as kava and could make one feel quite euphoric if taken in the proper amount).

He swirled the mixture around, added a splash of whiskey from his flask. "For taste," he said with a grin. None of the liquids seemed to blend particularly well with the others, but he tipped the glass back and let the concoction slide down his throat regardless. "Ah!" he cried, smacking his lips, after the involuntary shudder and sour expression had passed. "It could be a purple lime for all I care. As long as it continues to work as well as it does."

"It's really working?" she said with bemused amazement. "It's not just in your head?"

"I passed one kidney stone last night and one this morning," he said. "The deep *lomilomi* broke them up and this solution has helped their evacuation from my kidneys. You know, Nakata, that they have staff here for just such things?"

But their servant was not to be outdone by the attendants of the Haleiwa Hotel, and he had swooped in to scoop up the empty glass as soon as Jack had set it down. The speed of his motion frightened the gecko that had been hiding behind the teapot on the small side table and it fled for the safety of low ground, its chubby tail whipping a final question mark into the air.

"Nakata, wait!" The servant stopped at the sound of Charmian's voice at the entrance that led from the broad pondside porch, where they relaxed now, into the hotel lobby. "Bring me London-san's medicine bag, would you please."

He nodded and then disappeared through the louvered wooden doors, which swung back and forth after his departure.

"His people have a massage culture, too. D'you realize he's been with us for over nine years now? He really has grown into a fine man to be proud of."

"You can take all the Hawaiian cures you want," she told him in a mock-scolding tone, returning to the subject at hand, "and I'm glad if they bring you some relief, but I'm not going to let you stop taking your old-fashioned white-man medicine just like that." In fact, after the panic at the Nuuanu Pali Lookout and their return from the house of the *kahuna* she had increased his dosages. So he could praise *la'au lapa'au* healing all he wanted; she would quietly reserve her gratitude for the graduates of medical colleges who had filled that familiar leather bag.

They watched as several hotel guests in an outrigger-style canoe paddled under the bridge that crossed the pond at the bottom of the carefully manicured great lawn. The hotel itself was a three-story affair, painted white with green trim and roofing. As many hotels as she had seen with Jack all over the world through the years, this one was the most elegant and well appointed of them all. From the peacocks roaming the grounds to the tennis and badminton courts, from the tasteful guest quarters to the sumptuous dining room, the hotel stood as the symbol of highest taste in the whole of the Pacific. Although Haleiwa was considered the countryside by the citizenry of Oahu, this cosmopolitan outpost was currently filled with the high society of the islands; the bankers, lawyers, entrepreneurs, and military officials and even royals had all come to celebrate the seventy-first birthday of OR&L-and-sugar magnate B. F. Dillingham, who, through no coincidence, also owned the hotel. It was, however, a coincidence that the Londons had arrived in time for the celebration tomorrow, and an invitation to the fete had appeared soon after they had arrived. She had done everything she could to put the brakes on the Jack London Traveling Road Show—no Hobart, no beach boys, no entourage—only to arrive in the midst of the society event of the season.

"I know Mano appears to have no greater ambition than to be a beach boy until the end of his days," Jack said, "but did you notice how much pride he took in his association with the *kahuna*?"

She nodded.

"Not only that but I got the impression that the old man was quite sly about teaching Mano his art. Why, Mano knew where everything in the house was as the *kahuna* called for it. And he knew within an ingredient or so what was called for in potions. Yet he seemed to have no idea that the *kahuna* expected anything of him other than his assistance. But I believe that long before Mano has reached the age his mentor is now, he will have acquired all his skills and craft and become the great *kahuna* of Oahu, if not all of Hawaii. It's amazing how one can be on the path of his destiny and not know it. Mano's heritage, aptitude, and proximity have placed his way before him. While others, like myself, appear to have no destiny other than what they forge for themselves."

"You don't think you were destined to be a writer?"

"I don't think it was foretold based upon the circumstances of my heritage, nor the opportunities available to me, that I would be anything other than a laborer. Perhaps if I had not had to slake my burning thirst for knowledge I would have gone back to being a sailor after a while and someday would have risen to be captain of my own vessel. But I don't think you can look at the tale of my life and see a moment where destiny's hand opened a door and said, 'Hello, young Jack, it is time for you to stop canning salmon, and shoveling coal for the furnaces, and steaming huge piles of laundry, and pick up the pen.' No. I chose to enter the library. I chose to work as a janitor at the very institution where I finished my high school education at the age of twenty and to attend Berkeley. It was I who decided that college had nothing for me, nor for any man who understood how the world really works."

"I see your birthday has left you feeling rather reflective."

"I think it's natural to pause for deep reflection when something as momentous as a fortieth birthday rolls around." The screening of the Jack London pictures at the Popular the night before they had left had put him in a good mood. The pictures had sold out, and one after another, each had received standing ovations from the crowds. But she could tell that seeing *John Barleycorn* in particular had turned him pensive.

"Well," she said, "I know of at least three events in your biography that you didn't mention that might, and I only say 'might,' indicate the guiding hand of fate."

"Do tell."

"Well, for one, I know that even though your family was poor that your mother made sure you had a love for reading and an appreciation for the importance of the arts, especially writing."

"It's true that she thought very highly of writers," he agreed.

"Well then, it's also true that it was your own momentum that propelled you into the free libraries at an early age, but might it also have been the hand of destiny that placed Ina Coolbrith behind the desk there? Since she was able to call Mark Twain a great friend, I can only imagine the impact Ina must have had on your callow, impressionable young mind."

"There was nothing impressionable about me. I was seasoned at a young age," he grinned, obviously a little embarrassed. "Go on."

"I'd say the third instance of destiny applying itself to young Jack London was when he was welcomed into the heart and home of sweet, young Mabel Applegarth, his first muse."

"But not his last!"

She rose from her chaise and sat on the edge of his. "She was the first to see that underneath this muscled chest, this vulgar"—she placed one hand on either side of his shoulders so they were nearly nose to nose—"swaggering, uncouth"—she rose to her knees and slid her left leg across to his other side, straddling him—"smelly, foul-tempered sailor or prospector or hobo or what-have-you"—she kissed him lightly—"was the inheritor of the souls of Byron and Shelley"—she kissed him deeply, pressing her tongue into his mouth. He was receptive until he heard the low, shocked gasps. He pulled his head back, smiling shyly.

"People are watching."

"Jack, if I were to try to make love to you without people watching I would be a lonely old spinster."

She expected a grin, but instead she saw the quick flicker of a wince, and she knew in an instant why the day and the place had provoked such nostalgia in her as well as him. She rose from the chair as Nakata emerged with the medicine bag. Jack gave her a quick, fading smile, then focused his stare on the palm trees beyond the pond. Without a word she went about fixing his medicines, and after he had washed them down, he rose and announced, as if he had nothing else on his mind, that he was going to take his nap.

She listened to the distant roar of the great North Shore waves as they crashed upon the beach. Ever since Jack had gone upstairs she had smoked cigarette after cigarette and listened to the ocean meet the land. A waiter refreshed her gin and tonic. Nakata approached timidly.

"Is he asleep?" she asked, before he could speak.

"Yes. London-san is sleeping."

"Good, he needs some rest."

"Mrs. London is okay?"

"No, Nakata," she said, looking over her sunglasses at him. "Mrs. London just reminded London-san of the day she talked him into leaving the first Mrs. London."

"Oh." He stood at her side a little while longer while she sipped her drink. When it became apparent she had nothing more to say, he withdrew.

The hotel was so evocative of that day in Wake Robin near Glen Ellen, she inwardly chastised herself for not noticing it immediately. Even the lapping pond water was an echo of the whispering stream that had run through their camp where Jack and his family and friends had set up their tents.

Though Jack often promoted their love, through his writings and his actions, as a paragon of romance, the truth was that their love story was as average as most. Even as he'd tried to convince the world, and perhaps himself, that theirs was a love for the ages, she knew the truth, and the truth was that it was primarily based on their mutual sexual satisfaction.

It was ironic that she was considered the homewrecker, the other woman, because she had met Jack first, long before Bessie. Her uncle Roscoe managed the *Overland Monthly* magazine, and Charmian worked in the small office as the secretary. She could still clearly recall the Christmas of '98 and the horrid young tramp who had stormed in out of the San Francisco fog demanding to be paid or hell would be unleashed. She later found out that he'd had to pawn his overcoat to buy the round-trip ferry ticket from Oakland. "To be paid for what?" she'd asked innocently, certain that she'd not hired any day laborers recently.

"Why, I am Jack London," he'd said, but he'd said it with a smile and a wink as if she knew who he was, which of course she did, for the magazine had published his first stories, his tales of the Yukon. "To the Man on Trail" was his literary debut and the story for which he was demanding payment. The writing was so memorable. There were so many new writers she had read and thought only that they showed great promise. But Jack was promise fulfilled. And he was so young. She would never admit to herself that he had become handsome at that moment by virtue of declaring who he was, but he certainly became more interesting.

At the time he stood before Charmian he was actually engaged to another woman, Mabel. Mabel Applegarth. Poor little Mabel. Trapped in her little San Francisco middle-class, bourgeois life that Jack so wanted to be a part of. Jack had been raised in financial and intellectual poverty so extreme that he had never even been able to imagine anything like real wealth—to him the middle class was the goal. Bess would turn out to be a member of the same caste, of course.

Mabel had let her mother come between her and Jack; the woman had so poisoned Mabel against Jack that eventually she broke off the engagement. When Charmian heard about the breakup she had hoped to step into that place in his heart. But it was obvious Jack really wanted to make a social marriage and Charmian's aunt and uncle were only one generation removed from the Pit. But she had tried to catch his eye one last time.

She had her uncle set up a lunch for Jack and herself so she could interview him for the magazine. He skipped the lunch, leaving her sitting alone in the restaurant. Later she found out that he had gone and spent the day getting married to Bess: a pale version of the already pale Mabel. She was no partner for Jack, but he wanted his blond, blue-eyed little boys—his own little baseball team, he used to joke. Charmian saw him often enough around the bay. The Londons set up a little house in Piedmont, and it became the place to be. Back then, as his star rose, the Jack London Traveling Road Show became the greatest attraction in San Francisco and Oakland. Writers, artists, photographers, poets, socialists all rubbed shoulders with sailors, prospectors, hobos, and all the rest of Jack's true friends. And Bess was always there with a sour expression on her puss and harsh words about baby girls needing sleep. Especially after

The Call of the Wild was published and was just so madly successful. Charmian saw how Bess was, how she became strident, irritating, the woman of the rolling eyes. Charmian, who had given up hope, now saw that she might be given a second chance. She was a patient woman but not a believer in unrequited love—it never got anyone, especially a woman, anything but sorrow. So she hadn't spent the years pining for Jack. She had taken lovers. But she saw that he wasn't happy.

So when the event she would forever call her lucky break happened, she was ready. Her lucky break was literal. Jack broke his leg in a drunken carriage ride in the middle of the night. Riding home from a tavern with friends he'd decided to reenact his train-hopping days by clambering out and over the top of the carriage to the other door. What he'd forgotten was that when he'd achieved this feat in his younger days he hadn't had a bellyful of whiskey.

Bess and his girls were vacationing up in the country at the time. Charmian had set herself to caring for him. It was during those days, when he was laid up and alone, and she had him all to herself, that she was able to coax out of him the admission that he was in a loveless marriage. Other than his children, he felt he had made a terrible mistake and that he would never be free again. Above all he had grown to resent Bess for being just so . . . conventional.

Charmian knew there was still another woman in Jack's life, the woman he admired platonically—Anna Strunsky. Together they had anonymously published their correspondence, *The Kempton-Wace Letters,* a long-running argument about the conflict of romantic love and sexual attraction. She might have been the only woman whom Jack had ever respected as an artistic equal. Certainly Bess was jealous of that relationship. But of Charmian, whom she should have seen as a threat, a rival, Bess thought nothing. In fact, she sent letters of thanks to Charmian for helping out her husband during his convalescence. Charmian even took the time to write her back to tell her it was completely her pleasure.

When he was able she had taken Jack back up to the country to see his family. Of course his whole gang had gone ahead and set up camp around what was then just a little cabin, so there was plenty of diversion, which she knew was exactly what he wanted. Because by then they were in love. And the tension was destroying him.

One morning he came into Charmian's tent before the others arose. He told her that she had to leave, that she was destroying his life, that he loved his wife and children and that he would be moving them to the desert of Arizona to get away from all the distractions that being famous had brought him in San Francisco, including Charmian. Then he left to tell Bess his plan. Charmian had nearly taken him at his word; she knew that he was on the fence, torn between duty and desire. But when he had kissed her farewell, she felt the lips of a drowning man trying to snatch the air from hers.

It was a day just like today, she thought. There was a fragrance in the air and a quality to the light that was exactly like this. She'd had waited long enough and she knew her moment had come at last. When he'd emerged later from his family cabin she'd asked him to join her in a hammock near the stream. She'd whispered love into his ears for hours. The morning turned into the afternoon and in full view of his startled, gossiping friends, she told him all that she meant to him, and could do to him, and for him, and how much they loved each other, needed each other. She thought about the other things she had whispered to him, how her tongue had tickled his ear. She reminded him of the things she could do to him that Bess wouldn't, the way she'd put her mouth on him, the ways he'd had her. She teased him with possibilities that made him hard in his trousers. It was one of the ways she kept him from getting up in front of all of his friends, by keeping him so aroused, in such a pleasurable state of frustration and ache, that he couldn't rise for fear of mortifying, even injuring himself.

She'd talked like Jack wrote. She spoke with passion, honesty, and strength. By the end of that day Bess was the one he was leaving. She brushed some pollen from her dress. That's what she'd reminded him of today—the worst day of his life. Not that choosing Charmian was wrong for him. But the day a man leaves his children and their mother is not a day he wants to be reminded of. She sighed and sipped her drink. At length she rose, deciding it was time to see to her husband, to see if she couldn't find some way put him into a better mood.

Inside, the room was empty. Jack was gone. She hadn't seen him leave the hotel. Was it possible that he'd strolled right past her and not stopped for her? He'd been disappearing on her more and more often. Errands about which he'd say nothing. Moods that he'd vanish into, making him as good as gone. She remembered the admonishment of her uncle during the first public days of their affair, that there was no suspicion like that a woman would feel for a man who had left another woman for her. And doubly so for the woman who captured Jack London. She felt the panic rise up in her that she'd been suppressing for months. If their sex life had been the foundation for everything else they had built together, without it they would collapse. And a darker thought than even that one rose. Perhaps he no longer wanted sex with her and his ailments had become the lie he told both of them until he could find his way to the truth. She turned from the room into the hallway. She'd die before she lost him. She loved him too much, for too long, ever to let go.

She hastened through the lobby, only vaguely noticing that people appeared to be clustering in hushed groups. As she stepped onto the veranda, the setting sun dazzled her. She fumbled for her sunglasses. Once they were on, she quickly scanned the lawn, unable to see Jack. However, as she turned back to see if Jack might be at the bar, Harry Strange appeared, his mother on his arm. He wore a natty, perfectly tailored seersucker suit that was at odds with the morose expression on his face.

"Mrs. London," he said, tipping his boater. He appeared on the verge of tears. His mother daubed at her eyes with silk.

"Harry, what's wrong?" she asked, reaching out a hand to his.

"We've just had word from Mr. Ford, who's come up from Honolulu. Terrible news."

"What's happened?"

"It's Judge Wilder. He has hung himself."

CHAPTER EIGHTEEN

"O UR FAMILIES HAVE KNOWN each other for years."
"I saw him at the Low dinner just two weeks ago. There was no air of despair about him."

"How are his cousins, James and Gerrit? Have you spoken to either?"

"Who found him?"

"He was the most carefree person I've known."

"He was never the same after Rebecca died."

"Does no one worry about damnation anymore?"

So went the variations on the singular topic of conversations early that Sunday afternoon at the Dillingham luau. There was no one she or Jack spoke to who didn't have the name Wilder upon his or her lips.

"There's something about suicide in particular that frightens the herd," Jack said to her and Strange as they wandered the breeze-filled plantation house. "It speaks of an absolute disregard for everything they hold as sacred."

"You've written favorably about suicide before, haven't you? Doesn't Martin Eden commit suicide?" Harry asked.

"Well, yes. But I won't say that I was endorsing suicide. Martin was a young man with a young man's passion for life and when he realized life could not return his level of passion, it destroyed him. And Martin only ever had one goal in his life—to be a successful writer. And once he achieved that he had nothing else to do with his life. Love didn't come easily. So in effect, he renounced it. He stopped channeling his life into his writing because he found nothing in his life worth writing about and then he became a shell of himself. Even in his choice of self-death, though, he chooses a pathway of awareness to obliteration. By drowning himself, leaping from the ship into the sea, he is intensely aware of the life that slips away from him as he slips beneath the waves. He surrenders himself to the greater universe with his eyes wide open. Which I choose to think is in its own way rather life affirming. He chose another experience rather than an instantaneous end. Rather than being a cautionary tale about suicide, I intended to tell a cautionary tale about an artist losing his connections to the world around him. I suppose the same thing can happen to a judge. Desperation and disillusionment can crush the spirit."

They stepped onto the lawn and drank in the spectacular panorama of Dillingham opulence.

"Then again there are other men who don't know the meaning of the words," he said.

As they came down the steps into the yard, they were greeted by the sight of dozens of young Hawaiian women in rows dancing in the hula style—their undulating hands and roiling hips spinning legends of old Hawaii that no *haole* could ever interpret. A band swung ragtime tunes in the covered bandstand.

Steam and smoke rose from pits in the ground, like miniature versions of the Pacific volcanoes, where pigs had been roasting since before dawn in the traditional style, slathered in guava and draped with banana leaves to seal in the flavor and keep the flesh moist. When they were hoisted up and tipped over, the meat would slide right off the bone. Long tables held great bowls of tangy, purple poi from the ground taro root, and in addition to the rainbow of fresh tropical fruits in array was a particular favorite of hers, platters of pineapple dipped in brown sugar and baked. The salty *poke,* raw cubes of tuna mixed with onion and kukui-nut oil, chilled in tubs of ice. The total effect of all the food on display was a gentle reminder of the old island turn of phrase that a true Hawaiian doesn't eat until he is full, he eats until he is tired.

Jack, as usual, was in high demand. Word had gone round that Charmian had had the hotel restaurant cook a special meal for him to honor his birthday, and now everyone wanted to offer their congratulations on his achievement of turning forty. Delighted at the attention, he eagerly showed off the fine gold pocketwatch she had purchased as a gift for him.

Of course there were eventually other topics to discuss as the party wore on. Guests having taken the two-hour trip from Honolulu to Waialua on Dillingham's own OR&L railway had been delighted to see a massive pod of humpback whales frolicking in the choppy waters off Ka'ena Point. Others felt put out that there weren't enough rooms at the hotel and that they would have to return to Honolulu this evening. Dillingham had built the hotel as a way to increase the value of his railroad, which daily made the trip from his sugar mill to his warehouses. At one point Jack spun one of his favorite tales for a group of eager listeners.

Hearst had sent him to Japan to cover the impending war with Russia. Stifled by the restrictions on the press, Jack left Tokyo behind and crossed the storming sea of Japan to Korea in an open sampan. Then he traveled hundred of miles across the winter-stricken land on horseback to reach the Manchurian border and the war front, where he had spent the next two months traveling with the Japanese army and posting dispatch after dispatch. At some point during this adventure he had been arrested and was left to rot in a Korean jail. Then, and this was always the point where Jack paused for dramatic effect, "When all hope was lost and the firing squad was gathering I was saved by the last-minute intervention of the president of the United States, Theodore Roosevelt himself, who insisted that any harm that came to Jack London was an affront to America itself. Can you believe it? Of course, in exchange for my freedom I had to leave Japan immediately and never return. And I've never been back."

Jack always loved the reception that story received; its effect was guaranteed. She forced herself to laugh with the others, but the story only reminded her of how grateful she had been for the ocean's gulf between them. She had won Jack away from Bess, but the outrage, from their circle of friends, the citizens of Oakland and San Francisco, the national press, the world it seemed, had been more than she could withstand. At first the ire was directed at Jack's correspondent, Anna Strunsky, but soon enough her own name was circulated and she began to feel shunned. She had never minded being gossiped about, but this was out and out ostracization. She would purchase a newspaper to read

Jack's dispatches and have to turn past the latest developments in his divorce on page 1 to reach his story on page 3. So she had let Jack leave without saying good-bye, didn't answer his correspondence, and refused to meet him when he finally returned. It was only when she heard that he had been seen about town with a local actress, Miss Blanche Partington, that she began to write to him again; eventually she let him come back to her. They were married the next spring. All in all she felt that they were even now, each having inadvertently reminded the other of a painful memory. The only difference was she wasn't going to sulk about it—it was too pretty a day.

"Look at this," Jack said to her at one point. "There are representatives of half the races on earth here today, all mingling and happy. This is a model for all America right here."

"If all America could eat like this every day the model would probably stick," she replied. "Ever notice how well people get along when they're well fed?"

"All the same," he said, "I think we should consider moving from Glen Ellen to Oahu."

She turned to examine his expression closely, gauge his intent. "Are you serious?"

"I'm tired of all the furor at the Beauty Ranch. This life is so much easier and this place answers all the promises of California. I'm not saying it's perfection, but it's a lot closer than any other place we've been to. Will you think about it?"

She nodded. "Absolutely."

"Ho! Brudda Jack!" A hail from the crowd and Duke appeared, dressed as if his body were meant only to be showcasing the finest suits. He was free of the beach boys today but not without companionship; the woman on his arm was from a mainland socialite family that Charmian had heard of but whose name she could not recollect at the moment. Jack and Duke often joked about how a certain very upper-crust class of young ladies took an interest in the exotic Olympian. Today he was trying to persuade Jack to accompany him to observe the huge waves at Waimea Bay come sunset, that they were *maika'i*—good. Another man quietly joined them as Duke continued his sales pitch. Tall, thin, only a few years older than she and Jack. He was greeted warmly by the three, even though Jack and she knew James Dole, the pineapple king, only from having dined at his home in Wahiawa once nine years before on their *Snark* wanderings. He had aged well. In fact, though older than Jack, he now appeared younger, the result Jack would insist later of healthy industry, clean living, and the tropical lifestyle. Though his canned fruit was famous the world over, he kept a low profile on the island, perhaps to offset his cousin Sanford's leadership role in the overthrow of the monarchy in 1893, years before he himself had come to Oahu to make his fortune. As it stood now, though, he was by far the wealthiest man in Hawaii, even far outstripping B. F. Dillingham himself. In another, more subtle expression of tycoon one-upmanship, Dole's whiskers were nearly twice as long as Dillingham's, easily reaching his sternum.

"What are you working on now, Mr. London?" he asked in his usual whisper when a change of subject seemed appropriate.

"I can't say as yet," he said, with a sidelong glance at Charmian.

After much feasting, and after the downing of many rum drinks, more entertainment was offered to the guests. Even Jack had been enlisted. Waving to the applause he left Charmian's side, racing up the steps up into the bandstand. "I'm often considered the wolf writer," he said, his clear voice ringing out, after having delivered birthday wishes on behalf of the Londons. "For nearly twenty years I've been trying to live that title down. Now, in my dotage, I've realized that maybe being known forever as the author of *White Fang* and *The Call of the Wild* is not such a frightful legacy. After all, it's a better one than ever could have been predicted for me at the age of twenty. For a long time I've resisted all calls to give 'em more dog stories for that's what they want. 'NO,' I've insisted and resisted. 'They want my thoughts on truth and beauty and the nature of the Brotherhood of Man.' And, of course, some did. But what they really thirsted for were more dog stories. So, to that end, I would like to read a little from my first wolf novel in nearly twenty years, and one I think is in fact better than both *Fang* and *Call: Jerry of the Islands.*"

The thrilled response from the crowd roused a flock of nene birds. Jack adjusted his spectacles, ordered his manuscript pages—which Charmian had typed for him—took a great sip from his whiskey tumbler, and began to read. As his voice fell over the crowd and drew it into the tale of a dog who becomes the faithful friend to the captain of a ship full of dangerous men, she was reminded that no one ever left a Jack London reading early. Among other talents, he was able to slip in and out of distinct voices for all his characters as if he were a stage actor—and it was obvious as he read that he was his own biggest appreciator of his work.

But some in this crowd were unsettled by Jack's story. There were shiftings and murmurings. Jerry's world, like Buck's and White Fang's before him, was one in which men treated one another cruelly and the animals who accompanied them even more so. Jerry was a so-called nigger-dog, one of those unfortunate beasts, noble in every other way, but bred to harass and intimidate the Negro workers on the plantation where he was born. Jack's descriptions of Jerry setting about his chores were vivid and violent and portrayed without sentimentality or overt judgment. Some spectators went so far as to turn their backs on the reading and find other diversions. Far and away, though, most guests stayed, enthralled, until Jack reached the end of chapter 2. Dillingham, stout and creaky at seventy-one, red faced from food, drink, and sun, tottered up onto the bandstand to throw his arms around the beaming Jack to thank him. He led Jack back into the crowd, where admirers gathered to congratulate the author on what almost everyone seemed to agree was a return to fine form.

Charmian stood patiently by Jack's side, holding his hand with her right hand and his drink with her left, as he graciously continued to discuss this book and his other writings for close to an hour, even after Dillingham had been reluctantly pulled away. It seemed to her as if her husband was as charming as he had ever been in his life, more like the man she had met years before than he had been in such a long time. She was so proud of him and grateful for this moment. Sometimes she gently chided Jack about the romantic emotions he created for his women heroes, Avis, Saxon, and the others: the age-long bliss of an embrace, their thrill at being in the presence of pure, true manhood. Now she had to hand it to him; in those descriptions he had captured the way she felt right now perfectly—and it made her feel a little silly.

"I think that portraying as heroic a dog that has been trained to terrorize an already downtrodden race is offensive," spoke a womanly voice from the winnowed-down crowd. She was tall with blond curls piled high on her head, fashionably dressed and shielding herself from the sun with a fringed parasol. "The colored man deserves better treatment."

"Dear woman," Jack replied, "I was suckled at the breast of Mammy Prentiss, the finest Negress in Oakland and the daughter of a slave. So I am intimately acquainted with the situation of the colored man."

The woman's husband cleared his throat uncomfortably in the silence that followed as people looked from her to Jack. "Come, Alice, that's enough," he said. "Don't presume to understand the mechanics of literature as much as Mr. London here."

Before Jack could reply Charmian heard herself speaking. "I know you. You work at the Ewa Plantation. You were there when that field hand was burned."

"Hello, yes," the man replied, his head bobbing. "I'm Wayne Holdings, the assistant manager, and this is my wife, Alice."

Charmian recognized the young woman. "She's a friend of Hobart Bosworth," she said to Jack.

"That's right," Wayne said. "He was kind enough to befriend my wife on our voyage over. I was so very seasick."

The mention of Hobart's name had a strange effect on the young woman. Charmian was pretty certain she was the only one who saw the woman's glance quickly scour their surroundings, and she was absolutely positive that she was the only one who knew what it could mean. "Friends of his," she added, meeting Mrs. Holdings's haunted eyes as they returned to look at Jack and her. "It's a shame he wasn't invited to this luau, isn't it?" she asked the woman directly. The response was a discreetly relieved nod.

"I suppose," said another woman from directly behind them. She turned her head and her gaze fell upon young Leialoha, her dark skin glowing and beautiful against the white of her low-necked dress. All this Charmian beheld in an instant as the young woman continued to speak. "It could be argued that Mr. London's intent is to show the world exactly as it is, not how it should be. After all, he did not coin the phrase 'nigger-dog,' nor did he design their ugly behavior. Other men did."

"Exactly," Jack said, releasing Charmian's hand. "I am leaving it up to the reader to decide what is objectionable, just as it is up to the reader to decide what to do about it." He took Leialoha's hand. "It's a pleasure to see you here today."

"What are you working on next?" she asked.

"Everyone wants to know that," he replied with a smile, and Charmian anticipated his usual answer. But then he said, and quite profoundly, "My next book is a memoir. Like *John Barleycorn.* But instead of being about drink, this one I am writing will be about sex."

Charmian heard herself gasp.

"Is there an interesting story to be had there?" Leialoha said, looking directly at her.

"Should make a hell of a movie," he grinned, putting everyone at ease with a little laughter. "At the least it'll be scandalous."

"And you do love a scandal," Charmian declared archly.

Afterward Charmian would never be certain if it was the Holdings woman criticizing him or the appearance of the young Hawaiian royal that set Jack off and ruined the rest of the day. It was probably a combination. He increased his alcohol intake sharply, becoming louder and grander in a way she hadn't seen since back at the Beauty Ranch. He insisted that their small band stay together and drink. And once he had found Duke again, he remembered that he had to see the waves. Cars were ordered up.

"Jack," she pulled at him, "I don't want to go to Waimea."

"But why?" he asked, his lids hanging heavy over his stony eyes. "It's something to see."

"I want to go back to the hotel, Jack," she replied, pulling him from the view of the others behind one of the aptly named flame trees. Under the dense bower of its blazing flowers she kissed him. The red petals beneath their feet reflected the fiery glow above. The flame tree was the arboreal equivalent of the island's volcanoes, as if Pele had taken root. "I want to go back to the hotel and I want to have you. You say you're feeling better? I want you to show me." She held his jacket lapels and leaned against his body, rubbing him. "I want you to show me, Jack. I can't wait another minute."

He looked away from her for a moment and then looked back with his patented London grin. "After the waves," he said.

"No, Jack. I can't wait."

"I just want to see this."

"Please, Jack, please. Let's go back to the room and we'll do everything."

"Why can't you ever let me do what I want to do?" The alcohol was warm on his breath.

"Is that how you feel? Is that what you think?"

He looked away as he heard car tires crunching on the gravel, heard his name called. "I want to see the waves."

"Okay." She let go of him. "Let's go see the waves, Jack."

It took three cars to drive the party, which included the Holdings,

Duke and his companion, Henry Strange and his elderly mother, Mr. Ford, and a few other people she didn't really know, along the twisting shore road. All along the way the great waves crashed onto the beach. Charmian sat next to Jack, and he had invited Leialoha to sit next to her. Someone, probably Jack, had boosted a bottle of whiskey, which went round the car while favorite songs were sung.

The road, which had been rising gradually after passing the turn-off to Haleiwa, suddenly made a sharp right turn and dived down into a deep cleft. On one side, the steep walls of the cliff formed the nearly perfect V of a valley, which followed a curving river out of sight. On the other side of the road was the crescent of a small bay, not even as wide as Fern Lake back home. However, Fern Lake never even sprang whitecaps, let alone the monsters that periodically rose from the depths then stood higher than houses as they rushed the shore.

"My God!" Jack roared as the others fell silent. He was the first out of the car, dashing across the street and onto the rocks that led down to the thin strip of sandy beach below where the foam from the waves roiled like a cauldron.

Duke explained how the winds drove the water upon the rapidly shallowing coral reef to create such a spectacle. Each gigantic wave appeared only every fifteen minutes or so; the rest of the time the bay rocked with ripples as low and gentle as those at Waikiki on a calm day. The surfer clapped a hand on Jack's shoulder and exclaimed with pride, "There's always a good wave somewhere, brudda. You just have to look for it."

The great roar of a crashing wave drowned out the conversation. The surf seemed to be driven by an ill intention, as if it were trying to climb the rocky shore and drag them in.

"We call that Jumping Rock," Duke continued as the water eventually receded and a relative quiet was restored. He pointed out the great rocky pile that rose from the left side of the bay. Even the last massive wave had been unable to crest its summit. "In the summer, even the youngest boys, eight or nine, can climb up that and jump down into the water."

"How about during the winter?" Jack asked, passing the bottle to Leialoha, who politely set it down without sipping from it. He slipped off his jacket and loosened his tie.

"No. Not during the winter."

"What do you figure that drop is?"

"Fifteen feet when a wave is in. Forty when it's out."

Duke turned to speak with his companion for a moment. Long streaks of pink colored the sky as the sun began to fall behind the clouds massing on the horizon. Jack walked away from the group, and Charmian followed.

"I'm going," he said with a sly grin.

She laughed at first, but a look from him told her he was serious and the humor died in her chest. His eyes had lost their earlier dullness and were shining with wicked delight. "Jack!"

"I've got the timing of the waves figured."

"No."

Bounding away from her, he slid down the rocks to the shore as quickly as a monkey, pinwheeling arms helping him keep his balance.

"Duke!" she shouted twice. When the din of the breaking wave passed, the Hawaiian heard her and turned, then followed her gesture. On the beach, Jack already had his shoes and socks off and was stripping down to his light short-legged union suit. Duke sprang onto the rocks, heading down to the beach with the grace of a bobcat. By now the rest of the group had drawn together to watch.

Jack dove into the water and let the receding current draw him out toward the huge rock, striking with a crawl only when he appeared in danger of being swept past. He began climbing the rock even as Duke shrugged, picked up Jack's clothes, and clambered back up to the shoulder of the road. He reached Charmian's side, gave her a slight shrug, and handed her Jack's clothes. She understood: What was he to do? Swim after Jack? They would both drown.

She watched as the tiny figure that was Jack made his way to the head of the rock, near to the point where the monsters began their inevitable break. It seemed as if he was hesitating there forever until she realized he was trying to read the timing of the waves. She looked at the faces of the group; they were staring in shock and surprise. Then, when she thought he was about to jump, he instead began waving at them with both arms and pointing at the horizon. Then he clapped his hands over his head in a gesture of amazement. She could hear his shouting, but the first word, the one he repeated over and over again, made no sense.

"Gjöll! Gjöll!" he cried again and again. The others looked to her for explanation, but she had none.

"Look!" Mrs. Holdings pointed.

Emerging on the farthest edge of the ocean was a vast apparition of the deepest shade of dark indigo and of such immense size that it blocked out the setting sun. An indescribable fear stabbed at her heart as the vision hovered like some atrocious giant struggling to rear its head over the edge of the earth.

"The Twilight of the Gods!" she heard Jack yell. "The Twilight of the Gods!"

And then he jumped.

Part 3

"NO MENTOR BUT MYSELF"

—FROM A LETTER BY JACK LONDON

CHAPTER NINETEEN

"I HAD ANOTHER VISION," Jack said, sneaking observant glances over Professor Homer's snug university office, a well-appointed koa-wood-paneled cabana set to the far side of the campus. In his few visits he hadn't yet taken the time to give it a full examination, which meant carefully observing enough about it to be able to describe it accurately, vividly, in as few words as possible should the need ever arise for him to write about a professor's office. The collection of books and Hawaiian artifacts spoke to years of study spent in this room. To Jack it appeared as if the professor had dropped a taproot deep into the Hawaiian earth soon after his brass nameplate had appeared on the door. The windows of the professor's office were open and through the louvers Jack could see students gliding across the palm-tree-spotted lawn on their way to morning classes. Twin pangs of anger and regret poked at that tender spot under his heart. Once in his life he had wanted nothing more than to be one of those scholars, had worked harder than any man ought to earn the right, had swept floors at the same high school he'd had to attend to earn a diploma, years older than the middle-class youths in attendance, his ears burning as they laughed at him and his ambition as he set down his books after classes to pick up his broom. But Berkeley was his dream and he knew he could make it come true. Hard work. Long hours. Always tired. Always hungry. Always ashamed of his place. And then he'd been accepted, on one of the happiest days of his life. But it only took a few weeks for disillusionment to set in. The thought made him chuckle.

"Excuse me?" the professor asked.

Jack shook his head to reassure the worried-looking man that the thought that had crossed his mind was of no great consequence. "I was just thinking about what a terrible student I was during my brief university sojourn."

"Why is that?"

"It's very hard to teach anything to a young man who knows everything."

"I'm familiar with the type," the professor replied with a slight smile. "Why don't you tell me about your vision. Was it like the one you said you had on the North Shore last month?"

He cleared his throat, which felt full of phlegm, and lit a cigarette. "What happened at Waimea . . . I told you about that. I was tragically mistaken."

"Just because your vision there turned out to have a more physical than metaphysical explanation does not negate the fact that you did, in fact, experience a personal mystical revelation."

"Professor, I mistook the appearance of the island of Kauai being lit from behind by the setting sun for the mythological rock of Gjöll. I deluded myself into thinking I had discovered the rock that held fast the world-devouring wolf. I then nearly killed myself leaping into the ocean in my rapture. Clearly, I was in the grip of a neurotic complex, wouldn't you agree?"

"I'm not an alienist, Mr. London. I'm a professor of mythology."

"But you've read the books I gave you. The ones by Jung?"

"Which only persuades me yet again how ill equipped I am to discuss anything more than mythological events. Past and present."

He watched as the professor scribbled a few notes in a floppy leather book, really an Italian sketchbook he had commandeered for the experiment they had both begun the week after the New Year's celebration. The sound the pencil nubbin made as it scratched its way across the page was comforting—even before the call of the ocean and the tone of his wife's voice, this was the most persistent and reassuring aural presence in his life, something he was keenly attuned to. He had often wondered whether it was scientifically possible to discern what a person was writing by these sounds; could the creation of the letter *L* or *B* be perceived, for example? Was it possible to overhear the creation of one of his books?

"At the moment you saw Kauai," Professor Homer said, suddenly looking up from his writing, "you thought the universe was giving you a glimpse of its true nature and there's no reason to invalidate the impact that had on you. This is how a myth may be born. Let me put it to you this way. Let's say you were one of the guests at the wedding at which Christ made food and wine appear. Say that later you found out that the provisions had been brought secretly by his apostles and the whole effect was an illusion. You might be dissuaded from the experience of a miracle. But your belly would still be full."

Jack uttered a short laugh. "I like the way you reason, Professor." He let his eyes wander over the office. Though small, it was filled with Hawaiian antiquities and artifacts. In fact, it was more of what he would have expected to find in the *kahuna*'s home than he had found there. For some reason, this small campus office felt more authentically Hawaiian than the home of an actual Hawaiian. In some ways he felt it was a sad statement on the slow invasion by the *haole* of the islands. While they had taken as much of Hawaii as suited them and become more Hawaiian for it, they had at the same time forced the Hawaiians to take of them. And were the proud natives better off for being more white? He didn't think so. But then, he thought of Mano, learning the old ways while living in the new world, and that gave him hope.

"Well, what I've always believed, and your friend Jung seems to agree with me, is that mythologies are the ways we interpret the symbols of our lives—from the smallest details to the great mythic events. Now as I've told you, I'm not qualified to attempt an analysis on you or with you. It's why, as I told you at our last meeting, which was upsetting, I know, I refuse to engage you in your word-association play, though it seems to be a popular analysis tool. I doubt that there is anyone in Hawaii who knows much about this controversial new field of—I hesitate to call it science or medicine, but study. However, I do understand mythological symbolism enough to have these discussions with you about the meaning they may have for you. But as to whether or not these discussions give you any relief from complexes you claim you may or may not have—I'll have to leave that up to you and Mr. Jung. I think the question you have to concern yourself with is why do you think of all the things you could have interpreted Kauai as, including what it was, why did you choose Gjöll?"

"As opposed to?"

"A big rock? Leviathan? Poseidon's knuckle? The *Titanic*? You tell me."

"I guess I have a lot of Nordic culture on the brain right now. Nietzsche had made such a huge impression upon me when I was first starting out—I guess there are perfect books for perfect times in our lives. Rereading his works lately inspired me to investigate some of the Viking folk tales and I realized as I read them that the wolf referred to as Vánargand was the same character that I knew as Fenris Wolf from a book I had as a child. The wolf has great significance for me. Wolves and dogs have obviously been good for me as a writer of fiction."

"Why wolves?"

"I turned twenty-one years old in the middle of the Yukon winter in Charlie Taylor's cabin on the bank of Henderson Creek about a hundred miles south of Dawson City during the greatest adventure a man could have, the great Gold Rush. You can't imagine how cold it can get until you've spent a winter like that. Especially here surrounded by all this wonderful tropical heat. It got so I could tell the temperature by spitting. If my spit froze where it landed then it was fifty below. If it burst into ice shards in midair it was seventy-five below. Charlie's cabin was about as big as this office. Me, Charlie, my sister's husband, James, and whosoever stumbled in out of the endless white darkness. We accepted all comers. Some were friendly and some weren't but all of 'em were grateful for a little shelter, a little fire, and a little grub. All of 'em had at least one dog that needed tending to. And then there were our dogs, too. I never knew from dogs until then, 'cept for the curs that prowled the garbage heaps of Oakland, though I once had a dog named Rollo when we lived on a farm. I never knew 'em for the dedicated and devoted beasts they truly are until I seen, excuse me, saw how loyal and protective they were to their masters. How they'd die for 'em without even a thought to their own survival. But on the other hand how they'd fight to the end for their own survival under any other circumstances. I fell in love with dogs that winter 'cause I helped take care of them all—weren't, ah, excuse me again, wasn't much else to do but tell stories, play cards, drink, and take care of the dogs."

"Had you started writing then?"

"No. But I was realizin' my stories told better than just about any-body's. For example, if a prospector came by and told us how he'd been claim-jumped, why, when the next fella came in from the cold, I could tell the first fella's story in such a way that could make 'em both cry. So I begun to think that I might be able to write some of 'em down, both the true ones and the ones I was just makin' up out of whole cloth."

"Now what about the wolf?"

"Wolves. There were wolves in the forest. I knew less of wolves than of dogs; only that the ranchers near my father's farm in Alameda spoke of them as evil incarnate, fretted about them constantly."

"How old were you when you lived on the farm?"

"Just a boy. About seven or eight."

"A farm can be a hard life."

He laughed. "Hard? It was the happiest time of my life. I roamed the countryside with complete freedom. I didn't have to worry that I would be set upon by neighborhood toughs, because there were neither neigh-borhoods nor toughs to worry about. Rollo would retrieve the ducks and rabbits I shot. It broke my heart when we had to leave him. It was the last time I cried until Joy died."

"What happened?"

After a moment he uttered a single word. "Plume." The very sound of it surprised him.

"Excuse me?"

"An old friend of the family who has a lot to answer for," he said sharply, more so than he had intended. "But back to wolves," he said, slapping his thigh. "As the expression goes, there was a wolf at our door. Our cabin door. Actually, there was a pack that lived deep in the forest. We'd hear 'em at night. Set up a howlin' to scare dogs and man. I got used to it though. During the long twilight that passes for daytime, we could see their eyes glittering in the light of our torches just beyond the tree line. Only one of 'em was brave enough to show himself. Big fella, though not as big as some of our dogs. But lean. You know, that's the thing about wolves you don't realize until you see 'em is how slender they are—and built for speed. One of our bitches had gone into heat and that drew him out of the forest. Threw the other dogs into a frenzy. Now at this time there was just me and Charlie; James had gone hunting with a pair of other fellows. Charlie—he was plain terrified of the wolves. Like an old woman afraid of the devil. Got it into his head that they were going to kill us all in our sleep if we didn't get rid of the bitch. So I told him to cut her loose, but he wouldn't go outside. So out I went. She was a pretty gray and brown malamute. We already had her separated from the other dogs so they wouldn't fight over her. So I untied her and walked with her to the edge of the forest.

"Out he walked, like a king of the woodlands. Where I was up to my knees in crusted snow, he floated atop it. The pads of his feet were immense. He stared at me with eyes that seemed almost human in their comprehension of me—a startling sensation. It was as if he knew what I was doing—bringing him his bride, so to speak. And as we stood there, looking each other in the eye, I felt a kinship form between us. As if I knew what he thought and he knew me. I could hear his pack, snarling and yapping in the trees behind him. At any moment he could have lunged for my throat and killed me. Then they would have fallen on me and devoured my corpse. But he stayed them. I let the leather lead slip slowly from my fingers and the little malamute darted off into the woods without a trace of fear. After a moment more of watching me, the great beast turned and followed her. We never saw nor heard those wolves or that dog again."

"You know quite often in mythological tales, one of the first encounters the protagonist, usually a god or a hero, experiences is with an animal. This is quite a common occurrence in tales from cultures all over the world. Did you know that?"

Jack shook his head.

"This animal often provides some guidance, or its pelt for protection, or shelter from the elements in its belly and in some way shares its spirit with the hero of the story. I believe that symbolically this encounter helps prepare the hero to leave the realm of civilization behind and reconnect with the power of the natural world in which his adventuring takes place. Does that make sense to you?"

"You see?" Jack said, his voice rising, "You see? This is exactly what I was hoping to discover in our talks. I didn't know that, but it makes perfect sense to me."

"I'm glad you find it useful. Of course, there's a world of difference between an interesting natural phenomenon such as the one you experienced when you came face to face with the wolf and the nature of a mythological tale, you understand. But there are implications for each of us." The professor tapped tobacco into a cherry pipe bowl and held a lit match to it. Soon the rich smell of pipe smoke was mingling with the sharper smell of cigarettes. "As you know there are no wolves in Hawaii, but there have been dogs as long as there've been men here, some myths say even before. One such dog god is Poki, a brindle dog who is sometimes seen on the beaches south of Honolulu. If he walks with you then all is well, but if he lies across your path or passes you, then you should return home so as to avert disaster. Then there is the giant dog warrior, Kuilioloa, who fought with Kaulu, the trickster. The dog warrior was slain and his body broken into bits upon the sea where his spine became the island of Molokai."

"That's interesting. We're heading there tomorrow."

"Really?"

"Yes. Dr. Belko has asked us to take some medicine over to the colony. I've been itching to get out on the water again."

"You haven't yet told me about your more recent 'vision.'"

"A series of visions really. All in the same vein. And as real as the vision of Gjöll without the awkward mitigating factor of the subsequent intrusion of any realistically plausible explanation. They're different in the sense that while the rock appeared to me in the midst of an otherwise realistic environment, when these visions occur I am completely transported to another time and place."

"Can you tell me about them in sequence?"

"Well, the first once occurred while I was surfing. I was on the ocean, bobbing like a cork on the water with the beach laid out before me on a brilliant, blue-sky day. I was listening to the laughter of the beach boys. Then, it was as if they disappeared, as did everything recognizable about Waikiki altogether, and I was far out to sea with Oahu far ahead of me. Behind me, to the right and to the left, as far as I could see was a vast armada of war canoes. Hundreds of vessels, carrying thousands of warriors, their faces horrifyingly painted for battle. I realized that I was one of these soldiers—a son of the islands—and that my day of reckoning had arrived. I called out to one canoe in the distance, one that was pulling away from me. I felt anger and heartbreak. But the man in the boat wouldn't answer my calls. It was as real as all the world and put to shame the finest artistic recreations in the Bishop Museum. And then it was gone in an instant and I was upon my board again and about to catch a wave."

"Did this happen before or after our conversations began?"

"After. After the, um, our second meeting. Yes, that was when."

"We discussed Pele."

"That's right. Then I had another one while I was finishing writing one morning. I was in my little cottage when the walls simply dissolved away and I was on the beach, at the spot where the cottage had stood. I was seeking protection in the jungle, which extended right to the edge of the beach. Extending to the water were the fresh corpses of Hawaiian warriors—my brothers. The war canoes had made a landing on the beach and we were taking heavy fire from some cannons above the tree line. Men to the left and right of me were being torn to ribbons. I sent a party of warriors, brave men all, carrying guns, heading west into the jungle in an attempt to come around and flank the artillery. Then there was a huge explosion, sand was thrown into my eyes, and there I was at the writing desk again."

"What were you working on? Your memoir?"

"No. Notes for a screenplay for Hobart Bosworth."

"So you've decided to go ahead with that."

"I believe he'll get the picture made, and if he does, it could mean a lot of money for us. I think we've come to an understanding. So that's what I was working on that morning."

"Any other experiences?"

"One more—on the day I was going to visit Mano's *kahuna* to try and get some relief from my kidney stones. We had stopped for a picnic. I was off by myself near the Nuuanu Pali Lookout. I found myself lying on a mat in a clean, dark hut. It was early morning. There was a body next to me. I turned to find my slumbering wife."

"Charmian?"

"No. A Hawaiian woman. She was beautiful in repose. Thick black hair flowing over her smooth, nut-brown skin. I awoke her with a kiss, and her eyelids fluttered open. She looked at me with eyes as dark as obsidian. She kissed me tenderly with full lips and told me she loved me. Her body was warm and soft against mine. She was sleeping nude, as was I."

"Did you recognize her?"

"Her name is Leialoha. I know her. A relative of the Queen. A beautiful young woman. I believe she is betrothed to Mano—but they don't speak of it. Maybe they're not betrothed so much as destined for each other. She spoke one last thing to me before the dream changed, and then there I was creeping up the mountainside, carrying a club embedded with shark's teeth. There were screams before me—the cries of women, and children. Just as suddenly, I was alone in the jungle and good old Sailor Jack again."

"Interesting events."

"Do you believe in reincarnation?"

"No. But the transmigration of the spirit is a common element in mythologies, and resuscitation of the dead is quite common in Hawaiian lore, so I'm open to considering the underpinnings of the phenomenon. Are you inclined to think you're experiencing reincarnation?"

"Isn't it obvious? I am imbued with the spirit of King Kamehameha."

The professor cleared his throat.

"You're uncomfortable with that thought, I can tell," Jack interjected. "I can only try and convince you of the power and realism of these visions—like nothing else I've ever experienced in my life. These visions are of me reliving my victory over Kalanikupule at the Pali. At the end I was rushing toward the final stand at the cliff but I never made it. It was beyond the ability of my legs to carry me to the highest point."

"What do you think you would have found upon reaching its summit?"

"I don't want to see. I don't want to know. That's why I came to see you. I don't want to have any more visions. I don't want to see what happens in the end. I don't want to be a part of it."

"Why not? You know what happens."

"But don't you see, in each vision, I've been able to insinuate myself, as Jack, just a little. I called to the man in the boat. I sent the warriors into the jungle. These were decisions that I as Jack made. I awoke Leialoha with a kiss and I paused on the surge toward the cliffs to savor the taste of victory. What might happen to me at the cliffs—at that last battle? I feel I might find my end there."

"Well, you have to realize that these are only imaginings, and not real. I suppose you should consider what the crisis is, within yourself, that drives these incidents."

"But can't you help me with that?"

"I feel like I've made myself clear on that. It's why you left in such a high state of dudgeon last time with your word association list, vowing never to come back. It's up to you to apply our discussion of mythology to your specific areas of interest."

"Well, can you at least find someone in the body of mythology who experienced what I've experienced and let me know what happened to him?"

"I will do some research."

There was a long silence as both men smoked.

"I have to ask," Professor Homer said at last, "what was the sensation of jumping from the rock?"

He smiled. "It was a moment both fleeting and eternal. I think once was enough."

"And what was the reaction of the spectators?"

"Relief, I suppose, that they weren't to be involved in any police inquiry."

"And what did your wife say?"

"Actually, she hasn't spoken to me since." He gave the professor a wink. He was a married man, after all. But the professor didn't seem to catch the intent of his gesture because he continued his questioning.

"Do you think it's because of your actions at Waimea Bay? Or because you told her about your sexual memoir?"

"In the end, I don't think it really matters." Jack stood up. He felt it was time to head home, that there wasn't much more to talk about.

"One more thing, please, Mr. London?"

Jack paused.

"What was the last thing Leialoha said to you in your final vision?"

"She promised to bear me a son."

CHAPTER TWENTY

Moeʻuhane.

"Ho there, Hobart," he called as he turned the wheel of the *Will-o'-the-Wisp,* his hands attuned to the slight living sensations of the boat's response to wind, water, and his command. "Do you know what the Hawaiian word for 'dream' is?"

Hobart, who was coiling the anchor line in the prow of the yacht, some thirty feet away, shook his head.

"Moeʻuhane," Jack called back. "That's what this all is." He swept his left arm toward the receding island of Oahu, mist-shrouded greens and browns rising up from the purest cobalt. "One hell of a Hawaiian *moeʻuhane.* You know, you really should get to know a little Hawaiian while you're here."

"I'm trying, Jack," Hobart growled good-naturedly, "but I don't speak her language."

Jack roared with laughter. With a grin, Hobart returned to coiling the rope, making sure it was ready for tomorrow when they would drop anchor at the island of Molokai.

Jack heard a bumping from below. Charmian and Nakata were still stowing the supplies they had purchased in Honolulu in the small galley, which, while being no match for the spacious salon he had built on the *Snark,* was more than three times the size of the one aboard his first vessel, the *Razzle Dazzle.* He had bought that little oyster skiff when he was fourteen with three hundred dollars he had borrowed from his former wet-nurse, Mammy Prentiss. He had always been proud of how quickly he had paid back her investment and faith in him. As he listened to the below-deck murmurings of Nakata having more words with his wife than he had had since jumping off the rock, he thought of Mamie, the crew girl who was part of the *Razzle Dazzle* purchase price. He smiled to himself; now there was a girl who would have applauded a leap from a rock high above crashing waves, not waged a near-month-long campaign of stony silence. Of course, in many other ways, however, Charmian reminded him of Mamie—both were girls who liked to kiss and knew how to. Both were beautiful; Mamie's rough life hadn't robbed her of that, at least at the age of seventeen hers was a beauty born free and natural. The difference in the end was, he thought, that Charmian had had to cast off the bonds society places on a woman to find her true wild nature, but Mamie had always been feral. She had been known as the queen of the oyster pirates from one end of the bay to the other. Her skin had been as smooth and cool as the teak wheel under his fingertips, her hair dark and curly and Irish. Though he had tried to convince her to leave with him when he had sold the *Razzle Dazzle,* she insisted that the boat was her only home and where it went, so would she. He saw her only from time to time after that, as the skiff passed through the hands of other masters, her beauty and regal nature never diminished. She vanished from the waterfront soon after he married Bess, some told him the day of, and though he asked about her often, none of their old friends ever saw her or the *Razzle Dazzle* again. Whenever he brought a boat into harbor, he always cast an eye out for her fine lines, as if he would catch sight of her sleek form racing across its surface, darting in and out of the way of the larger boats like a gull in the rigging, bringing him one last glimpse of his black-haired first in every way.

The thought of Mamie made him sigh. He turned his attention to the day's journey. The sky was sparsely spotted with gentle clouds to the horizon line and the sea was even more deeply blue than the sky, especially as they entered the deeper water dividing the islands. It was apparent that it was going to be a slow sail across the Kalohi Channel; the wind was very light. They would be spending the night on the ocean. The gentle motion of the *Will-o'-the-Wisp* as it surged against the tide and the fizzy hiss of the wake churning beyond its stern filled him with peace and joy. Out here, like this, it didn't even matter that Charmian wasn't speaking to him. Still.

He decided it was time to test the water. "Hello down below," he bellowed. "How about some grub and some drink?"

His words were swallowed by the silence below. He sighed again. At least he'd had the good idea to invite Hobart along. They could bat some story ideas around while he considered whether or not he wanted to work with him again. And he knew that Charmian found the actor's presence an irritation, which was something of a bonus.

Finally the sound of something dropping below broke the stillness.

"Hobart?" Charmian called.

Hobart rose to his feet, grabbing the staysail sheet to steady himself. "Yes?"

"I think we've found something that belongs to you." She emerged from the dark cabin, blinking against the bright sunlight, pulling along an object providing resistance. Jack grinned at the sight, as Hobart groaned and clapped a hand to his head.

"Major!"

The stowaway hung his head, but the glint of defiance in his eyes told Jack he was ready to resist any punishment.

"I told you to stay at the hotel."

The boy gave no sign of comprehending.

"I don't know, Charmian," Hobart said, "I suppose we'll have to use him for shark bait."

"I've got a better idea," she said with a smile. "Why don't I send him down to the galley where he can help Nakata prepare some grub and some drink for the crew. Sound reasonable?"

"I suppose it will help him earn his berth. But I'm still tempted to hang him off one of those fishing poles."

"Well, we'll go fishing later; let's see if he's made himself useful by then," Jack said, adding to Charmian, "right?"

Not looking at him, she directed Major back down the ladder and uttered a few words of command to Nakata. Jack gritted his teeth, the wood of his dental plate pressing painfully into his gums. How much longer was she going to keep this up?

"Hobart," he said, as he watched her disappear into the galley, "are you familiar with the seven basic storylines?"

"What are those?" Hobart eased himself onto the lazarette. His light cotton shirt was open.

"All writers know them. To begin with there's man against the creatures of nature. Then man against another man. Man against the environment. Man against the supernatural. Man against machine. Man against God. And man against himself—his own seven deadly sins. I've recently added an eighth. Man against woman, because I have decided woman is so different as to not be interchangeable with man in any form."

"Couldn't she be considered a creature of nature?"

"Not in my book."

Nakata appeared in the galleyway, deftly balancing a tray of glasses filled with clear brown liquor over ice cubes and some sandwiches. "Here you are, London-san," he said, presenting the tray to Jack. "London-san," a title now as familiar to Jack as the mists rolling across the San Francisco hills. For nearly a decade, he had been London-san, ever since being introduced to the young man during his first visit to Honolulu. Immediately, Jack had been amazed at the ways Nakata functioned more as an extension of the boat than as a human, crewing it from the moment he stepped aboard. His footing was as sure as that of a burro high on a rocky trail. Instinctively he knew when a boom was swinging around behind him, or how to coax just a little more wind into a sail with the tug of a sheet. And when it came to creative uses of small shipboard coal stoves, no one could do more with one than he, and in his hands a single fresh fish could be transformed into five or six singularly distinctive, albeit small, dishes. However, he'd had to be trained in the proper amount of ice to add to whiskey.

"I'd love to take her around the north shore so you could see the sea cliffs," Jack said to Hobart. "They're sheer rock faces, higher even than those of Dover or Norway. But already we're going to be out here all night, so let's not find ourselves to the windward side of the island in pitch black."

Hobart nodded in agreement. The sails were listless.

"Do you mind taking the wheel? As long as the waters are so still, I'm going to go below and make up the writing I didn't get done this morning."

"Do you write every day?" Hobart asked, while relieving Jack from pilot's duty.

"Even when a storm's blowing," he replied, following Nakata down the stairs. The cabin below was cramped, with Charmian, Nakata, and the boy. "Nakata," he ordered, "why don't you teach the boy how to fish."

"Yes, London-san."

Major, giving every indication that he'd understood, eagerly followed Nakata up into the sunlight.

Jack opened his leather-bound folio and spread it upon the galley table. Charmian kept her back to him. He knew she was now faced with spending time with Hobart, whom she loathed, or him, whom she was angry with. "You know," he spoke, after a moment of tapping his pen against the table, "most wives would be grateful for such a Hawaiian adventure."

"Most wives don't have you for a husband," she snapped, taking her whiskey and heading up on deck.

Good, he smiled to himself. At least she's talking to me again.

After writing for a while, he lay down in the forward cabin to take his afternoon nap. Although his aches and pains were nowhere near their usual intensity (in spite of the silent treatment, Charmian had made sure he was still taking his medicine), his stamina was not what it once was and he felt the need for a nap about the same time every afternoon, whether or not he felt ill. The faint rocking of the light waves reminding him more of the journey downriver to Dawn he had once made on a raft he had built with his own two hands than a voyage on the open seas. He could hear Nakata just overhead patiently teaching Major to fish for the brilliant blue bonito. When the boy landed his first catch he heard the strangest sound, it must have been gurgling up from his throat, and Jack realized the youth was laughing with joy. Just before he drifted off to a Yukon *moe' uhane* in which he was waving from the raft to the astonished Inuit boys on the shore, he heard the murmured tones of Hobart, and then Charmian, finally engaging in conversation of some sort. Of course, he thought as he drifted down the river toward sleep, she's probably starved for decent conversation.

He awoke sometime later, the shadows having moved from one side of the cabin to the other. His dream had taken him to Dawson, and he had awoken with the memory that it was in that town he had received word that his stepfather, John London, the only man he had ever called father, had died, and that his great northern adventure would end. He rose and went on deck. The faces of the quartet above turned to him with surprise, as if they had forgotten he was on board. As was to be expected, Charmian rose immediately and pushed past him, down into the belly of the *Will-o'-the-Wisp*.

"Not much progress?" he remarked, nearly as a statement, to Hobart.

"Hardly. We're on tip," Hobart replied. His shirt was off and his skin was bronzing.

Jack looked to port and starboard—dark blue on one side and dark green to the other. The *Will-o'-the-Wisp* was on the seam where warmer waters collided with cooler streams. The sun was beginning to make its final descent into those cold waters at the edge of the world.

"Nakata," he said, "bring back those rods and make sure you give me the reels with the bronze wire fishing line. Then have the boy get that barrel of fish you've been filling there and start slicing them into chunks about this big. Make sure you don't lose any of the blood and guts, either."

Suddenly Charmian was making her way back up the ladder, as the two younger men set to following his orders. Her eyes, making direct contact with his for the first time in weeks, were bright and full of the fire of imminent adventure. "Nakata," she called out, as she studied the ocean line Jack was indicating. "Three rods."

"What are we doing?" Hobart asked.

"Along that riptide on the warm side, there you will find the great fish feeding: tunas, dolphinfish. On the other side, the cool side, there you'll find the predators lying in wait for them." Nakata came down to the stern with the heavy South Bend bamboo rods and as Jack took one, he said, "We are going to fish for sharks."

Charmian took her rod eagerly and Hobart received his. Nakata hurried to help the boy prepare the bait. Jack tied off the wheel. Nakata set the bucket of fish offal in the stern and began ladling it into the water. As he did so, Jack began affixing Major's slices of bonito to the large hooks at the end of the heavy wire leaders.

"If he strikes you keep your line tight, wear him down, and bring him up alongside the boat. I'll take care of the rest," Jack said, fastening a sheathed bowie knife to his belt.

"Got an extra one of those?" Hobart asked, making both him and Charmian laugh.

By the time the sun had set, the lines were in the water. The moon was brilliant and the water glowed with phosphorescence. Jack felt himself flushed with the thrill of anticipation that only fishing can bring, where one never knows what's going to happen in the very next moment. Then that moment has passed and nothing has happened, but another moment full of potential begins. All around could be heard the sounds of small plops as smaller fish leaped into the air to escape the bigger fish pursuing them through the black water.

"Hob," Jack said as they settled comfortably into the waiting that was part of fishing, "I've been thinking long about your proposition and I've decided there might be something to it for me."

Hobart laughed so hard he nearly spilled his drink and then he threw his arm around Jack and did spill a little. "Finally!" he cried.

At that moment Jack felt a tug on his line, the slightest vibration really. He tensed his body. "Reel in," he cried upon sensing a definite second response to the little jiggle he put into the pole. Instantly on both sides he was surrounded by the buzzing of winding reels. A third tug was violent and he responded by smoothly, swiftly jerking the rod back over his right shoulder. At that moment the line went taut, the rod curved over nearly double, and he felt the connection to a vital essence as it turned into a living thing in his hands. In the distance there was great churning and roiling as something splashed in the darkness, then the line snapped free and the rod turned into a simple dead pole again. Great groans of disappointment, cries of tragedy and injustice were raised, and curses to the gods were hurled. But moments later, all baited lines were back in the water again.

"The thing is," Jack told Hobart, when a diligent calm had settled back over the boat, "is that I was serious when I asked if you had any ideas. Because right now most of my creative energy is going into my memoir. I don't think I have anything suitably epic for you—nothing, at least, that I feel like applying myself toward. There's a fellow I've bought story plots from, Sinclair Lewis, but I don't think he's right for this particular project. So it comes down to you, Hob. What's your idea for the next big Jack London picture?"

Without a moment's hesitation, Hobart pointed and said, "Him."

"Major?"

"An American Mowgli," was his reply. "You've heard the tales of boys who run with wolves, I'm sure. Do you remember the tale of the wolf girl of Devil's River?"

It had only the ring of familiarity to both Jack and Charmian, so Hobart refreshed their memories. "Somewhere in Texas," he spoke, occasionally flexing his line so as to give the bonito flesh the appearance of life, "a young mother had been found dead in her lonely cabin surrounded by evidence of recent childbirth, but not child. The cabin was full of wolf tracks, and it was assumed that the infant had been devoured. However, there were rumors over the next few years of a girl seen in the company of a pack of wolves that plagued the cattlemen of the area. One rancher claimed he saw two large wolves and a girl bring down a cow. Finally, ten years after the grisly discovery in the cabin, a girl was captured in the woods. She was brought to a ranch where, during the night, she set up such a howl that the whole countryside was afraid. They say that that night a large pack of wolves descended on the ranch, terrifying the herd and the cowboys, and that in the confusion the girl was able to escape. She was only ever sighted once more—seven years later, and again in the company of wolves."

"Wouldn't the wolves have killed the child and devoured her?" Charmian asked.

Jack held up his hand. "Wolves can be astonishingly merciful. I've read other cases such as this one."

"So what if," Hobart continued, "instead of a girl it was a boy like Major. Let's suppose he falls in with them while young enough to have some memory of his humanity; there are cases where children up to three years old have been adopted by animals. After many adventures with his lupine brothers he is forced to choose between the life of a wolf or the life of a man. Which do you suppose he will choose? And what will life be like for him in either world as he moves from the carefree adventures of boyhood to that of manhood? Does that sound like enough of a story for you, Jack? Because it sounds like a hell of a one to me."

"You can't train a wolf to act," Charmian said.

"My audience won't know a big dog from a wolf. If I tell 'em it's a wolf, they'll believe it's a wolf. What do you say, Jack?"

"I have to say, I'm very intrigued."

With a tone of scorn, Charmian turned to Hobart and said, "Well, Hob, I see you'll find a use for anybody sooner or later. I expect you'll end up playing the boy? After all, you did play Jack in *John Barleycorn* and you were certainly too old for that."

"Of course not," he replied, "but I'm sure he'll have to have a father who loves him and is looking for him. That's up to the author. Now perhaps that's a part I could play."

"Don't you have a studio to run?" she snapped. "Shouldn't you be there instead of here?"

"Believe it or not, this is a matter of paramount importance to my studio. I find myself looking for a much happier ending out here than I could find back there," he responded with dramatic bravado. "No matter the cost in blood and treasure."

Charmian excused herself and went below.

"How long do you think it will take you?" Hobart asked, eagerly.

"As much time as it takes. I need to research. Take notes. Create an outline. Then find the words to fill in that outline. Now in the youth of my career I disciplined myself to approach writing as a bricklayer or any other tradesman would. I simply applied words to the paper one after another until my story was constructed. To make sure I had enough words each day I would write down new words from the dictionary and plant them around my room along my habitual route. When I came across them during the course of the day I would stop and make sure I had memorized the word, its origin, and its definition. Those were days when I was hungry and cold and in debt, and when one is in such straits, and the key to survival is to sell a construct of words, then there is no time for stalling, or agonizing, or staring at the walls waiting for art to happen, as appears to be the fashion of writers today.

"It could be a month, at least, before I have my notes together, my words chosen, so to speak, and then, given the attention I also intend to spend on my memoir, another month or so until I'm able to deliver a useful story. I'll write it as a story, or even a novella, if need be—then you adapt that for the screen. That way, if you're unable to make a movie of it, I can still publish it and see some return on my investment of time. And if you do get it made and I don't see any profit from your film, I can still make one from the story."

Even by the weak kerosene lamplight Jack could see Hobart's face darken, his eyes drawn away to the east as if he could see his little studio with all its attendant little problems from there. Jack felt a pang of sadness for him. But, such as they were, those were the terms.

"Surely, Jack, there's a way to speed up the writing of this story?" Having tired of being robbed of his bait, he handed the rod to an eager Nakata.

"Certainly there is," Jack replied. "All you have to do is abandon your desire for this to be a Jack London story and then you can hire any writer you so choose. Or write it yourself for that matter. Two months is not such a long time to wait for the story that will set your affairs in order, right? After all, I am supposed to be here on holiday."

"Will you be returning to the mainland to wait?" Charmian asked, reemerging.

"Was it Milton who wrote that it is better to wait in Paradise than wait in Hell? Or something of that sort, anyway. I think I'll stay and help keep you focused." This was said with the grin that had made him famous on stages around the world. "I've actually been thinking of taking you up on your challenge."

Nakata hooked a fish, the pole quivering with motion. Almost before Hobart realized what had happened, the Asian placed the rod in his hands.

"Challenge?" Jack asked, scratching his head, curious.

Hobart grunted. "You challenged me to turn any of your books into a play." Quickly he got his feet under him. Luck was with him, as it often is for the first-time fisherman. The shark ran straight toward the stern, its fin slashing like a silver knife through the water. "I've been reading *Before Adam.*" He reeled quickly, keeping tension and bringing the beast alongside.

His reactions were instinctive and good, Jack noted. The beast was a fine animal, a tiger shark, easily ninety to a hundred pounds. Nakata was ready. He dropped his rope in a loop in the water, attempting to lasso the fish at the tail. At the appearance of its snapping jaws, Hobart dropped the rod and stumbled back against the lazarette. In an instant, the rod and the shark were gone.

"I'll pay for that," he said after a long moment's silence.

Jack passed his rod to Nakata, indicating that the next shark he hooked, he should keep. He sat down across from Hobart. "You know, I have written several plays."

Charmian rolled her eyes and muttered something unfriendly about "those dreadful pastorals." He chose to take it as a new communication front.

"But, Jack," Hobart said, "my challenge is to create something new. I think I shall tell the tale of the dawn of man. And I'm thinking of using a mainly Hawaiian cast, as well."

"It costs money to mount a stage production," Charmian reminded him.

"That won't be a problem," he said. "I know *exactly* where to go to get what little money this will require."

"And how about a stage?" Jack asked.

"Again, not an issue. I have a standing invitation at the Popular—you might remember the ladies who own it? They were the women I was speaking with on New Year's when we bumped into each other? They've said they would put the theater at my disposal. All I need is your blessing."

"Why not?" Jack decided. After all, if it would cost him nothing then what was the harm of it? And perhaps Hobart would soon tire of all things Jack London and go home.

The action of the night seemed to quiet as the pursuers and their intended victims moved on to other parts of the ocean. Jack suddenly found himself tired again and decided to turn in. Charmian, huntress to the end, refused to turn in until she had had a real crack at one. He went below, frustrated by the lack of blood to satisfy his adventure lust, and found that she had laid out his medicines by the bed—so that's why she had gone below. Soon he was fast asleep, deeper than his earlier nap, and though he thought he heard some rumblings and thumpings, he was unable to rouse himself until the sails finally caught some wind and the *Will-o'-the-Wisp* gently heeled over in response.

On deck Charmian lay bundled under her quilt on one lazarette. On the other side of the wheel, snoring on the other lazarette, was Hobart. Nakata slept atop the cabin roof. Only the boy, Major, was awake. The deck was awash with streaks of drying blood. Jack beheld the most amazing sight. A great fish hung from the rigging. Easily one hundred fifty, two hundred pounds. Its maw was as great as the circumference of the wheel. The boy's face shone with exhausted pride. Jack had seen the same look in the eyes of soldiers on the battlefield after the charge is over. He pointed from the boy to the shark. "You?"

The boy shook his head, then whispered in a hoarse voice, "No."

At that moment, Jack knew without a doubt that he would write Hobart's picture.

Major pointed at Charmian and Jack realized why a slight smile was resting on her lips as she slept. He loved that smile and realized he hadn't seen it much, if at all, of late. Now her expression continuously seemed to be one of worry for him. He placed a hand on her shoulder, gently, and she stirred. He whispered gently in her ear. "Well done, Mate-Woman."

Her eyes opened slightly, just enough for him to see the gray light of the dawn reflected in them. She smiled, and finally, after three long weeks, spoke kindly to him.

"Thank you, Mate-Man."

CHAPTER TWENTY-ONE

A S JACK LISTENED TO the tale of Charmian against the monster of
the deep, he'd had to admit to himself he was growing a little
jealous. He was angry with himself for having slept through all the excitement, to be sure. But by the time he brought the *Will-o'-the-Wisp*
into the tiny port of Kaunakakai, he'd heard enough of the titanic
struggle in which she thought her arms might fall off while Nakata
and the boy lassoed the beast at the side of the boat and Hobart drove
the blade into its brain. More than anything he felt frustrated that
he'd not caught a shark of his own. But he was also irritated that the
commotion hadn't awakened him and disappointed that none of his
crew had made the effort to rouse him. He said as much to Charmian
in as polite a way as he could, not wanting to upset their tentative rap-
prochement.

"I didn't want to wake you until I had really caught it," she replied.
She was sitting in the stern sipping the last of the coffee. "You never like
to show your books until they're done."

"But a fish like that," Jack said while tying down the boom. "You
might have gotten hurt."

"Please," she said. "I was surrounded by men in their prime all willing to protect me." Hobart was passing the boxes of Dr. Belko's medicines over the rail to Major, who was silently stacking them. Nearby,
Nakata was negotiating the sale of most of Charmian's fish to a local

merchant, having carved off several choice hunks and placed them in the *Will-o'-the-Wisp's* icebox. Jack's stomach gurgled at the thought of what Nakata would do with those steaks on the journey back.

"Jack London! Ahoy aboard! Is that Jack London?"

"Goodness," Charmian said with a small laugh, "word of you always does travel in advance."

Jack grinned and watched the horseman approach down the dusty trail from the jungle beyond the small town. "That's our Nature Man," he replied with a smile.

"Let's hope the prophet of Piedmont Hills has bathed sometime in the last three or four seasons," she said, finishing her coffee and rising to watch his breakneck approach.

"Don't be silly, Charmian," he said, helping her down from the boat to the dock. "Hawaii doesn't have more than two seasons."

As he drew closer, all eyes on the docks turned toward the strange figure. The man was bare chested, his only garment a scrap of pants that hung from his hips and barely reached his thighs. He had the physique of a carved Adonis. His skin had been bronzed in the tropical sun, his golden hair rose and fell like a great tawny mane around his head and shoulders as he sped toward the dock. He drove his little horse right onto the dock, forcing the few townspeople who had drifted over to see who was aboard the yacht to step back to its very edge. In what seemed like a single movement Nature Man then leaped from the horse to the dock and had Jack clutched in his great arms, like steel cables, a second or two before Jack had a chance to realize just how rancid the man's smell actually was—like a junkyard dog on a hot summer day.

"It is me," the sun god cried in Jack's ear. "Your old friend, Ernest Darling!"

"So my letter found you."

"It did. I was here for you yesterday but when I saw how calm the waters were I knew you would be late. And you've brought your mate-woman, as well." He released Jack and turned toward Charmian, who preemptively offered her hand, which he accepted in a most gentleman-like fashion, placing a kiss upon it. Jack smiled as she then discreetly slipped her hand into her pocket. As if the only two people sharing the dock with him were Jack and Charmian, he spoke to them alone. "I've arranged for horses, just as you asked. They're stabled nearby."

Jack indicated the boxes of medical supplies. "We're ready when you are."

"Then wait here and I'll be right back."

The man mounted his tiny steed again and trotted off, proudly, in the direction of town. Jack realized, with some disgust, that he had left his scent behind, tenaciously clinging to his shirt.

"Well, Jack," Hobart said. He had finished passing the last of the medical supplies and had jumped down to the dock. "You always know the most interesting people. What the hell was that?"

"That's a genuine California eccentric," Jack said, taking out one of the cigarettes he had rolled this morning after completing his writing.

"He means San Francisco crazy," Charmian countered. "It's a particular breed."

Jack nodded as he finished lighting the cigarette. "Long before I met Charmian—before I was ever published in anything more than a letters to the editor column, I used to speak to the crowds in City Hall Park, up on my bench, lecturin' about the need for Socialism." He smiled. "Got arrested for it, too. Speakin' in public without a license. Whoever said there was free speech in this country was a dirty liar. That was just a citation, though. Not like the time I got thirty days in Erie Penn for vagrancy without any kind of a jury trial. Damn judge just passed sentence on the lot of us without even I had the chance to defend myself." He found himself as he had in the professor's office, sliding into the rough language of his youth, the rhythm and words coloring his story. It was surprising, but he couldn't seem to stop.

"Everyone in a certain circle knew that if you wanted to see some great free entertainment at lunchtime you had to go to see the Boy Socialist speaking," Charmian said with a smile, taking a cigarette from Jack. "Even as a raw and callow youth, great things were expected from our Jack London."

Jack shrugged, a little embarrassed, and continued, "Ernest Darling was another taking his stand in the park, though instead of promoting the brotherhood of man, he was ministering about the end of days. At that time he was skinny, dirty, thoroughly unhealthful, and dissolute. I had it on good authority that he was the scion of a wealthy family but his own inability to live comfortably amid comfort had driven him out of that world and he had sought his sanity and salvation by living in and with nature. So, of course, I took a liking to him. From far upwind, of course. For all his incompatibilities with society, he was quite sociable and agreeable, generally enthusiastic about his soul-saving mission.

"Then I left to make my fortune in the Klondike and upon my return found that he had vanished from San Francisco. Some time later I heard from my friends in the Piedmont Hills that they were often entertained by the shenanigans of a malodorous vagrant who ministered prophecy from the tops of the trees. Literally. And also he claimed to know me. So I rode my bicycle down to see this for myself and sure enough, there was my friend from City Hall Park. Still skinny, but healthier seeming by far than before. His nature life agreed with him. We spoke for hours about science and religion and how civilization was destroying man. I told him how I dreamed of a return to the land, to find my little Eden. Then, within days, he vanished again and was no more seen nor heard in those parts.

"On our *Snark* voyage we dropped anchor in Tahiti and there, of all places, I found our Nature Man yet again. He came down out of the mountains, strong and healthy, homesteading a jungle spot on the mountainside. Last year I received a letter from him that said he had been driven from that island and had settled here on Molokai, and should I ever need his assistance, to let him know.

"Oh, and Hobart, you should know that he is a terrific boxer, as well. One well-placed blow from him in Tahiti dropped me to my knees and gave me a headache that throbbed for days. You might consider sparring a few rounds with him."

"Next time I feel the urge to be torn apart by a savage I'll be sure and call upon your friend," Hobart said.

Nature Man returned, with five small horses and four mules. They were fastening the crates to the mules when Charmian, standing near Darling's own horse, suddenly shrieked, then burst into laughter. What Jack, and apparently Charmian, had first assumed to be an ugly black saddle upon the back of his dark pony was in fact the gutted carcass of a small black wild boar fastened by a rope around the girth of the horse. The animal had been freshly slaughtered, if the wet bloody streaks on the flanks of Nature Man's mount were any indication.

"How do you like my Mongol saddle?" Ernest Darling asked, as

Charmian convulsed with laughter. "I've been after that boar for months. She's been mucking up my watering hole. Well, I finally got her this morning." He rubbed his hands over the dead boar's bristles with something akin to affection. "Took her with a spear. You ever taken an animal down with a spear, Jack?"

Jack shook his head. "Can't say that I have."

Nature Man seemed a little disappointed, as if one of the many bonds he imagined he had with Jack had just snapped. "Well, you must have had some time catching that shark," he said, seeking to form another. The fishmonger Nakata had sold it to had arrived with a large wheelbarrow and an assistant, and together they were using the winch to lower the fish from the boat to the dock.

"I caught that," Charmian said as she wiped her eyes clear.

"Oh." Nature Man looked from her to Jack, then to her again. "You'll have to tell me about that. I've always wanted to catch a shark."

"Only if you'll tell me why, in heaven's name, you are using this as a saddle. What did you call it? A Mongol saddle?"

"In the days of Genghis Khan, the Mongol cavalry used this technique to tenderize their meat." Still chattering on about the boar, he helped Charmian aboard her horse.

Jack climbed aboard his pony, as irritated again now as he had been earlier in the morning. As he listened to Charmian and Ernest Darling compare notes on their sports, he realized that he needed a fresh kill story to tell. He wanted a new tale of blood. The next time he sat down with Professor Homer he would have to discuss this with him to determine whether Jung would agree with his theory that the sacrifice of an animal, in combat or upon the altar, became a metaphor for personal transformation. The professor would understand his lust to establish his own mortal primacy. He sighed, recalling how Hercules had faced a monster boar, and he kept his eyes focused on the sides of the upward-climbing trail for any evidence of an animal in motion and a chance to meet his own challenge.

The little caravan headed east toward Kamakou Peak, Charmian and Nature Man leading the way. Fortunately all could ride and it looked as if they would make good time. Jack was pleased to see Major could handle his horse well. The boy didn't seem to mind being observed, if he even noticed. Jack found that he had been keeping a watch on him a great deal, studying his mannerisms, his expressions, his eyes. Sometimes he seemed so bright it was almost startling, other times he seemed to be only about as intelligent as a well-trained dog.

By midafternoon, they had crossed the island, reaching the high cliffs of the northern side, and begun the descent down the sheer bluffs along the three-mile trail to the settlement Kalaupapa—their final destination. The going was slow and tedious. The treacherous switchbacks were terrifying to all except Ernest Darling, who kept up a steady stream of songs interrupted only by his wild philosophical musings.

Ahead of him, Hobart turned slightly in his saddle and said through gritted teeth, "So now I know why it is so difficult to get medical supplies to the people here. This trail is damn well impossible to traverse. But I don't understand why someone would live here in the first place."

"Because there is nowhere else for them. No one wants to live near a leper colony."

A weather-change blew across Hobart's face, draining what was left of the color from it. "Lepers!" he cried out, trying to stop his horse, but it knew that cool water and fresh grass lay at the bottom of the trail and it refused his commands.

"I thought you knew," Charmian called back.

"I had no goddamn clue," he cried angrily. "There is no way in hell I'm going near a leper."

"You won't catch anything from them," Jack said. "We've been among them before to no effect."

"Hell," Nature Man added, "Father Damien lived among them for years before he caught it."

"I'm sure he thanked God for his years of protection," Hobart spat out.

"Just use the antiseptic soap Dr. Belko sent along and you'll be fine," Jack answered.

Below them, between the meadow where wild horses roamed and the rocky cove inaccessible to all but the hardiest of small fishing boats, the features of the small colony, safe from the rest of the world behind the great wall of cliffs, grew close enough to distinguish. Wooden cottages and buildings, including Damien's quaint church topped with its white steeple, home to a population of six hundred or so souls, stood proudly on thin ribbons of tree-lined streets. Finally, with much relief, they reached the valley floor and Jack started a joyous race along the trail toward town, Hobart alone refusing to participate or enter the settlement, instead settling down to wait for them near a grove of trees.

"He's going to be surprised that we're spending the night," Jack said to Charmian as he dismounted.

She shrugged in response. "I suppose he'll be fine."

"He's not such a bad guy to have around, after all, is he?"

She shrugged again. "I suppose he's entertaining. And he was a big help with the shark."

People from the colony were approaching, Doctors Goodhue and Hollman leading the way. "I would have helped had you awakened me," Jack said.

"It's okay," she said, throwing a greeting wave toward the physicians. "Hobart was there."

Then they were surrounded by what seemed to be the entire population of the town. The afflicted, mostly Hawaiians, were dressed in simple, clean clothes, their diseased parts covered by fresh white bandages. It was a special occasion when anyone came to visit, but to have a celebrity like Jack among them, a man who promoted their dignity and dispelled misconceptions to the greater world, a friend, made this visit a great day. A luau was called for, Nature Man offering up his fully tenderized Mongol saddle as its centerpiece.

As the local health envoy gave a tour of their latest modest achievements—a new store here, an improved granary there—Jack took Charmian's hand and said, "It's a strange place to find Utopia, isn't it? Each man cares for his brother here. They own nothing but share everything, from the horses to the profits of their fishing labor, which also subsidizes their health care. They are organized and clean, with plumbing provided to each cottage and maintained by a small guild whose reward is provisions. Their common goal of survival has thwarted much of the idle strife that plagues, if I may be so bold, the rest of the world. Most importantly, all seem to be equal in one another's eyes, for the disease has made them so. They live more in the style of the old Hawaiians here without the restrictions of the old *kapu* system. It's as if the common bond of their ailment and the brutal facts of their exile had compelled them to form the perfect model of Socialism."

"I imagine most of them would trade their disease in an instant for a chance to return to the outside world," Charmian replied.

While the boar roasted in the *imu,* a baseball game was hastily organized. By the time it was finished, Jack's side having won in spite of his lackluster performance, the sun was setting and the luau was set to begin. This spelled the end to Hobart's exile, for there were men and women who had seen his pictures, knew of him, and desperately wanted to see him. Charmian disappeared into the outskirts of town for a while, finally coaxing him into an appearance by the light of the bonfire, where there was much applause.

Just as the tension was ebbing from Hobart's body and he seemed to be accepting the acclaim, a cry rang out from amidst the crowd, which fell instantly quiet. The old man staggered out of the night, bandaged and infirm, accusing Hobart of losing something he called "the tear."

"Who is that?" Jack whispered to Dr. Goodhue.

"A recent addition to our town. An old sailor delivered to us just after New Year's. The disease had come upon him quite suddenly and violently. We've had to amputate his fingers and part of his face. Sometimes it happens like that."

As the flames turned his damaged visage orange, the old sailor grew angrier, his badgering more aggressive, and red tears flowed down his ruined face. Hobart was quite stricken—horrified actually—until Dr. Goodhue gestured that enough was enough, and the sailor was led away to the infirmary, which was his home. Hobart protested his ignorance to Jack and Charmian, then fled the luau for the safety of his own camp near the foot of the trail.

"Why don't you go check on him," Jack suggested as the luau began to gather momentum again.

"I'd really rather not," Charmian insisted.

"He's just had a bit of a start. You could reassure him."

"Fine," she snapped. In a moment she had disappeared beyond the light of the fire.

Jack had no idea why the suggestion had irritated her so much. Before he could give it another thought, Ernest Darling had his arm in a powerful grip. The man was in high spirits, having been drinking the locally made gin since soon after their arrival. "London," he said in a conspiratorial whisper. "London, I have something for you that will alter your perceptions of reality." Jack winced; oftentimes a stranger offering him the opportunity to read one of his terrible stories began in a similar fashion.

He found himself again in the familiar iron embrace as Nature Man pulled him down to sit on one of the large logs set around the perimeter of the picnic grounds. Ernest Darling was damp with pungent sweat, droplets clinging to his long hair.

"Having fun, London?"

"I was never much one for dancing."

"No. Always with the words for you."

"I could have done what you did. I could have turned my back on civilization." Would have made more of it than *he* had, was the unspoken thought.

Nature Man roared with delight. "Oh London," he cried, "you could no more have trod my path than that boar could have."

"I certainly could have."

"No, sir. From the time you set up your soapbox in the park it was obvious that you wanted to be a leader of men to a better day more than to be a martyr of today. A part I had no problem playing."

A hundred, a thousand, a million responses all rose up in Jack's throat at once so that not one of them was able to escape, even though his mouth opened in expectation.

"We all knew young Jack London wanted to be rich and famous. You worked at speechifying too damned hard." Then, from some slender shred of garment, he withdrew a small leather bag and offered it for Jack to take.

"What's this?" Jack asked, accepting the bag.

"The seeds of the Hawaiian baby woodrose. Have you ever heard of it?"

Jack shook his head.

"It's the secret gift of the island. The woodrose grows only on the leeward side of the rocks on the windward side of this island and nowhere else in the entire world. Boil these in water for an hour, then strain the liquid into a teapot and drink it."

"Then what?"

"You'll see," he said, his eyes reflecting the bonfire's blaze. "It's like kissing Mother Nature. It reveals the hidden things." With that, and a good-natured solid slap on Jack's thigh, he leaped up like a whirlwind to rejoin the dance.

Jack slipped the pouch into his pocket without a second thought. He wished Charmian would hurry back. He was aching after the activity of the past few days and she knew exactly what medicine to give him. He closed his eyes. Soon, he felt another presence join him on the log. "Hello, Nakata," he said without opening his eyes.

"Hello London-san," came the quiet reply.

They sat in silence together for a long while, listening to the music. Then Jack heard the unmistakable sound of quiet sobbing. He opened his eyes to see tears streaming down his young friend's face. Greatly surprised he asked, "Nakata, what's the matter?"

"London-san, I am carrying a great weight in my heart. I have a suspicion that I should have told you about long ago."

"What is it? You know you can tell me anything."

He shook his head. "This is such a bad thing."

"What is it, Nakata?" He cupped the back of Nakata's head.

"On the night your Wolf House burned, I heard someone leave the house and take a horse from the stable before it happened."

"What are you saying?"

"I think Mrs. London set the house on fire."

"Why do you even think she would do such a thing?" Jack removed his hand.

"Maybe she was afraid that you were building such a big house for sons that she could not give you," he said in a voice that was just a whisper.

"Poor boy," Jack said. "Have you been carrying this with you all this time?"

Nakata nodded.

"Then it's time to put it to rest,' he said with soft authority. "Before it eats you alive. Wolf House is gone forever. Along with any dreams I may have had of filling it." He had grown very tired. After a moment he said, "It gives me some pain that you have harbored secret suspicions about her for so long, though I'm glad you've told me of them, for your own sake. You know she has suffered so much since marrying me, her name dragged through the mud by our friends, let alone strangers. But she's a good woman. Even though she detests Hobart Bosworth, she's gone to help him settle down in spite of the party here, and you know how she enjoys a party. That's the kind of woman she is."

Though the luau showed no sign of ending, he asked Nakata to help him to the small cottage Dr. Goodhue had prepared for them. Before collapsing into bed, he rummaged through the medicine sack, taking a few of the pills he recognized, hoping they were the ones that Charmian would have had him take. Then he fell asleep, awakened only once during the darkest period of night to find that Charmian still hadn't returned, though she was slumbering soundly by his side when the town's roosters heralded the start of their last day on Molokai.

CHAPTER TWENTY-TWO

"**D**ID YOU SEE THE elephant?" Leialoha asked him.

The young native islander wore a floral print sarong, draped from one shoulder, her other bare, skin as smooth and brown as oiled teak, her thick hair flowing over it like a black glacier. The simple engineering marvel of the perfect pinioning of her arm musculature to the carved definition of her collarbone swooping down to the rise of her breast beneath the green fabric was so fascinating to him, he found he had lost his breath when he tried to answer. "No," he managed to choke out, though Jack was pretty sure he had affected a measure of casualness. His heart was still racing, however, and he seemed to have no way to slow that down or disguise it from her. So far, she hadn't seemed to have noticed. Maybe she was used to having this effect on all men. Maybe she didn't realize the effect at all. "Tell me about it," he said quietly.

As she described the arrival and parade of the Honolulu Zoo's newest addition, how it had raced awkwardly down the gangplank at the pier, the way it had waved its trunk in greeting to those along the streets leading to the zoo, Jack finally drew his eyes away from her to scan the party for Charmian. He caught sight of her near the bar, speaking to Harry Strange, the man for whom the Parkers were throwing this farewell cocktail party at their seaside estate nestled into the rise of Diamond Head, the ancient volcano. The gathering took place in the style of the East Coast and could in no way but for the tropical locale be mistaken for a Hawaiian luau. First of all the servings of food were delicate, measured, and finite and only available when passed by waiters, not from a groaning table. Then there were the drinks, measured in jiggers and served over crushed ice.

Their good friend, and the guest of honor, had resigned his position at the Honolulu Gas Company in order to enlist in the Royal Navy. In all other respects a proper and reserved representative of his class and race, the young British expatriate had been infused with the ridiculous spirit of patriotism and answered the call to war. Jack, at Harry's mother's urging (though it hadn't taken much of that), had tried to dissuade the young man from his mission, describing in detail the gore, the horror, the privation, men stripped of humanity in ways the workhouse or prison never could do. Strange was unmoved. But Jack would try again tonight. As soon as he finished talking with this fascinating woman sitting on a stone wall as the stars rose over the ocean.

"Did you have time to visit the wolves?"

"No," she replied, her eyes lighting with interest.

"They have a marvelous pair of adult Great Plains wolves, a male and a female, and several cubs."

"You must love that."

"I've only had the chance to see them once since I've been back. I was struck by the serenity of the female. She was remarkably poised even as her litter swarmed around her. In fact, the she-wolf was so calm that she gave the impression she was a native Hawaiian."

Leialoha smiled. "You should give a lecture there sometime. I know many people would love to hear the great Jack London discussing wolves."

"Aw, I don't know as much as I make out," he said, a little embarrassed. "I'm no expert. I just watched 'em close up when I was in the Yukon and saw that they had some traits in common with the men there."

She shrugged and looked away, as if seeking a face in the crowd.

"I see your parents are here," he said, quickly. Mr. Kaai was well known in Honolulu as a practical politician—a Hawaiian who sought to reconcile his people with the reality of the American annexation.

She nodded.

"Your father must be very proud to have a daughter like you. My own daughters are much younger than you and give me nothing but heartache, though I am proud of how well they have turned out."

"Why the heartache, then?" she asked.

"They have taken their mother's side against me. They won't return my letters except to ask for money. I am seen as the great villain in their lives."

"Are you?"

He looked around the party again. "I suppose. Though I think a son would understand what I've done more than daughters, anyway."

"Which is what?"

"Charted my own course. Which is more than most men have done. That is what I would teach my own boy. How to walk a path beyond the ways trod by others."

"I think you would make a fine father to a son."

"I've always thought so, too. But it's not to be."

"Well, your father must have taught you the same lessons well and must be very proud of you."

He shrugged. "My father has never acknowledged my existence."

"What do you mean?"

"I mean, I am a bastard son. My father's name was Chaney. And he was a celebrated touring professor of astrology, if you can believe that such a position existed forty years ago. He drifted from one lecture hall to another, instructing people in the Universal Truths of Brotherhood, Righteousness, and Equality. Evidently he also took some time to instruct my mother in the truth of Free Love. The scandal of her pregnancy and his abandonment of her actually made the papers, for he was something of a celebrity," he said and hated himself for the note of vanity that crept into his voice.

He watched the gentle waves lapping the Waikiki shore far below. "Soon after my stepfather died, the man who adopted me and gave me the name London, I wrote Chaney a letter explaining that I was his son and would like to meet him."

"Did you?"

"I received a letter informing me that I must be mistaken, that he had no recollection of my mother and therefore could not be my father and that I should resist any further temptations to correspond with him. And that's what I did. Hell, I didn't even send flowers to his funeral."

"Then it was your stepfather who raised you to be the man you are."

Her eyes were dark and full of intent. He wondered why he hadn't noticed before how well-educated she had become. It was only happenstance that he had started a conversation with her this evening, and now he found himself fully entranced and engaged. Furthermore, when she touched his arm, as she had done to emphasize her comment a moment before, he felt a surging rush of power to his loins such as he hadn't felt in years. The feeling was invigorating. Like surfing, only more charged.

"He did," Jack admitted. He thought of their days spent together in the hills and fields hunting ducks and deer, of horse-drawn wagon trips to town on market day to sell their farm's small harvest, of the man's calming influence upon their mother when her unreasonable emotions got the better of her, as they so often did, and the old man's gentle, befuddled, uneducated presence in his life. "John London was a good man," he said, offering no better way to describe his stepfather.

"He must have been proud of you."

"He died while I was still nothing but a tramp."

"A good father knows that accomplishments are not always the measure of a man."

A warm wind whispered through the palms, making the flames of the torches dance. At the same time it carried a lock of hair across her forehead. Before realizing his action, his hand was reaching toward it to place it back in its ideal spot, though at the same time he admired its new position. She watched his fingers approach but made no motion to stop him. Suddenly, he heard his name called and quickly dropped his hand, as if he had been discovered in the middle of something untoward.

"London," Harry Strange again called his name, even while approaching him. Charmian walked by his side, helping Strange's mother, well into her seventies, navigate the coral stone path set into the lawn.

Jack reached for one of his cigarettes, offering one to Leialoha, who demurred politely. Of course she didn't smoke. Charmian plucked the spare cigarette from his fingers. Strange waved a newspaper under his nose.

"How could you?" he demanded.

"What exactly?"

"You've resigned from the Socialist Party? It's in the all newspapers." Strange's tone became good-natured.

"It is?" He took the paper and unfolded it, seeing an old photograph of himself printed alongside the open letter he had recently written announcing his resignation. "Well, look at that," he said to Charmian. "The front page. So there are still some pockets of civilization where I seem to matter."

"Why did you do it?" Strange asked, as Charmian brought a chair for Mother Strange.

"For you," Jack replied.

"Me?" the man cried with a startled laugh. "But you've been calling for the States to enter the war against the 'Great Beast of Europe,' as you yourself call Germany."

"Sure, I've called for Revolution. Social Revolution. With arms if necessary. Right now this is a war of the Oligarchs. This is capitalism under another name. It is being fought to preserve what already exists, not to create something new. The soldier finds a little more pride in his station and endeavor than the working man, but he's no less exploited and even more disposable. If only Socialism had stayed true to its intent then they would join this war and seize its aims and create a new world for all upon its conclusion. But they have no belly for a fight anymore. The structure of the old world is about to be burned away and all that will replace it will be more of the same unless men stand shoulder to shoulder and fight not for the Oligarchs, but for a better world. This is the moment, and my comrades have laid down their arms at the moment they should be shouldering them. So I'm done with them. And so should you be."

"But what is Jack London without Socialism?" Strange countered.

"Better to ask what is Socialism without Jack London," Charmian said.

"Exactly," Jack added. "This war would end in a week if those on both sides of the conflict who believed in Socialism as they claim to halted the means of the war's production. Not the soldiers, but those toiling in the foundries and the munitions factories. If they stood together, then the world would change more rapidly and neatly than any war could effect. So if you want to stop the war, my friend, stop your gas refineries. Others will follow your lead."

"Foolishness, Jack. Sheer foolishness."

"I suppose we shall never know." He flicked his cigarette over the edge toward the water somewhere in the black abyss below. "Unless tomorrow we awake to a world in which my words have finally taken root in the hearts and minds of men who can make a difference. Otherwise, what good am I really, as a writer?"

"While I appreciate the gesture on my behalf, more than you will ever know," Strange said, after a moment, "I still believe my place is at the battlements. There I can do the most good for my country."

"The Oligarchs."

"Those who refuse to place their necks under the boot of the Kaiser."

"Merely the same Oligarchs speaking a different tongue. For God's sakes, Strange, your King George and his enemy, the German Emperor Wilhelm, are first cousins! This is all a family dispute and the whole world must pay for it? Why won't you see that this war is merely a conspiracy between them to raise manufacturing and profits for each while thinning out an unruly population of those who might call for their overthrow? Please, Strange, I beg you, in your mother's name, and in the name of all that's best in the world that you yourself represent, don't go."

The young Englishman drew himself to his full height, substantially greater than Jack's. The invocation of his mother had touched a nerve. "I must do what my honor compels me to," he said gravely, and the great gray lady by his side stifled a sob with the handkerchief Charmian had loaned her.

Jack rose and embraced the young man, surprising him. "If you're going to be so damned British about it all," he whispered in the fellow's ear. "You come back home safe, you hear me?"

"You keep trying to find a way to end war, and I'll be certain to," his friend replied.

"I'll give it my level best." He released Strange and took a step back.

"Come on, Jack," Charmian said. "Why don't we go find some refreshments." She took his hand and led him toward the bar. "Perhaps the fair Hawaiian maiden will do more to persuade him to stay than your political soapboxing."

"Why would you say that?" he asked. He wanted to look back but felt as if the gesture might betray his newfound emotions.

"I suppose it's cruel to Mano even to suggest such a liaison, though," she continued, apparently oblivious to the sense of anxiety that he struggled to quell.

"Mano?"

"Wasn't it you who told me they were betrothed to each other? I mean, I'm certain I've heard that somewhere. As soon as he secures a position for himself beyond that of beach boy, I am sure that her father will give permission for them to marry."

"I hadn't heard."

"Oh, it's practically a done deal. Two scotches, please," she said to the bartender.

"Well, Strange is a married man. I don't see why he'd be interested."

"Mm-hmm," she said, eyeing him warily before reaching to take the drinks and handing him one. "How are you feeling?"

"Not well," he said, passing a hand through his hair. "The worms were at my brain again last night."

"Maybe you should take your medicine. I saw that you hadn't been taking it."

"I'm tired of taking it. I've been thinking that maybe I've grown too dependent on the stuff. Maybe if I don't take it, I'll feel like my old self again."

"If you say so," she said, sipping her drink, tossing a wave to someone behind him, then someone else. Her eyes finally fell upon him again. "You do what you like, Jack."

"Are you mad at me?"

She shook her head. "Not at all, lover. Just stating a fact."

He took her hand and together they made a tour of the party, stopping to speak with every little group, the ache in his head and down his back growing with each step, though he only sipped at the drink clutched in his hand. After a while Charmian was commanded by numerous acquaintances to grace them with her piano skills and she happily obliged, playing and singing with wild abandon that had the assembly swaying joyfully.

He slipped outside. The lawn was empty except for the help who were cleaning up. Those who hadn't already left had gone inside for the music. He made his way around to the side of the house, nearest the retaining wall, where he found several shrubs growing around a twisted scrub pine whose branches shielded him from the lights of the house. The golden flowers of the shrubs were trimmed with deep indigo. There his eyes could adjust and he could see the phosphorous of the ocean foam far below. He heard the soft crunch of a foot stepping lightly upon the blanket of pine needles.

"I thought you'd left," he said.

"I haven't," she replied. "I came to the lakana blossoms," she said, indicating the shrubs behind him. "They are my favorite flower in all the world. Jack Lakana. That shall be my secret name for you. I'll think of you whenever I see them."

He took a step on the edge of the wall, rocking back and forth a little. He heard her sharp intake of breath, but she made no move to stop him. Why should she?

"I'm still standing on Gjöll," he said, more to himself than to her. "Only this time I don't want to jump. The jump will kill me and all will be swallowed in the blackness."

He heard a rustle, felt her hand slip into his. "Then why should you jump?"

He listened to the waves crashing; the lift of the wind made him feel as if he were actually flying. "I don't know," he said and stepped down into her arms. Her lips found his, the softest he had ever kissed since Mamie. No, softer even than hers. The softest of all. The kiss fell apart only when he began to smile. Her forehead fell against his cheek and he knew she was smiling as well.

He still felt as if he were flying.

CHAPTER TWENTY-THREE

"It would suit your personal mythology to be present at the Twilight of the Gods, wouldn't it, Mr. London? That all the world would end with your apocalyptic finale? Is it that hard for you to imagine the world without you in it? The world will go on without you, Mr. London, indeed it will, as it will go on without me or any of us. So maybe what you should concentrate on is a way to unchain yourself from the rock." The professor, though maintaining an outward appearance of objectivity, still seemed to be glaring at him.

"You're saying I'm the Fenris Wolf?"

"I'm saying you've referred to yourself in symbolic terms and maybe that symbolism is the key to your relief. You say you're trapped on Gjöll. That is the station of the great wolf, isn't it? How would a wolf set itself free of that chain?"

"It would chew its own leg off." As if to emphasize his own point, Jack slipped his loafers off. His feet were aching a little after his walk to the professor's office this morning.

"There could be a less violent way."

"It could prove its loyalty to its captor."

"It would still be enslaved."

"It could transform."

"Into what?"

"It's a mythical beast? Anything it wants to, I suppose."

"I'll tell you this. What I've learned about mythology is that a careful reading of it shows that all of mythology is rooted in the concept of transformation. Of moving from one thing to another, from one state to another, from one plane of existence to another. The Twilight of the Gods is not the end of the world nor the end of man, it is the transformation of the myth-learner into the myth-teller. I think your anger toward the world is actually your anger toward yourself, over your inability to choose which transformation you want to undertake. Do you want to stay the wolf, full of wolf-rage and snarling at the world? Or do you want to transform into Kamehameha the bloodthirsty king? Or—"

"I am not a bloodthirsty man," Jack interrupted him. "I never meant to give you that impression."

"Then why are you so focused on the spilling of blood in the stories you've told me—be it shark or boar or your own?"

"I'm not."

"Bloodletting is a ritual of transformation, are you aware of that, Mr. London?"

He had no answer for the professor. Except for the sound of the rain dripping from the eaves outside the open windows, the room was silent.

"The wolf-rage is your libido, your own creative energy, Mr. London, and it is crying out for expression. How will you answer its call? After all these years, and all those words you've spilled across the pages, how will you satisfy its lust now that the words no longer answer?"

"The words always answer, Professor Homer. Always. They flow like the ink from my never-ending pen. Like water from a spigot."

"Then look to them, Mr. London. If your words once transformed you into Martin Eden, then look to them to transform you into something else yet again. Tell me, have you been writing your sexual memoir?"

Jack thought about the work he had done just that morning, describing the lack of passion in his first marriage. Of his appetites, and her passive reluctance. He'd had to tread the delicate line of not placing blame upon her but upon the conservative nature of her entire class. He had been unable to convince her of the joys of the physical acts. In the end, there was always only her shame, which brought him pain. "Yes."

"Will you be writing about Miss Kaai?"

"Ah, I see your game. Your bourgeois sensibilities are offended by the kiss I shared with Leialoha. I should have known better than to have confided that to you man to man. Or to think that a minister's son would understand. I thought an alienist wasn't supposed to judge his patient."

"I'm not an alienist, I'm a mythology professor. And you're not my patient."

"Then maybe you're asking about Leialoha because you're jealous."

The professor looked down at his hands. Jack could see that he was blushing.

"Don't wolves mate for life, Mr. London?" the professor said, looking up suddenly.

"I didn't marry a wolf," Jack said. In the next instant the worms stabbed at his brain. He clapped his hands to his eyes and cried out in agony.

"Mr. London!" He dimly heard the shock in the professor's voice.

Jack clutched the arm of the chair, trying to regain his composure.

"Let me call for one of my students to drive you home."

Jack took several deep breaths to fight the pain back, then waved off the professor's suggestion. "I can walk." He noticed that the professor's gaze had fallen toward his feet, and his face was crossed with concern. Jack had never replaced his shoes, and his feet had swollen so that his silk socks looked like the thin casing over sausage. "Some whiskey would suit, Professor," he said, his voice thin with the pain.

The professor quickly poured a glass for him and placed it in his trembling hands. Jack raised the crystal to his lips and sent John Barleycorn down into his gullet to join the fight. The explosion of whiskey fire in his belly drew the attention away from the swirling in his brain. He felt as if every part of his body was clenched, and bound, in a tightness that would never unwind. But he was able to breathe again, and think.

"I used to be so healthy," he said, after a moment. "I don't understand why this is happening to me. I used to be the strongest and the fastest of my all companions. My stomach used to digest scrap iron. I have lived a healthy life of sport and activity in the great outdoors. I gave up hard labor to escape this crumbling, collapsing fate. The workingman's fate. And still it has me." He pounded the arm of the chair. "I don't understand. I don't understand!" His hands were still trembling as he fought back against another wave of pain behind his eyes. The professor poured another drink and he choked it down, stifling a gasping sob. With the hand that had pounded the chair he now gripped the curve of the arm with a strength that turned the knuckles white and made deep indentations in the leather. In moments, the pain began to ebb, as it always did. He looked down at his feet. The swelling seemed to be subsiding somewhat. He took another deep breath. "I'm okay," he said at last.

The professor stood nervously by a foot-high statue bearing a fiendish expression, which rested on a small end table. Jack had noticed it before but never mentioned it. "What is that?" he asked now, wishing to direct the professor from his anxiety.

"This?" The professor ran his hand over the carving. "This is a Tiki statue. It was carved specially for me by a craftsman at the Dole pineapple plantation. He says it is the home of a spirit."

"Which one?"

"Does it matter?"

"I suppose not."

"Hawaiians say that Tiki was the original man, carved by the gods."

"You know, my education, my training in reason and logic, has not completely rid me of my mother's superstitions, I'm afraid," Jack said with a feeble laugh. "When a spell comes upon me like that I feel the cold hand of Plume clutching at me. I suppose it's because medical science has been unable to explain it, let alone cure me of it, that my mind takes a turn toward supernatural causes."

"Like a family curse."

"Exactly. I've told you how my mother was a spiritualist, right?"

"Yes."

"Have you ever attended a séance?"

"No."

"They were my mother's bread and butter. From the time I was six I used to hide under the table in our darkened parlor and provide the knocks and calls of the spirits of the dead in answer to her summonings. Do you understand? I was the voice of the dead. There were times when the presence of Plume was as real to me in that room as my own mother, even though I knew at that young age how impossible that was."

"Was that frightening to you?"

"Terrifying. Had I wanted to become a successor to Poe, it would have been easy." He gave a little laugh. "I feel like I've been dragged across the Yukon." He wiggled his toes, which no longer felt so engorged. He told the professor about how Plume had cursed him.

"You should tell my wife about your experiences sometime. She's fascinated by the spiritualist movement. But then again, she was raised Lutheran."

Jack smiled as the professor sat across from him in the other club chair. "You're happily married I take it?"

"I am."

"And you've always been faithful? You don't have to answer that if you don't want to. I'm sorry."

"No. You've been completely candid with me. I can only hope to be as honest with you. The answer is yes. I've been completely faithful throughout our marriage, and I hope she's been as well."

Jack nodded, thoughtfully. "I haven't been."

"I gathered as much."

"Charmian hasn't either."

"I'm sorry to hear that."

Jack lit a cigarette while the professor loaded and lit his pipe. "We were true to each other for the longest time. From the day we were married, through the earthquake, and the voyage of the *Snark,* and even after I first got sick in Australia. It was the happiest I have ever been, the happiest a woman has ever made me. But after Joy died, when she couldn't have children, she was so angry—at me. At the whole world. She couldn't be touched. She couldn't be soothed."

"So you looked elsewhere."

"In the end I had to."

"It was her fault."

"Oh, I wouldn't say that. That's not fair. I should say, too, by the way, that any infidelities I've undertaken have only been of an emotional sort, not physical, as my ailments have left me somewhat less . . ." He felt the sudden warmth of tears on his cheeks. "Less than the man I once was in the most important ways." He wiped the tears away and placed his hands over his face. Shame and exhaustion swept through him. "Even when she finally wanted me to touch her, I couldn't. You can imagine my anger, my howling goddamned rage, when I found her asleep in a haystack in the arms of one of my own cowhands early one morning while I was riding my Beauty Ranch. Of course, she'd had no choice. I knew that. She'd had to look elsewhere in the end. It was my fault. I can still smell his field stench on her.

"Jealousy," he continued, "is more powerful than love, for it is the twisted perversion of love itself forged over a fire of anger."

"What did you do?"

"You want me to tell you that I confronted him like the leader of a wolf pack? That I tore at his throat and snapped at his haunches as I chased him from my land? I wish I could tell you that. I left them sleeping. Later I had my sister fire the man."

"And what of your jealousy?"

He shrugged. "Like so many other things in my life I suppose it went up in flames with my Wolf House. So many of my deepest emotions, hurts, seem to have gone up with the smoke that night. After that night, when I had lost so much, I found what she had done to me was forgivable."

"And has she forgiven you?"

"Of course she has." He rose wearily, tentatively. "She's my Mate-Woman." As he drew himself up, a new sensation flooded through him and he turned to the doctor with a laugh. "They're gone."

"What are?"

"The maggots in my brain. They're gone. The pain is lifted. Dear God, Professor. I swear it's a miracle." He shook his head forcefully from side to side and experienced no pain. "See what you have done!"

"I've done nothing."

"You've been reading Jung again, haven't you? Look at me, you've cured me."

"I've done nothing, but I am glad you're feeling better."

Jack slipped his shoes back on; they slid over his socks easily.

"Shall I have one of my students take you home?"

"No. I think I shall walk after all."

He studied the Tiki statue for a long moment before turning toward the door. With his hand upon the doorknob he paused, and without looking at the professor he said, "When we lost our baby daughter, we nearly lost everything. Most importantly, each other. We're still trying to find our way back."

"Do the two of you ever speak of her?" the professor asked, his strange blue eyes offering an abundance of empathy.

"We don't even mention her name." Jack opened the door and glared at the rain as if it were a personal affront. Fortunately his umbrella still leaned against the trim white fence of the patio. "On the day she died, in my grief I wandered into a tavern for a drink to steady my nerves, where two of my most avid readers and stated admirers had been following my baby girl's travails in the newspaper, which had been publishing hourly updates. Upon seeing me, they took it upon themselves to explain how bad a father I was to abandon my wife in her hour of need. That they were probably right may explain why I submitted to the worst beating of my life. So Charmian and I were both in the hospital on the day of her funeral."

He wiped the tears away from his eyes. "Would that we had never called her Joy," he whispered, never sure after that whether or not the professor had heard him at all because he was closing the door as he said it.

CHAPTER TWENTY-FOUR

ACCORDING TO REPORTS FROM Duke's beach boys, by early May the large waves were receding from the North Shore and were due in Waikiki any day. Already the swells were much larger than they had been only the week before, and every day Duke and his boys paddled eagerly over the water, hunting for the next great ride. While they waited, they entertained both the beachgoers and themselves, not to mention padded their wallets, by letting swimmers ride tandem on their boards for a dollar.

Jack, who had not been feeling confident enough to join them, as if his current wellness were a fragile illusion, had taken to watching them from the long stone jetty near their cottage. On this particular morning, Nakata joined him with some fishing gear. Major followed at his heels like an obedient dog, the boy having taken a strong liking to the Asian.

The sun was strong and warm. The tourist season had begun and the sand dunes were full of pale, rich visitors from all over America, eagerly being tended to by Hawaii's genial service class. A figure on a surfboard waved to him. He asked Nakata for the field glasses and used them to bring Charmian into focus. She sat upon her board, the lone woman among a line of surf-sliding men, waiting for her turn to come. Her brown hair was slick with water, her smile was broad in her tanned, relaxed face.

The night before had been an interesting experience. At the insistence of some Russian aristocrats on an extended tour of the islands in order to avoid the troubles back in the Motherland, he and Charmian had attended an extravagant dinner at the Mauna Hotel, Jack London always having a strong base of appreciative readers in Russia. Jack had been thrilled to discover that one of the guests was the legendary British novelist Sir H. Rider Haggard, author of *King Solomon's Mines* and *She,* on the last days of his own tropical holiday. While the vodka had flowed and glasses broke and loyalties were pledged, the two writers had huddled over the cold beet soup and talked about writing, publishing, but most of all readers, until long after the last drunken Russian had slipped off into the night. Even Charmian had known better than to try to outlast Jack, bidding both of them good night not long before midnight. Other than a brief meeting with Samuel Clemens once on his way to lecture at Yale years before, Jack hadn't met many other authors of his stature, not that there were many to begin with. Kipling and Conrad he had corresponded with infrequently. To meet the writer whose tales of adventure, not to mention success, had inspired them all was a thrill beyond measure.

From the window of the hotel Jack had been able to point out all that had changed in Waikiki over the past nine years from the pristine shore he had first seen. Jack described the fields and marshes, crossed with little springs and creeks in which the natives found fish. He showed how once the tree line ran right down to where a row of lampposts, which seemed far older than a mere decade, now ran along a paved road. He was proudly still able to point out to Haggard the very site upon the shore where his countryman, Robert Louis Stevenson, had erected a small camp for a long period of time while he composed part of *In the South Seas* a generation ago.

Sir Harry, something of an amateur anthropologist, had informed Jack of the old Hawaiian rite of passage he had recently learned of during his travels, in which the boy's father and relatives, and a *kahuna* or shaman, would take the boy out in a canoe far beyond the surf line and throw him into the water, then paddle back to shore. If the boy made it back to the beach he was welcomed into the tribe as a man.

This morning, Jack reflected on this trial by water as he watched the surfers bobbing up and down. He couldn't help but wonder whether the great Kamehameha himself had been subjected to such a ritual.

The tide was low and their lures could nearly reach the edge of the coral reef, which had offered a good place to find fish that spring. Nakata was singing a refrain from the song "Red Wing," a folk song with a mandolin accompaniment that they had both grown attached to, as it had been the only recording to survive a storm aboard the *Snark,* and it had been played endlessly. Nakata must have been in a nostalgic mood to have recalled it on this morning. Jack joined him in singing the lyrics:

> *There once lived an Indian maid, / a shy little prairie*
> *maid. / Who sang a lay, / a love song gay, / As on the*
> *plain / she'd while away the day. / . . . While Red*
> *Wing's weeping her heart away.*

After a while Jack set down his rod and walked to the end of the jetty. He lit a cigarette and watched the endlessly fascinating surface of the rolling ocean. Somewhere on the other side of that was California. After flicking the stub into the sea he returned to Nakata's side. "I think I'm ready to go home."

Nakata nodded and obligingly began to reel in.

"Oh, I didn't mean back to the cottage," Jack said. "I meant that I want to go home. I'm ready to go back to the land of Glen Ellen—back to the Beauty Ranch in the Valley of the Moon."

Nakata stopped reeling. "I thought you were going to stay here?"

Jack shrugged. "As I was staring at the changing surface of the ocean, I realized that what I was missing was a certain constancy. The land changes slowly, if at all, and the view is dependable. I need a less tumultuous view to set my eyes upon, I think."

"When?"

"I'm not sure. After the fourth, I expect. I want to finish my memoir. So, I don't know for sure. We can't just pick up and leave—there are good-byes to be made, tickets to be purchased, a great many people to visit with. It could take us weeks and weeks."

Nakata's chin fell to his chest and he looked as if he might cry. "Dear friend!" Jack asked, "What is wrong?"

"London-san," Nakata answered, his voice cracking, "I was hoping you would stay in Hawaii. Then we could always be close."

"What are you saying, son?"

"I shall not be returning with you to America," he said.

"You're staying?"

He nodded.

"You're leaving us?"

He nodded again. "I have decided to stay here with my family. They want me to study to become a dentist. They feel it is time for me to end my adventures."

"And how do you feel?"

"I feel it is time for me to learn a trade. Maybe start a family of my own once I have established my practice."

Jack's own eyes filled with tears. "I never thought this day would ever come," he said with a rueful laugh. He'd watched this boy grow to manhood over the past nine years. Nakata had been a constant presence, every day, for nearly a decade now. Jack put his hands on Nakata's arms. "I've just realized," he said, "at this very moment, that you are not my servant anymore, you are my best friend."

"Thank you, London-san."

"And you'll make the best dentist Hawaii has ever seen. If only you'd decided to become one a few years earlier, you might have saved my teeth."

Together they resumed fishing and later all agreed that it was a spectacular morning for it. It turned into one of those very pleasant excursions, reminiscent of a carefree boyhood, that began with song and jokes, wandered into contemplation, and ended up in the stillness of camaraderie where the catching of a fish was celebrated by a nod and a smile, or a gentle clap on the back.

Only the increasing gains made by the ever more aggressive waves upon their dry spot finally drove them back to the safety of Beach Walk. "Look at that one," Jack laughed, as the water crashed mightily upon the spot where they had been fishing only moments ago. "We would have been soaked. Or washed away. There must be some storm churning out there."

"The swimmers are coming in," Nakata said.

"Do you see Charmian?" Jack asked. "Ah, there she is. On her way with the others." Although the great body of surfers, rafters, swimmers, and bathers was making its way to shore in a uniformity that reminded him of a flock of birds, one figure alone had cut free from them. "It looks like Duke is in no hurry."

The Hawaiian was paddling away from the beach, each stroke long and powerful, indicated by his speed against the current. He moved almost directly to the west, out to sea, to where the big waves were breaking. When he was just a tiny figure he pulled himself to a sitting position and faced the open ocean. Waiting.

"He's going to catch one of those monsters. Nakata!"

"Yes, London-san?"

"My field glasses, please! Hurry."

Duke had already passed on several swells before Jack had the glasses in his hand. He brought them to his eyes and adjusted the focus. The brown wood of the wet board matched the brown skin of its rider so perfectly that they appeared carved together out of the same miraculous and buoyant substance.

"My God," he heard himself whisper and he looked beyond the Hawaiian to see what had caused him to suddenly lie down on his board. Rapidly approaching the tiny figure was a long swell of magnificent proportions. It was a different beast than its cousins on the North Shore— large, yes, though not bearing the same threat of extreme violence. Still, it was more massive than anything he would care to ride.

He brought his eyes back to focus on the surfer. Duke was paddling and in the next instant the wave had lifted him high into the air. He popped up to his feet and the showboating surfer of earlier in the day was gone. In its place was the supreme athlete of the sport. The renowned Olympian. Through the field glasses Jack could see the man's expression of relaxed concentration, lips pulled back to reveal a satisfied grin. Foam from the curl of the wave fell over his shoulders. It all looked so fluid and smooth yet he knew how the man's board was vibrating under his feet.

"He's cutting to the right," he exclaimed to Nakata, though of course the man could see it almost as well as he could. The entire crowd on Waikiki and Beach Walk could see what was happening. Instead of riding toward shore, the surfer had altered his course, running parallel with the face of the rising water, letting a tube of green form behind him and crash just behind his board. The wave kept on coming and Duke kept on riding, a loose-limbed man standing on a runaway toboggan riding down the icy green slope of a glacier.

"He's been on there a full minute," he heard an onlooker shout and the word spread down the beach. Fully half the distance of Waikiki Bay had been traversed by now and it was apparent to all the spectators that they were witnessing an event that would never occur again. They had gone from cheers to silence to a raucous cry far beyond the definition of cheering. The cry of "A minute thirty!" rose above the din. At long last the wave began to founder, and the man far in the distance angled his craft into shore near the Surf Club. The people began a great stampede to greet him.

"At least a mile," Jack breathed to himself with vast pride for the accomplishment of his friend. "My God, I'm glad I was alive to see it."

He felt a hand slip around his waist and turned to find Charmian, wet and sun dazzled, at his side.

"Did you see that?" he asked her. "That was the birth of a legend. As long as there's a Hawaii, there'll be someone to tell that story."

"I'll never forget it." She was as delighted as he.

"God damn, but I'd love to be down there right now."

"I know Mate-Man. But your ankles are swollen again."

"But I've been taking my medicine."

"And see how much better you're doing. Why not come back to the cottage? Duke and the beach boys will be by soon enough. I think the celebration is only beginning."

"All right. Nakata can make up some punch."

"And ice some beers."

"Good idea."

Arm in arm they walked toward the cottage, even as the crowd surged past them, Nakata and Major forging quickly ahead.

"It was nice to see you out this morning," she said. "You've been so stealthy lately."

"What do you mean?"

"Oh, nothing." They came to the gate of their little home. "It's just that if you're not writing your mornings away on the first book you've never let me type for you then you're off on your little secret missions to God knows where."

They reached the lanai and he took a seat on the top step, sighing. He knew it was a matter of time before her curiosity got the better of her. "It's not a secret mission."

She leaned against the support column. "I've been wondering where you go. Should I be suspicious?"

"Not in the least. If you must know I've been exploring the psychology of my own unconscious mind."

"How on earth have you been doing that?"

"You remember Professor Homer, from the New Year's party? A couple of mornings a week we sit down together and he tells me tales of mythology."

"Oh."

"And I share tales of my life," he said casually.

"I beg your pardon?" she said sharply.

"Tales of mythology," he repeated.

"I heard that part," she said. "What about your life are you discussing with this professor?"

"Different things. Untold tales."

"About us?"

"It does come up from time to time."

"You're talking about our life with a complete stranger? You're telling him about me?"

"No, Charmian," he said, trying to fill his voice with reason, "I'm talking to him about me."

"I don't know why you're so intent on humiliating me in front of other people," she snapped, pushing past him into the house. "The impression you must have given him of me."

"I try to be as truthful as I can."

"Really, Jack." She turned, glaring at him from the doorway. "Why don't you try that with me. Why can't you?" She slammed the door.

He rubbed his forehead. Raindrops were plopping down around him. The storm had blown in before he had even had a chance to check the barometer. He was so tired of the unpredictable nature of things. He wanted to go home so badly, where at least the climate was predictable. At least she hadn't asked about his memoir.

It was only at that moment that Jack realized that Nakata's melody, "Red Wing," still hung in the air over the cottage. He turned his head to the left and saw that it was the boy, Major, sitting in the bay window, unaware that Jack was observing him as he watched the rain fall, quietly murmuring its sad refrain over and over again to himself:

While Red Wing's weeping her heart away.

CHAPTER TWENTY-FIVE

THE NIGHT WAS THICK with humidity and the perspiration had soaked through his shirt. His state of dampness, and the letter he had received earlier that day from his sister Eliza describing the sorry affairs of the Beauty Ranch, came so close to fully occupying his mental faculties that the startlingly beautiful fair woman who opened Hobart's door at the Hau Tree Hotel caught Jack completely off guard. Her blond hair was loose around her face and her full cheeks were flush with pink.

"Hello," he managed. Then, "I'm Jack London?"

"Of course you are," the woman said. She stared at him as if he were a museum piece. Jack generally stood eye to eye with most women. This one he looked up to.

"We've met before," she said. "At Benjamin Dillingham's birthday party?"

"Ah," he said. After a long moment in which sweat trickled down the back of his neck, he was able to add, "Of course."

"Alice Holdings?"

"That's right. You are," he said.

She blinked her blue eyes several times, as if to clear them. "I'm sorry. I'm in your way."

"Not at all."

Nevertheless, once she stepped aside he was able to enter the suite's sitting room. At the same time Hobart emerged from another room, apparently the bedroom. His shirt was loose and untucked and his feet were bare.

"London!" he called out. "What a pleasant surprise."

"I thought we had an appointment," Jack replied, inadvertently looking at the young woman, catching her in the act of twisting her wedding ring. This caused her to blush all over again.

"I was just leaving," she said, moving to collect some papers from the scraps strewn around the suite. The ones she snatched up she tucked into a binder bearing the gold stamp of the OR&L Railroad.

"Alice will be playing a key role in our production of *Before Adam*."

"Your production. What part will you be playing?" he asked the young woman.

"The narrator," she said.

"I didn't know there was one."

"Well, there has to be one. Monkeys can't speak," said Hobart.

"Not monkeys. Primitive man."

"Regardless. How can they carry the burden of your great ideas in dialogue that consists of grunts and pantomime? No. I decided a narrator was absolutely essential. And why not a woman to boot?" Hobart's voice lacked its usual smooth note, and the grand gestures, usually reflective of his theatrical nature, now only seemed to Jack to indicate some inner anxious condition. He felt his powers of perceiving the nature of character in others had grown through his discussions of his own personality with Professor Homer. Soon he would write a book to persuade everyone to seek the talking cure.

"And you've given me the best opening line for a play I believe I've ever had," Hobart continued. "From the ending of chapter four."

"Which is?"

"Show him, Alice!"

The girl reacted like a soldier, snapping to attention and barking, "I am a freak!"

"See?" Hobart grinned.

"Breathtaking," Jack admitted.

"It's almost a shame it shall only ever be seen by one audience. But that's the magic and nature of the theater. At least there will be some for whom the night of the Fourth of July, 1916, will always be remembered as the night they saw Hobart Bosworth's production of *Before Adam* by Jack London. Thank you, Narrator."

Released from her performance, Mrs. Holdings snatched up her broad-brimmed hat. "Hobart," she then said, "I mean to offer you a casting suggestion. I know you're having trouble finding your Swift One. Seeing Mr. London has reminded me of the most interesting young Hawaiian woman, whom I once met in his company." Jack noticed a new edge of steeliness in her eyes. "I believe her name is Leialoha Kaai and she lives here in Honolulu. I also understand that though she is a distant relative of the Queen's, she is given to performing from time to time. You might consider asking Jack to introduce her to you."

Jack turned to Hobart with a shrug. "Well, I don't really know her."

Hobart waved off the suggestion and Alice before Jack had even finished his protest. "I'll find the right girl," he said.

Jack noticed that Alice bit her lower lip.

"Good night, Hobart," she said.

He waved again, looking down at some costume sketches, barely noticing the door close.

Jack took a seat on the sofa and fanned himself with a handful of loose pages. "Bosworth," he said, "perhaps you should be the one to write a sexual biography."

"Don't smirk at me, London," Hobart said, adding the sketches to the pile of papers covering the dining table. "That is the wife of my financier."

"She's very shapely for a financier's wife," Jack said.

"I've noticed that's usually the case."

Hobart poured each of them a drink. "I'm glad you finally sent me a message asking if I had time to work on our picture project. To be honest, I was getting worried you were giving up on it."

"To be honest, I nearly had."

"Were you hoping I would just give up and go home?"

"Kind of."

"Well, I didn't. I won't. Hell, I can't! So why did you decide to give it another go?"

Jack rubbed his hands together. "You really think we can make some money doing this?"

Hobart leaned over the sofa, bringing his face close to Jack's. "A mint. Money problems, London?"

Jack ran his fingers through his hair. He thought of Eliza's letter, full of bleak descriptions of the circumstances of the farm, claims of dwindling streams of revenue from his book and magazine publishers, and pleas to rein in the seemingly extravagant spending of his wife whose wardrobe bills were only now finding their way across the Pacific. He looked around the suite and imagined how expensive it must be to maintain. "You couldn't begin to imagine."

Hobart sat heavily on the sofa next to him. "I'm sure I couldn't," he said, a great weariness creeping into his voice. "My financier does not realize just how much of this current Hobart Bosworth production his funds are producing."

Jack noticed that the other loveseat had been converted into a makeshift bed, with a pillow and blanket. "Where's Major?"

The actor shrugged. "I've not the foggiest notion. That boy comes and goes as he pleases and tells me nothing. If I lock the door, he comes in through the window. He's amazingly resourceful, with the gifts of a monkey."

"A useful model for your adaptation," Jack suggested.

"Ah, but he's wearing me down. I feel as if I have no more privacy. I don't know how long he expects me to be responsible for him. I don't know how long I can be."

Jack rose and wandered over to the table, pleased to see that the copy of the book Hobart was adapting was a first edition, though it had practically been ruined with all the annotations scribbled in the margins.

"I should get you to sign that," he heard Hobart mutter as he continued looking around, not so much for anything in particular, but as if to gain his bearings and fix upon something to discuss other than money.

"Are you here hat in hand?" he asked. "Or to gloat at my failure?"

"Charmian and I are leaving on the twenty-sixth of July."

"Oh." Hobart looked crestfallen.

"So that gives us a little more than two months to pull together a Hobart Bosworth production of the latest Jack London tale."

Hobart grinned and swallowed his drink. "How about calling it *The Son of the Wolf*?"

Jack laughed.

"What?"

"Your instincts are good. However, that was the name of my first published volume of stories."

"Well, then how about *Wolf Boy*?"

"Too specific."

Before Jack knew it Hobart's face was in his hands and he was trembling. Not tears. Not laughter. But some odd combination thereof.

"Bosworth?" Jack asked. "Bosworth! What is the matter?"

"I think I have it," he said.

"The title?"

"Leprosy!" He lifted his head, his face the shade of a gray cloud, then held up his hands. "My fingertips have been numb since we returned from Molokai."

Jack laughed. "Hobart, like most actors I've ever met you are only afflicted with a severe case of hypochondria. I assure you that the only reason your fingers are numb is because you've turned your hands into fists of tension."

"We need a title."

"Bosworth, is that really what's plaguing you? Our title? Titles are easy."

"They are?"

"They're the last thing I worry about. First thing we should be worrying about is what is our simple story."

"I thought we agreed that it was about a boy who runs with the wolves."

"That's just a sequence. What I think our story is about is a lost boy finding his way home. How does that sound?"

"Vague?"

"It's supposed to. From there it can only get interesting. Now we figure out how he gets lost. And in this way, we introduce who he is as a person. For example, Van Weyden's little boat sinks and he's picked up by the *Ghost* and he's cold, wet, and weak—we already know he's rich because he's told us so. And all that is in chapter one. So now, to begin with, let's give our young man a name. I've been thinking of Rodney Manning, what say you?"

Hobart was beginning to show some interest, his numb fingers apparently forgotten. He sat forward. At that moment there was a rustle in the window and Major clambered over the balcony and into the room. He looked at Jack in surprise. His hair was wet, his shirt was off, and his skin was glistening as if he had come from the ocean. He unrolled his shirt, which he carried under his arm, to reveal one of the island's strange purple dragon fruits. After a moment he took it to a corner of the room, sat down, peeled it open, and began to eat. "Do you feed the boy?" Jack asked Hobart.

"When he's around. Of course. But he likes to fend for himself."

Jack watched him devouring the fruit and an idea began to form in a tiny part of his brain not occupied by the story he was formulating. "We've an extra room at the cottage," he said to both Hobart and the boy. "How about letting him come stay with us for a while?"

"A done deal!" Hobart exclaimed.

"Of course, you may still come and go as you please." The boy looked at the two men and continued eating, giving no indication that he had understood the offer. Hobart gave Jack a baffled shrug, as if to say, Who knows what is on the lad's mind? Finally, they returned to their story.

"Let's fix his age," Jack suggested. "I say that the age of ten is a good age for a boy to have the wits to survive."

"I thought he would be a babe, like Mowgli."

"Ah, but if he's just a babe then we lose an essential ingredient, which is that Rodney must learn and change from his adventure. A baby lacks the ability to shed the shell of civilization—he hasn't even acquired it. A baby raised in the wild can only ever be wild. A boy who chooses to live in the wild is an adventurer. I see our boy as a wealthy scion of eastern society."

"Then how does he end up in the wilds of the West?"

"I think he's on a train trip with his parents. To visit relatives in San Francisco. At a whistle stop in the Rockies he ventures out of the train to explore an environment such as he's never seen before, that captivates his sense of wonder and revives in him the primal urge to see and know more. But he ventures too far and the train departs without him. He hears its whistle blow, chases after it, but gets lost in the woods, turned around, goes down when he should go up, but it's an effort in futility. Night is coming on and now this pampered youth will have to find a way to survive." He paused to sip some whiskey.

"After struggling through night and day and night again without food and water and several small dangers, our boy Rodney meets the wolf. He is son of the leader of his pack, who is himself the biggest wolf in the Rockies, and the most dangerous. The young wolf has left his pack behind to track this boy, but he is trapped in a snare long forgotten by a hunter. He struggles but cannot escape. It is only when he is exhausted by his struggles that the boy comes across him. At first the boy is going to kill him for food, but something about the wolf stays him from striking it with a rock. In their mutual distress, each recognizes the common bond that has always existed between man and canine. In another trap, he finds a freshly killed hare and it feeds both him and the injured wolf, whom he calls Odin. He nurses the wolf back to health, using the same traps to snare the animals needed to sustain them both. You see, he's resourceful, just like our Major."

"What happens next?" Hobart asked.

"The two help each other survive," Jack replied. "They have no choice."

"But what do they do?"

"I don't know. Yet. But I'll figure it out. I shall write it down and see what needs to happen next. I have an idea that the boy shall help Odin become the leader of the pack and that he shall run with them. I also fear that the hunter who placed those traps may play a tragic role, but I'm not sure yet."

"That hunter might be a good part for me."

"If he remains in the story."

"My pictures do better if I'm in them."

"I'll consider that in the creative balance."

"Will he find his way home?"

"Does anyone?"

"The writing of that you mentioned. When, uh, exactly do you think you'll start that?"

"Soon," Jack responded. "I'm still at work on my memoir, but I'll set it aside shortly to work on this."

"You're really writing that memoir? It's not some kind of dirty joke?"

"I hope not. Though you can't write about sex without somebody thinking it's dirty."

"You're not really known for writing smut."

"And I never will be. Not as long as my daughters are alive to read it. I've found that this particular book has required the greatest artistry on my part."

"So tell me, London," Hobart said, folding his hands behind his head and chuckling. "What is your simple story line? Another lost boy? Or is it just a gross litany of your conquests? Please, for God's sake, enlighten me. What have you learned about the fair sex?"

"Well, Bosworth," Jack said, "I know that we underestimate women when we place them above the rule of nature and refer to them as fair. A woman's base instincts can be as ruthless and destructive as the most brutish man, but they rely not on fists or weapons, but on guile and charm. Women hunt, Bosworth. Better than man, who, after all, is their prey."

"Ah," he said, chuckling, "it's a romance."

"There are tales of romance in it. It's not all animalistic analogies. Not that I'm a writer of analogies anyway, merely a journalist who turned to literature."

"Share one of those tales of romance with me."

"Then I'll tell you the tale of the wooing of Mabel Applegarth, the first woman I nearly married. Our love was young, pure, and beautiful. But her mother destroyed it. Because I was beneath their station and, according to her, 'didn't have much to offer a girl.' And while that may have been true at the time, it has been proven untrue many times over in the years since."

"A tragic tale."

"It was. You see, Mabel never married. I believe she never stopped loving me."

"Even now?"

"Now she's dead. I heard of it on the day of my birthday this year. Tuberculosis. Her mother, I'm sad to say, survived her."

"There is romance in that story, I'm sure. But where is the sex?"

"Well, she did not die a virgin."

"Ah. And you're going to write about that?"

"I tell of our long bicycle ride to our favorite picnic spot in the hills and how we lay with each other, naked chest to naked breast. One of the happiest, most beautiful days of my life. I thought that day that we would be bound together forever. But it was the beginning of our end, for she felt she had betrayed her family by being with me in that way. And that made her mother's assault on her easier."

Hobart sat forward. "Is it possible you've never stopped loving her either?"

"I should have saved Mabel from her mother and her fate. I should have. She should have been my wife. My one and only. But in the end she let me down by not overcoming the circumstances of her young life the way I had overcome mine. I wanted her to be stronger."

"More like you?"

"Why not?" He rubbed his forehead. An ache was growing there behind the skull. He found a spot and pressed the palm of his hand against it; the application of pressure seemed to help. Finally he looked down at Hobart. "Anyway, the moral of that chapter is that sex can't save love."

"What does?"

"I don't know. I haven't finished the book yet," he said with a rueful laugh. "I think it's time for me to be getting home before my wife starts to suspect yet another indiscretion."

"Let me ask your advice about casting for a moment," Hobart said, changing the subject. "This girl Alice has suggested. Is it true you know her?"

"Leialoha? I do know her."

"So what do you think? Should I cast her in my little diversion?"

"I think it's a paramount idea," Jack replied with a devilish grin.

"Well, rehearsals start in a week. If you wouldn't mind asking her to come by, I'd like to meet her."

"If I run into her sometime soon, I will mention it to her." He opened the door but stopped suddenly, detecting a lingering scent. He brought his fingers to his nostrils and realized he must have absorbed the unmistakable trace of fragrance from the sofa. "That's interesting," he remarked to Hobart.

"What is?"

"Mrs. Holdings and my wife both wear White Lilac. I buy it for Charmian directly from the California Perfume Company."

"It must be very popular, then."

"Indeed, I'll have to mention that to her. If I know her she'll want to switch fragrances immediately. She hates to think that her femininity isn't unique."

He walked home in quietude along Beach Walk, the only accompaniment his own footsteps, his mind fully occupied with wolves and women, two things that always made him very happy.

CHAPTER TWENTY-SIX

"MR. LONDON? ARE YOU all right?"
 "Mmm? Plume?"
"Mr. London? Are you all right?"
"Of course I am."
"Can I get you anything?"
"What do you mean? Why the fuss?"
"You fell asleep. Just there."
"I did?"
"In the middle of talking about booking your rooms on the *Matsonia* you began snoring."
"Really? I don't . . . How long?"
"Just a few moments."
"I beg your pardon, Professor. I suppose I'm not myself today."
"Not at all necessary."
Jack shook his head. The bright sunlight was streaming into the room, catching the dust and pollen in the air. "Did I tell you I have had a letter from Harry Strange?"
"No."
"He has completed his basic training and is to be assigned to a ship soon. I imagine he's already there since the letter was posted weeks ago." He rubbed his eyes, finding it hard to clear the mist before them. "I guess I did fall asleep. Odd. I saw Plume. Plume was in conversation

with a shadowy figure cloaked in black, and when I called his name, they both turned to look at me. He is in the company of the Noseless One. Oh, Professor, I swear, our discussions here in your office have dislodged some curious visions from my mind. So, tell me, friend, what does the Hawaiian mythological record say of this companion of Plume's? The Dark Angel."

"The Polynesians do not personify death. I think it's because of their close place in nature, they see death much more as a function of life—since everything around the Hawaiian is considered to be alive the transformation into the spirit life is only another way to live. To Jews, Death appears to Eve when she touches the tree of knowledge. Her first thought is that 'I shall die and Adam shall take another wife.' Though since there were only the two of them I can't imagine how he was going to do that. But it's interesting to see that, as a counterpoint to the Hawaiians, the tree acts to separate her, and later Adam, from nature. After all, how can you trust any tree ever again when you touch one and it introduces you to your mortality?"

"Does the Hawaiian fear death?"

"I'm sure the current Hawaiians fear death as much as any white man does. As for the ancient Hawaiians they probably did as well, though they had less to fear after death. No eternal damnation to worry about. Even if you view death as a transformation, pain is usually involved, isn't it? No ancient Hawaiian would welcome the pain and fear of dying. For example, suicide was an incomprehensible concept to the islanders before the coming of the *haole.* Now, I'm afraid, it's not uncommon to hear of a suicide, or even murder-suicide, among the natives."

"Another plague we've brought to Paradise. I saw the most interesting old native site last week. It was on Sunday, and Charmian had decided that we should picnic as we do back at the Beauty Ranch. Nakata had the day off to visit with his family and he had taken the boy with him, so while Charmian prepared a fried chicken luncheon, I borrowed a car. We decided to spend the day away from the ocean; there are just far too many people visiting the beach these days. So we drove into the interior—to the big valley where the high sugarcane plantations cede the ground to the low pineapple scrub and the earth turns red with rich mineral content.

"Earlier in the day, while I was writing, I had asked Charmian to play for me. She played Liszt, which she often does. When she finished, I set down my pen and told her, 'My life would have been so empty without you.'

"'Bull,' she replied, but with a smile. 'You would have continued to fill your days with friends and fun and nonsense and poetry just as you do now. You were always Jack London. You just let me be a part of that.'

"'Then that was the smartest decision I have ever made,' I said. 'You're the only one who could keep up with me.'

"'You're sure it's not the other way around? Maybe I'm setting the pace.'

"'Either way you've been the best companion a venturin' fella could hope for,' was my reply. When she went to the market I went to dress for our ride. While I was ransacking my room for some cologne I found a little pouch. In this was the mushroom smell of the baby woodrose plants that Nature Man had plucked for me. Remembering his instructions, I went to the kitchen and brewed it into a tea, which I set to cool with the addition of some ice. Then I poured it into my thermos.

"She drove. She likes to drive. I just lay my head back and watched the clouds drift overhead like loose bales of cotton. It's no surprise to me that the Hawaiians have a special relationship with the clouds. One feels very close to the sky here. We didn't speak much. Nakata's imminent departure is weighing on both of us. At one point she mentioned that she'd had a nice letter from our friend, Harry Houdini, who'd had such a good time at our Thanksgiving feast last year he was wondering if we were going to do it again this year.

"'I suppose we'll be home for it,' I told her.

"'That's good,' she said. 'I'd like to see him again.'

"We'd only just met him for the first time last year—right before we came out to Hawaii. He gave some performances over in Frisco. Charming man. And, I have to tell you, hands down the most entertaining dinner guest I've ever had at my table. Charmian found him very amusing as well. They've been corresponding ever since.

"I found myself humming that Liszt tune for a while. 'What was that piece you played today?' I asked.

"'It was *Liebestraum—Dream of Love.*'

"My greatest regret in life is that I was born without any musical aptitude whatsoever beyond appreciation. Had I been able to play the piano or guitar—to think of the times I would have actually been able to sing for my supper rather than to beg. The audiences I would have entertained. And to have been able to write music? What I would have accomplished then if I could have written appeals to the heart instead of the intellect.

"After driving a few more miles she said to me, 'You know there are lyrics to that piece?'

"I said that I didn't know that.

"She said, '*Love as much as you can, for someday . . .* ' She stopped and I saw her jaw clench as she caught her breath.

"'What is it, lover?' I asked. 'What's upset you?'

"'*Someday . . . Someday you will mourn at the grave.*' Behind her sunglasses I saw tears welling up in her eyes. I put my hand on her shoulder. She shrugged it off and said she was fine.

"We drove on for a while and then I asked her if she knew where she was going.

"'I have an idea,' was her only reply.

"We drove on past the military outpost at Wahiawa, the streets filled with young soldiers—so many boys from the cities of gloom back east now dazzled by the bright tropic sun. I said, 'If the Mad Dog of Europe decides to storm Waikiki Beach, Oahu will answer.'

"In a short while we rolled up the road to the valley plain, the lush vegetation vanishing in an instant, and she turned the car down a dirt road, barely even a road actually, more like a cattle trail. The saw grass grew tall on either side of us, and she slowed down to soften the rattling bumps. She steered us into a clearing and stopped the car.

"'Mrs. Strange told me about this place,' she said quietly.

"We were surrounded on all sides by massive orange-brown boulders, which formed a stone circle around the clearing. Each boulder stood taller than I and longer than our car. I can't imagine the work it took to bring them to this place. To begin with, I don't even know where on this island one could find a quarry to harvest them from. There is also a dearth of beasts of burden in the islands; horses came with the settlers and this site clearly predated them. The obvious conclusion is that they were dragged into the interior by men, probably a great number of them. I have the image of some lesser king telling his people, 'Today we begin the great rock-circle public works project.'

"'What is this place?' I asked.

"'These are the birthing stones,' she replied, climbing out of the car without taking her eyes from the sight. I followed her toward the high tree that formed a shaded canopy over the far end of the circle. 'This is where royal women had their babies. For seven centuries a chief would bring his wife here and she would deliver him a son while all around a great celebration took place. Men would pound the rocks. Women would sing. And a delegation of lesser chiefs would sever the umbilical cord. Think of it, Jack. The ground on which we're standing is soaked with the royal birth blood of generations.'"

The professor was watching him.

"Have you ever been there?" Jack asked.

"I've never heard of it."

"I put my hands to the earth, and then my face. I wanted to touch, feel, smell the royal ground. I, who have no concrete proof of my own progenitor, felt at last connected to the dirt, which sings a comforting song of forefathers." He drummed his fingers on the leather chair. Strange that soon he would never sit in this chair again. There was so much still to talk about. "We unfolded the blanket and ate our supper in the cool shade of that magnificent broad monkeypod tree. Mount Kaala was to our backs.

"'There's no one on earth who knows where we are right now,' she sighed. 'Isn't that wonderful?' She pressed her head against my chest. Again I could smell her White Lilac, mingling with the faint smell of pineapple in the air. 'You said earlier that you wondered what your life would have been like without me. I'm wondering what my life will be like without you.'

"'What do you mean by that?' I said, stroking her hair.

"'I'm so worried about your health,' she replied. 'You hardly touch your food.'

"'But look at all I've eaten here today,' I pointed out. 'And I eat a large breakfast each and every day. I'm getting older and doing less and my engine needs less fuel to keep this machinery moving. Especially here while I'm not ranching. Look at this belly.' I ask you, do you get this fat not eating? And she thinks I'm starving.

"'When was the last time we went for a swim together in the moonlight?'

"'It has been a while. But I've been writing so much and reading. I tell you what. Tonight, we'll swim and you'll see that I can still outpace you.'

"'Okay,' she said. 'And when we return will you promise me that you will see some of the doctors in San Francisco?'

"I started to protest that Dr. Belko was a real doctor but she said he was a drunk so I promised to see any doctor she wanted me to see. 'I won't lose you,' she said. 'I won't lose you to illness . . . or anything else.'

"'What does that mean?' I asked but she just looked at me with that stone-stubborn look of hers.

"'It means what I say that it means. You belong to me, Jack London. And I won't let you die, or fade away, or anything else.'

"'You are my Mate-Woman,' I agreed.

"'Then why won't you share your new writing with me?' she asked. 'Have you actually been writing a sexual variant on *John Barleycorn*?'

"'Yes,' I told her.

"'Oh, Jack,' she cried, 'you know you don't have to hide it from me.'

"I told her, 'Because it's an embarrassment.' I know it won't be when I'm finished with it, but it's a delicate work, and difficult to write. It may be the best I've written yet, but it's difficult. To share with readers the sway that various women have held over me. To speak bluntly about women I've treated rudely. To admit the disappointments women have caused me. It paints an amusing picture, to say the least, but it's not one that I'm prepared to share just yet.

"But I didn't tell Charmian this—there are things in it I'm not ready to show her yet. She knows a little of my dalliances. But to see the words on paper as they're written now will only cause her pain. I can prepare her for that. And I can smooth out the writing so it won't seem so blunt."

"But why write it at all?"

"I believe it's a story worth telling. I've learned as much from women as I've learned from nature. That's why I've written almost as much about women as about nature. Professor, it may shock you but I've been with nearly three hundred women in my life." He smiled at the man's obvious discomfort. "You forget, I became famous and successful at a very ripe age in a very liberated time."

"Can you recall all three hundred?"

"I'm trying to. What she would find right now is a list of the ones I can remember along with circumstances and reminiscences. For example, there's a woman I'm calling Melinda—a dancer I met in New York City. Right now, my notes about her following a physical description read 'Bold onstage. Demure offstage.' What is one to make of that? Or the Korean laundrywoman: 'Had rough hands,' the entry says."

"What is your point in writing this book?"

"To shake us loose from our sexual Puritanism. Our society likes to pretend that women can only enjoy sexual relations within the confines of a marriage, but if this many women are willing to be with me without being married to me then they must be enjoying the experience as much as any man. I want to show the world that sex is to be enjoyed. I want to free women. I want more women to be as free and uninhibited as Charmian is. The most marvelous woman I know is the one who has shed the restrictions of her class and had no fear learning the skills and techniques, even tricks, of lovemaking. How to use her hands, her mouth, every part of her femininity not just to please me, but please herself. I've been with enough women to know her forthrightness about pleasure is a rarity. It surprises me that Charmian shows so much concern over this manuscript, for in the end it really is a tribute to her and the gifts she's given me. But I probably haven't put it to her in that way because it formulated itself just now in my head.

"I could tell she was still upset about it so I brought out the thermos of baby woodrose tea and explained what it was to her and asked her if she would join me in an attempt to kiss nature. Ever adventurous, she readily agreed. I knew she would.

"The tea had a bitter taste, which was offset by its sweet smell of jasmine. At first there was no hint of anything. While I rested, and digested, for Charmian is right and my stomach has not been its old self, she wandered around the boulders, letting her fingertips drift over their surfaces. 'I wonder if you can hear the sounds of the mothers trapped within them,' she said, placing her ear against one. And it was at that point that I began to feel the sensation of an altered perception. The dappled sunlight through the leaves scattered slivers of gold upon the ground. The breeze that moved the trees made the slivers dance around me. I watched one play back and forth over the back of my hand, spotlighting a curious ant crawling there. I was mesmerized by the light, convinced that it was illuminating the blood in the veins raised there—revealing the motions and colors of the microscopic corpuscles.

"I found myself standing suddenly, hollering at the top of my lungs, 'I tell you I am standing on the edge of a world so new, so terrible, so wonderful, that I am almost afraid to look over into it!'

"Charmian was dancing slowly on top of one of the boulders, swaying to and fro to the Liszt dream music I was hearing all around us. 'Look into it!' she called back, her voice ringing gently on the air. 'Look, lover.' The long, late afternoon shadows cast by the boulders began to dance with her.

"'Do you know why we're here?' she whispered in my ear, behind me suddenly, her arms winding around my chest.

"'To be reborn as a king and queen,' I told her.

"She laughed and disappeared. Sometime later she was with me again. 'That's not it at all, delicious lover. I brought you here to hear the voices.'

"'Voices?'

"'Voices? No, that's wrong. It's not what I meant to say. I brought you here for Joy. I want us to free Joy. Let's release her. Let her go. Jack, we've never done this. Neither of us could even go to her funeral.' She was holding on to the lapels of my shirt, her expression was so urgent. Then there were tears. 'I miss my baby Joy,' was her cry. 'Let's say good-bye.'

"'I have,' I told her.

"'No, you haven't. I haven't. We've grieved, but we have to say good-bye now. Look. I have a candle I bought this morning when I went shopping. It's getting dark now. Let's light it for her on that boulder there. Then let's each say one thing that we wished we could have seen her grow up and do, the one thing that we wished for her, or wanted to know about her. Then we'll let go of that and say farewell. Please, Jack? Will you do it for me? I feel like we need to do this. Otherwise, I'll be lost forever and we'll end up losing each other. That's why you can't die on me, Jack. If you die then I'll be the only one who ever knew her at all. Do this for me. Say good-bye with me?'

"'I will. I will,' I said, taking her in my arms. She ran to her bag and withdrew the slender taper. I used my lighter to melt the bottom and affix it to the boulder. Then I lit the wick. As if it were ordained, the light breeze faded away and the flame caught hold. The sun fell behind the mountain.

"'My daughter,' she said, 'I wanted to hold your hand. I wanted to put a ribbon in your beautiful hair, which I never would have cut. I wanted to hear you laugh at one of your father's dumb jokes. I wanted to shop with you for your Christmas dress. I wanted to see you happy. I wanted to see you smile when you found a good man like I have found.' Her voice broke, and trembling, she fell against me. Great heaving sobs wracked her body. 'You go,' she whispered. 'Please.'

"'Joy,' I said to the night. 'I wanted to take you sailing. I wish you could have seen the world.'

"'She has. She has,' Charmian said. She pulled herself up and managed a brave smile. 'She's been with us every day, and seen all that we've seen. She'll be all right now. All right now. When the candle burns down I can let go of her. She'll always be here in my heart. But I won't be holding on anymore. No more.'

"We fell to the blanket and watched the flickering spot. The night grew mystical—stars fell from the sky. I read the next day that this outburst was the biggest meteor shower ever on record. But we didn't know that then and could barely have comprehended it in our state. All I knew was to us it looked as if heaven were falling apart. The night was warm, you remember? We began to strip articles of clothing off, at first for comfort, and then . . . Well, an altogether different kind of comfort. We spent the night there on the blanket, naked under the falling stars. When the last of the wax finally burned away we both whispered, 'Good-bye', and the still air was stirred again by the returning breeze, which caressed our skin but still kept us warm.

"'She's saying good-bye now,' Charmian said. 'Can you feel that? Can you feel her?'

"And I did feel something leave me. Like the rush of spirits in my mother's parlor when she claimed Plume was entering the room. Then a weight I hadn't even realized I was carrying was gone. We fell into the deepest slumber I think I've had in years. The next morning we arose and I must admit I felt better than I have in weeks. Charmian, too, seemed refreshed and cheerily embarrassed at our nudity, exclaiming that 'someone might see us.'

"I had to remind her that nobody on earth knew where we were and that we could be pretty sure that a visit to the birthing stones was on absolutely no one's Monday morning agenda."

CHAPTER TWENTY-SEVEN

HE STARED AT THE crumpled pink ball of paper in the palm of his hand. Only recently it had been a smooth rectangle, a calling card from his distant past come a-calling once again.

Where was he? Oh, yes. King Street. He turned left.

He was in shock. More than shock. The letter had arrived in the morning post. *Cosmopolitan* had refused the last story he had sent in— "When Alice Told Her Soul." The editor's note indicated, without directly saying as much, that the magazine was interested in something more adventurous, more in the nature of true Jack London.

The instant the pink note slid out of the envelope, Jack had been transported more than fifteen years back in time, to the small room he rented from the Italian widow where he had set upon the task of creating a new kind of writer from nothing but muscle, bone, will, and wit. Before his first taste of success had arrived he had papered his walls with the flurries of pink slips that blew in daily on the winds of the mail.

He hadn't walked far and briskly like this in weeks. It felt astonishingly good.

He had signed the contract with *Cosmopolitan* specifically for the security such an engagement offered. For two years the magazine had carried his name upon their masthead and a banner that cried, "Featuring Jack London" upon its cover. Circulation had expanded by thousands in those two years. Thousands! Because of him.

The noise of one of Honolulu's many new cars drew him back to the evening. Charmian had gone to have dinner with some of her lady friends in Diamond Head. Nakata was teaching Major a Japanese lullaby. The boy seemed to be able to communicate through music, at least with Nakata. Jack had grown restless. There was a torpor in the air, a humid stillness that was the harbinger of a great storm which would crash upon the little island. Jack could have gone round to see Hobart, or dropped in at the Surf Club. He probably could have even done some more writing. God knew he had enough unfinished on his platter.

Warren Street, at the foot of Punchbowl Basin.

He had declined Charmian's offer to attend yet another of her ladies' farewell cocktail parties and she had gone off without him, reluctant to pass up a party, particularly one in her honor. A restlessness gnawed at him as he lay in repose upon his little sleeping porch. Perhaps it was the heat. Far across the dark ocean he could see the herald of a storm. The flashes of lightning at the edge of the rising black mass spoke of imminent destruction. His adventurous blood had begun to boil.

As he strode up the hill he felt like a superb meteor in flight, every atom imbued with a magnificent glow. No one greeted him. He was perfectly anonymous. He was Jack London of Oakland, the young writer on the verge of catching the tiger, rather than the old man clinging greedily to its tail.

There it was just as she had described it in the Parkers' garden, a tidy white cottage with special blue trim in proximity to the Queen's residence. Without concern about who else might be there he took the steps two, three at a time, bounding up to the lanai, pounding on the door.

And she answered, her dark brown eyes filling with courage at the sight of him.

"Princess," said Jack, for that was the name he had come to know her as.

"Jack Lakana," she replied.

"I'm very lonely," he told her. "My thoughts have turned to you. May I come in?"

"I don't know if I should let you. It's very late."

"It's not. Not even at all. The moon has only just risen."

"I thought you would come sooner."

"I've tried to stay away."

He tried to enter but she placed a hand on his chest. "I won't let you in." He stepped back.

"Then will you walk with me? Before the storm comes. Will you?"

"Where will we go?"

"Take me somewhere I've never been before."

She made a short show of deciding, though he knew she already had. "All right," she said, closing the door behind her.

She took his arm and together they took Beretania Street west to Nuuanu Avenue, where the generation of Hawaiians who had left their villages behind now lived. Jack felt they were the only people moving in a city otherwise populated with statues. He asked her to participate in Bosworth's play and she seemed intrigued by the notion. The boulevard rose steeply along the side of the crater but to Jack it was a refreshing climb.

"I've been reading your books," she said.

"You have?" The admission made him happy. "Which ones?"

"I've read your dog books," she replied. "And now I'm reading *The Valley of the Moon*. It's a real place, right? Where you live? Your home?"

"It is."

"It has such a beautiful name."

"Sonoma."

"Sonoma," she repeated.

"That's the old Indian name for it. The Miwok tribe noted that in winter the moon appeared seven consecutive times between the two mountains that form the pass into the valley."

"Do I need to imagine what became of the Miwok people? How many remain in their beloved Sonoma? Sonoma." She said it again, and on her lips it sounded Hawaiian.

"It's a sad history, it's true. Writ long before I stepped foot upon the stage."

"Yet history has a way of setting the stage for its players nevertheless, doesn't it? I wasn't even born during the annexation and yet I still live as a conquered person in a conquered land."

"I don't believe you could be conquered."

She swept away from him. "Your writing makes California seem so very large and so very beautiful. Is that truth or is it a great writer's embellishment?"

"It is," he said and she laughed.

"Which?"

"Both. California will be the salvation of the nation. Every good idea, all the hardiest people, the attitudes toward labor and prosperity that will revolutionize America—all will come from my home state. You should see it. Though no one visit could ever do it justice. I've lived there most of my life and still know so very little of it."

"I have no desire to leave Hawaii. Everything I need is here."

"I'm leaving at the end of July."

Her response, telegraphed from her shoulder, down her arm to the fingers in his hand, felt like a shrug.

They walked along a granite wall in which seashells had been embedded. Soon they came upon an iron fence periodically interspersed with low walls of granite. Beyond it Jack could see what looked like a large garden spotted with amorphous, dimly glowing structures. She stopped before a gate in the wall and swung it open. It was well oiled and opened silently. They entered the yard.

"What is this place?" he asked her.

"The Royal Mausoleum," she replied. "The burial place of my ancestors."

Without speaking another word, she led him toward the greatest of the granite structures, a massive stone crypt, larger than Wolf House would have been. Over the doors, a crucifix was carved. Lanterns flickered eternally at the gates.

He ran a hand over the smooth arch. "I built one of these once."

"What happened?"

"It burned down. Does King Kamehameha rest here?"

"Not the first king, the great one. The first king to lay here is his son. Is this the kind of monument Jack Lakana will have erected to his memory? In thirty or forty years, of course."

"Of course. No. I'll tell you, on the ranch I own there is a little patch on a hill. I discovered it on a trail ride one day. This little patch is fenced in. Inside this little plot are two moss-covered wooden markers set fast in the earth. The first one of 'em says, 'Little David died 1876.' The second one says, 'Little Lillie died 1877.' Now I bought that piece of land from the township some years after the owner, an old pioneer named Greenlaw who'd homesteaded the land after the Civil War, was found dead and in arrears. So those two little Greenlaw children, they were all alone and abandoned up there. I cleared out that path myself and I drop by and visit once in a while. Sometime back I decided that I loved that land so much that I wanted to be buried there too, so I told

Charmian just to plant me on that hill and roll a big stone on me, and I'd keep company with those forgotten Greenlaw children for all eternity."

From out of the dark he felt her hand suddenly appear along the side of his face, tracing along lines of care and worry he knew she wouldn't have found only years before. Embarrassed, he gently took her hand in his, kissing her fingertips. They explored the silent grounds together and apart. At times he saw her drifting through the palm trees like a ghost. They came together again at a more modest monument, a stone table supported by marble columns. She leaned against it.

"If you had a son, what would you want him to be?"

"A tall and proud son of Hawaii."

"What would he know of his father? The Californian."

"That he is a man whose function is to live, not merely to exist. He would rather that his spark should burn out in a brilliant blaze than be stifled in dry rot. He would rather be ashes than dust!"

"And what of the son who could never meet his father? Would that not be sad for him?"

"He should know that unlike his grandfather, who denied his own son's existence to the world, that his own father would carry him foremost in his heart. And one day he would call him to California. Or meet him on some Hawaiian beach, should his mother insist."

"They would have to meet someday. A woman can only do so much. A boy should know his father. They would have to meet."

"They would. And what would his mother tell him of his father?"

"That he loved Hawaii with all his heart and soul. That he loved Hawaii like a native born."

He leaned in and kissed her again. She pressed her body against his. His hands burned on her volcanic skin, fingers tangled in the thick jungle of her hair, nostrils filled with the scent of a thousand tropical fruits, mouth tasting the rich, full red earth.

A flash of lightning indicated the oncoming rush of the storm at last. They made their way from the garden and just as the rain started they found themselves back on the porch of her little house. This time when she opened the door, she let him enter first, followed, then closed the door behind her.

CHAPTER TWENTY-EIGHT

"WHAT IF WRITING IS killing me?"

The storm that had struck the island the night he had gone for a walk with Leialoha still pounded away at the small island two days later. Ships had gone missing, houses had been washed away. The fresh walls of the newly begun Ala Wai Canal, which upon its completion would usher in a new era for a more stable and less waterlogged Waikiki, had collapsed. Sandbags against the ocean waves had been placed at strategic positions along Beach Road from Fort DeRussy to just past the aquarium at Kapiolani Park.

"What do you mean?" Professor Homer asked. How many times had he asked that?

"What if writing is killing me? What if the writing is why I'm sick?"

"Then stop writing."

"I can't. Here is what I'm talking about. I can't."

"No one's holding a gun to your head."

"No. My monthly expenses are more like a cannon. No, I'm afraid I won't be giving up the pen anytime soon. Why, God only knows what would happen to poor Charmian if I were to die suddenly. My finances are in a shambles. I imagine she would just sell off the Beauty Ranch to settle my debts, though I'd hate for her to have to do that. I'll have to keep grinding out stories for the magazines for many a year yet to finally secure myself. Unless Bosworth's picture strikes the mother lode. That's why, in the end, I agreed to work with him again—I'd always rather roll the dice and risk crapping out than not take the chance. It's the same thought I'm sure that comes to many an adventurer and storyteller. It's that moment that comes to you where you think to yourself, Am I going to make it out of this alive? Am I going to live to tell the tale?"

"I'm sure your readers hope so."

"Okay. I'm wondering if the outlay of vast mental capital that I expend on writing is to the detriment of my physical health. Is my brain sapping my limbs of energy just as I once foresaw that continuing to exert myself in manual labor for a dollar would cause my brain to wither and atrophy?"

"It's an interesting question. I'm not—"

"I know. You're not a physician. But I don't have any access to a doctor trained in theoretical medicine. So you, as my trained mythologist, will have to suffice. I've been lying to you all this time."

"How so? You're not Jack London? You're really Zane Grey?"

"Clever. What I meant, though, was that throughout our conversations about mythology, I have actually been using you as my alienist even though you had stated your reluctance to be seen as such. I don't think you've even been aware of it."

"You don't say. And what has this gained you?"

"Insight. Knowledge. A sense of understanding."

"Hmm. And to think that all this time I thought we were merely discussing mythology."

"Aha!"

"You have me there. Perhaps upon your return to California you will seek out a real physician—and continue what you have started."

"I don't think I'll be able to find anyone nearly as talented as you. I feel as if I should be so lucky as to find a doctor who can do for my body what we've done here for my mind. I had to hire a car here today, it's raining fiercely. But I've been hiring cars to go everywhere. Charmian thinks it's ridiculous since the trolley is only a block away. But it's just easier for me." He cracked the knuckles of his hands.

"Haven't I given my publishers, my audience, everything they wanted? Don't they know how hard it is? Do they not understand the toll it takes on me? To hack out words on paper like hacking a path through the jungle with only a pen for a machete?"

He rose to accept the crystal glass of whiskey the professor pressed into his hand. For the first time Jack realized that the man and he were the same size, almost exactly.

"Then why do it?" the professor asked. "Why do it at all?"

"Because otherwise I would have had to become a mailman." He gulped at the soothing liquor, feeling it expand through his body, firing his extremities with the white light.

"Why write?" the professor persisted.

"For the money."

"Bullshit."

He blinked at the professor's coarse outburst. The man had poured himself a drink as well, a tall one, and had walked back to his desk. "Tell me why you write," he said as he took his seat. Jack, however, remained standing. "You're a smart man. You're lifted yourself from poverty with your mind. With a brain like yours you could have chosen any industry and profession, and yet you chose a path that was offbeat, impractical at the least. You've made a success of it to be sure. But why do you do it? Why do you write?"

"Have you ever been poor?"

"No."

"When I was a kid I was so poor, so hungry, that one day at school I pulled a piece of meat, no bigger than my thumb and forefinger, from the garbage where it had been thrown by one of my classmates. I ate it down in front of the schoolyard while they jeered at me. I won't say that I didn't care. I cared so much I cried while I ate it, but that's how hungry I was. That's how hungry I always was."

"That's very sad."

"That's why I write."

"Because of the hunger?"

"Because I can give you a part of myself in words that makes you feel something. Sadness. Happiness. Excitement. I've always been able to tell of myself in this way. In a way that has an effect. Shall I describe to you how that bit of steak tasted? It was lined with fat and gristle, that's why the little girl threw it away. It wasn't suitable for her. But I hadn't tasted meat in weeks and to me I can still taste it, one of the finest pieces of steak I've ever had. Salted with my tears, no less. Do I need to tell you that even after I had finished it, with the schoolyard laughter ringing in my ears, that I licked the garbage dirt off my fingers to be able to taste just that little more flavor?"

"You're not that young man anymore."

Jack laughed. "Sir Harry told me that at a certain age you stop being a *wunderkind* and have to settle for *maestro*. But *wunderkind* is better. I was hungry, Professor Homer. I was hungry then and I'm hungry now though I can eat steak whenever I want."

His glass was empty and he filled it again. "I drink because I'm thirsty. I'm a devourer. A consumer." He was surprised to find the glass was empty and so he poured it full again. "So tell me, Professor. We've been through the mythological record. But tell me now again, who is the devourer of worlds?"

"I suppose you want me to say the Fenris Wolf."

"Call it what you will. I realize now why I've done the things I have done, the things I've tried to forget. The things that the Wolf Larsen side of my nature has done that my Van Weyden side recoils fearfully from and can't accept responsibility for."

"What are you talking about?"

"Wolf Larsen let himself be trapped in the *Ghost.* But not me. Like a great wolf I caught the scent of my own trap. I would have died there, you know. Trapped with only Charmian. But I freed myself in time to come here. Just in time. To discover my destiny. To meet Leialoha."

"Where, Jack? Where would you have died? I don't follow."

"I would have gone blind and mad alone there with her like Wolf Larsen. I realized even as each stone went up that I was building a prison to hold me that would last a thousand years. The local police and insurance inspectors suspected an unhappy employee. Eliza has always suspected Charmian's lover, the ranch hand. Nakata fears Charmian did this horrible thing, and I do feel bad about that. I certainly do. But Nakata was right, someone did take a horse from the stable that night."

"God, no."

"I carefully placed the rags during the day to make it look as if they had been carelessly left behind. Then I rode through the woods in the dark, those woods that I know like the back of my hand, to that place and entered. The echo of my footsteps was the echo I knew I would hear every day for the rest of my life. There would be no parole. No furlough. No pardon. There would be no children to fill it, no joy. I ask you, is that any way for Jack Lakana to live? For King Kame-hameha?

"The fire started so easily. I felt the horror of it deeply at the first instant. I even tried to put it out. But it was too late, the oil used to polish the floors was too fresh, the hot summer had dried the hardwood, so the flames spread like flowing lava in all directions. My fearful mind took hold, rejected my own actions, drove me home. But I remember now, Professor, thanks to you. Not only do I remember, but I accept my actions. My soul is no longer in turmoil. It is quiet. I recognize my dilemma. I, who have always been so dependably honest in my writings, have not been honest with myself, with what I have done."

The professor stared at him and gulped down the rest of his drink. "I need to hear you say what you did, Jack. What did you do?"

"Ain't it obvious? I put the torch to my prison and I transformed myself into an unchained wolf. I broke the bonds of Gjöll. I freed myself to stand upon the highest cliff and fly away to freedom if need be, or to devour worlds should blood demand it."

He set his empty glass down on the professor's desk. He hadn't realized it, but sometime in the past hour the storm had broken. Already streaks of purple twilight were visible through scraps of fast-moving clouds. He drew close to the professor, who was breathing heavily, as if in a panic, though his strange little eyes never left Jack's face.

"I burned down the Wolf House. I burned it down to the ground."

Part 4

"ALOHA 'OE, ALOHA 'OE"

—A BALLAD BY QUEEN LILIUOKALANI

CHAPTER TWENTY-NINE

"OKAY. MONKEY MEN LINE up to the left!"
God, he loved rehearsals.

The building that housed the small gymnasium at the Queen Lili-uokalani Elementary School and Orphan Home had been a small zoo only two years before, and Hobart was sure he could still sense the reek of animal piss. The headmaster, Mr. Gibson, had told him, with a laugh, of the exotic zebra that had lived in the yard whose stripes had to be re-painted after every rain. Perfect, Hobart had thought to himself as the priest had continued on the brief tour of the facility; I'm the guy who gets to follow the donkey who dreamed of being a zebra.

"Stage left," he shouted hoarsely and wearily as three of Red-Eye's tribe wandered to his right, "I meant stage left." Then he had to wait for the men to realize their mistake and for the rest of their castmates to have a se-rious laugh at their embarrassment as they tromped back across the boards, paper tape marking out the spot where various boulders and trees would be placed on stage. In the meantime he walked over to Morosco, busy at the central desk marking up Paramount Distribution papers.

"C'mon, Ben," he said, wearily plopping down in the chair next to him. "You're supposed to be my stage manager. Manage the stage."

Ben looked up from the columns of figures before him. "I have to get these receipts in today, Bos," he said in a voice that attempted to out-weary Hobart's.

"Christ, Ben. You've only got four theaters in the whole territory—"

"Six with Fiji and Tahiti."

"Okay, six. How hard can it be?"

"Look." Morosco set down his pen and pushed back his visor. "I know it's not the toughest job in the world, but I love it here. I don't want anybody back there even to remember I'm here so if that means I have to dot every *i* and cross every *t* in order not to call attention to myself, then that's what I shall do. Worst thing could ever happen to me is I get called back to California and sent somewhere cold like Chicago. I don't want to die in Chicago, Hobart. I want to die right here. So your little production is just going to do without me for a little while today so I can make the mail pouch on tonight's tide. Besides, you're the one who said this was going to be a walk in the park. You didn't have to turn it into the Hawaiian equivalent of *Birth of a Nation*."

"Then it wouldn't be a Hobart Bosworth production, would it?" he muttered, thrusting his hands in his pockets and leaning back in his chair.

"Took the words out of my mouth," was the equally muttered reply.

Hobart creaked in his chair for several moments while the Hawaiian actors he had cast began to settle down, then stir uncomfortably.

Morosco threw down his pen. "It's to be the *Cleveland Follies of 1899* all over again, is that it?"

Hobart squeezed another creak out of his chair.

"Then fine!" Morosco leaped to his feet. "Godammit monkey men! That is stage right. That is stage left." He grabbed up his play binder. "Let's start the scene from the top of page twelve. Get it right this time. Where's Boy? Ah, there he is. Now where the hell's Red-Eye?" As the actors scrambled for their spots he turned to Hobart. "Why are you even wasting your time with this?"

"Otherwise," he said, grinning up at his old friend's bright red face, "I'd go crazy waiting for London to finish writing my script." He settled the four feet of his chair on the floor.

"And the producing and directing fees don't hurt?"

"Not one bit. A man's gotta live." They had borrowed five thousand dollars from Wayne Holdings. If the production cost a thousand, he'd be shocked. That left four thousand on top of what he had left from Ruby, the film retrospective, and his luncheon speeches. While the money was more than enough to cover his living expenses, it was unfortunately not enough to fix the problems in his life. That power was still bottled up in London's pen. He rose. "And live well. Otherwise what's the point? Thank you, Ben." He turned, hearing the gym door slam shut. "Ah, and here's Red-Eye, just as you ordered."

Mano bowed his head at the loud sound the door had made behind him. "I'm sorry, Mr. Hobart."

"Find your spot, son," Morosco said. "We're going from the top of page twelve."

Hobart thumbed back to page 12. This was the scene where Boy, escaping the hardships of his home tribe in the trees, meets up with the cave people and is set upon by the fearsome Red-Eye, the leader of the tribe. Boy would be replaced after intermission by an older actor who would play Man, the adult character grown up and mature enough to fall in love with the lovely Swift One. He looked up at his jovial cast, mainly engineering students from Oahu College—not one among them could be considered fearsome. Except for Mano. He was perfectly cast. Gentle as a kitten, Hobart supposed, but cloaked in the hide of a warrior.

"All right," he said in his commanding voice. "You may begin." He sighed and, with little conscious thought, rubbed his belly. With each passing day its aching had increased a little more. On the occasions he had been able to send a telegram to Hollis, the man's replies had confirmed that all was well—no one had uncovered their subterfuge. And yet, Hobart worried. He had been away for months now and had nothing concrete to show for his efforts. If only he could get London to knuckle down and write. It wasn't that the trip to the islands hadn't been invigorating, even inspiring in some ways—but with each passing day he felt his studio slip farther away from him, saw Griffith's shadow growing longer in the distance. He hated to admit that he was even growing a little homesick for Los Angeles. But that would be his last reason for returning.

He watched the actors run through the scene. The Hawaiians were wonderfully enthusiastic; he felt his decision to cast them would be vindicated at the performance. They had a natural inclination to show off and no inhibitions about performing for one another. They attacked each rehearsal as if they were playing in front of an audience. He supposed some of it had to do with their culture of group dancing, the hula, which he had seen a number of times since his arrival. That, and the fact that they spent more than half of their lives in a state of seminudity, seemed to absolve them of any sense of inhibition. Not only were they all natural performers, they had the instincts of born comedians and were endlessly entertaining. They were certainly better actors than the cowboys he usually hired, who were generally more interested in drinking, fighting, and whoring on the set than these fellows were.

He paid close attention as the elementary school student who played Boy, Ikaika was his name, crept through the imaginary set. The headmaster told him that the translation of his name was "strong" and that he was a foundling, a baby left on the steps of Kawaiahao Church. He had been seven when Queen Liliuokalani had chartered this school, and like the other orphans, he lived here now and would stay here until he completed his schooling. He was ten years old and as lithe and graceful as a trained dancer. Ikaika had taken a particular shine to Mano because, unlike the college students who were in the process of leaving the old island ways behind and becoming Americanized, the tall native could speak Hawaiian. The headmaster had whispered to him that preserving the ancient tongue by teaching it to the Hobarts was the Queen's secret mandate. Hobart had approved of that idea wholeheartedly. It made the school seem like an abbey—an unassailable refuge of knowledge hidden from the barbarians in plain sight on a hilltop.

Mano sprang from the would-be wing and dropped to all fours with a savage roar that caught the attention of everyone in the room. Red-Eye menaced Boy. Ikaika suddenly broke character and stood up straight. When it was obvious he wasn't going to continue the scene, Mano straightened too.

"What's wrong?" Hobart asked.

Ikaika pointed at Mano's feet. "He's standing on *da kine*," he replied, using the common words for when the name for something had been forgotten.

Hobart looked down at the tape under Mano's feet. "He's right," he said. "You've landed in the bog."

"Bog," the kid whispered to himself, committing the name to memory. Originally Hobart had pictured Major Domo playing the part, since it required no line memorization or speaking, but the reality was that he would have been too much of a wild card, and after all this time Hobart was still unsure how much he took in and understood. At first he had been relieved when the youth had stopped creeping into his rooms at the hotel at all hours and had settled in at the London cottage. But he had come to miss his silent lurking presence in an odd way.

"But it's all right. I'm certain you won't miss it when there's a real set."

"No worries, Mr. Hobart," was Mano's muted response. Hobart had seen talents like his before: actors who could fill the rafters with their passion and stir the hardest longshoreman to tears, yet turned milquetoast upon exiting the stage door. Far preferable to the typical actress whose sense of drama only increased when the curtains fell. He had worked hard to capture Mano for Hobart Bosworth's production of Jack London's *Before Adam*. London had introduced them the one disastrous morning Hobart had tried surfing (thank God for Charmian's aloe gel, which had soothed his exquisitely sunburned skin) and met the legendary Duke Kahanamoku. Although shorter than Hobart, the Olympian's huge hand had engulfed his when they shook. It was as if the gods had destined him to be a water hero by blessing him with hands that reminded Hobart of a seal's flippers. London had already spoken highly of Mano and Hobart had been struck by his charismatic presence. Under other circumstances the man could have been a movie star. Hell, with a little training Hobart could transform him into a movie star. Maybe once London's picture put him back in business he would create a series of exotic island adventures featuring Mano and this whole company.

Upon undertaking this project, Hobart had tracked down Mano at the orphan school and asked him to join the cast, to no avail. Three subsequent visits had yielded no better results, though it had yielded an offer of this rehearsal space from the headmaster. One afternoon, soon after the rehearsals had started, he had found the Hawaiian skulking around the hallway outside the gymnasium. At first he had insisted that he was only keeping an eye on his star student, Ikaika. But then, in his soft, halting voice, he had asked Hobart if there was possibly still a chance that he might play a part. Hobart had agreed immediately and it was only upon following the line of Mano's darting eyes that he had noticed the recently cast Hawaiian beauty, Leialoha, rehearsing her part of Swift One in the gym, that he had understood the young man's interest in the dramatic arts.

Hobart had to admit that despite the loose nature of this production, it did feel good to be working on a live stage production again. The rhythms of theater were different than those of picture making, where everything was a rush to get the film in the can. A play offered a little more time to explore; the pace was less breathtaking and exciting, to be sure, but the integrity of the *da kine,* the whole thing, as the Hawaiians said, could be judged instantly rather than waiting for film to be developed and spliced together. It was nice to have the opportunity to change things he didn't like, which he couldn't really do on a picture after all the actors had gone home and the locations struck.

On the other hand, would it kill London to finish his goddamned script? Sure Oahu was beautiful and the accommodations exemplary. Hobart was a wanderer by nature; it was as much a part of his vocation as any other talent he possessed. To be an actor, or a sailor for that matter, meant one had to adapt to a gypsy life, not settle down too much in any one place, never set down a taproot, be prepared to leave on the next tide or trail. So he was accustomed to travel, even looked forward to it. But he had been stuck in Paradise for nearly six months.

He wanted to hear the sound of a herd of horses pawing at the earth as their riders waited for his arm to drop, signaling the start of a cavalry charge. He missed the whisper of crinoline rustling under the formal ball gowns of ladies twirling across a stage set. He wanted to smell the light green powder makeup they used to give the actors' faces the right hue again. He missed the hum and sputter and hiss of the great hot lamps they had recently started using to force more light through the lenses. More than anything he missed the whirring sound of film, expensive film, dangerously explosive silver nitrate film, but most of all precious film, rushing through a camera as the operator turned the crank. This play was just that—play. But making pictures—that was a man's art.

He heard a throat clearing behind his shoulder. Polite, but insistent, the throat was cleared again. At his back, out of sight, he'd had Ben place a few chairs for guests and actors taking a break. Two of his visitors today were Mrs. Blaisedell and Mrs. Wildemann, the owners of the Popular Theater where this production would be mounted on Independence Day. It was their first visit. The younger woman spoke, nervous though she appeared. "Is it all going well, Mr. Bosworth?"

Ben gave him a sidelong glance, a look he'd been receiving from the sweat-drenched little man for years. It meant, Tread lightly, the producers are worried. Though technically the ladies from the Popular Theater were not producers. They were venue hosts, as he liked to call them. He gave Ben a look back, which Ben knew meant, This is part of my job and by the way get the actors back to work before they start singing and dancing or doing something otherwise inappropriate and uncalled for that might further undermine my credibility here.

"Mrs. Blaisedell and Mrs. Wildemann, are you enjoying the rehearsals? It's going to be the most fabulous play, is it not?" He said this as grandly and with as much confidence as he could muster, leading them slowly back to their seats.

"I suppose," said Mrs. Blaisedell in a dubious tone. His work here was almost done already. He just had to get them seated.

"It just seems so unfinished, Mr. Bosworth," Mrs. Wildemann said, her voice dripping with dour antipathy. Her rigid body let it be known that she was not in a mood to be seated. "The performance is in two weeks."

"Let me explain to you about the nature of a production," he said, as patiently as he could. "A production is very much like a child's drawing of a mountain range, full of high peaks and deep valleys. At the beginning of production, it is an effort just to get up that first mountain, but once you're up there, the view is spectacular and your heart fills with energy and enthusiasm. Ah, but then you descend into the valley. And this valley is filled with despair and bad actors and drunken playwrights and thieving producers and designers who need more of the money the producers just stole, and many, many, many lose their way in this valley altogether. But a hardy few find their way to the next mountain and make it back to the top and all is as it was before. But then there is another descent into peril and ruin and people begin to panic. But experience is the guide that again finds the mountain path. And as the hardy crew soldiers ever onward," he swept his arm in an up and down motion to illustrate his next point, "they find that the mountains become hills and the valleys become meadows as it all evens out. There are still highs and lows to be sure, but the extremes are but memories."

"So what are we in?" said Mrs. Blaisedell in her sharp voice. He was really beginning to like her no-nonsense approach. He might have to bring her back with him as well to run Hobart Bosworth Productions. "A peak or a valley?"

"Why, dear Mrs. Blaisedell," he replied. "Can't you see? We're standing in a beautiful meadow. There are spring flowers all around us and only the gently rolling hills lie before us."

"Two weeks is not a lot of time, Mr. Bosworth," said the woman.

"In show business it's a lifetime."

"I hope this will be good. Our reputation in this community is at stake here. When we opened up our theater to you we were expecting something more along the lines of Shakespeare or even *Our Miss Gibbs.*"

"Or *The Country Boy,*" Mrs. Wildemann interjected.

"The Country Boy," Mrs. Blaisedell echoed.

He gave a little laugh. "And I gave some serious thought to staging one of those very fine plays. But there's a limit to the, how shall I put it, abilities of the local talent. Have some faith in our little London play, dear ladies, and I think you will see that faith dearly rewarded."

"But they're running around naked," Mrs. Blaisedell exclaimed.

"They're not naked. They have costumes. I have no interest in bringing burlesque to your fine establishment. But I am interested in mounting a play the likes of which have never been seen on this island before."

"I certainly hope so," Mrs. Blaisedell said starchily. "My brother will be joining us from Phoenix for this. And he's a priest."

"Then he should find this most enlightening as well as entertaining," he shot back. Out of the corner of his eye he saw Red-Eye hit his mark perfectly this time, missing the bog. Having done it just as he had been directed, Hobart realized now that the scene would have to be restaged. Though distracted by thoughts of how to maximize the terrifying impact of Red-Eye's appearance, he said, "I'm glad you invited your brother and I look forward to meeting him."

"Pssh," she snapped. "He invited himself when he read about it in the paper. He's an admirer of Jack London's."

"He's sure to be entertained then. I'm so glad you came today but if you'll excuse me I have to get back to rehearsing. Only two weeks, you know."

"I thought you said that was plenty of time?"

"I hope it will be," he said and left them finally taking their seats. He stepped back to the table and Morosco's side. Hobart took a deep breath to regain his center and rubbed his hands through his hair, thoroughly mussing it, though it made his scalp tingle, which in turn energized his brain. "How did Mrs. Blaisedell's brother read about this show? Have you been sending out press releases? To a paper in Phoenix?"

"No."

"Okay. Good." He smoothed down his hair.

"Just to a few of the Hawaiian papers."

"Do you think it's possible that they just might, I stress might, have put the story on the wires?"

"I suppose it's possible. But I asked them not to."

"You asked a journalist to keep a secret?"

"Sure."

"Shit."

"What's the problem? I'm trying to make sure we have a full house."

"Ben, it's a single performance. The families of our cast alone could fill the house for one night."

"I guess I couldn't help myself."

"Well, it can't be helped now. Please, for God's sake, no more releases, please!"

"Sure thing."

"Christ. You were right about one thing." Hobart sighed.

"What's that?"

"Now it really is turning into the *Cleveland Follies of 1899* all over again."

"Yeah. At least this time you're not sleeping with your star."

At that moment the scene came to an end. The faces of the young actors turned to look at him expectantly, waiting for the approval that all performers crave from their audience whether it's two or two thousand. "Pretty good," he said after thinking through the dozens of things he had to change in this scene alone. "Pretty good." He turned and whispered to Morosco. "Why don't you let them knock off for the day?"

"Okay." Ben turned to the ensemble. "Okay, boys. Good work today. We'll see you all next on Wednesday at ten sharp."

"Rehearsals don't start until eleven," Hobart whispered again.

"Ever hear of Hawaiian time?"

"No."

"Then, please, just let me do my job." He raised his voice again. "Ten o'clock, fellas. Please. Don't be late." He dropped into his low voice again for Hobart's ears. "If I tell 'em ten I'll have most of 'em here by eleven."

"Hawaiian time?"

"Now you got it."

As the cast filed out, joking with one another and thrilled to have the evening free at last, Hobart felt a soft touch on his shoulder. He tilted his head, knowing who was there.

"Alice."

Morosco scooped up his binder in a sudden rush and headed over to intercept Mrs. Blaisedell and Mrs. Wildemann.

"I spent all day in the corner over there working on my needlepoint like an old woman."

"I'm sorry. I thought we'd get to you today. But I have you all day tomorrow."

"I don't mind about that, Hobart. But you never even once came over to say hello to me."

"I saw you this morning."

"That's true, you did say good morning to me. Not a word after that, though. You even took lunch by yourself, as did I. Are you ignoring me?"

"How could I do that? We're here together all the time. And I have you all day tomorrow."

"I just thought we would be spending a little more time together."

"Time, yes. Well time seems to be the currency everyone's worried about my spending today." Morosco gave him a wave as he ushered the ladies out the door.

She stroked his tie and leaned in close, now that they were alone. "I've been watching the show come together and I have some ideas if you want to hear them."

"You know, I can't wait to hear them. And we have—"

"All day tomorrow. So I've heard." She let his tie drop. "I don't suppose you have the time to join me for a quick supper before I head back to Ewa?"

"I can't tonight. I really have so much work to get done and I have to drop in at the Londons' tonight to see what progress Jack has made. If any."

"All right," she said, in a tone that was anything but. "All day tomorrow, then."

"Absolutely."

He focused on writing down his thoughts as notes he would incorporate into the next rehearsal as she slowly left the room, seemingly stopping to examine every angle and floor gap on her way. He gave her a good half hour after her disappearance before he finished up his notes, closed his binder, and called it a day.

He walked through the warm tropical evening down the hill from the school. He paused between 'Iolani Palace and Washington Place. The streets were full of busy bicycles and cars. Already red, white, and blue banners were strung from the lampposts and crepe ribbons festooned the palm trees. The Fourth of July was imminent. Two weeks.

At least sometimes Honolulu could feel a little like Los Angeles, so he wasn't completely homesick. He didn't head for the London cottage as he had told Alice. Instead he made straight for the hotel. A group of peacocked American naval officers were drinking in the bar and singing loudly. He left their roar behind and reached the safety of his room, locking the door behind him.

A warm ocean breeze made the thin white muslin drapes fill and flutter like luffing sails. He tossed his binder on the sofa and walked to the French doors to watch the sunset turn the sky scarlet and vermillion. He took his coat off and loosened his tie.

"Are you here?" he said at last, never taking his eyes off the foaming surf.

After a moment came the response from the bedroom. "Yes."

He nodded to himself. Smiled. Good.

Charmian spoke again. "I'm here."

CHAPTER THIRTY

Hᴵˢ ᴾʀᴏʙʟᴇᴍ ᴡᴀˢ Aʟɪᴄᴇ.
It wasn't that he was tired of the affair, nor that she constantly reminded him of her husband's comparatively minuscule investment to fund the play. It wasn't because he was now involved with Charmian.

It was because Alice couldn't act.

He'd seen this before. When the lights came up or the camera faded in on her, all the wonderful angles of the beautiful face would vanish, the curves of the attractive body would melt away, and the mellifluous voice, which could send shivers up the spine of any man, grew hard and grating. Vocal problems were never an issue with the pictures. But on the stage, Alice's voice had to carry the bulk of the narration, and her stiff presentation was painful to hear. Even Morosco, immune to the artistry of stagecraft, winced every time she began a passage. Hobart had tried everything he could to get his young star to act well, but his direction seemed to roll over her as easily as the gentle waves lapping against the protected sands of Ala Moana Beach.

He knew she was trying her damnedest. He had given her breathing exercises, forcing her to focus on her diaphragm, and he had seen her pacing behind him in the gymnasium while he rehearsed other scenes, raising and lowering her arms while murmuring her lines as he had shown her. But when cued, the conscious effort of breathing only made her line readings sound even more strained. He'd tried motivation in every guise, from intimate coaxing to energetic coaching, and still every line was delivered in that flat midwestern accent of hers that was driving spikes into his brain. As Morosco had put it after the all-day rehearsal a day earlier, she had a great voice for still-life pageants.

"Again," he snapped at the cast, as they rehearsed the final scene, where the Narrator described the happy union of her primitive ancestry while Boy and the monkey men dramatized it. Yesterday had been a long, hard day, today even worse. He buried his head in his hands as she began again. Perhaps with his eyes closed, without actually seeing her stiff poses and pained expressions, he would at least hear the promise of some good acting.

It was Morosco who at last came to the conclusion he himself had been trying to avoid for two days. With his eyes still closed he smelled the man's bay rum cologne and felt his warm breath on his ear as Morosco drew close and whispered, "She can't do it, can she?"

It's one performance, he thought to himself. Just one. What would it matter in the grand scale? Not a bit. Except that his name was on it. He was responsible. It was his job not to make it good enough but to make it great. One performance or a thousand, it didn't matter. Good enough was not good enough—and she wasn't even good. He lifted up his head and looked at Morosco, whose head still hung close to his own. "No," he said with resignation. "She can't."

"What are you going to do?"

"Cleveland."

"Oh. Damn."

Hobart stood up, raising a hand to stop the performance, which ground slowly to stillness as the actors shed their characterizations. Even at this point, he was surprised at the transformation the Hawaiians were achieving; they seemed to evolve before his very eyes. He focused his gaze on Alice and began to pace, trying to find the right words. She shifted from foot to foot, her face growing red.

He began to speak, never taking his eyes from her:

> *To-morrow, and to-morrow, and to-morrow, / Creeps in*
> *this petty pace from day to day / To the last syllable of*
> *recorded time, / And all our yesterdays have lighted fools*
> */ The way to dusty death.*

He watched as she angrily set her jaw and her flushed, trembling face grew white but for two red spots on her cheeks. He continued:

> *Out, out, brief candle! / Life's but a walking shadow; a*
> *poor player / That struts and frets his hour upon the*
> *stage / And then is heard no more: it is a tale / Told by*
> *an idiot, full of sound and fury, / Signifying nothing.*

She blinked, but the tears welled up in spite of her effort. "Go home," he said at last. "Come back tomorrow. And be prepared to do some acting, for Christ's sake." Though Alice hadn't moved at all even though the others swarmed to the exit, he spoke to her from the table. "You stay."

"Christ, Bosworth," Morosco said, eyes down. "You can sure be a son of a bitch."

He offered no response as the little man left. Still Alice stood there, rooted to the spot with the same stoic tenacity with which her forefathers stood upon the wintry plains of Wisconsin. "You don't have to humiliate me," she said at last.

"You're the one doing the humiliating," he yelled back at her. The force of his outburst startled her and she took two steps away from him. "You're humiliating yourself and you're humiliating me."

"You?"

"Yes! Godammit, yes! It's my goddamn show!"

"You don't have to swear at me, Hobie."

"Sorry if it offends your delicate sensibilities, but that's what we do in show business. We swear! We screw and we swear and every now and then we put on a show. But it has to be a good show, otherwise they take away the screwing part."

"Please stop."

"Now I know you can do one, but I don't know if you can do the other. Can you swear? I want to know if you can swear. I want to hear it. Let me see if you've got it in you."

"No."

"Come on, Alice. Let me hear you say 'godammit.'"

"No."

"Dig down deep and find it in yourself to say 'bullshit'!" He pounded his fist on the table. "Say it and you'll be an actress, I swear to God it will make you an actress. Say it."

"No! Hob. No! Stop it! Stop badgering me."

"I'm not badgering you. I'm trying to get you to act."

"I'm not an actress."

He folded his arms. "I'm not arguing with you. Now I'm going to have to recast your part. You know that, right?"

This brought the tears. She rushed into his arms and he could feel the wetness soaking almost instantly through his light linen shirt.

"Please, don't do that to me, Hob. Please."

"It's not just for the good of the show, Alice. It's for your own good, believe me. People will laugh at you. You don't want that, do you?"

"I don't want to quit."

"I'm not asking you to."

"Please, Hob. I want to do it right. I know I can."

He placed his hand gently under her face and tilted it up so he could look down into her startling blue eyes, glowing even brighter now that they were outlined in red and glazed in tears. This was partly done so she could see his expression more clearly, and partly done to salvage his shirt before any permanent staining took place. "It takes a certain permissiveness, a freedom of spirit, to be an actress, darling," he said. "Desire isn't enough. You need to have a talent for it."

"But I can do it," she sobbed.

"Even if you could, what did you expect? That I was going to sweep you away from your husband and whisk you back to Hollywood and put you in the pictures? Please, Mrs. Holdings, that was never going to happen."

She pushed away from him and daubed her eyes dry. He again saw her set her jaw in that stiff manner that betrayed her anger. "Is there another woman?"

"What? No."

"You're giving my part to Leialoha, aren't you? I knew I shouldn't have introduced you to her. You're . . . You're . . . You're screwing her, aren't you?"

"Why would you think that?"

"Answer my question!"

"Of course I'm not."

"I bet you are. I bet you are and that's why you're replacing me."

"I'm not. And I haven't decided who's replacing you anyway."

"My husband will never stand for this. He'll want his money back. I'll see to it."

"Your husband signed a contract, and when he sees Ben's projected box office numbers he's going to be very happy that he's going to more than double his money."

She sneered at him. Now she turns in a good performance, he thought. "I can make him break it, you mark my words."

"And when I tell him I broke his wife in for him? What do you think he'll say about that? Should I tell him that his wife has made a cuckold out of him as long as he's been on this island?"

Her expression turned from anger to shock and then she bared her teeth. "You wouldn't," she hissed at him.

"Go home, Alice. Go to your husband and tell him that you're disgusted by the world of theater and want no more to do with it or me. We'll put on our little play and pay your husband back royally, then soon I'll return to California and you can go about the business of having babies and helping Mr. Holdings succeed in the exploitation of the sugar peasants." Peasants. Far too much time in the company of the Boy Socialist, he thought.

"Don't talk to me like I'm beneath you," she said, pulling herself together and rising to her full height. "You're beneath me. You . . . You . . . Actor!"

"There. I knew you could swear."

She flung the papers from the table at him. He stepped aside to dodge his own heavy binder. Then she walked briskly, proudly even, across the room to her needlepoint bag, her blue skirt swirling around her dramatically. Hobart crossed his arms to watch her. Her hair was coming undone and spilling down around her shoulders and her eyes were blazing. He was almost immediately a little regretful that he had had to end all contact with her like this; even now he found himself being aroused by her. But it was for the best. Best for the show and certainly it would make the situation with Charmian a little less complicated than it already was. Besides, when it came to women he had recovered from worse setbacks than this. One thing he had learned about women was that their own emotions confused them. In a week she wouldn't remember the specifics of her anger toward him, just that he had aroused a deep feeling within her. All he would have to do would be to remind her of that feeling and she would tumble for him all over again.

She stopped briefly at the door as if to say one final thing, but then gathered her dignity and crashed through the door with a noise that would probably wake the sleeping orphan babies on the other side of the building. He sat down on the table and breathed a huge sigh of relief. Now he only had to recast, and he had an actor in mind for that already. He lay down on the table, feeling at peace, groaning only slightly as the icicle in his stomach twisted again.

Charmian.

Good God in heaven, what was he thinking? Charmian London. Of all the women on the island, including the perfectly gorgeous one who had just made her stormy exit? Charmian?

The thought of her made him grin. Strong emotions at play again. She'd gone from hating him to wanting him. It had started innocently enough on Molokai. Seeing the old sailor again among the lepers had certainly thrown him, and he'd wanted to put as much distance between the whole damned, pestilent lot and himself so he'd camped at the edge of the settlement. Sensing his distress, she'd come to his fireside that night, only to keep him company. The night had ended with passionate kissing as the embers burned low and the trumpeting of the wild boars had echoed off the cliff sides. She'd kept her distance on the boat on the way back the following night, even as they found themselves alone on the deck. But he could sense her conflict. He knew there was nothing he could do about her choice, which could go for or against him, so the best thing to do was steer clear. Which is exactly what he tried to do. He made it a point only to go over to the cottage when he knew she would be out at a luncheon and to otherwise have London over to his rooms. Which is exactly where she had turned up one morning.

He hadn't let her in at first. She'd insisted on a conversation to clear the air, before things got anymore complicated. Finally, he'd agreed and let her in. Turned out in the end she'd had very little to say. Before or since. Except in bed.

He could see why London had thrown over his family for this woman. She was exactly as aggressive and entertaining sensually as

Mrs. Holdings had been pedestrian and domesticated. She communicated to him what she wanted, where his tongue and fingers should go, what his hands should do. She seemed as satisfied by their lovemaking as he did when it was over and they would lie on each other, rivulets of sweat running down their bodies. Then she would quickly leave. The times he was in the presence of both her and Jack she gave no glimmer of awareness of having anything other than a professional interest in him. He had to appreciate that. She made it clear where her attachments lay. And he knew that anyway they would be talking soon enough. It always came to that, so he'd enjoy it while he could.

His reverie was interrupted by the door creaking. "Ben?"

But the voice that answered, "Uh, no, Mr. Hobart," wasn't Ben's.

He sat up and saw Mano standing sheepishly in the doorway.

"Mano. What can I do for you, son?"

Mano swayed uncertainly, looking embarrassed and somewhat befuddled.

"What is it, Mano? I'm very busy." He stretched his arms and cracked his neck with a twist to the left and right.

The young man walked toward him, each step hesitant and unsure. He held a mason jar of brown liquid in his hands, which he suddenly thrust out toward Hobart. "I made this for you. For your stomach. It's from the noni plant."

Hobart took the jar from him, opened it, and gave it a sniff. It smelled agreeable enough. "How did you know my stomach was bothering me?"

"I can tell about things like that," was the reply. "I see you sometimes wit' your hand on the gut. Like my uncle after he eats too much *lau lau*."

"That much pork and fish is a bad combination for anyone, not just your uncle."

"This will help you."

"Well, thank you very much, Mano. I appreciate it. Should I . . . ?"

"You can drink some now if you want to. But drink a little every night and every morning. If you want more I bring you more."

He took a swig of the tangy liquid, which tasted a bit like cherry soda gone flat. *"Mahalo,"* he said after swallowing and capping the jar. "Not too bad."

"Yeah," said Mano, staring at a spot on the floor between his sandaled feet.

"Is there something else on your mind?"

"Mr. Hobart, I think I'm gonna have to not be in your show."

Hobart groaned and fell back on the table with a resounding thud. Then he sat up again right away, startling the young man.

"Can't."

"But I think I'm gonna have to."

"Won't hear of it. Why? Is it work? I can talk to your boss, if you want. Is it money? You knew there was no pay involved going into this. But I could maybe talk to Ben . . ."

"It's not any of that."

"But you're doing so great. You're a natural actor. I tell everybody who listens about this major discovery I've made here in the middle of the Pacific. You cannot be shy now. You're doing such a superb job. The audience is going to love you, son. Just love you. Not to mention the women."

"That's my problem, Mr. Hobart," Mano said. "Women."

"You and me both, son. You and me both. That's the actor's curse. You'll have to get used to it. Too many to handle."

"I can't get her to talk to me." The words spilled out of him, shameful and confused.

"Who?"

"Leialoha."

"Swift One?" he asked, identifying her by the part she played.

"She's supposed to be my girl, Mr. Hobart. Since we were little we've been together. I love her and she loves me. It's always been that way. But all of a sudden she won't talk to me and I didn't do anything. I don't think she wants me around so I think I should quit."

Hobart rubbed his scalp until it tingled. "Mano, my friend," he said, leaping from the table, "let's take our worries for a walk."

Outside they stood with the three-story sandstone building at their backs and looked down the hill at Honolulu spread out below them, lush green acres cut into neat squares by crisscrossing boulevards of gray. He could see as far as the miniature navy ships making their way in and out of Pearl Harbor, smoke spilling like puffy black chenille from tiny stacks, the blue sea a blanket of crystal-cut sapphires. "You could find all the answers here," he said at long last, the wind tousling his loose hair, carrying the scent of the ocean and the rich, perfumed essence of the jungle to tickle his nose. "If you looked hard."

"No," was Mano's response. "You have to listen."

"You're lucky to live here, you know that, right?" He found that the top of his head only reached the Hawaiian's muscular shoulder.

"My *makua kane*, he wouldn't know the place anymore," the young man replied. "You know, there are only forty thousand of us real Hawaiians left? Many more whites now. Almost as many Japanese. My father was right, we're a dying breed."

After a moment, Mano began to walk along the path skirting the orphan school and Hobart followed, the sweeping panorama remaining to starboard. He followed the young man to a rough wooden shed, really just a roof supported by stripped tree trunks on the grounds about twenty yards from the building beside the outfield of the small, dusty baseball diamond. Sawdust and wood curlings crunched beneath their feet and the tangy smell of lumber filled his nose. A dirty brown muslin tarp covered a long object supported by two sawhorses. Mano gripped the head of the cloth and cautiously peeled back the covering. Then he stood back, quietly proud.

"You built this?" Hobart asked.

Mano nodded. "Me and the students." The sunlight danced over the oiled wood, making it glisten as if the outrigger canoe had just been pulled from the water, though it obviously had yet to take its maiden voyage. The only markings came from a row of round white dots painted in a line from stem to stern. "It's nearly finished," Mano said. The pride in his voice was unmistakable. "We carved it from a single piece of koa tree. The place where it grew is *la'a*. Sacred. It's a secret where these trees are grown but I know. My *makua kane* took me there when I was a boy. It's where I found the wood for Duke's surfboard, too. For a long time after my *makua kane* died I forgot where it was and I was very sad. But I never stopped looking and one day I found it. They grew the wood there for the chiefs only. Now no one goes there. But the trees waited for me."

From the modest tool table Hobart picked up a foot-long model, an exact replica of the streamlined vessel. "How did you learn to do this?"

"From my grandfather. He knew the old ways. He taught me how to carve the models. I have carved so many of them that I have to sell them to the *haole* to get rid of them now," he said with a laugh. "He told me everything I need to learn about building the big ones I learn by building the small ones. Only this is heavier. When we are done with it I am going to take it out on the ocean like my ancestors did and visit all the islands of my home and learn everything there is to learn. Then I will come back here and teach these children. And my children. I love Leialoha," he said at length in his low voice. "I always have. And she used to love me."

"Then she must still."

Mano shrugged off Hobart's observation.

"Love's a strange thing," Hobart continued. "It offers the promise of solving all problems, but seems to only cause them."

Now Mano nodded.

"We're driven to obtain that thing that can destroy our independence, our health, our minds. Why? It's more than a biological imperative, I'll tell you that. I think we try to find love because every now and then it makes us happier than anything else we've known. I've been in love more than a time or two." He sniffed at an indescribable fragrance in the air. "I'll tell you, I don't miss it."

He felt the young man's eyes gazing down on him.

"Don't mistake that for a lack of passion in my life. I'm passionate about women. I'm passionate about film. But I'm not in love with any one woman—and that's probably for the best."

"I think love should be easy," Mano said.

"You're young," he replied. "Everything's easy to the young."

Somewhere in the orphan school behind them someone began to play hula music on the ukulele, the ubiquitous Hawaiian musical instrument. The sound made him smile. "You think you and, uh, Swift One are meant to be together?"

"Leialoha."

"Right. Leialoha. You're supposed to be with her. Raise lots of little Hawaiian babies. Grow old together."

"Yes."

"Does she know that?"

"What?"

"Well, it sounds as if she might need some reminding. Listen. Women, especially beautiful women such as her, never assume how you feel about them. You constantly have to tell them. Otherwise they get worried and move on to someone who will tell them. Easy there, son," stressing calm as the big man began to tremble. "I'm not saying that's what's happening. It's up to you to make sure that it doesn't."

"How?"

"I don't know. Woo her? I see all you Hawaiians in rehearsal. You all like to joke around and hope that it attracts the attention of the ladies. Try not clowning around so much. Show her your serious side when you're with your friends. Bring her out here and tell her you love her when the sun's setting. That's what I would do. But you won't be able to do any of that if you quit now."

"Is that what you did with the Narrator?"

"Who? What? Oh, Alice. Oh, Goddamn no. You heard some of that, huh?"

"I was waiting to talk to you."

"God, can't anyone take direction anymore? I told you to go home."

"Sorry."

"Oh, don't worry about it. For the record, no, I did not woo her. She wooed herself my way."

"Oh."

"Anyway, here's what else I can do for you. There's going to be a few casting changes to be made. Why don't I switch you into the part of Man and give Johnny—hell, I can't even pronounce his last name—the part of Red-Eye. That way you can have the love scene with Swift One, which you can rehearse with her until the—I don't know if you Hawaiians have a phrase for it—until the dolphins swim home. You're a better actor than Johnny what's-his-name anyhow, and who wants to play the villain? You're a leading man. We wouldn't want you to get typecast. Sound good?"

"*Mahalo.*"

"Ain't no thing."

"Ay, now you talkin' Hawaiian!" With a thump, the man smacked Hobart on the back, and he knew the man wasn't going to quit.

"You think?" he said with a grin.

"Finally, brudda Hobart. Finally."

They grew silent as the sun began its last descent into the Pacific.

"They say you can sometimes see a flash of green race across the sky as the sun vanishes," Hobart said, his voice low as if he raised it too much it might frighten the phenomenon away.

"Oh. I never heard that."

A few minutes later Hobart quietly said, "Did you see it?"

"No. Did you?"

"No."

"Was that . . . ?"

"Shh," the Hawaiian cautioned, now only a shadow. "Listen brudda."

CHAPTER THIRTY-ONE

"So now it's to be Hobart Bosworth Presents Jack London's *Before Eden* Starring Hobart Bosworth'?" Jack asked.

"Rolls off the tongue, doesn't it?" Hobart Bosworth responded. "Morosco says it will bring an additional twenty-five percent to the box office and wants me to consider adding a second show."

"What do you want to do?"

"I want to go home."

"Yeah," Jack sighed, shuffling from his writing desk to recline on the chaise. "Me too."

"Not feeling well?"

"I'm fine."

He sounded convincing but to Hobart's eyes he didn't look at all well. He hadn't thought it was possible for anyone to go pale in Hawaii, but Jack's rugged tan had faded from bronze to a shade of thin cream as if he hadn't been outside at all recently. His movements were slow and measured, as if the extra pounds he had put on were weighing him down. Outside the beach dog bayed at some swimmers.

"Is that Jerry?"

"Poki. I've renamed him. He must be chasing some hotel guests."

"Oh."

Jack lit a cigarette.

"Where's Charmian tonight?" Hobart asked, casually.

Jack waved his hand in the direction of Diamond Head. "She's off visiting our friend, Mrs. Strange. Her son Harry was killed when his destroyer was torpedoed by a submarine in the North Sea near Jutland at the beginning of June. We received word only a few days ago. It's been devastating."

"Was he a friend of yours?"

Jack nodded.

"I'm sorry. If you don't feel like working I understand."

"No. That's fine. It keeps my mind occupied. Why don't you pour us a drink and we'll see what we can get going."

"All right." He rose and went to the side table and poured a couple of tumblers of whiskey, being sure to water his own glass down. He wasn't able to drink it unadulterated as the writer could.

Jack swung his feet to the floor and sat up as Hobart delivered the glass. "Though to be honest I haven't done much."

Hobart groaned inwardly, but said, "With something like this on your mind, how could you?"

"It's not just about dear Harry. My sexual monograph is occupying much of my mental and emotional time."

"Can't that wait?"

"Apparently not. I can only write what words come to me."

"Oh. You ever worry about not having enough words?"

"Does a fish worry about not having enough water to swim in?" he replied with a laugh. "I worry about not having enough time to write all the words I have in my brain. But never about having enough words." He picked up a letter from a stack of mail on the side table. "You know there's a waterfront strike in San Francisco?"

"I hadn't heard."

"Four thousand men on the line. It's the largest organization ever seen there. They want me to lend my name and pen to the cause. Write letters to the newspapers championing their cause."

"Will you?"

"Honestly, I don't know. At my age I'm realizing that I've gone from *wunderkind* to *maestro*. It's not the words nor the battle. I don't know if I have the time for the fight. I've found that the things I write tend to have an explosive effect, and the fuse I'm holding the match to is never far enough away from the powder keg to keep me from being blasted."

"You cast a long shadow, Jack. I know what it's like to toil in the shadow of another. Standing in Griffith's as I always seem to find myself. But when you're the one casting the shadow, it means you're the one being burned by the sun."

Major entered the room as confidently as if he owned it and walked over to a mahogany cabinet created in the Louis XV style. Hobart recognized the design because pictures featuring the fall of the French nobility were becoming very much the rage back east. The boy opened the front of the cabinet while Jack watched with bemusement. He withdrew a square envelope that contained a twelve-inch disc. He opened the lid of the cabinet and placed the disc on the round drum. Then he reached to the side of the cabinet and found the crank, which he spun violently. Finally, he lowered the needle arm onto the record and took his seat in front of the silk screen that was part of the cabinet facing. A few moments passed and Hobart heard the distinct low strain of a familiar orchestral piece flow out of the phonograph.

"*Das Rheingold?*" he asked.

Jack nodded in confirmation. "The boy loves music, you know. He won't talk, but he sure can sing."

"Really." He watched the boy, who in turn was focusing all his rapt attention on the cabinet. So much so that he was unprepared for Jack's next question.

"Has Leialoha asked about me?"

"I'm sorry. Who?"

"Leialoha. She's in our play, isn't she?"

"Oh. Swift One. I guess I'm the only one who thinks of her like that."

"Swift One. Right."

He laughed. "Goodness knows she appears to be on a lot of minds right now. You know, she almost cost me my best actor?"

Jack's eyes grew narrow, nearly vanishing in the low evening light. Pretty soon they would have to turn up the lamps if they were to keep working, though the flames in the fireplace were enough for now. "How so?"

"Mano is quite smitten with her but she has not been forthcoming with her favors and it's causing him some distress."

Jack smiled and rose to his feet. "Mano is just a boy," he said. "Leialoha is too much woman for him." He hummed along with the music as he fixed another drink.

"I thought you liked the boy."

He wrinkled his nose. "I suppose he's a credit to his race."

"He's fashioned the most amazing outrigger canoe in the style of his elders."

"Really?"

"Yes, you should come up to the orphan school and have a look. He's going to launch it soon."

"What say you, Major? Want to go look at Mano's little boat?"

The boy looked over his shoulder at Jack and gave a quick nod.

"Well, there you have it. We'll pay a visit."

"Come up tomorrow."

"Can I see some of the rehearsal?"

"Oh no, I never let anyone watch my rehearsals. I wouldn't want anyone to get the wrong impression."

"Ah."

"You know, it's funny about Leialoha. When I let Mrs. Holdings go, she accused me of having an affair with the girl."

London gulped down his entire drink. "Are you?"

"God no. I can't even remember her name other than Swift One half the time. She's attractive enough, I suppose, but I fancy a good old-fashioned American girl all the same."

"Good."

Hobart took a small sip of his whiskey and then said, "So London, where do we stand with your screen story?"

"Making progress."

"Do you think we'll be done before you sail on the twenty-fifth?"

"Is that our deadline?"

"Before is good, too."

"I've never liked deadlines all that much—at least those imposed by editors. Oh, don't look so glum, Bosworth. You'll have it before I leave and with time to spare."

"But when will it be finished?"

"It will be done when the last word is on the page."

"I could have written it myself by now."

"But you couldn't put the name Jack London on it, now could you?"

Jack took a seat at his writing desk. There were three stacks of paper on the table. The tallest, several inches high, was a mass of blank paper waiting to be written upon. The second highest Jack patted fondly and then pushed to the side. The third, the thin stack, was the one he picked up, tapping its edges against the surface to even out all the pages. "See, here we are. Act I."

Hobart reached to take the pages from Jack's hands but Jack pulled them back at the last moment. The writer's eyes twinkled with mischief.

"I don't usually let people read something that's not finished."

"Come on, Jack. I'm dying to know."

He moved to put the papers away. "I wouldn't want you to get the wrong impression."

Hobart rubbed the stubble on his jaw for a moment. Then he said, "Maybe it wouldn't be such a bad idea for you to visit a rehearsal."

"Really?"

"Everyone would be so thrilled."

"That sounds like a wonderful treat. I'll clear my calendar."

And with that Hobart found the precious pages in his hands. He had just begun reading when he was startled by a clatter upon the lanai. Charmian's home, is the thought that crossed his mind, and his body went cold as he prepared to perform a character study in nonchalance. He relaxed a moment later when he heard a man's voice bellowing Jack's name and Jack rose to open the door for the unsteady, vast form of Dr. Belko.

"Hello, Sailor Jack," was his greeting as he crashed against the doorjamb on his way into the room. "Ah good! I see you're still serving! And Hobart. Everyone's talking about your Fourth of July pageant."

"Actually, we're working on it right now," Hobart said.

"I can see that," Belko replied, suspiciously eyeballing the tumblers of liquor the two men held. "I've already ordered my ticket." He poured himself a drink, draining the bottle and indicating a little dismay over that before sighting a fresh bottle on the small credenza. "Saw Mrs. London walking on Waikiki Road evening last," he said on the tail end of a glass-draining gulp.

Hobart's icicle twisted in his gut. He had seen Charmian last night, too.

"I don't think so," Jack replied. "She was tending to Mrs. Strange last night."

"Sad business." The physician shook his great head. "Nevertheless, I saw her in the gathering gloom taking a constitutional. I called to her but she did not answer. I guess she didn't hear me. It reminded me that I've been meaning to call on my dear friend Jack London for some time and since I found myself out this way tonight, I thought I'd pay a house call on my favorite patient." He set down his glass. "And not a moment too soon, I see. Good Lord, Jack. What's happened to you?"

Jack held out his arms. "Nothing. I'm fine."

"Fine, my ass. Stand up. Let me take a look at you."

The needle reached the end of the record, bounding repeatedly against the final groove. Hobart looked over to see that Major Domo had withdrawn from the room at the doctor's entrance. As Dr. Belko began poking and prodding at Jack's neck and back, he walked over to the phonograph cabinet and removed the record, taking care to place it back in its sleeve. In the dim light of the hallway, he could see the form of the boy, cowering in the corner by the bedroom.

"Major?" he whispered, taking a few steps forward. "What's the matter?"

He followed the boy's frightened eyes back to Belko.

"The doctor?" he asked. The boy nodded slightly. Hobart approached and crouched down before him, studying his eyes. "I forgot you were there," he said. "Don't be afraid of the doctor. What he did that day— that man was in a lot of pain and he wasn't going to get better. Do you understand that?"

The boy nodded.

"What he did was take the man's suffering away. That's why the man died."

The boy gave a minute shake of the head.

"It's what's known as mercy," Hobart said.

Major settled in against the wall, his little form relaxing a bit. His eyes finally left the doctor and settled on Hobart. His hand reached up to ruffle his own blond hair and Hobart realized he was imitating his own habitual gesture.

Hobart smiled. "You know, Major, I think this was our first real conversation. We should have more like it."

"John." The voice was like a quiet croak from the throat of a little frog.

"John is your name?"

The boy nodded. "Major." His lips struggled around the word, but he smiled even as he said it.

"But you like being called Major?"

The boy nodded again and Hobart reached out and tousled his hair for him. "I think I'll keep calling you that, then."

He stood up, the popping of his knees prompting a giggle from the boy. "Laugh now," he told the boy. "Someday you'll be old like me." He thought for a moment. "I wonder what you'll be like."

Major drew his fingers in the air then pointed at Jack.

"A writer? Like London? Not a filmmaker?"

The boy shook his head.

"Well, there's plenty of time to come to your senses."

He walked back into the living room and turned on the lights. The two men blinked, not having realized how dark it had become. Jack was putting his shirt back on.

"Like I told you, Doc," Jack was telling Belko, "strong as an ox."

"Bred for the slaughter," Dr. Belko replied.

"Look, I don't know what you physicians want from me. I do what you tell me and you're still not happy with me."

"You're still drinking."

"Only a little for medicinal purposes."

Belko scratched at his greasy beard. "What other medicines are you taking, Jack?"

"I don't know. Whatever Charmian tells me to."

"Can I see?"

"Sure." Jack slowly left the room, tucking his shirt in as he went.

Belko turned toward Hobart, who was just sitting down with the sheaf of papers. Hobart studiously ignored him, though it was apparent the man wanted to talk. He struggled to focus on the words on page 1 but the doctor's incessant throat clearing grew too irritating. He slapped the papers down. "What is it?"

"Uremia."

"And what," he said while issuing a silent prayer for patience so he could pay attention to the script he'd waited months and risked all to read, "is uremia?"

"When the kidneys don't flush the waste out in the urine properly and it stays in the blood, growing toxic."

"You think he has that?"

"I think he shows some early signs of it. But I'm not sure."

"And how does one come by uremia?"

The doctor looked at his empty glass and set it down. After a moment Hobart put his down as well.

Jack entered again carrying a leather satchel, which he opened, presenting its contents to the doctor. Belko pawed through the bottles, holding up one after another, occasionally muttering alien words such as "bismuth," and "Largactil" and "Butalgen." Finally he took Jack aside, though Hobart could hear his voice; a drunk man is notoriously unable to whisper. "Friend," he was overheard to say, "I have to ask you if you suffer from the disease of syphilis?"

"God no!" was Jack's startled reply.

"Then does your wife?"

"Absolutely not." He shook off the man's conspiratorial hand.

"Then you should throw this all out."

"I don't take all of these. We have them in case of emergency. And these medicines," he set aside several bottles, "were prescribed to me by the Australian doctors who saved my life."

Belko swept up one of the bottles. "Algospasmin."

"For my stomach."

"Salvarsan? This has to be injected."

"I don't. I just mix it in some water and drink it down."

Belko pulled his hand down his face. "When do you take these?"

"Every morning. Charmian prepares it for me."

"You have to stop. Right away. You have to stop."

"But these are what's holding my illness at bay. Without them my stomach becomes a mass of pain and I spend all day in the toilet."

"Jack, these medicines are poisons. I'm begging you to stop taking them, as your physician."

"You're not my physician. You're an outpost infirmary medic practicing first aid among the savages."

"Come on now, Jack." Hobart tossed down the papers and stood up. "That's uncalled for. The man's a doctor. You should listen to him. He's trying to help you."

Jack glared at them both for a long moment and Hobart readied himself to pull the man from the doctor's throat before too long. Instead, he withdrew his rage back into himself. "Belko," he said at last, "I'm sorry. I owe you an apology."

Hobart had to give it to the bloated physician. He took the apology graciously and professionally. "Accepted," he replied. "On the condition that you listen to me very carefully."

"Agreed." Jack's breathing was growing more steady and measured. He sat down at the dining table, packing the bottles away.

"Salvarsan is an arsenic-based medicine and it's very dangerous. I don't like to give it to my patients unless their syphilis is advanced."

"I told you I'm clean and so is Charmian. We do not have syphilis."

"I know. I've examined you both at one time or another. I'm just trying to figure out why you're taking this."

"The Australians prescribed this to prevent gastritis."

"And do you have gastritis?"

"No."

"Then stop taking it. Those damned Australians think everyone is syphilitic. Stop taking everything."

"Even the Algospasmin?"

"The key ingredient in Algospasmin is opium. Take that carefully and only when you have symptoms. Stop taking the Salvarsan, Jack, and I believe you'll start feeling better within the week."

Jack looked up at the doctor with a sudden expression on his face that Hobart had never seen before but understood. His eyes spoke of an eagerness to believe, intensely deep and nearly religious in their desire for hope. "Really?"

"Before I test your kidneys for anything else I believe you should start here." He placed his hands on Jack's shoulders. "These medicines are making you sick, Jack. And if you don't stop taking them they will kill you. It's that easy."

Jack placed his head in his hands and Hobart realized the man was crying. He looked to Belko for some response, but the doctor stared down at his hands, refusing to meet his gaze. No man liked to be in the presence of a crying man. Hobart turned at the creak of a floorboard to see Major appearing stealthily from the dark hallway. He crept toward Jack and placed his head against the man's rocking back. Jack, choking down a sob, placed one of his arms around the boy's shoulders. At last he lifted his head. "All this time I've been thinking it was my own damn body."

"That may well yet be the case," Belko said. "But this is a good place to start and I won't have to cut you open to find out."

"Charmian's going to kill me."

"What do you mean?" Hobart asked.

"She's a big believer in these medicines. She thinks they saved my life. She's going to raise holy hell when I tell her I'm not taking them."

"Tell her it's doctor's orders."

"That's not exactly going to carry a lot of water with her."

Dr. Belko poured himself another glass and drank it all. "You know, I did study medicine at Harvard. You might mention that to her."

"Really?" said Hobart. "How'd you end up here?"

"I didn't say I graduated, did I?"

"Ah, well. At least you're in Paradise."

"Oh don't call it that!" Belko held up his hands and Hobart could see his appeal was serious. "The moment you realize you're in Paradise is the moment it's ruined." He walked to the front door before turning to Hobart. "I think our patient needs a little rest."

"All right."

"You don't have to leave," Jack said. "I'd really like to make it up to you for my horrible words."

"Then come see me next week. I want to see how you're doing. If it's well, like I think, then I'll let you buy me all the rum in Ewa."

"Done."

Hobart felt the big man's arms circle around his shoulders, ushering him out the door. Belko had dragged him quite a way down Beach Walk, inquiring lasciviously after Lillian Gish, before Hobart realized he had left the pages of the screenplay behind and unread.

CHAPTER THIRTY-TWO

"I COULD WRITE SOMETHING for you."

Hobart was half asleep. "Hmm?"

"If something happened to Jack and you still wanted a Jack London screenplay, I could write it."

He opened his eyes and focused on the hotel room's slowly rotating ceiling fan. The belt drive was nearly worn through and looked as if someone had been chewing on it. He felt that if he had only been able to sleep a little longer he would have awoken with a solution for more artfully staging the battle that ended the second act. But the answer vanished as if it had been swept away by the blades of the whirling fan and he was left with only the original problem—the violence was too frightful for the audience to bear.

A gecko climbed across the ceiling, defying the law of gravity. It paused near the fan as if to study the two shapes beneath the sheets on the bed below. We must look like two snow-covered mountains rising out of a wintry plain, he thought to himself.

"I've rewritten Jack's work before," Charmian continued. "Sometimes he lets me when he's moved on to something else and lost interest. And I write in my journal every day."

He smiled. "Writing in a journal doesn't make one a great writer like Jack." He turned over toward her. "And what are you getting at, anyway? There's nothing wrong with him that can't be fixed."

"I know. It's just that his finances are such a mess; if something were to happen to him, the discovery of some new Jack London manuscripts or screenplays might be helpful. He's appeared well and then had relapses before," she said. "I need to be prepared."

He shrugged.

"Have you ever tried psychoanalysis?" she asked, suddenly.

"I'm an actor. If I tried something like that and people found out I'd be the laughingstock of Hollywood."

"I've been reading some of Jack's books on the subject and it's not all smoke and hokum. Some of it is really fascinating. As if these men really know how we work. Wouldn't you want to know that?"

"Everything I need to know about how we work can be found in Shakespeare."

"Dreams, for example," she continued. "Tell me one of your dreams and I'll interpret it."

"Oh for Pete's sake. There are few things as tedious as someone recounting one of his dreams. If we're going to play parlor games let's play something I'm good at, like charades."

She poked him. "Tell me the last dream you had."

"I dreamed I was drowning, okay? I had fallen, or leaped, from a boat in a storm and I was swimming downward to a depth where it would be impossible for me to reach the surface. And yet I kept going until in the dark depths below me I began to see swirling colorful lights, and music filled my ears even as my lungs emptied of air. That's it. I wake up. End of story. Care to analyze?"

"Pff. Too obvious."

"Oh, you think? Well then, tell me yours."

"I'm in San Francisco and it's right after the big quake. The fires are over, there is only smoke and rubble all around. There are no corpses, as there actually were, and no one roaming the streets with that dazed expression on his face as I saw in the days that followed. There is no sign of any person. I look down and I realize I'm in a pinafore—that I'm a little girl. I'm carrying a doll I lost when I was ten. She had a blue dress on like mine, and a painted china head with blond ringlets, which I always wanted to have instead of this flat brown.

"The city is still filled with smoke and dust and I can see great plumes of the stuff rising from the districts where the fires were the worst. I'm walking down Van Ness, away from city hall, and I come to what's left of St. Mary's Cathedral. All that's left is its beautiful pipe organ. I can hear it as I approach. Someone's playing. But it's not a requiem. I hear the 'Maple Leaf Rag.' You know that tune? There's a man furiously working the stops and pedals. He's covered in smoky residue and oil from head to toe. He's a black man, too, so this gives him the appearance of being darker than night. He's flailing away at the organ but stops when he hears me. He turns to me and he says, 'Your dollie's broke.' Then he goes back to playing as if I weren't there. I look down and he's right, the doll's head has a huge crack in it. 'It doesn't matter,' I tell the blackest black man. 'I still love her.'

"'But nobody else will,' he says and then he hits all the keys with his fists and this great chord just wipes the streets clean. And that's how my dream ended."

"When did you have that?"

"Last night."

"Jesus, that's grim."

"Better than committing suicide."

"I suppose."

"What do you think it means?"

"I don't know."

"Come on, just tell me what you think."

"If I were trying to divine the great theme, I'd say the black man was Jack and the doll was your marriage. But what do I know? Maybe," he said with a yawn, "if he gets better, he'll be able to satisfy you more than once or twice a year. Maybe you'll be able to be happy with him again."

"You're a son of a bitch, you know that?" She turned her back to him.

"So I've been told." He rolled over on his belly and closed his eyes. Perhaps he could find his way back to that dramatic solution.

She sat up, the setting sun edging her silk slip with an indigo glow he could see through one parted eyelid. "Be nice to me, Hobart. I just committed adultery with you." She got up and went to the balcony. "It's not easy being married to a force of nature. There is always temptation for him. Liquor. Women. There are always rumors. But for most of our marriage I've chosen not to believe in them. I want to believe that the man Jack London claims to be is the one he is." She began to wring her hands together as her anger faded to anxiety. "We're mated together for our whole lives. I believe that, too."

"But?"

She sat on the edge of the bed. "But what if he falls in love with someone else? I wonder. In a way that's not just about infatuation or availability or free love. What if he truly falls in love with someone else? I'm not young anymore. My thighs are not as strong as they used to be. My skin not as smooth as it once was."

"Are those the qualifications for love?"

"Maybe they're the reasons he won't be with me."

"I thought you said he couldn't."

"In the end it's the same to me. Ever since the Wolf House burned. For two years, except," she added softly, almost to herself, "for one weak night."

"I suppose he might leave you then. Just as you might leave him."

"I will never leave him." She shook her head gently. "Never."

"Do you trust that he feels the same way about you? Are you worried at all about that new book of his? His sexual memoirs?"

"*The Liberation?*"

"Is that what he's calling it?"

She nodded. "I hate the thought of that book. The very thought of it. It's as if he's deliberately setting out to humiliate me."

"I don't think it's really about you."

"Shows what you know about us," she sniffed.

"I really and truly believe that Jack thinks writing the memoir will help him gain control of his sexual powers the same way that *John Barleycorn* gave him control over his drinking."

"He's only drunk more since writing that book. Anyway, Jack London is mine and if he falls in love with another woman I'll do what I've always done with Jack London. Find another way to keep him."

He watched her as she slowly got dressed. She made it as unconsciously tantalizing as she did conspicuously undressing. She paused, hearing a sound brought in on the breeze.

"That damn dog," she said, grimacing at the far-distant baying. "Someone ought to put him out of my misery."

"Dr. Belko saw you coming here the other night," he said as she returned to fastening the silver buttons that ran up the side of her skirt. "Though he didn't actually see you entering the hotel and you could've been going anywhere."

"Belko's a drunkard."

"Just in case. Be careful how you leave."

"Should I leave through the service exit like some used-up show-girl?"

"Fine," he said. "Walk proudly through the crowded lobby. Hold your head high. Announce your presence."

"Don't direct my exit, Hobart," she said dismissively. "I know how to make it gracefully. I'll cross the lobby and no one will notice me unless I want them to."

After she left he lay in bed for a while, listening to a bird squabble over what was left of their supper, which they had taken on the balcony. When he arose to close the doors, wrapping the sheet around him, he found that the bird was gone along with their dinner rolls. He thought about Charmian gliding through the lobby, beautiful but unseen.

He had a solution.

The next morning he set the scene for the climactic act 2 battle, which featured every actor. Before he let the actors begin he spoke to them. "In one week we open. Tomorrow we enter the theater for the first time. Today we're going to fix what's wrong with this play."

As the morning went on he set about it, little by little sweeping actors off the stage and out of the ugly and violent scene until only Swift One remained, while Morosco breathed sighs of relief at the savings in copious amounts of now unnecessary stage blood this new blocking would provide. The girl was light on her toes and adept at pantomiming her terror and using her body and face to convey the complex emotions of the offstage horrors she was witnessing. Hobart began to understand Mano's infatuation with her and why Jack was constantly asking after her. Her hand gestures were fluid, sensual. Leialoha's arms would reach the end of their motion and then the hands and fingers would continue to dance and gesture with little flicks or twists that seemed to convey hidden meanings. Watching her thick jet-black hair swirl around her face he found her grace and commitment to her own motions mesmerizing, nearly intoxicating. More importantly, he knew the audience would too.

At a break, she looked up at him with eyes as dark as obsidian, like Pele's tear. He felt suddenly not at all like the captain of a crew of performers, but like a grimy stagehand approaching the starring actress. He drew a deep breath. "I've heard you're a performer."

"Sometimes I sing the old Hawaiian songs," she replied. "For the Hawaiians. Am I doing something wrong?"

"Not at all. You're doing very well, in fact. I'm very pleased."

"Good." She smiled, her teeth white as stars, her smile inviting and youthful.

"You move very well, too. Have you had dance training?"

"Oh, that?" she said, as if surprised he had noticed. "That's just a little hula. I hope you don't mind it."

"Hula? The dance they do at luaus?"

Her face grew a little darker, but the attitude only added to her beauty. "That's 'auana for the *haole*. My *kumu hula* taught me *kahiko*—the traditional way."

"Sorry, *kumu hula*?"

"The teacher who has knowledge of the hula. When the missionaries came they saw the *hula kahiko* and it frightened them. So they declared it evil and had it forbidden. But some people never forgot and they continued to teach the dance even though they could be put in jail if they were caught. It was King David Kalakaua who gave permission for hula again but by then so much had been forgotten that the new *hula 'auana* had to be created from all the little bits and pieces that were remembered. But some still knew the ancient ways. Would you like me to show you?"

"Yes, please."

She threw her towel to the floor. Then she stood next to him and held her arms out parallel to the gentle roll of her left hip. "Stand like this," she said.

"What?"

"I can't show you hula unless you do it with me."

"I couldn't."

"I've seen you dance around here a little, Mr. Bosworth. You're a very graceful man. I can teach you a little hula."

"Have it your way," he said, returning her grin. He removed his jacket and loosened his tie. "Very well," he said, striking the pose. "Show me the hula."

"Okay. Take a step and a step and another step."

"Like that?"

"Not like that at all. Here." Before he knew it her light footsteps had taken her around him and she stood behind him with her hands on his hands. "Move your hips. Roll them, like this, with each step to the toe and then the heel. Ready? Step, and roll. Step, and roll. That's it. *Maikaʻi. Nui maikaʻi.*"

"What does that mean?"

"It means good, Mr. Bosworth. Very good."

"I am?"

"Now back the other way. Good."

Her hands on his hips were firm, but each movement of every finger was delicious. He could feel her warm breath on the back of his neck and smell her exotic skin lotion. Every eye in the room had found them now and he could see the good-natured smiles and laughs. Someone broke out one of those ubiquitous ukuleles and began to strum out a snappy tune, while others began to clap the rhythm.

"They're watching," he said through gritted teeth.

"Then keep dancing," she replied.

She moved to his side again, hips swaying seductively, beyond his abilities. He moved his arms and hands in a poor imitation of hers. And yet he felt his heart pounding in tempo and his body moving with the cadence. He felt a connection with the hula, more than he had when surfing. This was language as musical performance. This he understood.

He kept his eyes locked on hers. The rafters rang with laughter. In moments the Hawaiians had fallen into line with them and their precision movements amazed him. Against the wall he saw Mano, crouching, his eyes intent upon her, his face clouded. Hobart faltered, then stumbled out of the line to the amusement of the dancers and the spectators. He took a bow to the applause of them all. When he stood up, he saw Jack and Charmian London in the doorway, politely applauding as well. He reached out and took Leialoha's hand, drawing her down in an exaggerated bow, her fingers lingering for a moment afterward.

"Ladies and gentlemen," he announced to his cast, "the great Jack London and his wife." The applause turned their way and Jack broke into his familiar grin. Morosco ushered the couple in and gave them seats at the table. Major slipped in, nearly unnoticed, to sit cross-legged on the floor. "Let's show them what we've accomplished today. Act two everyone."

Still breathless, he took his seat next to Jack. "Hula," he said.

"You've gone native, I think. You're practically *kamaaina,*" Jack responded, then leaned in and whispered, "She's entrancing, isn't she?"

Hobart nodded, at the same time giving Morosco the go-ahead signal. He sat back in his chair as the Londons both leaned forward. Jack's coloring was healthier and he didn't seem so drained of vital energy. Perhaps Belko had hit the nail on the head after all.

The new staging played exactly as he had expected it would. He contributed his lines from his seat as he was still unsure of exactly where he was going to place himself on the stage. But that was a minor issue compared to the work they had achieved this day. Several times Jack turned to him with an expression of delight and pleasure. Charmian remained intent on the play, never once looking across to him. When it concluded, the author sprang to his feet and gave the cast a rousing ovation. He asked for Hobart's permission to speak and received the very same go-ahead signal.

"Of all my books," he told them, "I would have considered *Before Adam* to be the least likely to succeed in any other medium than the one in which it was created. But from what I've seen you all do here today I find it hard to believe that it was created in any other way than for the stage. I applaud you all." Then he spent the next half an hour graciously glad-handing with the cast and signing autographs.

Hobart leaned over Charmian's shoulder. "What did you think?"

"Monkeys," she sniffed. "Nothing but monkeys."

He called Mano over and presented him to Jack. "How about our star here, huh? Some performance? Might have to take him back to Hollywood."

Jack shook his hand rather formally, Hobart thought, considering how much time they had spent together surfing. "Hobart was telling me about your canoe."

Mano ducked his head bashfully. "Ain't no thing."

"How about showing it to us."

Mano looked at Hobart.

"It's okay, we're done for today here."

"Okay."

"Swift One," Hobart called to the girl as Mano led Jack and Charmian and a few of his Hawaiian friends out of the room. "Come along and see what Mano's built."

In the time since Hobart had last seen the boat, Mano had made fast the cross supports holding the outrigger pontoon. "She's ready to launch?" he asked Mano as the covering was peeled back.

"Pretty much."

"Isn't she a beauty?" he asked Jack.

"I'll say." Jack was impressed, he could see.

Leialoha walked around the canoe, admiring it from every angle. *"Nani,"* he heard her murmuring again and again. *"Nani."*

He leaned in to Mano, whose chest was swollen with pride and asked, "What she's saying. What does that mean?"

"Beautiful. She's saying it's beautiful."

"That's *maika'i,* right?"

The Hawaiian smiled. Leialoha, thinking the smile was for her, as she had just happened to look toward him at that instant, smiled back.

"Hey!" Jack's voice distracted them all. "Nothing sorrier than a boat on land, I always say. Why don't we give this beauty a shakedown cruise."

"I don't know," Mano said.

"Sure, we could take her out tomorrow. You'd come, right, Bosworth?"

"We have to rehearse tomorrow."

"Then we'll go early. Before rehearsal. We'll borrow Duke's truck to bring her down to the beach. I'll get some champagne and we'll give her a proper christening. Leialoha here can do the honors."

Mano looked at her. "Would you?"

"Yes," she responded.

His eyes quickly darted to Jack, then back to the girl. "I guess we'll do it."

Hobart turned to see Jack's volley but the man had grown silent. His eyes had narrowed and were trained on Leialoha. He had an instant realization.

Jack London was in love with Leialoha.

Quickly he looked at Charmian just as her gaze left Leialoha and fell on Jack. The expression that flashed across her face in the space of a heartbeat was unmistakable to him. She had seen the look her husband had given the Hawaiian girl.

She knew.

CHAPTER THIRTY-THREE

THE WATERS OF THE Pacific were placid at dawn, pure liquid blue lapping as gently on the deserted beach of Waikiki as the ripples against the edge of a cat's bowl of milk. From a distance, the outrigger had looked like a dark, long-limbed water bug poised to pounce as it rested upon the white sands of the shore. They'd had to unlash the outriggers to get all the pieces into Duke's truck and then stand back and watch as Mano painstakingly retied the complex system of knots that held the pontoon rig to the canoe.

In the end it was only the three of them, Mano, Jack, and himself, who had arrived for the maiden voyage. Jack told them that Charmian had chosen to sleep late that morning, and Leialoha was nowhere to be seen. "Maybe it's for the best after all," he told them. "Women can be such a distraction on a true adventure."

"Brudda Hobart," Mano said, "I saw you in Chinatown last night. I waved but you didn't wave back."

"Me?" Hobart shook his head. He hadn't been anywhere near the other side of Honolulu in weeks. "Had to be a look-alike," he said with an innocent shrug, though Mano gave him a knowing nod as if together they would keep a secret.

Instead of breaking the bottle of Gauthier champagne over the bow of the boat, they had passed it from one to another, sipping the bubbles from the bottle while admiring what Mano had accomplished. All agreed that she was a thing of rare beauty.

Then Jack surprised Hobart by repeating a prayer that he had heard many a sailor offer up as a vessel had left the safe harbor of a port behind. He said, in a loud, strong voice, "They that go down to the sea in ships, and occupy their business in great waters; These men see the works of the Lord, and His wonders in the deep. For at His word the stormy wind ariseth, which lifteth up the waves thereof. They are carried up to the heaven, and down again to the deep; their soul melteth away because of the trouble. They reel to and fro, and stagger like a drunken man, and are at their wits' end. So when they cry unto the Lord in their trouble, He delivereth them out of their distress. For He maketh the storm to cease, so that the waves thereof are still. Then are they glad, because they are at rest; and so He bringeth them unto the haven where they would be."

"Amen," Hobart had murmured along with Jack.

Then Mano added, "I called upon proud Kane during the building of my canoe. Now I call upon mighty Kanaloa for the sailing of it."

"I suppose that's all that needs to be said," Jack had said, finishing. "Let's weigh anchor and shove off."

They had carried the heavy canoe into the gentle, warm waters, schools of tiny silver fish the size of minnows and little crabs darting away from their feet as the men scraped purchase in the wet sand. Mano had steadied the boat at the stern while first Hobart, then Jack hoisted himself up and onto the individual benches that ran laterally across the beam of the outrigger. After Mano had entered the boat they each took their own seat. The canoe itself was remarkably seaworthy, thanks to the pontoon. There was very little of the customary rocking sensation found on even the largest vessels, just a steady communion with the water itself. Mano, farthest back, distributed the smooth koa paddles which he had lashed to the gunwale for the launch, and on his count, the three men had silently, but joyously, dug into the bright water and the boat shot away from the shore like a falcon seeking prey. They bobbed easily over the surf rising and falling over the outer edge of the reef, and as they entered open waters the ocean took on a darker, richer hue of blue. Sea turtles bobbed curiously all around them, craning their long necks like seals to catch a brief glimpse before sinking back into the depths. They continued on in a southeasterly direction, always keeping Diamond Head just off the port side as the canoe sluiced across the water. Mano described how the Polynesians of old, who had first discovered and settled the Hawaiian chain, had built massive canoes like this one, on which the *ali'i* could ride on a chair upon the outrigger platform and a sail would have propelled the boat on a mast rising from the hull. These vessels could have carried twenty or more warriors and provisions and were similar in size to the boats used to create Kamehameha's great invasion fleet. With no other ship in sight and no distinguishable man-made structure on shore, the arrival at the islands must have appeared very much then as it did now, Hobart pointed out.

Mano spoke of his proposed journey to the islands.

"Where will you go?" Hobart asked.

"As far north as Midway, the last island in the chain. Many miles away. There are nineteen islands of Hawaii. I want to see them all. Maybe there are even islands out beyond Midway that no one has discovered yet."

They pressed on, the huge cone of Diamond Head crater looming nearer now. The quiet plip and plop as their oars dipped in and out of the water provided a soothing accompaniment to their progress.

"Oh, you've built a fine ocean steed," Jack cried at one point as a flock of albatrosses pinwheeled overhead. "Puts me in the mind of riding my own shire stallion, Neuadd Hillside, over the hills of my ranch. You should see this great gentleman of a horse, Hobart. He weighs a solid ton and was the grand champion horse of all of California."

"Sounds like a wonder."

"Oh, he is that."

"What does that mean? Neuadd Hillside?" Mano asked.

"Neuadd is Welsh for hall, or gathering place," Jack replied. "So the horse's name literally means a hall on the hill."

"Oh." The Hawaiian paddled for a while and then said, "Funny name."

"I guess it is," Jack replied. "Have you thought about a name for this boat?"

"Does it need one?"

"Well, we Westerners like to name our ships. Many times we name them after women, because boats are inherently feminine, but there are many other names as well. In the navy they often name them after important places or significant presidents. I've owned boats named the

Razzle Dazzle, and the *Snark,* and the *Roamer.* I think a strong ship like this needs a good name. Something that's important to you. Like your mother or the Queen."

"Hmm." Mano thought for a good long time. "Maybe Leialoha? That's a good name."

Hobart noticed as Jack's paddle missed its bite into the water and slipped a little in his hands. This little gesture told everything Hobart wanted to know. Still watching Jack closely he answered, saying, "That it is."

"Good. Then that's the name. *Leialoha.*"

"Very pretty," Jack said without looking back.

Hobart said, "I could see she was fairly impressed with what you've built here."

"I think so," Mano said. "She sure smiled."

"Didn't she though?"

"What do you expect her to do while you go exploring?" Jack asked. "Do you think she'll wait for you?"

"I hope so," Mano responded.

"Charmian waits for you, doesn't she, London?" Hobart asked.

Jack, paddling, never looking back. "That she does, Hob. She does."

"Then of course Leialoha will."

"She's a fair catch on these islands, is what I'm thinking."

It was from behind this time that Hobart heard the clunk of the blade of the oar against the hull below the water line. Mano had faltered.

"If someone loves you they'll wait for you."

"Not forever," Jack said.

"Yes," he replied. "Forever."

After a while they all picked up their oars and drifted across the windless sea, drawn on only by the current.

"It's hard to think about the one at home when you're the one off having the adventure," Jack said, opening the hamper of food Nakata had spent a busy night preparing once he had been informed of the odyssey. "Sometimes you can nearly forget that there's a home to go back to." He passed them delicious spiced pork sandwiches on hearty rolls spread with butter and lined with watercress and pickled carrots wrapped in paper. Jack nibbled at his while Hobart spent a few moments examining the feminine curves of the new Coca-Cola hobble skirt bottles, introduced only a few months ago.

"How are you feeling there, old sailor?" Hobart patted him on the back.

"Not as good as the doctor made it seem I would."

"Well, give it time. You've been taking the medicine for quite some time. What did Charmian say?"

"What do you think she said?"

Hobart wasn't sure how to answer until Jack turned around, grinning.

"She said, 'It's your funeral.'" He took a swig from the cola bottle. "And did she ever mean it!"

The canoe exploded in laughter as all three men doubled over. Jack's timing had been impeccable, funnier than his response, and the wicked gleam in his eye as he had delivered Charmian's line had sealed it for the trio. Hobart was soon gasping for air, tears streaming from his eyes. "Oh, I can hear her saying it," he laughed.

"Could you now?" Jack was eyeing him sharply.

He shrugged in response.

"Just imagine," Jack said. "King Kamehameha riding in one of these while spread out behind him are thousands more, turning the ocean black. The largest invasion force ever assembled in these islands. The greatest army Oahu has ever seen. He would have stood up right here and looked out across his armada, inspiring them with the power of his presence. He held his arm out like this, as the statue before the courthouse has it, indicating the way to glory. How the islanders would have trembled as they saw the approach of such a sight. They must have thought that Lono indeed had returned as he had prophesied but instead of appearing on an island of white it was a black island, dark and disastrous, an approaching typhoon.

"Outwardly Kamehameha appeared sure of his victory but there was turmoil in his heart. His great heart. For even as he held his hand upon the great prize before him, the reward for all his years of planning, he felt the stab of betrayal as he recognized Kaiana's canoe. Beached. All his worst fears had come true. His friend had stolen his wife and his trust. But did he let that stop him from striving toward his destiny? No, he did not! With a mighty roar he dropped his arm, signaling that all warriors should dig in, drive on, and seize the island. He would pursue his betrayer to the top of the Nuuanu Pali, letting nothing come between them." He was clutching the shaft of the oar with fingers that were white with strain. Finally he set it down.

"Before he was grown to manhood, though, he would have undertaken a right of passage native to Hawaii. Mano? When you were a young boy did your father ever take you out in a boat like this and throw you into the water, making you swim to shore or drown?"

"No. *Da kine* is a very old Hawaiian tradition. For the old ones a long time ago."

Jack peeled off his shirt. "I've wondered how I would fare."

"London, what are you doing?"

Next he took off his canvas shoes and loosened his belt, sliding his linen pants off, leaving only his undershorts on. "I've wondered if I would have survived the test of the *ali'i*." Without saying another word he dove from the prow of the canoe, slicing neatly into the water.

Hobart called after him; Mano as well.

Jack's head broke water just off the outrigger. He spat out some seawater. "Did you know at birth Kamehameha's name was Paiea? He was named for a crab."

"London, get back in the canoe."

"Come on, Hob. Come on a swim with me."

"It's over a couple of miles."

"The water's warm and the current is with us."

"You're nuts, London."

"Come on. Let's see if a couple of old men can pass a test for boys. Let's become men all over again."

"No."

"What are you, yella?"

"I've seen the size of the sharks they've got out here," he said, recalling the monster Charmian had landed. "No thanks."

"Sharks are night feeders. Like wolves." He gave Hobart a little splash. "Let's swim to the shore of the crater."

Hobart rubbed his jaw thoughtfully. In the rising heat of the morning the water did look inviting. He began to take his clothes off. "Okay," he called. Jack's grinning head looked like a jack-o'-lantern bobbing on the low waves. "But it's no race. We swim in together."

"Deal."

As Hobart took off his shoes, he turned to Mano. "Keep a rope handy." Then he added, "The long one."

The water was even more electrifying than it appeared. As he reached the deepest part of his dive he paused, swirling his arms gently to hold him in place while he looked around. He'd never swum in open water before and was surprised how quickly the blue water turned inky black below him. The water seemed empty and endless. He kicked to the surface, holding on to the hull for a little support. He licked the salt water off his lips and flipped the hair out of his ears.

Jack was treading water. "What would Charmian say?"

"'It's your funeral.'"

"That's right."

"You ready?"

"Yeah. You?"

"Uh-huh."

"Then let's go. Last one on dry land buys the drinks." His kicks splashed water in Hobart's face.

"I thought we weren't racing?" he yelled after the flurry of the receding swimmer. Then, after one last look underwater for roaming predators, he pushed off, determined to catch up.

The going was easy in the gentle waters. Jack was a good swimmer, but he had started off too eagerly and soon had to slow down. Hobart caught up with him as he floated with his head just above the waterline in a fair imitation of the turtles they had watched earlier. He turned and waved at Mano, a hundred yards away.

"Canoe's kind of big for a single paddler," he said to Jack.

"He'll have to rig a sail to see all the islands by himself."

"Maybe Leialoha will go with him."

Jack stared as if he were seeing something far beyond the outrigger's position.

"Have we made any progress?" Hobart asked him.

London turned and looked at the crater, a brown, treeless cone. "I think we're going against the tide a little."

"A little?"

"I didn't take that into account."

"Maybe we should swim back to the canoe?"

"I'm not."

"Okay, then. Start swimming."

Together they began to strike the water seriously, Trudgen style, arms wheeling one after the other, head turning for air on alternate strokes, legs snapping open and shut.

"You doing good there, Hob?"

"As good as walking, sailor. How about you?"

"As natural as a fish." He flipped over on his back. "How's your back-stroke?"

Hobart did likewise. "Olympian."

After some distance in silence, Jack rolled over again. "Breast-stroke?"

"Best of all."

Something hard bumped against his leg and he stopped swimming. "Jesus. What was that?" Another hard jolt caught the small of his back. "Jack?"

Jack started laughing. "Sea turtles!"

He ducked his head into the water. About fifty feet below he could make out the sandy floor of the ocean bottom, sloping away toward the darkness of the deeper waters. That was a relief. Suspended at various levels were the turtles, dozens in the pod, some as big as four feet in length, hovering at a variety of depths, their great flippers lazily flapping as easily as birds' wings in the air. The one he had felt drifted into him once more and he laughed at its somewhat surprised expression as he shoved it away. It reminded him of a cow interrupted in its grazing on his father's farm.

"Can you see Mano?" Jack called to him.

He twisted around but as they had reached the shallower water the size of the waves had increased relatively. It was hard to see any great distance. "No," he called back.

"Then I guess we've no choice. Onward."

Now he was beginning to feel the burn in his arms and legs, across his back. The water seemed a little colder, his hands and feet chilled. He couldn't tell if the shore, and the crater above it, seemed closer, or if it was his imagination. He stuck with the breaststroke as it made it easier to keep his head above water as he swam forward. He began to feel like one of the turtles they had left behind, held motionless in space. When he looked below the water now he could see the reef with its gorgeous living mosaic of blue tangs, green mandarinfish, and orange and white striped clownfish. That had to be a good sign but land still seemed so unforgivingly far away.

"I can see people on the beach," Jack called out to him.

Hobart swam closer to the writer, who was resting by treading water.

His face seemed drained of energy. Hobart looked but couldn't make out any human shapes. "I don't see anything."

"They're there. We're making progress. I just wish the damn tide wasn't against us."

"Should have thought of that before you jumped."

"Wouldn't have been much of a challenge then, would it?"

"I still can't see any people." He was using his hand to shield his eyes, but the sparkling reflection of the water was nearly blinding. "I don't see how you can."

"I've always had extraordinary senses. I still don't need glasses, though I'm over forty. I could read a page from a book across the room. I can smell like a wolf, too. Always could. I can tell when the grapes are ready for picking from the breeze that blows through my bedroom window. And I can tell the difference between White Lilac perfume and Babcock's Japanese Rose. That's what your Alice Holdings wears, by the way. Japanese Rose. Charmian wears White Lilac. I can smell her on you."

Hobart was too tired to move away from Jack and Jack seemed too tired to move forward. So they hung there in the warm waters of the ocean, staring upon each other.

"Until she closed herself off to me I was completely faithful in every way. In my heart I've always been faithful to her. And I wish it had been anyone but you, Hob. I really do."

"It's you she needs."

"Oh, don't tell me what you think she needs. I know."

"Then why don't you?"

"Because she can't give me what I need."

"What's that?"

"A son. That's all I want. All I've ever wanted. It's what we promised each other we would have. Ah, it's all my fault. I drove myself too hard. Dreamed too big. I've ruined her. I've destroyed us."

"What are you going to do, Jack?"

"What do you want me to do, Hob? Do you think I'll drown you? Despite my reputation I'm not a bloodthirsty man. I suppose there'll be another divorce. The papers'll love that. Hell!" He began swimming again, crawling at top speed across the water.

"Jack!" Hobart yelled after him. "Jack!" He began to swim as hard as he could. He felt the tide working against him, but he felt the gentle push of the waves behind him, finally giving his aching, breathless body an assist. He saw an explosion of foam ahead of him and then Jack disappeared beneath the water.

He dove down, seeing the man clutching at his leg, bubbles leaking from his mouth. Mustering his spent reserves he kicked as hard as he could toward the sinking figure. His ears felt as if someone were driving chopsticks into them as his fingers closed around Jack's surprisingly dense and muscular upper arm. Pulling desperately he struggled to get them to the surface.

"Cramp!" he heard Jack sputter.

"I've got you." He twisted Jack so he could get his arm around his torso, keeping his head above water and supporting Jack's body with his own floating beneath it. Jack was coughing up water and gasping for air.

"Let me drown," he coughed.

"I won't."

"Goddamn you, Bosworth."

"That's right. God damn me."

He began to sidestroke with his free arm toward shore. Jack was too exhausted to put up much of a struggle. Onward and on he pulled the writer along. Stroke after stroke, kick after kick. Several times he nearly inhaled seawater too, but he was able to clear his lungs quickly. He felt his foot drag across coral, shocked at the sensation of flesh being torn from his toes and the fire that engulfed his foot. He could hear breakers.

"Almost there," he gasped. His lungs, straining for air. His stomach aching.

"Yeah," said Jack. "I know." He slipped free of Hobart's grasp and floated on his back, letting the waves carry him in to shore.

"You're okay?"

He paddled toward the beach. "You know what I learned in my hobo days is never pass up a free ride."

"I could have drowned."

Wordlessly, Jack swam into the shallows. Hobart threw himself upon his unsuspecting back. "Son of a bitch! I thought you were drowning."

"Wouldn't it have been better for you if I had?" Jack shrugged him off.

"Dammit no. Jack! You're my friend."

"You've got a strange way of showing it. I'm your meal ticket, Hobart. That's all I am to anyone these days. A meal ticket."

"You're my friend." He staggered in the surf and then was knocked by the incoming wave up the beach until he was sitting on the sand. He looked down at his foot; blood was flowing from the wound caused by the coral scrape and trickling down to mix with the swirling waters. His toes felt like they were burning.

Exhausted, Jack collapsed nearby. "There's Mano," he said, pointing out the Hawaiian paddling furiously toward them through the surf. "I'd say it was a successful maiden voyage." After a little while longer he said, "I don't know about you but I feel like a new man." He used his hand to scoop some of the salty sand close to his face and inhaled deeply. "God damn, but I do love it here."

"Jack," Hobart said. "The thing with Charmian was just a big mess. I regret it and I know she does too."

"No," Jack sighed. "That's the thing you don't know about her. She doesn't. I wouldn't want her if she did." He lay back on the sand staring at the clouds. "She and I, we know how gods are made."

Hobart rose and waded into the surf to help Mano bring the canoe in. The Hawaiian was apologetic about his difficulties keeping the boat nearer to them. Hobart told him it was all right.

"Where's brudda Jack going?" Mano asked. Hobart saw Jack wandering away from them down the beach.

"He's going home to his wife. Finally."

CHAPTER THIRTY-FOUR

HOBART HAD A QUIET dinner by himself at a small restaurant near the beach, eating only rice and drinking a little thin tea. His arms ached so that turning the pages of the play required effort.

Afterward, he walked slowly and stiffly back to the hotel to find a note waiting for him at the front desk:

There's been an accident.
Please find me in Room 202 at the hospital. Ben M.

An image of his friend, red faced and anxiety ridden, passed before his eyes and Hobart knew in a heartbeat that Ben had suffered a heart attack. The doorman hailed a cab for him and they drove quickly to the small hospital. He limped up the steps to the lobby and soon found himself on the second floor. As he reached an intersection of the corridors and was reading the signs to divine whether Ben's room was to the left or to the right, he heard his name called. He turned to see Ben, not in a hospital gown but in his street clothes, dashing down the hallway toward him. His face wore an expression of relief and delight, and he caught Hobart up in a strong, healthy embrace.

"You're all right?" Hobart asked.

"You're all right," Ben said, at almost the same moment. "I kept telling them it wasn't you."

"Who? What is going on?"

"Come on." Ben began pulling him down the hall. "You have to see this." They entered room 202. There was a man lying on the bed, his face partially covered in bandages. A policeman, a young Hawaiian, sat in a chair. He stood as Hobart entered the room. "Tell him your name," Ben said to Hobart.

Without hesitation, Hobart spoke his name.

"There," Ben said triumphantly to the officer. "This is Hobart Bosworth." He pointed to the patient. "This man was beaten up in a bar brawl. The police had reason to think it was you. A friend on the force knew I knew you so they called me."

Hobart looked at the unconscious figure. He was long and tall, exactly as he was built, and about the same age. The man's suit, which had evidently been stripped from him by the hospital staff, hung on a hanger next to the bed—expensive brown linen. Tailor made. Hobart had one just like it back in Los Angeles. "Why do they think this was me?"

"Because witnesses said that the man who attacked you . . . him," the young officer stammered, "called out your name before the fight. Actually, there wasn't much of a fight. This man had been drinking and the other man obviously had had some boxing training."

"Who would do that?" Hobart asked.

"We briefly arrested a suspect. But there was a call from Mr. Dillingham himself, so all the charges against him were dropped."

"Who?"

"Wayne Holdings," Ben sighed. "Our investor."

"Oh," Hobart replied, as innocent as a lamb. "Why would he have a beef with me?"

"I can't imagine," Ben replied, as innocent as the lamb's brother. This was now a performance for an audience of one. "Creative differences?"

"That has to be it," Hobart nodded. "Mr. Holdings is one of our investors in Hobart Bosworth Presents Jack London's *Before Eden*."

"Starring Hobart Bosworth," Ben added quickly.

"This is a show-business squabble, I'm sure of it. Sometimes during the production of a play or a picture, tensions run high over the way it's coming together. I'm sure he disagreed with some of my decisions. Or he may have been worried about his profit margins. In fact, there aren't any, right?"

"Oh, it's been an outright disaster," Morosco replied. "An absolute bloodbath. It's going to end up losing us money."

"I imagine Mr. Holdings's frustration must have compelled him to search out a bar and start drinking . . ."

"Heavily," Ben added.

"And in his state he must have mistaken this poor man for me and one thing led to another."

He looked at the man, his chest rising and falling gently. Hobart hoped the sedation was heavy.

"This kind of thing happens all the time," Hobart continued.

"In fact, something very similar happened to us in Cleveland," Ben said.

"It did," Hobart nodded. Morosco neglected to tell the cop that in Cleveland the husband had taken out his wrath on Ben, and Ben had been the one spending a few nights in the hospital.

"Okay," the policeman paused, unsure if there was any reason to further pursue an inquiry. Hobart held his breath. Finally, the young man held out his police notebook. "Mr. Bosworth, could I have your autograph?"

"Of course!" Hobart signed the blank page and handed it back.

The officer looked down at the slumbering figure. "So you have no idea who this man is?"

"Of course not," Hobart lied to the officer before bidding farewell. "Is he going to be okay?"

"The doctors say he will."

Ben at his side, Hobart walked down the hallway. When they reached the stairs, Hobart turned to his friend. "If I were you I'd get out the good books today and hide the bad ones. Frank Garbutt's in town."

Morosco peered sharply at him. "You sure?"

"No doubt about it." Hobart nodded, then looked back down the hall toward the man in the hospital bed. "He must have been pretty drunk for a bantamweight like Wayne Holdings to take him to town like that. Guess his wife wasn't kidding about his temper." He shook his head. "That poor son of a bitch was always one sad excuse for a boxer."

"You know that guy?"

"Yeah," he replied in a low voice. "It was me."

"Come again?"

"Hollis Willoughby."

"Oh. I thought you said, 'It was me.'"

"I did."

"I don't understand."

"Don't worry about it. That fella in there was an ace that Garbutt was going to play. But because Hollis Willoughby never learned how to keep his face out of the way of a punch and wandered into the wrong bar at the wrong time I now know that Frank Garbutt is here in Hawaii." The aching weariness in his bones was draining away. "What I want to know is how many aces he has left."

CHAPTER THIRTY-FIVE

"THIS SHOW IS SO good we should take it on tour," Morosco remarked to Hobart in the downtime after the matinee.

"Hmm?" His foot was throbbing to the point of distraction. He had spilled bottles of iodine over his toes but the coral cuts still ached as if they were fresh instead of two days old.

"It was just a brilliant choice to play the Narrator seated," Morosco continued. "Really makes the audience focus on you."

"Yes."

"I can see the tour now: *Hobart's Hawaiians.* Can you imagine what people will pay to see something so exotic? We'll pack them in from coast to coast."

"I thought you never wanted to leave Paradise?"

"If Zukor fires me I won't have much of a choice now, will I?" In spite of Hobart's prediction, Frank Garbutt had not appeared in Morosco's office. But that hadn't shaken Hobart of his conviction that the man was on Oahu. "So we may as well take this show on the road."

Hobart styled his hair and looked at himself in the mirror positioned over the makeup table in the small dressing room backstage at the Popular Theater. Outside, down the wooden staircase, he could hear the cast relaxing and joking with one another as they played among the canisters of films shown long ago and never to be seen again. They were hidden behind the large projection screen that Mrs. Blaisedell and Mrs. Wildemann had dropped for a repeat showing of the Jack London films between the two performances. *Martin Eden* had just begun. Hobart was pleased; the afternoon debut had gone off perfectly. There were only a few notes to review with the players before the evening performance began just after sunset; the show that really mattered.

He stood up and limped to the door where he could see the back of the screen and the shadows of the action that shone through. He could see Martin Eden dancing on the beach with the tropical maidens, a scene he had shot on Baker Beach outside of San Francisco. He smiled, remembering how much trouble it had been to find palm trees that day. He had wanted two dozen. They had found two and had had to keep moving them around from shot to shot to create the illusion of a coconut grove.

"No," he said at last. "The magic of the play is in its evanescence. When it's over, all that will be left is its memory. Years from now people will remember that they saw it but that's all they'll have of it. A memory. It all ends tonight."

"A shame." Morosco sadly shook his head.

"That's theater," he replied.

Even through the thick walls of the theater he could hear the booming of the fireworks in and above the streets outside. Honolulu had embraced Independence Day with a passion. The festivities would last until dawn. In the spirit of the celebration, the young actors had opened several old film canisters and were in the process of draping the coils of film like streamers from the backstage rigging.

Behind the silver screen stood the set he had designed for the play. The architecture students at Oahu College had done a great job at recreating a primordial jungle from papier-mâché and chicken wire. Trees rose from the stage floor and vines hung from the makeshift lighting grid. They had even managed to create a drinking hole by coating muslin with a combination of paste wax and tung oil and molding it into the shape of a pond.

Behind the stage setting he had hung a cyc, a wall made of flat curtain, upon which the upperclass students at the orphan school had painted the jungle landscape. Backstage of that was the narrow area upon which his cast rested and ate while waiting for the second performance. His gaze fell upon Mano and Leialoha, perched together atop, and surrounded by, the crates bearing stenciled labels that declared each one individually as the various properties of Paramount Distributors, the Universal Film Manufacturing Company, the Fox Film Corporation, Keystone Film Company, Essanay Studios, Mutual Film Corporation, the Biograph Company, the sum whole of Hollywood standing in mute attention. A crate of Hobart Bosworth Productions pictures stood open on top of some of the others. The ladies of the Popular had taken great pleasure in showing him their Hobart Bosworth collection. Mano gently, wordlessly, took Leialoha's hand. Hobart felt a twinge of satisfaction. Apparently he'd leave a little more than a memory behind.

"Do you think London will come tonight?"

"I couldn't say." The last he'd seen of Jack was his back as he'd disappeared up the beach.

"It'd be a shame if he missed this. I promised the press that he'd make a speech."

"Guess you'll have to play the part."

Morosco laughed nervously, unsure whether Hobart was serious or not.

A rectangular sliver of light caught Hobart's eye as the backstage door was opened for a moment.

Ben recognized the form silhouetted in the doorway before he did. "Your investor," he whispered as Wayne Holdings entered cautiously and shut the door behind him. One of the actors pointed out Hobart's location to him and he came forward. "Only a matter of time before he showed his face."

"Good." Hobart turned as Holdings approached the staircase. "Hello Wayne." He descended toward the man. "I'm kind of in the middle of something right now. Perhaps you'd like to rough up one of these innocent bystanders in the meantime."

Holdings's fist caught him hard in the stomach, crushing the icicle within into a thousand tiny daggers exploding in all directions. As Hobart crumpled against the banister the man hissed, "That's for what you did to my Alice."

"I'm sorry," he gasped, catching the wind that had been knocked out of him. "She's just not a very good actress."

The second punch caught him in the cheek, and his vision turned scarlet. He heard Morosco shout and other voices suddenly raised.

"That's not what I meant!" Holdings held up his fists in a caricature of a classic gentleman boxer. It was comical. "She told me everything.

You seduced her! You corrupted her!" Hobart saw the odd sight of monkey men scrambling to his rescue, grabbing Wayne's arms. Someone helped Hobart to his feet and he faced his restrained attacker.

"What do you have to say for yourself?" Holdings snarled at him, struggling against the strength of the Hawaiians.

Bosworth withdrew a handkerchief and held it to the side of his head. He'd been hit harder, but it was never pleasant. "Like I said, she wasn't that good."

Wayne's demeanor slackened.

"Go home, Mr. Holdings," Hobart said, leaning in to whisper quietly in the man's ear. "Don't give Mr. Dillingham more cause to fire you, to have your career thrown away. Go on home and try to be a man to someone who gives a good goddamn."

Holdings looked around at the assembled faces nearly surrounding him; becostumed and made-up the dark Hawaiians looked fearsomely terrifying in the shifting silver light filtering through the screen. His shoulders sank and his chest deflated. Several big men stood between Hobart and himself. Without looking back, he turned and walked toward the stage door. He turned once and paused, as if thinking about charging again. Instead, in a gesture of twisted futility, he kicked the box of Hobart Bosworth Production pictures as hard as he could. Dozens of film cans clattered to the floor, bursting open upon impact, their contents spewing out across the stage like shiny black ribbons. Then Wayne Holdings turned and made his exit.

Hobart felt the eyes of the ensemble turn toward him. He held up his hands. "A critic," he said simply, receiving the laughs he knew he would. He moved grandly back up the stairs to his dressing room, shutting the door behind him, silently refusing even Ben's entreaties as he assessed his bruised cheek. He'd give orders to have the follow spot dimmed slightly, giving him a mysterious cast. His jaw might ache a little during the longer passages, but it would take his mind off the pain in his foot. How many of your affairs have ended just this way? he thought to himself. Not as many as should have or could have, was his answer.

He heard sobs and gasps from the audience and that drew him out of the dressing room. He knew what they were responding to, though he had never seen it in reverse; watching it from backstage almost created the illusion of a picture he hadn't seen dozens of times before. He watched as Lawrence Peyton playing Martin Eden stood on the deck of the ship staring out to sea. The young writer gave a desultory salute to life and climbed gracefully over the railing. Eden hung there for a moment, taking one last look. Hobart remembered that shot. He'd struggled so hard to get Peyton to properly convey the depths of Eden's passion. What he had settled for was passable; it fooled audiences, but it was never what Hobart had really wanted. Then Martin Eden let go of the railing and dropped out of sight into the ocean and the oblivion of the depths. Hobart smiled at the gasps.

Hobart's own cast was as rapt as the audience. He could see tears on the faces of some and he knew he would see the same if he peeked out at the audience. Hell, it was a good picture. Honest. With none of Griffith's melodramatic preciousness. In his own opinion. Hobart listened to the applause rolling in now like an ocean wave. His own cast was clapping for him as he descended to the stage floor. Behind the proscenium arch he caught sight of the stagehand running the rigging, bringing the scarlet curtain with gold tassels down in front of the projection screen. In a few moments he would raise the screen up and the rest of the audience would be seated and the stage would be set for the second and last performance. All it awaited was his signal.

Morosco met him at the bottom of the staircase. "How ya' feelin'?"

"I'll make it."

"I saw him." Ben blurted out, excitedly.

"Who?"

"London. Jack London. And Mrs. London. They're here."

He rubbed his jaw. "Ain't that something. Send word that they're welcome to join us backstage at anytime."

Ben turned to deliver that word, then stopped and turned again, facing Hobart. "I know you're going back to Hollywood when this is all over. And I know you're not going to take this show on tour. You're probably not even going to come back to Hawaii."

"Ben . . ."

"I just want you to know how much fun it's been to be part of the magic again. Sitting behind a desk all day, even if that desk is in Paradise, I've forgotten how much fun it all was. How much fun we used to have. We had fun."

"Of course we did. Ben, why are you acting so goddamned sentimental? It's not like you."

"I've gotta go. Gotta go speak to Jack London." He turned and walked swiftly to the stage door, announcing as he did so, "Ten minutes, people! Curtain up in ten minutes!"

Hobart parted the curtain a little. Mrs. Blaisedell and Mrs. Wildemann had delivered Honolulu as promised. The auditorium was packed, standing room only. Even the balcony had people sitting in the aisles. The small chamber orchestra kept the crowd entertained with some popular favorites and everyone seemed filled with their special brand of Hawaiian holiday conviviality. It was more than that they enjoyed a celebration. They enjoyed celebrating with one another.

At last he spotted Jack and Charmian. He wore his customary tailor-made cream suit, and his face seemed paler than it had a few days ago. She wore an extravagant silk crepe de chine with a yoke of silver lace and trimmed with satin ribbon. It was impossible not to notice her; he wondered how he could have missed her now as she listened to Morosco deliver his message to Jack. Her expression was polite and she shook his hand as the stage manager took his leave of them. She laced her arm into Jack's and the two of them walked down the aisle toward the reserved seats. He walked slowly. Was she helping him? Hobart couldn't be certain. Following them down the aisle at some distance were Nakata and Major Domo, Hobart pleased to see that Major was wearing the suit that he had had tailored for him. A scattering of applause broke out and then the whole theater took to its feet as a mass to honor Jack London. He bowed politely and waved more than once, flashing them the London grin they really wanted.

Behind him the cast was taking their places as Morosco had ordered, and the anticipation level was rising. They whispered among each other nervously. Hobart was about to let the edge of the curtain fall back and take his place on his chair when something at the back of the theater caught his eye. Ben was showing another man to a seat in the back row. The man was tall and dressed in a dark suit unsuited for the tropics. Hobart watched as Morosco shook the man's hand and seated him. He couldn't quite be sure about the stranger; he was seated far back, and the lights were shining in his eyes. Hobart could be wrong, maybe this was just a friend of Ben's. He continued trying to peer into the darkness of the theater until Morosco reappeared and took his place at the stage manager's podium.

"Places everyone," he hissed. Glancing at his watch he added, "Two minutes to curtain." Realizing that Hobart hadn't moved and was staring at him he said, "Places, Hobart. Curtain's about to go up."

"Was that Garbutt?"

Morosco nodded. "I was going to tell you he was here after the show. I didn't want it to throw you."

"Nothing can throw me before a show, Ben," he said with a weak smile, his stomach churning. "What'd he say?"

"He said to tell you to break a leg." Ben smiled. Then he cried, "Curtain going up," cuing the cast. The lighting operator heard as well, throwing the great switches, two at a time, to set the stage lights for the opening scene, sparks drifting from the contact points to the floor.

Moments later, the curtain ratcheted up and Hobart spat out his first line, "I am a freak!" causing some gasps among the audience, who may have been expecting a more genteel opening. His heart was racing and he could feel it adding to the throbbing in his foot and head. Shards of shattered ice still floated in his gut. He took a breath, and then another, inhaling the fragrances of the crowd, hearing the final, nervous expectorations as the audience settled in. They were here to see him. Hobart Bosworth.

As he began to talk, as the words began to flow, Jack's words became his words. He made eye contact with Jack, on the aisle in the third row, then Charmian. Both met his gaze with interest but no emotion. As he spoke the players began to move onstage behind him, the lighting operator throwing the levers, raising the green and blue tinted lights, the play beginning to take on a life of its own, an organic existence that would last for only two short hours before dying away.

As the curtain fell for intermission, he remained seated, drained to the point of being dazed. He could hear the rumble as the audience on the other side of the curtain headed outside for drinks and cigarettes, perhaps to catch a glimpse of the fireworks bursting all across the city's night sky. At last he rose and went backstage, his feet sliding on unspooled film. Someone would have to wind those up, he thought. He could see the exhaustion in the eyes of his actors. Their boisterous energy had dissipated and they waited mostly in silence for the final act to begin, each lost in his or her own thoughts. The stage door opened; it was behind him, but he heard it.

"Hello Frank," he said, without looking.

"Hobart," Garbutt replied, his voice thin and scratchy.

"Enjoying the show?" Hobart turned to see the man pluck his ever-present cigar from his lips.

"It's fine," came the response, as if carried on the cloud of cigar smoke oozing from his lips. "For a play." The man's voice suited his cadaverous, angular form, his prominent, bushy eyebrows furrowed into a single straight gray line across his forehead. Perspiration rolled down his pale, white face—the suit he was wearing was much too warm for the climate.

"If you're looking for Hollis," Hobart said, "he's in the hospital. Doctors say he'll make a full recovery."

"Your boozehound pal gave you up months ago," he said, dragging his forearm across his face, turning the blue wool black with damp. "He went on a bender the likes of which Hollywood has rarely seen. Can't believe you left him with all that cash and trusted him to watch your ass. But that's you in a nutshell—always making the poorest choices in associates. We've known for a long time that you weren't in Hollywood, we just didn't know where you were. It was just luck that I happened to read in the newspaper that you were putting on a show in Hawaii. Of course, I had to come see what my business partner was up to."

"Just trying to keep busy."

"Mr. Zukor is more than happy to have you act in any of his pictures. Starring roles even. He's even open to you directing."

"But not for Hobart Bosworth Productions."

"Famous Players and Lasky Productions." He said it as one name.

Hobart's heart sank. "They merged? I hadn't heard."

"Several months ago. Don't you get *Variety* out here?"

"So who's running Paramount now? Zukor or Lasky?"

"Who do you think?"

"Well, I'll shut my studio down permanently before I let you and Zukor take it."

Garbutt laughed. "Take it? Hell, Hobart, wake up! We already own it. He's owned it from the moment we made a deal with him. You just refused to realize it. Everything was fine as long as you were making your little Jack London pictures and the money was coming in. It's a shame you're not in the Jack London picture business anymore."

"Oh, but Hobart Bosworth is most definitely in the Jack London business," Jack said, stepping forward from the shadows, Charmian at his side, holding his hand.

Garbutt's reaction of surprise was to raise his eyebrows so high they actually parted, something Hobart had never see them do before.

Jack looked up at the tall man. "I'm writing a picture for him right now. It's going to be a huge blockbuster. It has wolves in it. That's what the public wants. They want that peculiar combination of my stories told through Hobart's lens. They know the real deal. You can't hire another director to do it. Not even Griffith. They like that our pictures are a little bit dangerous." Hobart was proud to hear Jack make reference to "our pictures."

Garbutt didn't hesitate to negotiate. "What is he paying you?"

"We're splitting the profits."

"Because that worked out so well for you before?"

"It's going to be different this time. It's going to be such a big hit even you're not going to be able to hide the profits, Frank."

"I'll pay you ten thousand dollars for your screenplay."

"You already owe me fifteen thousand."

"Twenty-five thousand on top of the fifteen you're owed."

Hobart saw Charmian stiffen and her hand gripped Jack's even more tightly.

"No."

Garbutt reached into his jacket and pulled out a slim leather booklet and a pen. "Mr. London, I am prepared to write you a check right now for seventy-five thousand dollars for the screenplay you are writing."

"Take it," Hobart told him, without hesitation. "Don't be a fool, Jack. Take the money."

"I won't lie to you, we could use it."

Garbutt opened his checkbook and began to write.

"But if artists can't stand together against the Oligarchs, how can we expect to inspire the working man to?"

Garbutt tore the check loose and held it out to Jack. "Think about it, Mr. London. This money could wipe away so many of your cares, and it's an offer that's about to expire." He pulled his cigar from his lips and held the ember to the corner of the slip of paper. "Mrs. London, you've always seemed to me to be the sensible one."

"Me?" Charmian gave a little laugh of genuine surprise. "Imagine that. I was just hoping that that was a Jack London cigar you were smoking," she said as a tiny flame began chewing its way up the check.

Garbutt pulled the cigar away to show her the brand. "Partagás," he said, tapping the ash from the end.

Hobart watched it drift to the floor, where it sprinkled like gray snow across the uncoiled film Holdings had knocked across the floor. No one had cleaned up the loops and coils that ran every which way. Instantly, Hobart's eyes snapped back to the flame devouring the check.

"Stop!" Hobart heard himself yell even as Garbutt made the dismissive motion that flicked the glowing spark into the air. He heard Jack's words again—"our pictures are a little bit dangerous." Hobart's eyes met London's and held the writer's gaze for one incalculably brief, excruciatingly eternal moment.

Garbutt's gesture was intended to end the discussion. In a way it did.

The silver nitrate film lying in great spools on the floor didn't ignite so much as burst into little rivulets of intense white light flowing after and devouring the black. The fire spread out in long paths past crates, under rope and canvas and muslin, always intersecting with more ribbons, spreading in rapid dazzling flashes of silver brilliance, flaring heat, and noxious smoke.

"Get out! Out now!" he shouted, choking and coughing, trying to push people out the door. He could hear the alarm being spread beyond the curtain, panic breaking out. There were figures running through the smoke, screaming, trying to avoid the roaring flames breaking out all across the stage. He lost his way. Where was the door? He felt someone grab him by the shoulders as he had been grabbing people only a moment before. He could just make out his rescuer's face.

"Mano," he choked out.

"This way, brudda Hobart."

There was the door. Hobart had been turned around. Mano gave him a rough shove and he stumbled out into fresh air, onto his knees and gasping. He reached behind him for Mano, but the man had rolled away. The sounds of terror filled his ears, the roar of the inferno, the cries of the frightened and injured, the wails of the fire brigade sirens—thank God for those. Staggering to his feet he looked around, trying to account for his cast, his people. There were still figures making their way through the smoke-filled door to safety. He grabbed at their dazed forms and pulled them out. He tried to reenter the theater but people were grabbing at him. Through the haze and heat he thought he could see someone moving, but maybe it was only sandbags falling from the rigging. Then the cyc burst into flames and the firemen were rushing past him, pulling him back.

Clearing his eyes he saw Jack and Charmian standing on the sidewalk. He dashed to them. "Mano? Have you seen Mano?"

Jack looked shocked. "No."

"He threw me out and then I lost him."

Together they began to search the crowd, calling for Mano, twisting people around to see their faces. A sense of desperation began to grow in him, edging out the hope that his call would be answered. This couldn't be happening.

A wailing filled the sky, ridiculously incongruous against the boisterous fireworks. He saw figures emerging from the stage door, smoke swirling around them. The three firefighters were carrying a prone figure between them.

"No, no, no," he heard Jack moan as they pushed toward the firemen. The firefighters lay the man down as he and Jack arrived at their side. Someone began to wail. Leialoha, her fingers raking at her face. Jack gripped Hobart's arm.

Mano's handsome face was covered in burns, and his fine form, so bursting with life only an hour before, seemed deflated, corroded. But the great mass of tattoos on his legs remained unscathed. Jack dropped to his knees, tears streaming down his face as he took Mano's lifeless head in his hands, blood staining his shirt. Hobart's legs buckled under him and he fell to the cool grass, oblivious now to the people swirling around them. Jack rocked to and fro, holding the young man. Eventually Hobart became aware of someone standing just behind him. He turned and dimly saw the oddest-looking man, not a hair out of place in spite of the pandemonium, dressed for a night at the theater, wearing glasses that reflected the raging fire.

"Jack," the man said, tenderly, his voice somehow cutting through all the emotion and confusion. Jack looked up as if prodded and instant recognition filled his face.

"Jack," the man repeated.

Jack lay down Mano's head and rose, even as Leialoha dropped to the fallen man's side, weeping.

"You see, Professor—" Jack choked on a sob, then cleared his throat, his mouth chewing around the words he finally spat out. "This is the end of the world at last."

"Jack!" cried the man who Jack had called Professor. "Jack!"

But Jack turned away from them all and within a moment had disappeared into the crowd.

CHAPTER THIRTY-SIX

THE HOURS HOBART SPENT wandering the streets of Honolulu passed in a blur of drunken revelers, fireworks, music, and laughter, all of it washing over him like waves crashing over the jetty near the London cottage. The people celebrating the Fourth of July on King Street, they hadn't heard, didn't know, couldn't care. It was Independence Day—a carnival. Something burned? Fires happened. Someone died? That's a shame. Have another drink? Yes, please. Though his body ached with each step, his feet never stopped moving, he never even thought about stopping, couldn't if he had tried.

The young navy officers staying at the hotel had turned the lounge there into their exclusive club room and filled it with friends and the island's comeliest young socialites. Endless streams of rum punch and champagne had spilled over the banks of their bowls and bottles and glasses and flowed in little rivulets across the damp wood floor, as if making their way to merge with one another into a single river of liquor and then find its way to the sea at last. Hobart stood in the doorway and at last his feet stopped moving. He felt a thought trying to turn over in his mind like an out of time car engine. The idea sputtered to life—he should drink some whiskey. That would steady him. He noticed that he was catching the eyes of the officers and their guests, quick glimpses. How did he look? He ran his fingers through his hair, trying to straighten up. A mirror would help. A reflection. Was he covered in soot and smoke and blood? Mano's blood—was his shirt stained by it? Grasping the fabric he craned his neck down to see, but the shirt was remarkably clean, as were his hands—even the fingernails were free of grit. He caught sight of himself in the angled glass behind the bar; even in his disheveled state, his clothes hung perfectly and there was nothing about his appearance that would betray the events of hours ago.

A tap fell on his shoulder; he should have known to expect trouble from the sailors. This one was about to find out that he had picked the wrong actor at the wrong time and Hobart spun around, ready to use his fists to pour out all his rage upon a lowly ensign. Drawing his right fist back he grabbed at the man with his other, drawing him forward out of the shadows, light falling across the stranger's surprised face. Hobart froze.

"Nakata?" He lowered his fist.

"Bosworth-san," the man replied, calmly regaining his composure. Unlike Hobart, at some point he had changed out of his theater garb and into his dungarees.

"How's Major?" Hobart asked. "Is he okay?"

"Yes, Bosworth-san." The Japanese man was staring at him.

"What's wrong, Nakata?"

"Please, Bosworth-san. London-san has not come home. Mrs. London is very upset and I have looked everywhere. Come, please."

"What? To the cottage?"

"Yes, please." A note of urgent desperation crept into Nakata's voice.

"Oh, I don't think so."

"Please, Bosworth-san, please. I am very worried."

"Nakata, London's probably doing what I plan to do—getting stinking ripped. He'll be home sometime after the sun comes up."

Nakata gripped his arm tightly, with more strength than his wiry body would indicate. "Please."

Hobart looked longingly at the distant bottles, calling to him with subdued displays of twinkling light in various hues of amber.

"It's a big city. Hell, Nakata, it's a huge island. How would we even know where to look?"

"Please, come to the cottage."

He sighed. "All right."

They walked along the beach path, leaving the hotel gaiety behind. Out of its earshot, Hobart noted that the rest of the city seemed finally to be turning in, growing quiet; the lights in most of the houses were out. Honolulu was preparing for the Fifth of July by getting a few hours of well-deserved sleep. The only sound was the pounding of the surf. The waves at Waikiki had been rising steadily for the past few days as the summer swells, stirred by distant typhoons, moved in. A throbbing in his foot required that he stop for a few moments. He put his hands behind his head and let out a great sigh of exhaustion. He turned to Nakata. "So? What'd you think?"

"Think?"

"Of my play?"

Nakata spoke only after a long thoughtful silence. "Tell me, in the end, does the boy kill Red-Eye?"

"No. Red-Eye survives. He lives on, lurking, while Boy and Swift One move on, evolve, into the world. He's a throwback to our earliest natures, an atavism. Red-Eye always lurks in the darkness, waiting." Hobart's throat closed up on him and he could speak no more.

The cottage was glowing, with lights on in every room, the house standing like a beacon against the darkness, the slight mist blowing in from the sea surrounding it in a soft glow.

"London-san took the car he's been borrowing," Nakata said. As he led the way up the path he stopped, hearing Hobart's steps falter.

"Are you okay?"

"No." And Hobart threw up into the shrub. After long moments spent heaving, he straightened up, his vision blurry, his head swimming. Nakata's hands were on his back and waist, steadying him. He withdrew his handkerchief, already a veteran of the night, and wiped his eyes and mouth.

"Hello, Hobart." Charmian was standing on the porch, the light from the living room surrounding her as it spilled out of the door.

"I could use a drink," he replied.

"Come in," she said. "We're pouring."

She vanished into the light and he followed Nakata in after her. Major was curled up on the loveseat, sound asleep and snoring lightly.

"How is he?" Hobart asked Charmian.

"How does one know?" she said with a shrug, handing him a tumbler of whiskey she had readied as he entered. Their eyes met and held on each other as he took a long drink.

"No sign of London?"

She dropped her gaze and shook her head. "No. He had taken the car by the time we got here."

"I guess we should put together a list of places he might have gone."

"I believe I know where he went," said a man's voice. Hobart looked to the kitchen, where the odd little man who had spoken to Jack outside the theater was emerging with a cup of coffee. Hobart took an instant dislike to the man; he didn't like his imperious presence in this house, nor the way his spectacles kept reflecting the lamps, making it difficult to see his eyes.

"Who are you?" he asked, drawing himself up to full height.

"This is Professor Homer," Charmian answered.

"Professor of what?"

"Mythology," the little man responded.

"He's been spending time with Jack."

"We've been exploring some of the underlying mythologies in his work and his life."

"You're an alienist?"

"I'm not." Professor Homer removed his glasses and rubbed at his eyes. When he blinked and opened them, Hobart could see that the man looked weary and sad. "And yet Mr. London still has shared much about his state of mind with me." He brought his coffee into the room and sat down on the edge of the sofa, then replaced his glasses and again Hobart lost sight of his eyes behind them. "Mr. London believes he is cursed."

"Plume," Hobart said, remembering the story Eliza had told at the Beauty Ranch.

"His mother's spirit guide? Jack is not that superstitious," Charmian insisted. "He's a rational man."

"He is. While he may not believe that a spirit from the beyond has cursed him, the truth is he does hear that curse, in his mother's voice, ringing in his ears. Tonight's tragedy is yet another manifestation of his mother's words haunting him. They accrue weight with each misadventure that befalls him. This fantasy is very strong and over the years he has allowed it to penetrate the fabric of his reality. Literally tearing through the fabric, in fact."

"Do you know where the hell he's gone or not?" Charmian snapped.

"I believe he's gone to the Nuuanu Pali."

"The Pali?" Charmian asked. "Why?"

"To stand where Kamehameha stood," Hobart answered. "On the cliff, remember? To break the hex. To take the leap."

"I think that this evening's tragedy may have startled Mr. London into seeking refuge in the symbols of Kamehameha, symbols that represent courage and strength. Mythological symbols that he was already substituting for those of his own."

"Jack has an abundance of both those qualities," Charmian said.

"Excuse me, I didn't fully explain myself. I mean to say that Kamehameha's symbols are more primitive in nature, not tempered by the civilizing effects of Mr. London's mercy, tenderness, and sentimentality. Immersing himself in Kamehameha's symbols may be the only way he has of coping with the grief of losing someone he was so fond of."

"He's spoken to you of Mano?" Charmian asked.

"He spoke of him as a son."

At this she lost her composure and Hobart stepped in to support her. "Is your car here?" he asked the professor.

The streets were nearly abandoned in the near-dawn blackness, only awaiting the arrival of the street cleaners to restore proper order. The professor's little car sputtered along toward the looming mountain range. Hobart sat in the backseat while Charmian rode up front with the professor.

"Professor," he said, as they reached the outskirts of Honolulu, "why aren't we all about to throw ourselves over the Pali? Sorry Charmian. Why does London get to be the dramatic one?"

"Christ, Hob," Charmian scolded, "now is not the time to be jealous."

"I'm not jealous. I just want to know why Jack can't crawl into a bottle of whiskey like the rest of us. Why does he have to turn this into another crisis? We should be mourning Mano, not looking for the wild man on the mountain."

Charmian grew quiet.

"Believe it or not," the professor said, after looking at her for a moment, "Mr. London is not trying to be the center of attention. He's struggling to free himself from some traps of his own making."

"Such as?"

"You'll have to ask him, Mrs. London."

They continued onward and now upward in silence, the twisted, dark shapes of the jungle trees streaking by, reaching for them then disappearing. Hobart tried to doze; he had forgotten what a long, jolting trip this was, but minutes after closing his eyes the image of Mano, sometimes alive and full of joy, or dead on the ground outside the theater, would appear to him, forcing him awake. With rising panic he worried that he would see the man's face forevermore and would never be able to sleep again. But then again, that might only be fair.

"There's our car," Charmian said, as the headlights from the professor's car illuminated it at the side of the road.

"We're still a couple of miles from the lookout." The professor pulled over and parked behind the Londons' car. "He must be reexperiencing Kamehameha's final assault." He opened his car door.

"What are you doing?" Charmian asked.

"I'm going to start looking."

"Why don't we just wait for him at the overlook? I mean, that's where he's heading."

"But he may have become lost in the jungle."

"My husband trekked the Yukon and piloted his own boat across the Pacific. He'll be able to find where he's going."

The professor closed the door with a shrug and pulled back onto the highway. As they crested the summit, Hobart could see a slim line of pink tinge the eastern edge of the world. "Red sky at morning, sailor take warning," he whispered to himself, following the other two out of the car. "Jack!" he joined them in calling out, again and again. As they moved toward the jungle line, he walked toward the cliff. Looking over into the inky blackness of the valley below he realized that if Jack had stumbled over the edge no one would know from this height even when the sun came up.

He imagined what it would feel like to fall. Would his mind be overwhelmed by fear or would he be able to comprehend fully the sensation of flying? At night, in particular, he'd have no way of knowing when the end would rush up to meet him.

"Jack?" he yelled once into the void.

"Bosworth? That you?"

Hobart was so startled to hear a response from beyond the edge of the cliff that his knees buckled and for a moment he thought he might topple over himself.

"London? Where the hell are you?"

The voice, weary though it was, came from somewhere below Hobart and to his right. Suddenly he heard his name whispered, as softly said as if the wind had spoken it.

Jack stood at the edge of the lookout. Hobart could make out his shape, black against the vermillion beginning to crack through the blackness on the edge of the eastern sea. He raised his lantern and caught a glimpse of the man's stricken countenance, tears having cut lines through the grime on his cheeks. This was the look Hobart had tried to pry out of Peyton's Martin Eden. Hobart saw true despair written in every line of Jack's face.

"Don't take the leap," Hobart said, urgently. "Don't make a move."

Jack turned his face to the horizon where night struggled to give bloody birth to the new day. Hobart couldn't tell whether or not Jack had been able to understand him. His eyes had seemed to drive through Hobart's very head. He crept closer. Jack had stepped beyond the barricade, just several feet from the cliff's edge.

"Jack," he said, mustering as much calm as he could command. "That way only leads to oblivion. It's not the way for you."

"It's always been the way," Jack said, after a long moment in which Hobart drew even closer. "I've always known that somehow, I would be the instrument of my own destruction."

"You're not responsible for what happened. It was all a horrible mistake. If anyone's to blame it's me."

London turned to look at him again, those stony eyes betraying no thought or emotion beyond his pain. Then he turned away again. "Maybe I won't fall," he said. "Maybe the spirits of the ancestors will carry me away."

"You mean us, don't you?" Charmian emerged from the darkness and walked directly toward the edge. "After all, it's lovers who also take the leap."

Hobart watched as Jack tried to speak her name, gave a slight shake of the head. She crossed past Hobart as if he had never existed and stepped confidently over the rail. Jack took a step away from her, closer to the edge. She stopped for only a moment but then took several steps toward him. The sky behind them both was a curtain of scarlet and gray. A sudden wind whipped around them.

"I'm sorry," he said. "I've done terrible, awful things to you."

"So have I to you," she answered him, reaching out her hand. "Shall we let the spirits decide our fate?"

His fingers twined with hers. "In the darkness as I stood here, I heard the cries of men, women, and children as they went over. Hundreds of them, screaming at me for my hand. Begging me for one last chance to live."

"I have your hand now. I won't let go."

"I want to tell you the most horrible thing I've done."

"Tell me."

"Then you can decide whether you want to hold my hand or let go."

"I will."

He took a deep breath. "What happened to Wolf House was my fault."

Hobart felt as if someone had slapped him across the face. He could only imagine how Charmian felt, he couldn't see her expression. Her face was turned from him slightly, looking down into the abyss, her hair fluttering wildly around her face.

"I set it on fire. I came to see it as a trap. I burned it, Charmian, to the ground."

Charmian turned toward Jack. She took his other hand and they stood as lovers will, face to face. "I think I have always known."

"I said it was the most horrible thing. But I'm sorry, Mate-Woman. I'm sorry, Charmian."

"You were right to do it," she said at last, as tears fell from her eyes. "It's wrong to keep a wolf captive."

"You haven't let go," Jack said, looking at her hands in amazement.

"I never will. Until the end, I never will."

"I'll build us a new home, a house of laughing walls, the one you've always dreamed of. A home that suits us and not my ambitions. And that will be a home that will never be a trap. Will you come into that home with me? Will you hold my hands for the rest of my life and never let me go and never let me leap?"

"I will," she said, "if you do one thing for me. Make me one promise."

"Anything," he nodded.

She leaned her head against his breast and he dropped his ear close to her lips. After a moment Hobart thought he saw Jack nod in affirmation, but they were now too close together and too far for Hobart to overhear anything more. That was fine with him; he'd heard more than he had ever wanted to.

Hobart sat down heavily on a large rock. After a while, the professor emerged from the woods. Though he was startled to see the couple standing on the edge, he took Hobart's raised hand as a cautionary signal and held back. As the sun finally burst forth over the Pacific, Jack London slipped his arm around his wife's waist and Charmian wound hers around her husband.

CHAPTER THIRTY-SEVEN

FOR MOST OF MANO'S funeral Hobart had stood by himself. No one, it seemed, had wanted to be near him. Considering that he was one of the few whites amid all the Hawaiians, it didn't surprise him. Even the Londons had ceded any claim to a place of honor and stood near the back of the assembled gathering of fifty or so around the grave site. It hadn't taken Hobart long to realize how unwelcome he was; when he'd taken a seat in the chapel's pew, the people in his row had risen to find other seats.

In his solitude at the grave, while the minister spoke of Christ's love and the resurrection, Hobart had taken in the faces. First there were the young orphans from the school, sober though restless. It must be hardest for them, he had thought, to accept another loss in their lives. Their teachers stood with them beside the headmaster and other students. Next there were the beach boys, fronted by Duke, their muscular forms compressed into their Western suits, their tan faces ashen in the haze of the morning, all traces of their inherent native joviality suppressed—he saw in their faces the noble burden of a conquered race. The Londons had been stoic in their presence; Charmian's face remained nearly hidden under the shadow of a new hat. Jack's face was careworn and his movements, when he made them, seemed tired and slow.

The gathering of elderly women who sobbed softly he had assumed to be relatives; they had dabbed at their eyes with lace silks and seemed to take solace in the offered prayers. Then there were all the others, friends from a life Hobart could barely imagine. The three immensely fat Samoan brothers who supported one another, how had Mano known them? The tall, silver-haired gentleman in the gray suit and his fair-skinned wife, what was their connection? He would never know.

During Duke's brief eulogy he had finally felt a presence nearby. "Hello, Major," he had whispered, looking down at the small figure who had materialized by his side. He was astonished at how much the boy had grown and thrived during his time on Oahu; his head nearly reached Hobart's shoulder. He had been wearing the same suit Hobart had seen him in at the theater. "It's hard to say good-bye, isn't it?"

Major nodded and leaned against him and Hobart felt a lump form in his throat; his words had carried more meaning than he had intended. He placed his hand on the boy's back. He felt the boy shudder as he released a sob and looked down to find his big blue eyes brimming with tears. Then Major looked away.

Looking through the crowd, Hobart had sighted Leialoha, beautiful as ever even in her grief. Her thick black hair was pulled to one side and she stood supported by a handsome couple that Hobart could only assume were her parents. She had lifted her eyes to gaze directly at him, as if she had sensed his appraisal, and the look was dark and unforgiving. Then she turned her face to the coffin and placed an orchid lei upon it. Soon after that he had realized that Major had slipped away again, vanishing into the crowd.

His head had begun to throb in the island heat, his body still aching from the various wounds so recently inflicted—his foot in particular still raw from the coral scrape. Finding himself completely alone, he had turned and sought shelter on a low bench under a broad jacaranda tree, its blooms purple and scented. He must have dozed off for a brief time for when he had awakened, the mourners had drifted away, leaving the brown coffin strewn with flowers from every corner of the island. One lone figure had remained standing directly at the head of the coffin and Hobart had heard a lonely haunting song in an ancient tongue rising from the chest of the man. He had recognized him instantly as Mano's *kahuna* whom they had once taken Jack to see long ago in the jungle on the other side of the island. He had swayed and chanted, removing his jacket and shirt to reveal his tattooed, old, yet still-muscled body performing a ritual of lament that Hobart would never understand though he listened as long as he could.

When he had stood up he heard someone behind him on the other side of the large tree. He found Leialoha standing in the shade, her arms wrapped around her body.

"Hello," he had said to her.

"Hello." She wiped away her tears.

"I didn't know you were there."

"I was," she gestured around the small cemetery, "walking around. It is too bad the old ways have been outlawed. He should have had a true burial ceremony."

"What would that have been like?"

"Mano's *iwi* held great *mana*."

"Excuse me? What's that?"

"His bones are magic and would bring great power to a warrior who owned them. The priest would chant over him, singing much these same songs. After burning in a fire for ten days, the flesh would be peeled away and sent out to sea. His skull and long bones would be wrapped in leaves and given to the new *ali'i* and kept in a sacred *hale*, sorry, house. The children would be told that the rest of the flesh and the bones would have been transformed into a new god."

"He died saving lives, you know that? I saw him pushing people out of the theater."

"And what about the lives he leaves behind?" She stared at him. Leaning against the tree she whispered, "What about the life he will never know?"

He shook his head, not that it mattered, as her eyes were closed and her hands were upon her belly. It was a gesture he had directed actresses to make for years.

"Leialoha," he had said softly. "Are you pregnant?"

"Yes," she had replied with a forlorn sigh. She couldn't be very far along, he thought. Nothing about her physical appearance seemed to have changed. "With Mano's child."

With her eyes still closed she had breathed, "I will call him Lakana, after a flower that I love. Lakana Mano will be his name and I'll raise him to be strong and everyone will know he is his father's son." She choked back a sob and fell into his arms and wept from the pain of her broken heart. Then, as the *kahuna*'s chant faded, she slipped away from him and never looked back.

Following the funeral he'd had an appointment.

"There he is!" Garbutt announced as he walked through the door.

The Paramount Distributors' office was as neat and clean as if it had only just opened—Morosco had gone out of his way to create the appearance of professional order. Frank Garbutt sat in the chair behind Morosco's desk while Morosco stood behind Garbutt, blocking the view out the window.

"You know what they're calling him back home? The dean of Hollywood, can you believe it? Hobart Bosworth, the dean of Hollywood."

Hobart took a seat in the old leather club chair. He couldn't help his fingers plucking at a tear.

"Did you know Adele is back in town?"

"Really? I hadn't heard."

"She's already moved back into her house."

"My house."

"The two of you didn't have any children, right?"

"Not that I'd heard."

"Well, family is an important thing, I've found. You know, we've always considered what we're building at Paramount is a family."

"If Zukor's the father, then what does that make you?"

"The rich uncle."

"Ah."

"The marriage of Famous Players and Lasky is an important one for Paramount. We're even changing the name now—to Paramount Pictures. To them, Hobart Bosworth Productions is like a wayward child, a prodigal son, and we'd like to bring that child home now. What you have to understand now is that Paramount is no longer in the business of distributing pictures made by other studios, like yours. Paramount Pictures is now in the business of producing and distributing its own pictures, made internally by the studio, and distributed by the studio."

"So you own it all."

"That's right."

"Including my studio."

"Honestly, and I don't mean to shine you on here, your studio was never more than a vanity outfit. It's too small to survive on its own, especially with no distributor."

"I can find another distributor."

"Hobart, the days of the little picture studios are over, don't you see it yet?"

"I'll distribute myself."

"To where, Hobart? In a few years Paramount pictures, produced at Paramount Studios and distributed by Paramount Distributors will only be able to be seen in a Paramount theater. We're all starting chains now and buying the theaters where we can't build 'em. Are you going to start your own theater in addition to running your own little studio?"

"No."

"Of course you're not. What you are going to do is let Paramount Pictures settle all your debts for the price of your studio and by that I mean your rundown sets and costumes, not that little warehouse of yours. And your talent contracts, of course. And we'll extend you a services contract and we'll be happy to have you act in any of our pictures. Honored even."

"What about directing?"

"Hobart. Your pictures don't make money."

"But they're great," Morosco interjected. "The best. Better than Griffith's."

Garbutt cleared his throat and Morosco's enthusiasm withered on the vine. "I'm not saying they weren't good. I'm saying the only pictures of yours people gave a damn about, enough to pay a lot of money to see, were the London pictures. Now, when we resolve the debt on your studio, we'll be able to settle those outstanding profit issues as well— maybe get the Londons a little something finally for all their investment with you."

"I have another thought about that."

"Which is?"

"I have a London picture that's going to be a smash. That'll erase all my debts and create a demand for more Hobart Bosworth pictures."

"I'm sure it'll be very successful."

"Damn right."

"At the one Paramount theater that it's distributed to. Maybe it'll be out here in the islands, though it's a shame we just lost the most popular venue in Hawaii. I think we're buying a theater in Fiji, right, Benjamin?"

"Yes." Morosco's tone was that of a chastened boy.

"I have an idea, too. Maybe we'll have Ben manage it and then he can throw a gala opening-night party for you and your cast. Maybe the Londons will even come for that.

"If you make your London movie at Paramount Pictures, instead of with Hobart Bosworth Productions, I can guarantee you broad distribution, and if it's a hit, like you think, we'll give you a five-year directing contract as well. Come on home to Paramount, Bosworth."

Hobart finally freed the tiny strip of leather from the arm of the chair. It felt good because for the last minute he had been pouring all of his concentration into the effort.

"So," Garbutt said, with a smile that reminded Hobart uncomfortably of the night of shark hunting, "tell me about your Jack London picture. What's it called?"

"We don't have a title yet."

"Why not?"

"Just wasn't important."

"Okay." Garbutt intertwined his fingers and placed his hands, club-like, on the desk. "Then just tell me the story."

So Hobart told him. There was no reason not to, there was nothing to hide. He could tell Garbutt was pleased as he described the ending, just as London had described it to him.

"That sounds brilliant," Garbutt exclaimed when he was done.

"Better than *Birth of a Nation.*"

"And cheaper than *Intolerance.* You should see the monstrosity of a set Griffith is building downtown. The ancient Hanging Gardens of Babylon!"

"But it's not going to be inexpensive."

"No, not at all. But one can see where money should be spent. And it's not on a set." Garbutt looked at his watch. "I have to call the mainland in a few minutes," he said in a way that let Hobart know he was being dismissed. "I am leaving tomorrow and I would love to read the screenplay on the voyage home."

"I don't have it yet."

"You don't have it? Then get it. As soon as possible. You can't make a Jack London picture without a Jack London screenplay. I mean that literally, by the way," he added as Hobart rose.

"I'll be back in Hollywood on August fifth," Hobart responded. "I'll bring it straightaway."

"If not, then the final absorption of Hobart Bosworth Productions into Paramount Pictures will begin on the sixth."

Hobart nodded.

"By the way, Bosworth," he spoke again as Hobart's hand fell upon the doorknob, "how did you ever manage to survive in such a godforsaken place for so long? Didn't you feel like Robinson Crusoe?"

"Are you kidding?" Hobart replied. "This is Paradise. It's too bad you didn't notice."

Morosco called out to him as he reached the staircase. He stopped and waited for the man to puff down the hall. "Hob," he said, "I just wanted to say I'm sorry—sorry about that Hawaiian boy. I didn't get a chance to say that."

"Yeah," he replied. "He was one of the good ones."

The next morning Hobart hired a cab to take him to the London cottage. Once there, he asked the driver to wait while he carried a small object wrapped in canvas into the little house. The Londons were out, paying one of their many obligatory farewell calls to some acquaintance. Nakata was busy emptying the contents of the home into the many crates that littered the floors of every room. While Nakata was out of the room Hobart rattled Jack's writing desk ever so slightly, but the drawer was locked shut. Oh well, he thought, there's some time now. His heart skipped a beat as he realized how much he was looking forward to making a picture again.

Nakata entered the room again, now with Major at his side, carrying a small valise. Hobart held out the covered package and the boy took it from him. He unwrapped it and as the canvas fell away, the trim outlines of the little outrigger canoe model Mano had made were revealed. It had been part of the final stop Hobart had made yesterday afternoon. Major's eyes shone with delight.

"It's time to go, Major," Hobart said.

The boy didn't even pause for a moment. Trustingly, he followed the two men out of the house and into the waiting cab, taking care to hold the little craft gently on his knees. As the driver pulled away from the curb, they caught sight of Dr. Belko strolling along Beach Walk.

Major murmured something unintelligible and Hobart asked him to repeat it. "Poison," the boy slowly chewed out, looking back at the cottage, though not at the receding figure of the physician. "Poison."

"Why do you say poison?" Hobart asked, but the boy had no other answer for him and sat playing with the model. When they reached the Queen Liliuokalani Elementary School and Orphan Home, Hobart held the canoe for Major while he stepped onto the pavement, looking up at the building before him. The headmaster stood at the top of the steps, smiling warmly.

"Major," Hobart said, "there's something I want to show you." His arm around the boy's shoulders, he took him around to the back of the building, motioning for the headmaster and Nakata to wait behind. He brought Major to the canopy under which Mano's outrigger canoe had been placed respectfully. It had been draped with dozens of colorful leis, its fine lines still speaking of the dream of island visits to be made and a life spent on the water.

"You know, the man who built this wanted to discover everything there was to know about Hawaii," Hobart told Major. "You could do that now. This is yours. I've asked the headmaster, and he's agreed, that if you stay here you can have this. It's yours now, John."

"See you?" the boy said, pointing at the boat and then at Hobart.

"It's a big ocean. Who knows? The Polynesians traveled thousands of miles in these things. Someday, when you're older, perhaps. I can always use a good *chargé d'affaires*."

Major, now John, approached the boat slowly, running his hands over its smooth finish, examining every notch and knot, and comparing it to the smaller model. In a little while Nakata joined Hobart.

"You'll drop in on him from time to time?"

"Yes."

"And you'll let me know if he needs any money for books or clothes or . . . ?" Hobart's words stuck thickly in his throat.

"Yes."

They watched the boy for a while longer and then Nakata said, "I wonder what he will grow up to be. Maybe a doctor, or a teacher like Mano? What do you think he will be?"

Realizing he would never see the boy again and would never know, Hobart quietly answered, "Hawaiian."

CHAPTER THIRTY-EIGHT

JACK'S FAREWELL LUAU TOOK place at the cottage. After some thought Hobart had decided to accept the invitation—if the Londons were leaving on the morning tide then tonight must be the night that Jack would hand over the screenplay.

He joined the forty or so guests in the backyard as the late-afternoon shadows began to stretch their cooling shade over the lawn and garden. He found it hard to believe the amount of food the Hawaiian girls Charmian had hired were able to deliver out of the small kitchen. As it was impossible for a luau to occur without a roasted pig, a small *imu* had been dug in the yard, and when the swine was finally released from the banana leaves surrounding it, the sweet flesh rolled right off the bone and onto the awaiting platters. Meanwhile, the thick, smoky aroma hovered deliciously in the air. Dish after dish of delights materialized on the long table, from fried fish to savory lau lau, while the cottage itself was filled with the yeasty smell of baking breadfruit, which, Hobart discovered, tasted much like the San Francisco sourdough bread he admired.

An eclectic mix of chairs had been borrowed from around the neighborhood, and when two of them collapsed, one right after the other, under the weight of their ample occupants, the roars of laughter could be heard up and down Beach Walk. The Queen of the Islands, Liliuokalani herself, sat at the head of the table with Jack at her right side, while Charmian, the luminous hostess, sat at the opposite end. Next to her sat Mr. Ford, Jack's cofounder of the Outrigger Club. Hobart sat somewhere near the middle, across from the dark mourning shade of Mrs. Strange.

Every so often the sound of silverware clinking against crystal would stop conversation and a toast would be made: to Jack's health and longevity, to the books he had yet to write, for the gracious consideration he had shown the Queen and the great injustices done to her, for his *aloha 'aina*. At last it was Jack's turn to respond and he rose slowly, swaying slightly, though Hobart had noticed him nursing the same glass of wine all afternoon. He wore, Hobart noted with approval, a striking white suit and white shirt accented by the slim black slash of his tie.

"Aloha, friends all," he began. "Charmian and I thank you for your generous hospitality and for helping us turn what could be a sad occasion into a happy one. You've all done so much more than make us feel welcome during our stay here, you've made us feel at home."

"You're *kamaaina,* London! One of us," someone called, and the other guests roared their confirmation.

He stood there, embarrassed, and then said, "I thought I had prepared my thoughts for this. But I am at a loss for words. Finally. Thank you—I love you all." And to a standing ovation, even the Queen rose to her feet, Jack sat down, his head bowed. Duke, seated next to him, put a hand on his shoulder, which shook several times. Respecting his need for a moment of privacy, the guests began to turn to one another for conversation.

They grew quiet again soon as the Queen rose. This time there were no ringing sounds of crystal; her presence was enough to draw attention. As the silence fell there was a rustling from nearby as a band of musicians, dressed in traditional Hawaiian garb, descended upon the lawn from the house. Charmian stiffened noticeably as Leialoha, dressed in a formal island gown, took a position at the front of the players.

"My dear friend, Jack," the Queen said, her voice melodious with wisdom and the special island intonation. "As a way of saying *mahalo* for your years of friendship I have asked our good friend, Mary Low, to create a *mele.* You know what that is?"

"A song?"

She smiled with the warmth of an indulgent parent. "A song, yes. A hula chant, yes. When an *ali'i* would travel around his lands, a *mele* would be written afterward so he could tell others what he had seen. This, Jack London, is a *hula mele* for you so that others may be told of the things you have seen and done here. I know Leialoha Kaai is a particular friend of yours as she is to me and I have asked her to sing the song for you—and all she asks in return"—was Hobart mistaken, or had Jack's hands trembled and his face blanched?—"is an autographed copy of *The Cruise of the Snark.*" Laughter and smiles broke out all around. The Queen held up her hand again. For a moment her face seemed to take on a hard edge, and Hobart caught a glimpse of the warrior spirit who had held her nation together though subjugated by the mightiest force on the planet. "This *mele* is for you and your *Lakana wahine.*" Eyes fell on Charmian, who nodded graciously; not all eyes, though, for Hobart noted that both Jack's and the Queen's steely brown eyes had flickered from each other to Leialoha. Hobart instantly reached for the decanter and filled his glass to the brim with wine.

The Queen continued. "Now I shall try to translate this chant for Jack London, but I'm afraid my voice won't carry to all of you and if you are not sitting next to one who speaks the language, I am afraid you may not understand all that you hear. However if you will indulge me I shall jump ahead to the very end, a feat I'm sure our writer friend here would disapprove of in any other circumstances than these, and introduce the song by giving you its end. *Hainaia mai ana ka puana, No Keaka Lakana neia inoa*—'This song is then echoed, 'tis in honor of Jack London.'"

There was a scattering of applause as she sat down and then the musicians began to strum their ukuleles while the dancers began their intricate swaying, their grass skirts swishing around their bare ankles. Then Leialoha began to sing and her voice and gestures were so pure and synchronized that it became difficult to tell whether the ethereal voice they all heard issued from her throat, the fingertips of her graceful hands, or the trees themselves.

As Hobart downed gulps of wine from his glass he watched carefully as the Queen whispered in Jack's ear, his head nodding with comprehension, his glittering eyes never leaving the entrancing form that had captivated them. When he turned his head to the other end of the table, Charmian sat like a marble statue, white face set in grim repose, spots of red anger burning on each cheek as she watched her husband. All the while the servers continued to bring heaping platters of food to the table and murmured conversations took place, for Hawaiian *meles* are lengthy. Each gulp of wine churned like lava in the pit of his stomach, but he couldn't stop; a spasm racked him so hard he had to grip the table and close his eyes and hope neither guest to his left or right would speak to him, or notice the sweat suddenly drenching him. And still he drank.

Jack rose again, offering his grateful applause to the performers as the hula ended. "I remembered what I was going to say," he said after a moment and great laughter broke out. "I, too, have a gift to make, this one to my Mate-Woman. My Charmian." He raised his glass to her and there were gentlemanly cries of "Hear! Hear!" in her honor. Jack set down his glass (Hobart had required a refill before draining his for the toast) and picked up a thick envelope, one of the manila ones Hobart had noticed on Jack's desk the day he had delivered Major to the orphan home. "This is a love story I have written for you," he said directly to her and she responded with a tight smile. Jack hefted its weight for a moment, as if by that he could convey something of the quality of its content. "Perhaps the greatest I've ever written. It's certainly as close to the truth as I've ever come." There was an excited hum in anticipation of one of Jack London's lauded readings.

He began to walk around the table and into the yard. "I thought about making it a gift to you, but what can I do? I've dedicated enough books to you that you might even find it tiresome."

She demurred and shook her head.

"But with this book, I know that the greatest dedication I can make to you is to dedicate it to the spirits of this great land and let its words be whispered on the breeze as it rustles through the coconut palms and in the waves as they lap at the shores just beyond our beloved cottage."

With a swift flip of his wrist he grabbed the envelope by one end and let the pages slide out in a flurry of white leaves onto the still smoldering embers of the *imu* pit. There were cries of shock and horror as some of the pages burst into flames, while others simply curled up, charring brown, then black. Meanwhile, Jack smiled at Charmian and she nodded back as white smoke drifted into the colorful sky of the setting sun like the fountain of all clouds.

Evening had turned to night by the time Jack was finally able to rise from the table. He looked around for the girl, Leialoha, but she was nowhere to be seen.

"I have our title." Hobart heard Jack's voice just before the man's hands clapped down roughly from behind on his shoulders. The lava in his stomach lurched into his esophagus.

"Jesus Christ, London, you scared the hell out of me," he said, gasping.

"Don't you want to know what it is?"

"Of course I do."

"The Wolf Hunter."

"I like it."

"I knew you would."

"When do I get it, Jack?"

"Are you going to come see us off tomorrow?"

"I guess so."

"Then I'll give it to you then."

"Why not now?"

"Because if I give it to you now, you'll read it tonight and by tomorrow morning you'll have a list of notes for me to work on before I board the *Matsonia*. If I give it to you tomorrow I won't have to change a word." Hobart could see him grinning in the flickering light of the newly lit torches.

"You win, Jack."

"We both win, Hob. Don't you see? I'm giving you the opportunity to make a picture, the likes of which has never been seen before."

"It's hard to imagine that it's that original."

"I assure you it is. Nothing like it. Going to take a brave man to film it. Braver than Griffith for sure," he said with a smile, lighting a cigarette, the stench of the smoke nearly causing Hobart to retch.

Through an effort of sheer force of will he managed to keep his stomach in check.

"Did you hear the news?" Jack said, changing subject.

"About what?"

"Little Lady of the Big House. It's already in its second printing."

"Congratulations."

"Looks like there's still some life in the old dog after all and some rabbits left to run down. They're even talking about a national book tour in the fall. I haven't done one of those in a long time."

"Jack," Hobart said, "what has passed between you and the girl?"

"What girl?"

"You know. Swift One," he said, in case anyone was listening.

"What has happened, Hobart, is that I've left my heart on this island. She is keeping it for me. This is literally my expression of *aloha 'aina*."

"Jack."

"They want me to stay. She and the Queen, did you see?"

"Yes."

"Don't look so shocked, Hob. I know it's not conventional, but we're not conventional people. I thought you would understand most of all."

As he studied Jack's pale countenance, an unformed thought pricked at the back of his mind. Something Major had said. He looked around for Charmian but could not catch sight of her. He thought he saw her standing near the small group of Hawaiian musicians, but before he could tell for sure the Queen herself approached.

He had never seen a face so careworn, the smooth brown skin folded into thick deep creases.

"Princess Cupid." Jack extended his arm for her, which she accepted gratefully, and with a gentle pat. Though she seemed spry for her age, there was a perpetual weariness about her. "May I present Hobart Bosworth."

"The famous tragedian," she said, in flawless, unaccented English.

"That," Jack said grandly, "is a matter of point of view, now isn't it? In his point of view we are all just players in his drama—whether tragedy or comedy."

Hobart felt her dark eyes appraising him before she spoke again. "One is reminded of the admonishment to beware of actors, they should be seen, not known."

Jack coughed. "Come, my dear," he said to the Queen. "Let us take one more walk together. Hobart, if you'll excuse us now I will see you tomorrow at the quickening of the tide. Your Highness?"

"My Lakana," she said and took his arm.

Before turning away, he grinned at Hobart, the beaming glow of a truly happy man. "Don't look so glum, Hob. Listen to the music playing. You're in Paradise, friend."

Together they walked away from Hobart, the last Queen and the great writer, swallowed up by the great colorful swirl of the dancers.

Hobart looked around, unable to find a friendly face, for all the eyes that met his seemed to be judging him. He felt isolated, unable to blend in. Trapped in a spotlight. He decided it was time to make a graceful exit and soon he was back in his room at the hotel, where, even though he would not be leaving for another week, his bags were already packed. He barely slept.

The happy sounds of the Royal Hawaiian Band mingled with the roar of the crowd greeted him as he approached the waterfront the next morning. Boat Day was always a big event in Honolulu ever since the days when the wooden ships of discovery had been greeted by scores of canoes. The ground was strewn with flowers and ribbons thrown from the decks of the *Matsonia,* which rose into view, its immense smokestack already billowing out great clouds of thick black smoke, as Hobart approached the pier. In the waters off the port side little brown children dove after handfuls of coins flung by passengers. Pushing himself through the crowd, he presented himself to the chief cabin steward at the top of the gangway, who in turn directed one of his staff to accommodate Mr. Bosworth.

The steward led Hobart through the corridors full of confused passengers. Finally they arrived at a cabin door, Hobart tipped the man and then knocked.

"Come in," a muffled voice said from within.

He opened the door into the cabin, which was spacious and furnished with an elegant, dark wood four-poster bed and a dining table, writing desk, chairs, and wardrobes to match. Inside he saw Charmian, sitting cross-legged on the bed, holding hands with Nakata, who sat on one of the chairs pulled close. Both had been crying.

"Hello Hobart," she said, pulling her hand away to pick up a handkerchief and wipe her eyes.

"I'm sorry," he said. "Jack said to meet him."

"I know," she replied. "I think he's in the salon trying to finish some letters before we sail while Nakata helped me unpack." She blew her nose again then stood up. Nakata followed her lead.

"I'll just go look for him, then."

"It's okay, Hob. Nakata and I were just saying good-bye."

Nakata looked stricken; tears fell from his eyes like heavy drops of rain. Tenderly she put her arms around him and held him tight. "Remember what London-san always says," he overheard her choked whisper, "there is always song somewhere."

Nakata nodded and sobbed and she squeezed him tighter. Then he stepped back from her and with a nod of his head he quickly pushed past Hobart through the open door and down the corridor. Hobart turned his attention to her when she blew her nose again.

"Come to get your screenplay, I suppose?"

"And to say good-bye."

"To me or to Jack?"

"To the both of you."

"Though I don't suppose he'd be delighted to find us alone together."

"Probably not." He looked down the corridor, which was only now beginning to empty of passengers.

"Well, this is what you've come for." He found her holding another thick manila envelope. He tried to keep from snatching it from her, instead taking it with something akin to disinterest. Though he was frantic to open it and begin reading he paid attention only to the note written in Jack's hand on the exterior:

> *Hobart,*
> *I think this is my masterpiece.*
> *It's in your hands now.*
> *Do with it what you will.*
> *Do with it what an artist would.*
> *Treat it as a friend would.*
> *Jack*

As he held the package nonchalantly at his side, relief spreading through his body, she lifted a bag onto the writing desk: the medicine bag. "We never did get to properly say good-bye, did we?"

"I suppose not," he replied.

"Well, there is much we have to leave behind us on this trip. Perhaps too much. Are you all right?"

"My stomach has been bothering me a lot lately."

"I might have something for that." She opened the satchel.

"That's okay," he said.

"Not at all," she insisted, setting a few bottles on the table while she dug deep.

With shock he recognized a bottle and took several steps into the cabin. Poison. The meaning of Major's word struck him like a hammer. Poison. "Salvarsan? You're not still giving him this, are you?"

She continued to root through the bag, not looking at him.

"Charmian."

"What? What?"

"You're not . . ."

"Of course I am, damn you! Of course." She snatched up the bottle. "Do you think I care about the opinion of some drunk doctor? This Salvarsan keeps him alive."

"It's poison. You're keeping Jack sick."

"It keeps my husband from straying. It keeps him home. He's sick, he needs me to take care of him."

He gasped as a tremendous ball of hot gas exploded in his stomach. He gripped the table for support and gasped, "Charmian, you're killing him."

"This won't kill him." She withdrew the morphine needle. "But this would. If I wanted kill him I'd use this like Belko showed us that night he ended the sugar farmer's misery. His body weight ratio formula is seared in my brain. Will you ever forget it? They'll suspect uremia. Or even suicide, I suppose. God knows, he's written enough about suicide for me to be able to plausibly convince someone that that's what he died of. If I were to kill him."

"Why would you even think of something like that?"

"There are rumors again," she said. "I'm sure you must know of them. About a young Hawaiian lady. And the boy she carries. If the child is pure Hawaiian, I think it may break his heart. And if it's half Hawaiian, it would break mine."

"It's not what you think," he gasped. "It's a misunderstanding."

"It always is with my Mate-Man. My Keaka Lakana," she spat the words out before regaining her calm magisterial bearing. "Don't look at me with such horror, Hobart. This would only come to pass if Jack begged me to end his pain as the sugar farmer pleaded for an end to his. I promised to hold his hand to the end. If he chooses an end of his own design, I will still hold on. I could do this for Jack, if he asked—to show him how much I love him."

He gripped his stomach tighter.

"Ah." She held up a bottle. "This might help you."

"No."

He lurched into the corridor. She called his name but he turned from her. He had to find Jack—tell him to stop taking the Salvarsan. Without a porthole it was difficult to say which way was fore and which aft. He heard the whistle blast for final boarding as he found a staircase. Up he went. The hatch was sealed. But there was another corridor up here. He turned down it and before long he was in the dining hall, which was deserted but for the waiters tending to the elaborate table settings of the first luncheon at sea.

"Sir!" He had caught the attention of an officer, who cut through the islands of great round tables toward him.

"Thank God," he said to the officer. "You have to help me find Jack London—the writer."

"Sir, this dining room is closed right now. I'll have to ask you to leave."

"You have to help me! Where is the main salon? I need to find Jack London."

The officer looked at him with suspicion. "May I see your boarding pass, sir?"

"I'm not a passenger. I just need to speak with Mr. London."

"Sir, we are just about to throw hawsers. If you're not a passenger then I need to ask you to leave this vessel."

"And I am telling you I need to find Jack London."

He tried to push past the sailor but the man was young and strong, seizing Hobart's arm with a force that wrenched his torso around, causing his stomach to burn. His knees buckling, the officer snapped his fingers at the gaping waiters and two of them rapidly came forward.

"Yes, you have to help me find . . ."

The waiters grabbed his arms. They were pulling him now, with inarguable force, propelling him across the floor of the dining room.

"No." He struggled, but the men were strong and his own strength had faded. As they reached the upper deck outside the dining room he began to call out. "Jack! Jack London!" Maybe he would be heard. "Jack!" The damn band was so loud and all the people cheering and throwing streamers and flowers. "London!" So much noise and confusion. He was being dragged down the gangplank, not even the passenger gangplank, but the one reserved for baggage and food. Then there were police at the bottom, preventing him from reboarding, not listening to him.

He pushed along the length of the pier, parallel to the ship, scanning the faces of the beaming passengers as they waved and yelled, "Aloha!"

and the band played the familiar song "Aloha 'Oe." He thought he saw Jack and Charmian far ahead, toward the bow of the ship. There were so many people in his way. Someone knocked him to his feet and he rolled to avoid being trampled, still clutching his envelope. A sensation of great nausea swept over him and he staggered dizzily to his feet. His limbs felt weak.

The gangplanks were falling away and the great ropes were unwound from their moorings, splashing into the water and winding toward great spools on the ship's deck. He found his feet again and pressed forward. Was that Nakata? He grabbed at the Asian man, only to find him unfamiliar and hostile. There on the upper deck—Jack and Charmian. Waving. Who was Jack waving to? Hobart thought he caught a glimpse of Leialoha. Onward he staggered, ignoring the elbows and curses thrown at him. With a great churning of foam at the stern, the mighty vessel began to edge away from the pier.

"Jack!" he shouted, his voice thin, unable to project. "Jack London!"

It was them, he was sure of it, so far away.

"Jack!"

Charmian saw him. She tapped Jack on the shoulder. He looked at her and smiled. She kissed him—a long and lingering kiss of passion. Then she directed his attention toward Diamond Head, and the sea. After Jack had looked away she glanced back once more to look down at Hobart before turning her face from him forever.

An electric pain ran up Hobart's shoulder, as if he had been stabbed. He clutched his stomach, feeling his fingers grow wet with the sweat soaking through the shirt. There was nowhere solid to steady himself. The ship floated hazily in front of his eyes. There were people all around. Someone asked him if was drunk.

Then he was falling.

CHAPTER THIRTY-NINE

"H OBART?"
Willoughby.

"Hobart?"

Willoughby had come to visit Hobart every day since his release from the hospital. For a brief time the two had actually shared a room, but Hobart had thrown such a morphine-fueled fit that the next day his former friend had checked out against doctor's orders. Still, he came every day while Hobart lay in his bed. And every day, Hobart ignored him until he went away. Today, though, it took longer than usual before his former friend took the hint and left.

It was late November.

The ulcer, which had perforated the lining of his stomach the morning the *Matsonia* had sailed and left him prostrate, unconscious on the pier, required three surgeries to repair. He ate his first meal of solid food, a little bit of shredded pork after weeks of eating nothing but sour poi, on All Hallows' Eve. All the while the brown manila envelope, his only possession, sat nearby in a drawer in the table beside his bed. He had read the contents once and then set it aside.

Hobart knew that somewhere in the drug haze he had said good-bye to Morosco, now assigned to Florida. All that Ben left behind was a telegram to Hobart from Universal that had come to Morosco's office. Even through the fog of drugs and pain Hobart knew that meant that his whereabouts were now general knowledge. The telegram offered an acting contract that would pay three hundred dollars a week. Twelve hundred lousy dollars a month.

The hospital let him make all his travel arrangements from an office two flights down. It was as if they were testing him to see if he was well enough to leave by making him walk the stairs. He had his clothes and belongings brought over from the hotel, where they had been sitting in storage. Good thing, too, he was told, for the premises had been sold and a big renovation was beginning to transform it into a more luxurious destination to be known as the Halekulani Hotel. The thought of his charming little hotel being razed depressed him—but growth and change seemed to be the twin plagues on the land and there was nothing he could do about it.

The money was nearly gone. The hospital had cleaned him out. But, if he was frugal, he could get home on his remaining two hundred dollars. He spent the last night in the hospital rereading Jack's masterpiece. Then, early in the morning, he packed it away in its envelope and tried to sleep. In the morning, there was a message waiting for him.

He met her at the Honolulu Zoo. Hobart sat down beside Leialoha on a wooden bench overlooking the wolf pen. Her belly, though larger, was hidden by the fabric of her dress, and her face, which radiated the glow of a healthy pregnancy, was nevertheless darkened by a shadow of loss that could never be concealed. They watched the wolves through the iron bars for a long period of silence. The large one, evidently the male, lay in a cool spot of shade near a pile of slate watching two pups frolic roughly, twisting around and around each other as if they were one ball of fur. The mother sat nearby, thin and patient, keeping an eye on her offspring.

"There were three cubs at first," she said at last. "But one of them died."

"That's sad."

"I've heard that wolves sometimes eat their young," she continued. "I hope that's not what happened, but no one will tell me. I came one day and he was gone. The littlest one. Maybe it's for the best. What else did he have to look forward to than spending his life right here in this cage? I like to think that he escaped. Now he roams free through the islands and I'll hear him howling in the night."

He nodded. "I like the sound of that."

She fell silent again for a long while. "Did you read the newspaper today?" she asked.

"I don't follow the news much," he replied with a shrug. "There's nothing in it for me."

She was staring at him, her eyes glossy obsidian in their blackness.

"What happened?" he asked.

"Nothing," she said quickly. Her gaze fell back on the wolves. "You're right. There's nothing there for you."

"I'm leaving for Los Angeles tomorrow evening," he said.

She nodded.

"I have to get to Hilo today." He felt for her hand. It was soft and warm. "I could stay," he said in a low voice that sounded thinner the more he spoke. "I could stay with you here in Paradise and we could raise your son together."

"No," she said without even looking at him "No." She pulled her hand away.

In the cage, the she-wolf growled as the cubs' play grew too rough. They scampered for the security of their dozing father, who acted as if he didn't notice their cavorting presence.

"Well," he said, rising. "I do have a boat to catch."

She nodded. There were tears on her smooth cheeks. He wished he could say something to make his leaving less painful for her. But of course she would be broken up about it and there was really nothing left to say.

She looked up, but past him, still at the wolves. "I wrote to him."

"You probably shouldn't have done that."

"I had to."

"What did you say?"

"I told him that the baby I'm carrying belongs only to Mano and no other."

"You believe that?"

"Some days. That's what my heart tells me, and what he tells me." She rubbed her belly. "He talks to me in my dreams."

"It looks like we're both protecting Jack's secrets."

"What do you mean?"

He shook his head as if what he meant didn't matter. "Why did you send the letter?"

"It's for the best if he never comes back to Hawaii. Now he has one less reason to."

"Yes," he agreed. "I suppose you're right."

"No," she said with a shake of her head, the tears still flowing. "You're the one who's right. I shouldn't have written to him."

He waited to see if there was anything else she had to say to him, but she closed her eyes and leaned back against the bench. He watched as the golden sunlight smoothed the care from her face. Hobart left her with the wolves, his feet echoing lifelessly in the otherwise deserted park.

The trail deposited him on the Waikiki boardwalk, which was otherwise deserted. He could see gray clouds hanging ominously on the horizon. The water was as still and featureless as a piece of slate and he watched as Duke paddled over its surface, frustrated in his search for one good wave.

For ten dollars Hobart arranged for a fishing boat to take him to the Big Island. The fall seas between the two islands grew rough but the pods of migrating humpback whales seemed not to mind. He made landfall that night. The next morning he left his bags with the bell captain and hired a car from the hotel's garage. The day was even more overcast than the one before, with menacing, growling clouds.

"I've got no umbrella for you," the mechanic said, glancing up at the sky. He grabbed up a newspaper, *The Pacific Commercial Advertiser,* and handed it to Hobart. "All I can offer you."

"It'll have to do." Hobart took it and was about to throw it into the backseat when the partially exposed photograph above the fold caught his eye. Slowly he unfolded it.

"Aw hell," he said, slumping against the front fender of the car. It felt as if all his insides were swirling around and being sucked out at once. He put his hand to his face. "Oh hell."

The mechanic wiped his grimy hands on his overalls and looked over Hobart's shoulder. "Yeah," he said, "the dog writer."

"Wolf writer, actually," Hobart sighed.

"Who knew he spent so much time in Hawaii? Wished I'd a known. I loved *White Fang.*"

"Me too," Hobart said quietly, scanning the headline again before throwing the paper into the car.

JACK LONDON DEAD

Long-time Uremia Illness Triumphs Over Medical Skill; Servant Finds Young Genius Unconscious. Novelist Good Friend of Hawaii and Intended to Make His Home Here.

He drove up the windward side, following the occasional sign, toward the rim of the volcano. The object in his pocket was warm and hard, its weight pressing against his thigh. A trick of the imagination he decided. Wind from the sea buffeted the car. He saw a sign on his right for Kamila Beach and a fork in the road, one branch heading down toward the distant water and the other rising up into the mists surrounding the volcano.

He never saw the rock, but only felt it as the jolt threw the front of the car up into the air and then down with a thud that snapped something metal. Instinctively he threw the wheel to the right and the car coasted down the road, steam pouring from the hood, the steering wheel now nearly locked in its final position, the car gliding steadily nearer to the beach as his foot worked the brake, the only control he had left over the car. He guided it to a stop by some rocks. As he climbed out, the newspaper fell to the ground.

He was surrounded by desolation. The only sound of life was the distant cawing of the black albatrosses. There was no point in opening the hood or crawling under the car to see what was wrong; he knew nothing about engines or mechanics. He would have to wait for someone to come by.

He looked up; the volcano was miles away. He would never make it there now, and his ship was leaving the next morning. Hobart unfastened his shoulder bag and withdrew Jack's envelope. Then he walked out onto the beach. There was an uncomfortable crunching and snapping beneath his feet. He looked down. The beach itself was black—lava stone ground into powder by the incessant pounding of the waves. Covering the black were thin patches of weeds and something else, something that looked like tufts of black grass. Hobart took a step aside from one and with a sickening glance realized what it was. The corpses of hundreds of the ugly albatrosses littered the beach. This must be their nesting site in the spring, he thought. The elements and scavengers had reduced the bodies to little more than bone and feather. He looked at the nearest bird, the one he had stepped on. Where its stomach had once been there was now a tin army dog tag, complete with chain. Each bird had some similar man-made object in its gullet, taking up room required for food.

The beach was littered with every piece of man-made debris that could float and be carried ashore on the morning and evening tides. Toothbrushes and wooden toys, fishing gear and a hundred miles of fishing wire, empty wine and cola bottles, combs, razors, compacts, shiny buttons by the bucketful. All this garbage had filled the tiny stomachs of the fledgling albatrosses, starving them to death by the thousands and tens of thousands. This, finally, was the outer rim of the world and the refuse of humanity washed upon its shores.

Hobart withdrew the tear of Pele. He threw it as far and as hard as he could; if he couldn't return it to the goddess, he would at least leave it at her graveyard. He didn't see where it dropped, but he was happy to be rid of it.

Next Hobart opened the manila envelope and withdrew the sheaf of paper. "A brave man," Jack had told him, would be required to handle it.

"Yes, Jack," he said. "I'm a brave man. But not so brave that I can protect *The Liberation.*" He drew his finger across the title. He had read the memoir twice and knew why Jack had given it to him while burning *The Wolf Hunter.* It was a masterpiece.

"I'm not that brave," he whispered, though there was no one to hear him on that horrible shore. He spread his fingers and let the wind take the pages, a strange flurry of white exploding suddenly on the beach, some pages heading out to sea, others for the sky. It began to rain and he had a long way to walk before he might be found. By the car his eyes fell again on the newspaper. The heavy raindrops were causing the ink that had printed the familiar face to run, the dark eyes under the Western hat gleaming intently at eternity while the slight smile accepted it. Hobart swept the water from his face and tore his gaze away from the photograph. Far away on the heaving ocean, something caught his attention. It rose, then fell, hidden for an instant behind the very wave that seemed to reveal it in the next. Hobart squinted through the rain, trying to see clearly even as the howling storm clouded his vision. But he couldn't tell for sure if the object streaking across the black, foam-flecked water toward the most distant and mysterious islands in the Hawaiian chain was an outrigger canoe. Then he lost sight of it altogether.

ACKNOWLEDGMENTS

Research and inspiration were found in *Jack London, Sailor on Horseback* by Irving Stone, *Jack London: A Life* by Alex Kershaw, *Jack London in Aloha-land* by Charmian Kittredge London, *The Other Side of Salvation* by John B. Buescher, *Myths and Legends of Hawai'i* by William D. Westervelt, *Hawaiian Mythology* by Martha Beckwith, *O'ahu's Hidden History* by William H. Dorrance, and *Psychology of the Unconscious* by C. G. Jung, not to mention the timeless classics written by the man himself.

Assistance and information were provided by Sue Hodson, the curator of literary manuscripts at the Huntington Library, the largest archive of Jack London's papers. Her staff, including Gayle M. Richardson and Natalie Russell, were always gracious about helping me track down another piece of paper. Thanks also to the staff at Jack London State Historic Park for their help. While I'm on the subject of the park—thanks to Judith Zissman for hiking it on one of the hottest days Glen Ellen saw in 2006. And thanks to Dolores Gelertner for giving me the time to cool off with cold beers at Heinold's First and Last Chance Bar in Jack London Square. Lastly, the grand dames at the Hawaiian Historical Society library were endlessly patient.

On the subject of advice, let me thank Mirena Rada for pointing me to that most valuable of all research tools: the 1916 edition Sears, Roebuck and Co. catalog, and for her wardrobe suggestions. April Grover, thanks for teaching us how to surf. At the C. G. Jung Foundation, my appreciation goes to Morgan Stebbens and his class.

For encouragement and guidance, not to mention enthusiasm, I have to thank my editor Marysue Rucci. My gratitude goes out to David Rosenthal and Victoria Meyers and all the exceptional professionals at Simon & Schuster. Thanks also to Casey Panell. Writing the word "professionals" reminds me how supportive my coworkers at R/GA have been, so thanks again to Bob Greenberg, Chapin Clark, Dan Harvey, John Antinori, Andy Clark, Scott Weiland, Elyse Epstein, Sean Farrel, Steve Caputo, Trevor Eld, Chris Dugan, Joe Jaffe, Ross Morrison, Ray Fallon and all the terrific copywriters, too many to list, whom I have such respect for.

And on, finally, to friends and family. Dean Lorey and Anton Salaks, thanks for reading the drafts and helping me figure out what needed to be done. Gabby Sasson, you're such a great help. Susan Golomb, my great agent, what can I ever say but thanks again? And to my wife, Audrey, and boys, Nathaniel and Wesley, *mahalo*. I hope you enjoy this one, final souvenir from our great Hawaiian adventure.

ABOUT THE AUTHOR

Paul Malmont works in advertising. He attended the Interlochen Arts Academy and New York University and now lives in New Jersey with his wife and two children. This is his second book.

MY BROWN BEAR BARNEY

By Dorothy Butler
Illustrated by Elizabeth Fuller

GREENWILLOW BOOKS, NEW YORK

Library of Congress Cataloging-in-Publication Data
Butler, Dorothy (date)
My brown bear Barney/by Dorothy Butler;
illustrated by Elizabeth Fuller.
p. cm.
Summary: On her many travels,
a small girl takes many things,
especially her brown bear Barney.
ISBN 0-688-08567-9.
ISBN 0-688-08568-7 (lib. bdg.)
[1. Teddy bears—Fiction.]
I. Fuller, Elizabeth (Elizabeth A.), ill.
II. Title.   PZ7.B976My 1989
[E]—dc19   88-21199   CIP   AC

When I go shopping, I take . . .

my mother, my little brother, my yellow basket,
my red umbrella

and my brown bear Barney.

When I play with my friend Fred,
I take . . .

my bike, our old dog Charlie, two apples from our tree,
my boots

and my brown bear Barney.

When I go gardening, I take . . .

my father, my straw hat, my wheelbarrow, my spade

and my brown bear Barney.

When I go to the beach, I take . . .

my mother, my father, my little brother, special things to eat,
my sunglasses

and my brown bear Barney.

When I go to my grandmother's,
I take . . .

my pajamas in a suitcase, a flower in green paper,
a tasty tidbit for her cat, some carrots from my garden

and my brown bear Barney.

When I go to bed, I take . . .

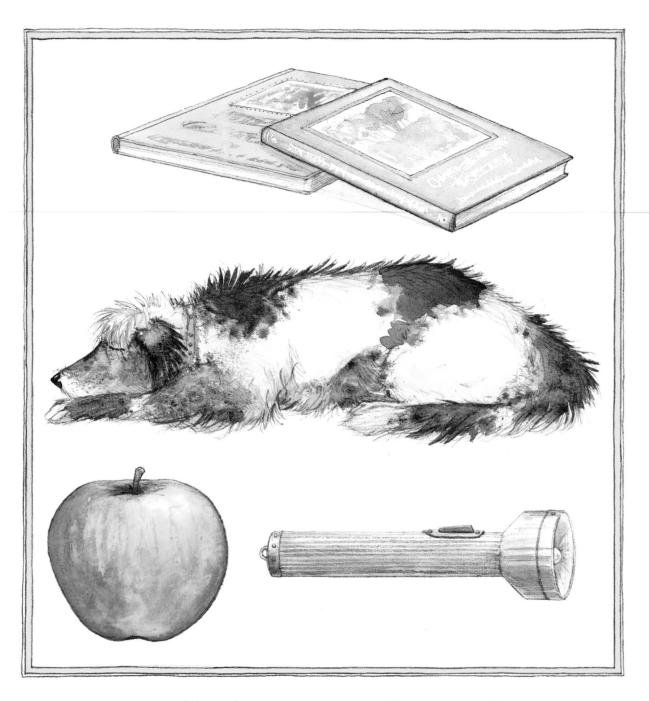

a good book or two, our old dog Charlie,
an apple for the morning, my big silver flashlight

and my brown bear Barney.

When I go to school, next year or the next,
I'll take . . .

a new school bag, some lunch, my dinosaur badge and
a pencil with an eraser on the end.

But not my brown bear Barney.
My mother says that bears don't go to school.

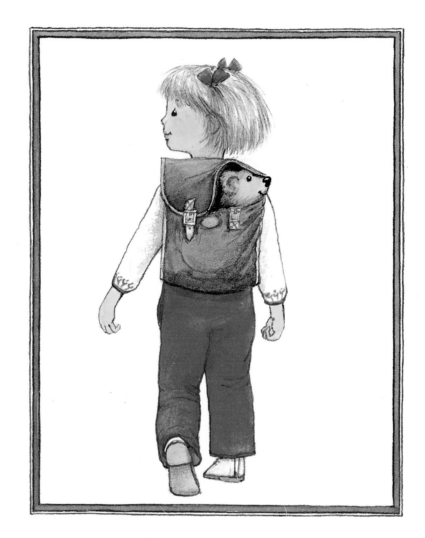

We'll see about that!